COVENANT

A NOVEL

LARRY L. BAILEY

DDP Literary Press

Covenant

Published in the United States of America by DDP Literary Press, a division of Double Dragon Publishing, Markham, Ontario Canada.

A DDP Literary Press Book

Published by
Double Dragon Publishing
PO Box 54016
1-5762 Highway 7 East
Markham, Ontario L3P 7Y4 Canada
http://www.double-dragon-ebooks.com

ISBN: 1-55404-032-9

A DDP First Edition March 2, 2003

Book Layout and
Cover Art by Deron Douglas

For my Native friends and neighbors from the Colville reservation who have taught me much about the earth and her peoples, two-legged and four-legged and of the salmon people who sustained us all.

CHAPTER I

Harry looked at his hands. The cold felt good to them, made them alive. He moved his fingers, felt the strength in them. His hands always had embarrassed him. Farmer's hands. They were too thick, the nails too tough, to be mistaken for a piano player's, or a banker's.

Long ago he had learned to hide his hands in his field jacket pockets or wear gloves or just keep them out of sight. It had begun in Junior High School when the worst, most degrading thing you could be called in the rural towns was "Farmer." It had replaced "moron" and "idiot" and "fool."

Now his future was certainly in these farmer's hands. He hoped they were as good as the old man's hands. With his own hands Harry's grandfather had built and nurtured an entire homestead after he had turned sixty.

Harry thought of Dad's sticky hand on the cold Beretta. He shivered and reached down to pat Reject and wondered if the dog remembered, too. Reject licked Harry's fingers, his tongue hot against the chilled skin.

Harry opened the pickup door for the dog, then followed him in. He started the engine and sat for a few minutes, watched the dawn lighten the snowy wheat fields on the heights far across the river. Below, it was dark where the walls of the great coulee broke in four-hundred-foot cliffs down to the still-shadowed Columbia.

He pulled onto the thick ice of the road and was pleased. Loaded as it was, the old International crept down the treacherous grade without a slip. Harry was glad he had switched the good winter tires from the Chevy the bank had sold at the auction. They owed him that much at least.

The San Poil River, too, was dark when he got to the bottom, but it was warmer here on the canyon floor, the highway nearly clear of snow. As he turned north, upriver, a large bird, a raven or owl or an eagle flapped quickly out of his headlight beams.

He drove more slowly, tried to make a plan, but everything tumbled into his mind at once. Judith and the kids. The old mare to move. He would need feed for her, and shelter. And shelter for himself, the pickup was a little cramped for a home. And he couldn't afford to eat in restaurants for long on the fifteen hundred dollars he had left.

Besides, he had ground to work. Soil and water and time seemed suddenly like blessings, although he had long taken them for granted. He had no machinery now, of course, and no tractor. That was all gone in the auction.

He did have the old mare, but some might say she never would pull again. He had heard of horses that had worked even older and she was the old man's mare, no one knew more about them or raised finer.

He remembered hayfields along the river when he and Judith were last there. He needed to meet the neighbors. "The whole world depends on neighbors," he heard the old man say in his mind. There had been a time, after the old man died, when Harry had been afraid that voice would go away. Now he was sure it never would leave him.

Daylight touched the tops of the tallest Ponderosa Pines and Black Cottonwoods and glowed from the fogbanks caught in the river bends. Already it felt a little like home. He thought of Judith's ancestors, his children's ancestors, who had walked and ridden and canoed this Valley of the Cliffs for many thousands of years. He always would be a newcomer.

The valley widened and yard lights shown from scattered farms. Eyes sparkled and he slowed. A doe bounded away, faded into the grayness. Harry could think only of Judith's eyes.

He missed her and Rebecca and Little Joe more than he had admitted. As with a mortal wound,his mind had not accepted pain it could not bear. Now, here in their valley, eased by the hope of seeing them soon, he felt the loss, found himself crying. He looked in the rearview mirror and brushed away the tears, felt Reject lick the salt from his fingers.

The further up the valley he drove, the deeper the snow. He was more than two miles past the Cache Creek turnoff when he realized he had gone too far. He turned back but could not find a break in the banks thrown up by the snowplows. The road to the little bridge was just a faint depression alongside a field. It would not be passable until after breakup unless he could get it plowed. He remembered a store a few miles up the river.

The store still was dark and the sign said "Closed." He thought of driving all the way to Republic but decided it made more sense to wait. He saw a pay telephone and looked at his watch. 7:27. Judith might not be gone. He searched his pockets for change but came up with less than a dollar.

The operator would not let him bill the call to his parents' number because no one was there to confirm the charge. Finally he gave her Uncle Paul's number and after a brief silence she told him the charge was approved. The line rang several times then he heard Rebecca's voice but he could not make her understand who he was. Judith came on.

"Who is this?"

"Harry," he said and felt the constriction of his voice.

"Oh, Harry. What do you want?"

"Just to talk for a minute."

"We're almost late," I have to go."

"But last night you said..."

"This is morning,I have a job interview and kids to get to daycare."

He said nothing.

"Call me this evening," she said finally. "We'll be here by six-thirty."

He started to say something, stopped and hung up the receiver.

He sat in the pickup again and watched the snow fall through the bright circle cast by a single streetlight. He felt himself fall with the snow and half-expected to be buried by the storm. He shook himself awake and wished for coffee. Still no sign of life in the store.

He decided to call Uncle Paul. He hated to go back there where they all knew him and would ask about Mom and Dad and the auction and the funeral. But if anyone would help him it was Uncle Paul. He was the closest thing to the old man left alive.

As he walked back to the telephone, a log truck roared in from the north, it's trailer loaded piggyback. The truck stopped and the driver got out, left the engine racing, blowing out thick, half-burned diesel that swirled the snowflakes.

As Harry dialed, the driver stood near the telephone booth, watched him intently. Harry turned away and waited several rings until Uncle Paul answered.

"Harry. Where you at?"

"Some store up here on the river," Harry said. There's a lot of snow up here."

"The San Poil gets lots of water, at least compared to this desert."

"I don't know if I can find a place for the old mare up here. Or hay."

"You could bring her here, but that could cause trouble."

"I bought her fair and square," Harry said.

"You know the banker," Uncle Paul said. He laughed in his dry way and Harry thought of the scar across his uncle's eye that always made it seem like he was winking.

"What can he do? I have a bill of sale."

"You have to admit that the bill of sale was obtained through coercion. At least from the story you told me."

Harry laughed. "I didn't hurt him. I don't think he'd testify against me. By the time he heard the deputy ask about the body, he wasn't even going to remember where he was." Harry was surprised that already he could make a joke about his own father's body.

"They'd pay him off," Uncle Paul said, "just to get at you. They're still pissed-off about the trailer. They already called this mornin' to say they're goin' to pick it up today. 'Don't touch anything,' the banker said."

"That bastard. The bank will get their money, now, from Dad's insurance."

"But they don't have it yet, and until they do, they can try to collect from the survivors. And the insurance company will try to beat it, claim suicide isn't covered, or somethin'."

A movement caught Harry's eye and he turned to see the log truck driver dance in his shiny cowboy boots, impatient for the phone. Harry gave him a look that backed him off a little.

"Well," he said to Uncle Paul, "they won't get the old mare back. I need to move her out of there today, before that asshole finds out we got her back."

"You can use my truck. But you should find another place. Find a neighbor up there. Someone must have an extra stall and hay."

The truck driver managed to get Harry's attention again, knocked the snow from his wide hat and stamped his feet.

"I've got to go," Harry said. "I'll see what I can do up here. Can I store some stuff at your place? Judith's loom and grandma's cookstove and some other stuff I don't have shelter for?"

"No problem," Uncle Paul said.

The truck driver glared at Harry and Harry glared back at him, made a little mock-bow as he left the telephone booth. He heard the door slam. He hoped that wasn't one of the neighbors.

The snowfall lessened and he turned off the windshield wipers, watched for the farmhouse just below his turnoff. The house sat back from the road at least two hundred feet, but the drive was well plowed. The house was old, made of logs with a stone porch. It was spacious, as though it once had been a hunting-lodge or rich man's retreat. There was a large steel machine-shed and beyond it a classic board-and-bat barn with a high loft and wide overhangs. Cows with new calves ate hay from a wooden feeder along one side of a large pole corral.

Harry parked and looked for someone. Two dogs charged at the pickup and Reject barked at them. Harry soothed him and got out, held him in while he closed the door. One of the dogs nipped at his leg and he kicked at it. These were not the usual farm-dogs, all noise. These two were stocky with large heads and clearly did not like strangers. Some German breed, Harry thought. He watched them closely as he walked towards the house.

He heard a voice and turned. A large red-faced man in a cowboy hat hailed him from the door of the steel building. Harry walked towards him and the dogs growled on each side of him. The man chewed a toothpick at Harry for a moment then said,"Come inside here. I got this cow down with a breech calf."

Harry followed him in and saw the cow in question. She lay on the floor, halter-tied to a post. The legs of a calf protruded from under her tail and she was in great distress. The rancher had hung a block-and-tackle from another post and hooked it onto the calf's legs with a slipknot. He pulled out the slack and gave it another pull. The cow bawled and struggled. He held the rope and poked her in the ribs with the toe of his boot and she wobbled to her feet. He pulled again and the cow nearly went down.

The rancher was covered with sweat, looked at Harry. "Give me a hand, here, son," he said and held out the free end of the rope.

Harry looked at the cow and the upward angle of the calf's legs. "You'll have an easier time if you slack off and turn the calf."

"You ever pulled a calf?"

"Quite a few," Harry said. "Without killin' the cow."

The rancher slacked the rope. "Be my guest."

Harry touched the cow on the hip and she trembled. He stroked her until she quieted a little, then he talked to her. "Take it easy, girl. We'll take care of you."

He took hold of the calf's legs and pushed it gently back into the cow. She had a contraction and it pushed against him and he held the calf still until it was over. He could feel faint movements in the tiny legs as the calf struggled for birth. He pushed again, tried to turn it but could not.

He worked one of his hands into the birth canal and held against another contraction and tried again. The third time he felt it turn, then more, but could only turn it halfway. He remembered a time the old man had a similar problem.

"Give a pull," Harry said, "but get rid of that come-along."

The rancher unhooked the rope and pulled the calf's legs.

"Easy." Harry said.

As the rancher pulled, he turned and the calf began to slide out. They gained more with a new contraction and in the lull, Harry managed to turn it a little further. On the next contraction the cow gave a great bawl and the calf came out with a rush, nearly sprawled them in the bloody straw.

The rancher looked at Harry. "Thanks. You're pretty good at that. You a vet or somethin'?"

"No," Harry said. "Just what my granddad taught me. He was a farmer."

The rancher dug in his overalls, came out with a dented flask, held it out to Harry. "Old Granddad. Have a nip."

"No, thanks," Harry said. "It's a little early for me."

"Suit yourself." He unscrewed the cap, tipped up the flask and swallowed a couple of times. He waved the flask towards the cow. "I just don't have the time to baby 'em like that. I yank 'em out and take my chances. I got two more waitin' out there that may need help, too."

"How many head you got?"

"Four hundred. Takes that many to make any money anymore."

"That's a lot of cows. You got any help?"

"Just my kid, and he's pretty much worthless. Can't afford no hired help. What brings you out here anyway?"

"Lookin' for hay," Harry said. "And a place for a horse."

"Way out here? This somebody else's horse?"

"No, she's mine. I've got a bill-of-sale."

"So why do you want your horse way out here?"

"I've got a little place," Harry said. "It belongs to some relatives. Just up the river."

"Where's that?" the rancher looked at him closely. "How far up the river."

"Across from your hayfield there, where that little bridge crosses."

"How big of a place did you say it was?"

Harry laughed. "I didn't. It's a hundred and sixty acres."

The rancher studied him. "You talkin' about that Indian place?"

"They're Colvilles," Harry said.

"You're not Indian."

"No. My wife is."

"Oh," the rancher said. "I thought they were all dead and gone." He shook his head. "Well I got no place to keep horses. Don't care for 'em much. When I was a kid I had to feed the horses before I could eat. Kind of soured me on 'em."

"I might be able to rig a pen, over on my place, if I could buy some hay."

"Can't help you. I may be truckin' in feed myself before spring."

"You know any other neighbors might help me?"

"Nope. Well there's some hippies up a mile that used to have some horses. I think they still have a corral and kind of a shed."

"Well, thanks. I'm Harry Isaacson." He held out his hand.

"Carlson," the rancher said and briefly shook his hand. "John Carlson." He held the door open and Harry went out.

The two dogs harassed Reject who barked furiously in the pickup's windshield. "Shut up," Harry said to the one on the driver's side. It backed away, head down. He got in and it barked again as he pulled away.

He looked for the place a mile up the river and didn't find it at first. Finally he saw a small A-frame cabin back in a thick patch of scrub pine. The driveway was blocked but the snowplow had turned around there and cleared a place wide enough to park off the road.

Harry climbed over the snowbank and walked towards the cabin. There was a thin drift of woodsmoke from a metal chimney and he saw a long gray bus with no wheels on the far side of the small clearing. There was an old Volvo, covered with snow, and a van someone had swept part of the snow from.

A German Shepherd-looking dog bounded out to meet him, growled and barked playfully, then escorted him to the door.

Harry knocked, but there was no sound. He waited, knocked again. He thought he heard movement and tried again.

Finally, as he walked away, the door cracked open and a woman's voice asked, "Who are you?"

"Hi," Harry said. "I'm a new neighbor." He saw a face appear between dirty curtains on the window in the door. She wiped a hole in the film of condensation and he saw that she tried to look beyond him.

"Who are you?" she asked again.

"I'm moving in. Down below Cache Creek."

"Carlson's?" she asked suspiciously.

"Across the road," Harry said.

"There's no house there," she said, tried to wipe a larger peephole.

"There will be. Can I come in?"

The curtains closed together and he heard her call to someone. "It's some guy. Says he's movin' in down by Carlson's. He ain't from Welfare."

Harry heard a male voice answer gruffly. After a few minutes the door opened slightly and an eye peered through. Then it opened wider.

"What do you want?" the male voice asked.

"I'm moving in down the river a ways. Carlson said you might be able to keep a horse for me for a while."

"You a friend of Carlson's" The door opened a little wider and Harry could see two eyes and a scruffy beard.

"No," Harry said. "Just met him. Helped him pull a calf. It's a little cold out here."

The door opened hesitantly.

"Come in," the guy said, seemed reluctant. He was tall and gangly, dressed in jeans and a thermal underwear top. The woman disappeared into the back.

Harry noticed several marijuana roaches in an ugly clay ashtray and some empty beer bottles nearby. He looked for a place to sit, gave up.

"I've got a place across the road from Carlson's hayfield. I need someone to keep a horse for me for a while. I can pay something and buy some hay."

"That Indian place? You don't look Indian."

"My wife is," Harry said.

"We ain't got no place for no horse. Besides we're goin' to Seattle. Soon as she gets her check. Shoulda been here last week."

"Anyone else in the area?" Harry asked. "It's just one old draft horse."

"Naw." He shook his head. Then he looked at Harry. "Well, there's Eliot. I think he's back already. Always spends the winter back east or California or somewhere. He's got his racehorses. You can't see the place from the road."

"Eliot. That his first name or last?"

"I don't know. Just Eliot."

"How do I find Eliot?"

"It's about two more miles up. All you can see is the driveway. No mailbox or nothin'."

"So, two miles up." Which side?"

"Same side. There's just this driveway, winds around behind some rocks then up a ways. Big fuckin' house up on a ridge."

"Thanks," Harry said.

He drove the two miles upriver and found the nicely plowed driveway. He turned onto it and followed it around a couple of tight bends and up a steep grade. The house was huge, newly built, two stories with lots of glass and bright pine siding. Woodsmoke boiled from twin chimneys set at each end. There was a matching barn surrounded by neatly fenced paddocks. If there were horses there, they were inside, out of the cold.

Harry walked up the freshly swept stone steps and pushed the doorbell button. There was no answer but he felt he was watched. He heard Reject bark and turned to see a Doberman-Pinscher charge at him. The dog was silent, acted like he meant business. Harry turned to face the charge and the dog stopped at the bottom of the steps and growled softly. Harry kept an eye on the dog and pushed the doorbell again. He could hear chimes sound deep in the house.

Finally there were soft footsteps and the door opened. A rather short man about his own age stood there, dressed in jeans and cowboy boots with a work-shirt but Harry noticed that his hands were soft and white.

"Mr. Eliot?"

"Close enough," the man said and waited.

"Some people down the river sent me up," Harry explained. "I'm looking for a place to keep a horse for a while. While I get set up."

"Set up?"

"I've got a place on the river. My wife's family does. We're moving in."

"What place is that?"

"Across from Carlson's. The Indian place."

"I know the place. Nice spot. What kind of horse."

"An old mare. A Percheron. I'm planning to farm with her."

"That'd be a trick. I can't take in any strays. Those big horses just bulldoze through corrals and stuff. I've got a lot of money into this place."

"She's real gentle. My granddad worked her for almost twenty years."

"Sorry, can't help you," Eliot said, started to close the door.

"Do you know anyone else?"

"You talked to Carlson?"

Harry nodded.

"The only other people right around here... besides those hippies... are those old people." He thought for a minute. "Davis, I think their name is. But I don't know if you could even get in there. They don't come out in the winter. You might try up around Republic. There's a couple of Dude Ranches up there."

"These Davises. How do I find them?"

"They're right in there behind the place you're talking about, the Indian place," Eliot said. "You cross that little bridge and follow it in. No one else in there."

"I know the bridge," Harry said. "Thanks."

Eliot silently closed the door.

There wasn't enough room to get the pickup out of the driving lane where the road over the bridge left the highway so Harry took a run at it and got his right wheels well into the snowbank. Snow came up above the passenger side window. He hoped it wouldn't melt and leak inside. He might have to chain-up to get out again.

He whistled Reject out and locked the doors. He thought about taking a rifle along but decided against it. He checked the load in the back and locked the canopy. He climbed over the snowbank the plows had made and as he walked towards the bridge he thought about the stuff in the back of his pickup.

There was Judith's loom. He had so often watched her sing to herself as she wove on it, the children quietly at play near her. Her patterns seemed to emerge from nothingness, growing out of her mind. And there was Grandma's cookstove, a blue enameled Monarch that had come with them from Kansas. He couldn't begin to count the wonderful meals he had eaten that she had cooked on it or the number of times he'd warmed himself by it as he listened to the old man talk. And there was the old man's forge. He wished now that he'd paid more attention all the times he'd watched his grandfather heat and shape horseshoes or hammer out parts to repair his equipment.

Harry was determined to remember all that he could and find someone to teach him what he couldn't remember. He knew now that these few simple things were his real birthright, a legacy greater than the farm and all the equipment and tools sold at yesterday's auction. These things and the memories and skills that went with them.

He felt a little sorry for Mom, but he had begun to feel nothing but relief that the farm was gone with its mountain of debt. A new start was what he needed, no matter how small or difficult. Something he could do with his own hands. He shoved his hands deep into the pockets of the old man's black wool coat.

The little bridge was buried under the snow. It was as though he walked a snowbank across the sparkling little river. A light mist rose from the water and he noticed that the sky had lightened, the clouds might break.

He walked on, passed the spot where he and Judith had made love so long ago on a green summer day. He shook his head as he remembered how he had gotten depressed afterwards and left her to go back to the city, sure she never would marry him.

He thought of Judith as she had sounded this morning, harried, almost desperate, but doing her best to cope with the city and the children. Alone. He felt sick at the thought of the children in day-care, then school, and then day-care again as they waited for her. He had to get them, bring them here. Judith had said she had a job interview, as though she didn't believe their conversation last night when he'd said he would come for them. Well, he supposed she had good enough reason to doubt him. That would change.

The road almost was invisible, just a soft depression in the snow bounded by small pines. It wound through the flat river bottom then began to climb. He reached a cleared field and saw tracks, horse and human. A wisp of smoke rose from the trees beyond the field.

The little house made of silvered wood and covered with snow, blended into the background. The barn, too, seemed to have grown where it stood. Like the old man's house, it faced south. Harry smiled to himself. He was sure the floor plan would be the same, too, bedrooms on the east to catch the morning sun, livingroom on the west for evening light. He wondered if the cookstove was a Monarch.

Horses, big ones, munched hay in the pole corral, and Harry saw cattle along a feeder just beyond. Reject's ears went forward and the hair along his back bristled. Harry looked where the dog looked and saw a Border Collie charge towards them. He stopped and waited, Reject stopped beside him. The dog slowed as he neared them, then came nose to nose with Reject. They sniffed suspiciously, slowly relaxed.

Harry moved on, thought he saw someone near the barn. A man turned towards him. His black wool coat nearly matched the one Harry wore, the one he'd taken from the old man's house after the auction. Sparse gray hair showed beneath a battered Stetson. His eyes appraised Harry, then smiled in welcome.

"Don't get much company this time of year. How can I help you?"

Harry smiled back. "I'm plannin' to move in, on that place over by your bridge. I've got a horse I need to board for a while."

"What sort of a horse?"

"An old mare, a Percheron. She belonged to my Granddad."

The man looked at Harry with new interest. "What you doin' with a horse like that? Nobody has draft horses anymore except beer companies and crazy old coots like me."

"Well," Harry said with a grin, "I'm not from a beer company."

"You plannin' to work her?"

"I hope so. I want to learn how, if I can."

"Nothin' to it. So how long you need to board her?"

"I'm not sure. Until the weather breaks. I need to get a place built and get my wife and kids."

"New neighbors," the man said with obvious pleasure. "Come inside and meet the wife. By the way, my name is Davis, Walt Davis."

"Harry Isaacson," Harry said as they shook hands.

Harry was right about the floor plan. With a few differences it might have been his grandparents' house. And the cookstove was a Monarch, shiny chrome and green enamel. A Dripolator steamed with fresh coffee beneath the warming ovens.

"Frances, come meet our new neighbor," Walt said and she came in, wiped her hands on a gingham apron. "He's movin' in to the old McTavish place. Wife and kids, too."

"Bill and Martha would be happy to know there was young folks movin' in there." She shook hands with Harry and smiled sweetly. "I'll get you a cup of coffee. Cold out there this mornin'."

"Bill and Martha helped us get started here when we were just young folks," Walt said.

They sat at the kitchen table and Harry had a hard time concentrating on the conversation. Everything was so similar, so comforting, almost uncanny. Walt would be happy to keep the old mare for him, had plenty of hay. He offered to plow out the road with his drag.

"Don't usually bother with plowin' it this time of year. No reason to go to town anyway. And it keeps the hunters out."

When finally they went back outside it had cleared and the little farm sparkled under an intense sky. Harry hoped his new place would someday look as good. The brightness blinded him and he shaded his eyes as they talked. He said he would be back the next day or at worst the day after.

Reject had found a friend and the two dogs chased each other up and down the road. Harry had to whistle several times before Reject broke it off. He licked Harry's hands and danced around him. Harry led the way back towards the pickup with a brisker step and lighter heart.

CHAPTER 2

The roads were wet as the new snow melted rapidly under the sun. Harry didn't need the load for weight any longer but he knew that he'd kept it as much to have it all close to him as for traction. He would leave it at Uncle Paul's except his clothes and personal stuff. He had decided that after he moved the old mare he would make the trip to Seattle. He half hoped that Judith and the kids would come back with him although he did not know where they all would stay.

It was hard to believe that Rebecca was almost seven and that little Joe would turn four in a couple of weeks. He had hoped by the time they were in school he would be able to provide a stable, secure home, one where they could spend at least all of their school-years. But here he was, nearly forty, starting out again with nothing. He didn't mind for himself or even for Judith, but he had wanted to give his children more than struggle and uncertainty.

It had been nearly noon when he'd left the Davises so it was after one when he crossed the bridge below Grand Coulee Dam. Very little water went over the broad spillway and the enormous concrete face was streaked and stained by the minerals in the water. From below, the outflow from the great turbines boiled up and the river flowed on. But the dam divided the river now into a great millpond stretching more than a hundred miles into British Columbia which was called Lake Roosevelt and a still-live river below which welcomed dwindling salmon runs. Above the dam the salmon were entirely gone and with them a way of life.

He realized that he hadn't eaten anything since lunch the day before so he stopped at the Wildlife Cafe in Grand Coulee. When the waitress brought the menu, Harry gave a little start; she looked so much like Judith. He wondered for a minute if it was one of her sisters, but he knew them too well. A cousin, he decided or more distant relation.

By the time the food came, Harry wished he had gone somewhere else. Everything about the Wildlife reminded him of Judith. They had come here many times and everyone who worked here knew her. None of them seemed to recognize him and he didn't remind them.

He left two dollars for the waitress and wrapped the remains of his hamburger in a napkin for Reject. As he paid his check, he felt a little panic at how fast the fifteen hundred dollars would be gone. Just to haul the old mare would cost fifty dollars or more in gas, then the trip to Seattle. With the old mare taken care of maybe he could get a job on the coast, save up a little. But it cost so much to live there. Maybe he could stay with Judith.

Water splashed down the coulee walls and flowed across the highway as he drove south. By the time he reached Dry Falls, green showed through the thin snow. Soon it would be time to plow in the Basin. Farmers would be putting the final touches on machinery repairs and filling their bulk-tanks with fuel. It would be very strange not to be part of that.

Uncle Paul walked through his fields, surveyed the new crop of rocks that emerged from under the fading snow. He saw Harry pull in and came to greet him. His dog danced around the pickup, urged Reject to come out and play. Harry let him out and the two dogs raced across the field.

"Afternoon."

"Afternoon. Truck's all gassed up and ready to go. I'd get her out of there right away if I was you."

"It's a little late to get back up to the San Poil today," Harry said. "Roads will be slick as glass in a couple of hours."

"You could park here overnight, take off before daylight."

"Sounds like a plan," Harry said. "You heard from the banker."

"Not his highness, himself, but two guys from the RV place came out and got your Dad's trailer this mornin'. Acted like I might shoot them or somethin'."

"You got time to ride over with me?"

"Sure. Can't do nothin' here yet. Have to spend a week pickin' up rocks before I can plow. Good crop of rocks, this spring." He laughed and shook his head.

Harry laughed, too. "Too bad the market's down."

"That's a fact. You know, Harry, if you hadn't told me about that big flood, back in the Ice Age, I'd think these rocks were a special curse, just for me and these other poor bastards out here."

"You could sell this place. With what it's worth now you could make a down-payment on a unit out in one of the new blocks, somethin' with five feet of topsoil."

"Then I'd have payments again," Paul said. "Besides, this is home. I wouldn't know what to do with myself without these rocks." He looked seriously at Harry. "We better get goin', before that fuckin' banker gets any funny ideas."

No one was around when they got there. Mom must have gone to Jack and Diane's after all. Vehicle tracks led towards the old place and he knew the coroner must have been there to get Dad's body. Harry shivered and looked at Paul.

Paul reached over and touched his shoulder. "Nothin' you could have done."

The old mare stood alone in the corral, tossed her head and neighed gently at them. Paul backed the truck into the loading chute while Harry directed him. They'd thrown a bale of hay in the back and Harry climbed up and broke it, shook a flake at the mare. She started towards him, stopped at the bottom of the chute and swung her head back and forth. Paul climbed into the corral and gave her a gentle nudge on the hip. She balked momentarily, then slowly worked her way up the chute and into the truck. Paul closed the gate behind her.

"Couldn't be easier."

"I hope she'll work for me as easy as that."

"She will. The old man's horses always loved to work."

As they pulled away Harry noticed a gray Mercedes pull into the lane from the county road. "The banker," he hissed.

"Duck down," Paul said. "I'll handle him."

Paul stopped the truck at the end of the lane and waited. Harry heard the Mercedes come alongside and Paul rolled down the window.

"Howdy."

Harry tensed when he heard the young banker's voice.

"Hello, Paul." You hauling horses, now?"

"She's mine. I bought her from the guy who bought her at the auction."

"That isn't the story I heard. I heard Harry had something to do with it."

"Not that I know of. I just wanted a keepsake. She belonged to my Dad, you know."

"She belonged to the bank," the banker said. "Until yesterday."

"Well, not no more," Paul said and started to move.

"If you see Harry, tell him he'd better stop interfering or he will be in a lot of trouble. I heard the sheriff wants to talk to him."

"I'll let him know, if I see him," Paul said and drove off.

"That asshole," Harry said when Paul motioned to him that it was safe to sit up. "You'd think he'd have somethin' useful to do."

Harry left for the San Poil before daylight the next morning. There had been no more hassles from the young banker and he saw no one as he drove north. The roads were slick again, but the truck handled it easily. He stopped for coffee and a cinnamon roll at the Wildlife. He couldn't seem to stay out of the place.

He checked on the old mare several times and she seemed content. He'd left her enough rope to reach the hay and she munched it and calmly eyed him each time he climbed the side of the truck to look at her. He took the switchbacks on Manila Creek slowly so he didn't throw her off her feet.

The road across the bridge was plowed as promised and he pulled into the Davises' yard at mid-morning. It had begun to snow again. The old mare unloaded easily and Walt helped him put her in a small pen near the large corral so she could get to know his Belgians across the fence. If they seemed to get along he would put her in with them in a few days. Walt asked Harry if he wanted her bred to his papered stud and Harry said that was fine. He hoped she took. Walt's Belgians were beautiful.

They went in the house for a cup of coffee. Frances had fresh-baked muffins and sat with them to talk. They told him of their history and asked for his.

They had come there in the late thirties, wanted a place to raise a family. Walt was from Oklahoma, had wound up in Kansas City, trying to stay alive. Frances had been a schoolgirl then, had fallen in love with the soft-spoken farm boy, determined to follow him on the trip west he had long planned.

Frances found a job as a waitress; Walt was a good carpenter. After a few months they'd saved enough to head west, Seattle, to see how things were there. It was okay, Walt said, but it was just Kansas City with more rain and seagulls. He wanted to farm. He'd left Frances in a rooming house on Capitol Hill with a little money and a promise that he would find them a farm. He worked the grain harvest from Pasco up the Columbia to the high plateau around Wilbur. There someone had told him about the San Poil Valley and he'd borrowed a saddle horse for the trip.

Bill McTavish sold produce from a little stand by the wagon road that later became the San Poil Highway and had the finest draft-horses Walt had ever seen. Times were good for McTavish and he said he could use a hand. Walt offered to work for food and a place to build a cabin. The bargain was struck. Walt said he'd be there with his wife in the early spring, as soon as they could plow.

They never had left, since that spring. McTavish had helped them buy their place after a few years and had traded Walt a team of Belgians for work. They had remained the best of friends and neighbors until Bill and Martha had passed on. It'd been a little lonely since then, Frances said, with their own kids grown and gone. It would be nice to have neighbors again.

"How about you?" Walt asked. "I hear somethin' sounds like home in your voice."

"Kansas," Harry said. "Western Kansas on the Arkansas. I've got family all along Highway Fifty. We left there in fifty-eight, my parents and grandparents and my Uncle Paul. That's his truck I'm drivin'. We farmed down in block eighty-eight since then. Until day before yesterday." He paused and looked at them, shrugged. "We lost the place."

"To the bank?" Walt asked him gently.

"Yeah. The place, the equipment, the stock. Just about everything except what's in my pickup and that old mare."

"How're your folks takin' it?" Frances asked him.

"My Mom's fine," Harry said, got control of himself. "But my Dad, he shot himself, after the auction."

Everyone was quiet. When Harry looked at Frances he saw tears in her eyes. She poured him another cup of coffee.

"You're a young man," Walt said finally, "You've got plenty of time to start over. Just don't get in hock to the bank. They'll own everything soon. They don't like us small farmers. We don't play their game right. Too hard to control."

"You should have your family here," Frances said. "People have to stick together through these things."

"Yeah. But I messed that up too." He told them about Judith, about his own drinking, how he'd signed her name to an agreement, pledged her horses as collateral on the farm loan.

"They'd be gone, if some of her relatives hadn't showed up and bought them back. I think she probably hates me, now."

"People make mistakes," Frances said. "That's why the good Lord talks so much about forgiveness."

"I don't know," Harry said. "I talked to her twice yesterday and I think she's changin' her mind. About comin' back over here. I can't blame her."

"You should go to her," Frances said. "Tell her what you just told us. She'll understand. We know her family, they're good people."

"I've got to get a cabin built, or there won't be anything to come to."

"You can't do that right now," Walt said, "Ground's frozen. We'll take care of your horse. When breakup comes I'll give you a hand with the cabin. Frances is right, you need your family."

They talked late into the afternoon. Harry finally looked out the window.

"I better be goin'. I'll be drivin' in the dark as it is."

"Why don't you stay with us," Frances said. "You can go early tomorrow mornin'."

"No, you've done enough. I'm afraid I've overstayed my welcome, as it is."

But they insisted, said they loved to have company, especially in the winter. Harry drove to the store and called Uncle Paul to let him know. Paul said the banker had come by his place.

"He was peerin' through the windows of your rig when I saw him," Paul said. "Tryin' to see what you'd stolen, I guess. I ran him off quick. Your mother called, too. She was lookin' for you. Said she needed to talk to you."

"Talk at me, most likely. I'll go by Jack and Diane's tomorrow."

Harry sat up talking to Walt and Frances by the warm stove late into the evening and slept better than he had in a while. When the dawn's light awakened him the next morning he thought for an instant that he was in his grandparents' house, years before, and the world was right.

It was mid-morning when Uncle Paul helped Harry unload the old man's forge and a few remaining tools, grandma's cookstove and Judith's loom into his storage shed. They covered it all with tarps. Harry thought about leaving his guns, too, but at the last minute decided to keep them. At least for now.

He drank a cup of coffee with Paul, tried to pay him for the use of the truck but Paul wouldn't hear it.

"You're family. Shit there's little enough family out there as it is." He wanted to know if Harry was going to see his mother.

"I guess I have to, not that it will serve any purpose."

"She was real agitated when she called me," Paul said. "Somethin' must be up."

"Everything's an emergency with her."

He had some trouble finding Jack's house at first. All the houses in Desert Aire looked the same to him. He finally found the number and parked. He sat in the pickup for a while then slowly walked to the door.

Diane answered the bell. "Well it's about time you showed up, Harry."

"Nice to see you, too. Is Mom here?"

"She's here, all right," Diane said with exasperation.

Harry followed her through the entryway decorated with gold foil wallpaper and fake plants.

Mom looked at Harry then back at the television. "Just a minute. I want to see if this woman really had an affair with her son-in-law." She watched avidly as the host interviewed a middle-aged woman with too much make-up. Harry sat on a green-and-gold overstuffed chair and waited.

"I knew it," Mom said. "She didn't do it. Her daughter was just jealous of her." She turned towards him. "Harry," she said as if she'd just realized he was there. "We need to talk."

"Here I am."

"We expected you yesterday, at least I did."

"Had to see a man about a horse."

"They're asking a lot of questions. I don't know what to tell them."

"Who's asking questions?"

"The banker. And the sheriff, and the man from the insurance company. And the coroner won't sign the death certificate. He says there are irregularities."

"What irregularities?"

"I don't know," Mom said. "You need to talk to them."

"I'm on my way to Seattle."

"I need you to do this for me, Harry. I'm all alone now." She started to tear up.

"Jack can handle it."

"The sheriff said he wanted to talk to you," Mom said.

"About what?"

"I don't know. They just said they needed to talk to you. You were the one who found the body."

"Yeah," Harry said. "I get all the good jobs."

"They won't release anything until they talk to you. I don't even have enough money to get my hair done. For the funeral. The funeral's on Friday."

"Get Diane to do it."

Mom looked at Diane then back at Harry. "I can't ask her to do that. She's done so much already."

Diane glared at the two of them.

"I need to get my own place," Mom said. "I can't stay here."

"So who am I supposed to talk to?" Harry asked.

"The sheriff left this number," she said, dug in her purse for something, finally handed him a torn scrap of paper.

He looked at Diane. "You can use the phone in the kitchen," she said.

Harry dialed the number and a dispatcher answered.

"This is Harry Isaacson."

"Um, just a minute." The line went dead. Harry waited.

Finally a different voice came on. "Mr. Isaacson?"

"This is Harry Isaacson. I understand someone there needed to talk to me."

"Sure do," the voice said. "Could you come down to the department."

"I guess so. I'm kind of in a hurry."

"Oh?" the voice said. "What kind of a hurry?"

"I'm on my way to the coast."

"I wouldn't make any plans like that. Not until this is settled. Can you come down now?"

"Sure," Harry said, "I'll be right down."

Harry gave his name at the counter and the clerk took him down a hallway and opened a door.

"Wait right here," the clerk said, "Someone will be with you in a while."

The room was nearly bare, just a table and three chairs. There was one window, near the ceiling, with heavy wire mesh on the outside. Harry shivered a little as he recognized it as an interrogation room. When the clerk left he tried the door. It was not locked.

He sat in one of the chairs and waited. It was nearly half an hour before the door finally opened and a man about Harry's age in civilian clothes came in. Another, older man, followed him.

"Mr. Isaacson?" the first man read from a manila folder he carried.

"Yes."

"Ah, just a few questions. You have the right to remain silent," he began, then smiled, "but you've heard all this before."

Harry just looked at him, said nothing, so he finished with the Miranda-rights spiel, asked Harry if he understood.

Harry nodded.

The two men sat down across from him. The one with the folder looked through several sheets of paper.

"So", he said, finally, "You're the son of the deceased?"

"Yes," Harry answered.

"You close to your father?"

"I guess so. We were partners. In the farm."

"Yes, I see that. But did you get along?"

"Well enough, I guess. What are you driving at?"

"We'll ask the questions," the older man said.

"Your mother says you were the last one to see him alive," the first man said. "And the one who found the body."

"I found the body," Harry said, "but the last time I saw him he was with some friends."

"Who would that be?"

"Chuck Henry. And Harold Raines, and Jim Thompson."

"They said the last they saw of him he was walking up towards the old shack. And that the two of you were arguing."

"Not really arguing," Harry said. "I just told him my mother wanted to see him."

"They said you were blaming him for losing the farm."

"It was his fault, but I was long past arguing about it."

They both looked at him for a while.

Finally the older one said, "Funny you knew just where to find him, the body."

"It's not hard to follow tracks in new snow. Are you trying to say I had something to do with it?"

"Just trying to find out what really happened."

"It's pretty obvious," Harry said.

"Sometimes the obvious isn't the real answer," the older man said.

"Your mother said you and your father had been fighting quite a lot," the younger man said.

"No more than usual," Harry said and wished he hadn't.

The older man raised his eyebrows. "Your pastor, Reverend Hale, said you always hated your father, didn't get along with him at all. He says you have a real violent streak."

"He's not my pastor," Harry said. "He hung around my mother a lot. Actually my Dad didn't have much use for him either."

"You had quite a lot to gain," the younger man said. "From your father's death."

"Not me. The bank did."

"The banker says you would have had a pile of debt. Now you may even get some money. Could be quite a bit of money."

Harry just looked at them.

"The coroner isn't sure just what happened out there," the younger man said. "He says the angle of the bullet, and the point of entry, pretty hard for a man to do that to himself."

"I don't know, I didn't have anything to do with it."

The younger man looked through the file. "I understand you've got a pretty hot temper."

"Not that I know of."

"It says here you spent some time in Western State Hospital. After an assault on a doctor. Heavy drug use."

"Just after Viet Nam. I was a little messed up back then."

"All better now?" the older man asked.

Harry glared at him.

"And an arrest for suspected rape?"

Harry felt his blood rise. "That was complete bullshit. They found that out. I had nothing to do with it."

"Then, a fellow tells us you threatened to cut his throat, just last night. Over a horse. You seem to be a real non-violent type of guy," the younger man said.

Harry didn't answer.

"All this seems to add up to something," the older man said. "We'll have to make our report to the prosecutor and he'll decide whether to charge you. Meanwhile, we can't tell you not to go to the coast but I would advise you to stay in touch. If you are charged it will be better for you if you cooperate. You sure you don't want to make a statement now, save some time?"

"I told you what I know."

"You have a telephone number on the coast where we can reach you?"

"No."

"We'll let your brother know when we need to talk to you again," the older man said. "Stay in touch."

"Sure," Harry said.

CHAPTER 3

Snoqualmie Pass was a sea of slush as Harry reached the summit. He swung into the left lane to get around a string of semis, fishtailed and decided against it. He would just have to follow them down. There had been several inches of new snow which cascaded from the trees in sloppy white clouds.

He had told Uncle Paul about the interrogation at the Sheriff's office and Paul had told him to be very careful and not talk to them again without a lawyer. They had pieced together a chronology of the afternoon of the auction as well as they could and listed all the witnesses who had seen Harry both before and after he'd found his father's body. Paul kept a copy of it in case something happened to Harry's. Paul promised to dig around and see what he could find out.

The slush was gone above North Bend and Harry finally passed the line of trucks and sped towards Seattle. He hadn't called Judith. Their telephone conversations were not pleasant lately and he wanted to see her in person. He had just about decided to stay on the coast and work for a couple of months, raise a little money to take back when they went.

With his late start he was in rush-hour traffic by the time he reached Issaquah. It was bad, but when he looked across at the eastbound lanes leading away from Seattle he realized he had the best of it. He was not used to city traffic. His heart raced and he tasted adrenaline. It surprised him. He'd spent years dashing around the Seattle freeways without a second thought. Now it seemed like something only the insane would do.

The traffic was worse as he crossed Mercer Island and commuter busses pulled in and out of the lanes. The roadway narrowed to cross the Floating Bridge and there were several near misses as drivers made last-second lane changes. A strong chop beat against the north side of the bridge. He watched for the Rainier Avenue exit, nearly took the northbound ramp by accident. He relaxed a little on what the traffic reporters called "surface streets" as though the freeways were suspended in the air.

He couldn't remember exactly where Holly Point was, somewhere just off Rainier. He knew he'd driven by it, but never imagined that he would know anyone who lived there. He remembered that it reminded him of military housing, rows of identical wood-frame buildings with tiny yards between.

There were more dark faces in cars and on the sidewalks as he drove south and the buildings were more dilapidated. He stopped at a stoplight and a group of adolescents crossed in front of him. One pointed towards him and they all laughed. Harry ignored them.

A sign identified the project but it was covered with graffiti and barely could be read. He turned in and looked for the building number Judith had given him. It nearly was dark and many of the numbers had been painted over. He found a space to park in an almost full lot. He started to walk away then went back to lock both doors and check the canopy. He noticed several people watch him.

Music and voices came from open windows as he searched for Judith's building. Gangs of children played in the torn up area that served as a playground. He wondered if his two were among them.

He would get them away from here as soon as possible. He could not find the building, finally asked two women who sat on a cracked concrete step and one of them pointed towards the far side of the playground. As he walked that direction he could hear the women laugh.

He found the building number and went in. Several people talked on the stairway and he had to squeeze by. On the second floor he found the apartment and knocked. He heard Judith say, "Joseph, don't you open that door."

He knocked again.

Finally the door opened a crack and Judith said, "Yes."

"It's me."

"Harry?" she questioned.

"It's me," he said again.

He heard the rattle of a chain, the click of a dead-bolt, and the door opened.

"Daddy," Little Joe said and ran to him. Harry picked up his son and felt tears spring into his eyes. Rebecca looked at him silently.

"Why didn't you call?" Judith asked.

He looked at her. Strain showed in her dark face but she was as beautiful as he remembered.

"I wanted to surprise you."

"I don't need any more surprises right now."

"I'm sorry. I needed to see you."

"Where are you staying?" she asked him.

"I don't know. I'll find some place. I can sleep in the pickup."

"You shouldn't have come, Harry. I've got more than I can take care of, now."

"You don't have to take care of me."

She just looked at him.

He put down Little Joe and the boy clung to his leg.

"I'm going to get a job, save up some money."

"You can't stay here. They'll put us out."

"I can find a place."

"It isn't that easy. Rent is really high. Most of what they build now are 'luxury' apartments."

"I could probably stay with Ron," Harry said. "He's got a place on the East Side somewhere."

"Do whatever you want to do."

"Shadow and the colt are on Cache Creek."

"I know," Judith said, "Nathan called."

Harry looked at her, shook his head.

"Don't say it. If it wasn't for Nathan and Little Eagle I would have lost them."

"You don't have to remind me," Harry said. "I found a place for the old man's mare. Some people that knew Bill McTavish. Walt and Frances Davis. They live back behind."

"I remember them. I didn't know they were still there."

"I stayed with them. Last night. They'll help us build a cabin."

Judith had a faraway look in her eyes. "I'd love to live there, Harry. But I can't drag these kids back and forth. If they're going to have to live in the city, it's better they get used to it now."

"We'll make it there. Walt says we can use some of his equipment and he'll teach me how to handle draft horses. It may be hard, but we can do it."

"It couldn't be as hard as this. I don't mind hard. I just want some stability for the kids. I'm afraid we'll get up there and then you'll change your mind or something will happen."

"You know I don't mind hard work," Harry said. "You've seen that."

"I know. It isn't the work. It's the communication. I can't trust you to tell me the truth."

"I won't ever lie to you again. And I won't drink at all. I know I can't handle it."

"I thought just us Indians couldn't handle liquor," she said with a hint of a smile.

Harry laughed. "Maybe it's the other way around."

"I don't know, Harry," she was serious again. "I'll have to think about it. I hate the city, but at least here I can get some help. Up there, if you're not a tribe member, you have to go all the way to Colville for Food Stamps."

"You could be enrolled," Harry said. "You're half."

"I won't do that, Harry. The tribe has enough to worry about. I decided a long time ago I would never take anything from them. They have too many 'little bit' Indians as it is."

"We can make it," Harry said. "We can grow our own food, and sell the extra. We might not have much money but we can survive."

Judith turned at a knock on the door.

"Judith," a woman's voice called. "It's Valerie."

Judith opened the door a little.

Little Joe took Harry's hand and led him into his bedroom. He held up a shiny dump truck. "Grampa sent."

Harry heard the woman ask Judith, "Who's the red-neck?"

"My husband."

Harry could hear the disbelief in the woman's voice. "Your husband? No wonder you left him. Listen, we're havin' a little party tonight. Tony wanted me to invite you."

He couldn't hear what Judith said.

"Looked to me like the two of you were gettin' along pretty good the other night," Valerie said. "He's a nice brother. Has a good job and everything. Get rid of that man and come on over. Sharla says she'll watch all the kids."

"I don't think so," Judith said. "I've got too much to do."

"Well you know where we are," Valerie said. "Your husband!" she giggled.

"Harry," Judith called and he came back into the livingroom. "I've got some things to do."

"Yeah," Harry said. "I heard."

"Not that. I'm not in much of a party mood. I promised Rebecca I would cut her hair. And Joseph needs a bath."

"I could help," Harry offered.

"Not tonight. They need to stay in their routine."

A group of kids surrounded his pickup when Harry got back to the parking lot and he saw one try the canopy door. He realized they must have seen the guns. It was stupid to have left them in plain sight over here. He was lucky they hadn't gotten in yet. In the farm country no one would even have noticed.

He started to yell at them, but decided against it. He unlocked the door and they scattered except for one kid with dreadlocks who sat on the hood and glared at him. Harry said nothing, started the engine and put it in gear. As he started to move the kid slid off onto the ground and slapped the side of the pickup. Harry ignored him.

The traffic had lessened and he made good time back across the Floating Bridge and Mercer Island and turned north on 405. He wasn't sure where Ron lived or if he was back on the coast but he had a phone number for him. He stopped at a mini-mart and called, got an answering machine. He decided not to leave a message.

He took the Evergreen Point Bridge back across Lake Washington and got off in the University District. There were several new high-rise buildings in the Health Sciences complex along the ship canal and more under construction. He could see more new buildings going up on the main campus. Just in the eight years since he'd left school the university enrollment had more than doubled.

He cruised University Way, looked for some place to eat. The Greek place he and Judith had gone to so often still was there but it looked very crowded. He drove on north, noticed that the Century Tavern had become some kind of sports bar. He didn't need a tavern, anyway. He finally decided on Pagliacci Pizza and stood in line to get his food. Almost no seating was open so he carried it back to the pickup and ate there.

The District had changed a lot. All the hippies were gone. Students looked more like they had in the middle sixties when he'd first been there, all business and short hair. The Reaganites must be happy with their Great War against long hair and useless knowledge.

The Sureco building where Judith had worked when he met her was the same, but there weren't many good memories there. This area had long been his home but already he felt like an alien. He drove around a little more, looked for something familiar and comforting, but the more he drove the worse he felt.

He stopped to call Ron again and this time Ron answered. "Hey, buddy, where you at."

"The U. District."

"Better get over here in God's country," Ron said. "Nothin' there but freaks and fairies."

Harry tried to laugh with him. "That invitation still open?"

"You mean a place to stay? You bet. Come on over. You know Kirkland?"

"I built a couple of houses there. We lived in Redmond."

"That's right," Ron remembered. "Well this place is just up behind the new Post Office. Some new buildings, couple of years old. It's called Coventry East. There's four fourplexes; I'm in the second one from the north, the one with red trim. Upstairs on the right."

"I'll be right over."

The buildings were European-styled with steep shake roofs and garages underneath. He found the one with red trim and walked up two flights and knocked at the door on the right. Ron answered, was clearly happy to see him.

"Hey, buddy, you hungry? I was about to go eat."

"I already ate."

"Well, come on and eat again. Looks like you could use it."

"I'll wait."

"I'm payin', I'm the guy with the money."

Harry laughed. "I'm the guy without any."

"We'll get along fine."

They ate at a new broiler on the Kirkland waterfront. Ron insisted that he try the mesquite-grilled swordfish and Harry had to admit it was very good. Ron drank wine and tried to get some for Harry but he refused.

"One thing I don't need is alcohol."

"I got somethin' better than that." Ron winked.

"That either," Harry said. He told Ron about the Davises and the encounter with the Sheriff's Department.

"Those bastards. I was with you until they started sellin' the stock. Then I had to take off."

"Well, that just left me time to run up there and shoot him."

"Anyone else see you?"

"Just the banker," Harry said. "And some friend of his. Some CIA asshole that tried to recruit me to go to El Salvador. They aren't going to help. The Sheriff already talked to the banker. And to Mom. Sounds like she's the one made them think I did it, tellin' them we were fightin'."

"There must be someone. There was a lot of people there."

"Maybe," Harry said. "I know someone who might be able to say what really happened," he remembered how Nathan and Long Joe had appeared suddenly out of the darkness behind the corrals. "But I don't know if they'll talk. They don't have much use for the white man's law."

"You mean those relatives of Judith's?"

"Yeah. I need to talk to them."

They drove around the Eastside for a while. Ron tried to get Harry to take a hit of some fine cocaine he carried but Harry refused. Ron also wanted to stop at one of the "pussy bars" for a drink or two but Harry wasn't up for that either.

"Shit," Ron said finally, "You're as much fun as my old man. You're not that old yet."

"Just tired, I guess. They're havin' my Dad's funeral tomorrow."

"Oh, fuck, I'm sorry." Ron looked at him. "Don't you want to go?"

"No. Doesn't seem to be much point in it."

"No," Ron said, "I guess there wouldn't be."

The morning was blustery and wet as a late-winter storm blew through Puget Sound. Ron called his father's office and told them he wouldn't be in.

"Any excuse to stay away from Radford Retirement Environments," he said to Harry. "I hate it worse every day."

Ron had agreed to help Harry find a job. They left early, had an espresso and pastry at a little bakery and picked up a Seattle Post-Intelligencer. Harry looked through the help-wanted ads. There were quite a few construction jobs on the Eastside.

He put in several applications but was disappointed that most of the jobs paid less than five dollars an hour. He wouldn't be able to save money at those wages, especially if he had to rent a place. Finally one concrete company owner who interviewed him looked at his qualifications, his years with Arne Olson, his stint as a job superintendent for United Homes, and asked him why he didn't get a subcontractor's license.

"That's how it's all done, now," he said. "The general contractors don't want to hire their own labor. They want someone's ass on the line in case anything goes wrong. And they squeeze the hell out of us. But you can make good money if you work day and night."

They went back to Ron's and Harry called the State to see what the subcontractor license procedure was. There really weren't many requirements except for a bond. They couldn't tell him how much that would cost but they did give him the names of some bonding companies. He called two of them in Bellevue and they told him to come in and pick-up applications.

Ron drove him down and Harry filled out the applications and did a quick interview. It all looked like it would be routine. Except for the five thousand dollars each wanted. Ron told him not to worry about the money. He could help with that.

Harry wasn't sure what specialty to license in; he really could do almost anything in construction. Ron recommended electrical.

"It's inside, after the building's up. And then it's all covered up so no one sees anything."

Harry visited Judith and the kids twice in the next few days but things didn't get any better. Little Joe always was happy to see him but Rebecca would hardly say a word to him. Judith remained evasive and distant. He always left the project feeling worse than he had before he went there.

Both bonding companies rejected his applications, cited credit problems from the farm. Harry asked them what that had to do with the quality of his work, but they said it wasn't about that, it was about money.

Ron offered again to hire him to work for the Radfords' nursing-home company, but Harry could not imagine himself there. Ron admitted that it was a terrible place to work but the money was good. He offered to set up a sub-contractor partnership and put the bond in his name but Harry wouldn't agree.

Harry went to the employment office at the University of Washington to see if he could get on the grounds crew where he'd worked as an undergraduate but they weren't hiring. He thought of finishing up his Masters' degree in Anthropology, but he knew he never again could adjust to the stifling world of academics. He longed for the country, for solitude, for self-reliance.

He knew that Ron tired of his company and Harry couldn't blame him. Depression is contagious and Ron had enough trouble adjusting to life away from the farm. Harry knew his friend's brave show of urbanization was a thin veneer and at times Ron would admit that he would take their old life back in a minute. Harry knew he had to make some kind of move.

Finally he asked Judith if he could spend some time at her place, in the daytime, to read and think and make some decisions. He would be glad to watch the kids for her. She said if she didn't send them to daycare she might lose her grant and not be able to get it again. She did say that he could stay there in the daytime, but he had to leave in the early evening so she could keep the kids lives regular. If she wasn't there he was not to answer the door or the telephone, no matter what, and he was to tell no one he was her husband. He agreed.

Judith still pursued her own search for work although Harry knew it wore on her. She had been a rising star in Sureco's underwriting department less than ten years before and now, it seemed, she had joined the ranks of the unemployable. She got one offer, at minimum wage, as a keyboard entry clerk for a hardware chain but when she calculated her take-home pay it was far less than she got from welfare. She remained happy and confident when the children were around, but sometimes, when they were gone, her face was drawn and she looked much older than she was.

Harry tried to reach her, to re-establish their relationship but she was cold towards him. He knew she didn't dare trust him and he did not know how to change that. He was determined not to make it worse and did his best to help her however he could. The one thing he could not provide was money and that was what she needed most of all.

One day as they sat at the kitchen table to talk and it seemed like he had made some progress, there was a knock at the door.

"Who is it?" Judith asked without opening it.

"Jack Barnes," a male voice answered. "We're from the Department of Social and Health Services. We need to discuss your eligibility."

Harry saw a fearful look cross Judith's face and she motioned him into the bedroom. She closed the bedroom door and he heard her let the DSHS people in.

"We understand your husband has moved in here. We need a new application. This could affect your eligibility."

Judith denied that her husband lived there and assured them that she was making every effort to find work. A woman's voice joined with the man's as they questioned her about Harry's whereabouts. She told them he was somewhere in Eastern Washington, she wasn't sure where. Harry checked out the closet, made sure he could hide in there if they came to the bedroom.

They shifted direction, asked Judith about support, whether there was a decree or court order. When she said there wasn't, they told her that she would have to file for divorce or separation and get a child-support decree or she would lose her eligibility. She said that she didn't want anything from him but they told her that it wasn't her he owed, but the State, and the State wanted their money.

By the time they left Harry trembled and was short of breath. He had never felt so humiliated and was sure that Judith felt the same. He could hardly look at her when she opened the bedroom door.

"Now do you understand?"

He just nodded.

When Harry told Ron about the DSHS visit, Ron said, "Why don't you just go ahead with the divorce? It would be better for both of you. It doesn't sound like you're doing any good there, anyway. Besides, no one stays married anymore. You need to get on with your life."

Ron took him out for dinner, tried to get him interested in other women, but it all seemed unreal. He made a weak attempt to flirt with a waitress, but she looked at him like he was some old geezer. He felt like one.

After they got back to Ron's apartment, the telephone rang. Ron answered and turned to Harry. "Judith," he mouthed.

Harry was excited. It was the first time Judith had called him since he'd been on the coast.

"Hi," he said to her.

"Hello, Harry. I wondered if you wanted to come to dinner tomorrow. Little Eagle and Nathan will be here."

"Harry's heart dropped. "I don't think Nathan wants me around. I'd just be in his way."

"Nathan's the one who wanted me to invite you," Judith said sharply. "You need to get off of that."

"I'm sorry. Sure, I'll come. What time?"

"Around seven."

"Should I bring something?"

"Just yourself."

He looked forward to the dinner all day. He wanted to talk to Long Joe, Judith's distant cousin whom she called Little Eagle. Long Joe always had something important to say, something Harry needed to hear. And Nathan had wanted Harry to come. Maybe he would finally drop his old crush on Judith, accept her marriage to Harry. At the auction Nathan had said all he wanted was for Harry to take care of Judith and the kids. Maybe he'd meant it.

Harry knocked on Judith's door a few minutes early. She smiled at him and it was like water to a man dying of thirst. He wasn't sure if it was a mirage. He tried to smile back, afraid it was just a grimace.

Long Joe and Nathan were there, sat on the couch and nodded greetings. Harry sat in a chair near Long Joe and looked into the little man's eyes. So many times, it seemed, those eyes held answers.

"Harry," Long Joe said quietly. "It is good to see you."

"I'm surprised to see you over here."

"No more than I am surprised to see you. We took Judith's horses up to Cache Creek and decided to come visit her. What is your excuse."

"I'm not sure. It seemed like a good idea at the time."

"You do not seem happy here," Long Joe said.

"I hate it," Harry replied. "This used to be my home, now it feels like an alien planet."

"Home is funny that way," Long Joe said. "A rich man once told me his home was everywhere, that he was a planetary citizen. I told him he was homeless. To have a home is to know a place intimately, for a long time."

"I don't want to know this place intimately."

"No one does," Long Joe said. "It is just an outlaws' camp."

"When are you going to start on your cabin?" Nathan asked him.

"I don't know," Harry said. "I wanted to get a job over here, save some money. All I've done is spend money."

"You don't need a lot of money," Nathan said. "We can find what you need. I told you I would help. And you promised me."

"I don't know if there's a reason to build a cabin. I can live anywhere, by myself."

Nathan and Long Joe looked at Judith and she looked away. "She does not trust you anymore, Harry," Long Joe said. "It is hard for her to try again, to make a new start when she has been hurt before."

"She needs a sign," Nathan said, "proof that you are changed."

"Don't talk about me like I wasn't here," Judith said angrily.

"Are you here?" Long Joe asked. "I thought you had gone to your own world."

"It's the only world I have. I have to take care of myself and my kids. No one else is going to do it."

"No one can do everything all alone," Long Joe said. "That is the white man's illusion. That way you always fail."

"I feel every day like all I do is fail."

"Congratulations," Long Joe said. "You have figured it out. That is how you are supposed to feel. They take away your means of support then say, 'See there, you are useless, you cannot even feed yourself.'"

"It's not her fault," Harry said.

"Of course it is her fault," Long Joe said. "She is the one who chose to live in an outlaws' camp."

"It's just the way the world is," Harry said. "No one can stand alone against it."

"It is hard to win another man's game," Long Joe said.

"That's fine to say," Harry said, "but you have to be part of your own time. No one can choose the world they are born into."

"But we all choose our own lives, Harry," Long Joe said. "We all make our own deaths. You said you understood that just a few days ago."

"I thought I did. But then the real world crashes down on me."

"This is not a real world. What will these outlaws do, Harry?" Long Joe asked, "when they can't steal their living any more? That's all they've done for at least a thousand years. For the last five hundred years they have stolen from the dark people of the earth, first the land, then the trees and grass and water and the minerals underground. They even stole our bodies to do their labor. But they have all of it, now. They can steal from each other for a little while. But soon there will only be a few rich and everyone else will be poor. Then who do they steal from? They tried to go to other planets and could not. There is nothing left to steal. For outlaws, that is a problem because the whole system depends on more and more and more loot."

"Then what?" Harry asked. "What happens then?"

"War and riots and starvation and epidemics. Any band of outlaws can work together during a robbery, but what happens when it is time to split up the loot? They fight."

"So what's the answer? Everyone wants a better life."

Long Joe looked at him for a while. "The way our people lived, in the old days, we never suffered from want. We had needs, which we filled as we could, where we could. But we did not want. The white man brought that concept, to want. Want is an addiction to needless, useless things. To fill this unfillable void, the white man placed a tax on the entire planet. Not just on human production, but on the bones, blood and skin of our Mother. He has ravaged the planet and now wants to tax us all again so he can pretend to clean it up. What the planet needs is to be left alone. To the most extreme extent possible. That is obvious, inescapable to a rational mind. The brave white man leads us in looking away while our Mother is butchered, like an addict who winces at the moment the needle breaks the vein."

"We can't all go to the woods," Harry said. "There are too many of us, now."

"That is not true," Long Joe said. "Even now. That is another of the big lies. If everyone would settle for what they need—food, water, air, a place to raise happy children, there is still room enough for all. It is not what we need that is the problem. It is what we want. The whites brought a culture of fear and want. The only thing that sometimes kept them from committing unspeakable acts was the fear that they would burn in hell or that the law would come and hang them. At first we thought that these whites who came here were sick and had been exiled by their own people. We kept expecting that some day we would meet 'normal' whites. We never did." He paused and looked seriously at them. "The covenants are broken," he said. "The covenant between parents and children, the covenant between man and woman, the covenant between people and the Earth. All broken."

Harry laughed. "Well you certainly made me feel better."

Long Joe smiled at him. "I will not preach anymore. At least not tonight. Judith has made us a fine dinner and I am hungry."

"I'm not sure I am," Harry said.

"Suit yourself," Nathan said. "I'm starved. I haven't had any decent food since we've been over here."

When he sat down at the table Harry was hungry after all. Judith had bought two free-range chickens and roasted them with potatoes and carrots and mushrooms. There was a huge green salad and apple pie for dessert. She was silent at dinner, seemed deep in thought.

Little Joe idolized Long Joe and Nathan and chattered incessantly. Even Rebecca smiled and talked although sometimes when she looked at Harry she grew as silent as her mother.

Nathan talked of the cabin they would build and where they could find materials. He seemed determined to be Harry's friend and even Harry found it hard to believe he still carried a torch for Judith.

Long Joe talked of the seminars he had lined up in Oregon and California and of another planned appearance at the Experimental College where Harry had first realized that there was more to the little man than the "Patient Joseph Longeaux" he'd met at Western State. Harry knew this was his real family, not the quarreling group whose only common thread was the last name of Isaacson.

That family had died with the old man.

When Judith went to put the kids to bed, Harry told Long Joe and Nathan about his problem with the Sheriff's Department. "I think they know I didn't do it," he said. "It's just another hassle from the bank."

"We know you did not do it, Harry," Long Joe said.

"What do you mean?"

"We saw it," Nathan said. "Almost. We saw your father go into the old house, then we heard the gunshot. You were still at the corral."

"We will tell them," Long Joe said. "When we go back home we will go to the sheriffs and tell them."

"They might not believe you."

"Because we're Indians?" Nathan asked.

"And because you're related to my wife. Besides, murder is better for the department than suicide."

"They will believe us," Long Joe said, "Because we tell the truth."

"I hope you're right," Harry said.

Long Joe and Nathan left. Harry offered them a ride, but they made it clear that Harry was to stay, to talk to Judith. There was an awkward silence when they were gone.

Finally Judith said, "I heard what you told them, Harry. How can anyone think you would do that?"

"They don't," Harry said. "At least most of them. They just need someone to hang it on. I'm not their favorite person."

"You should have told me, Harry."

"You have enough to worry about."

"But I'm your wife."

"Are you?" he asked, felt tears in his eyes.

"I want to be. Sometimes I don't know how."

"I'm the one who doesn't know how. I'm not sure I know anything."

"I love you, Harry," she said suddenly. "I can't pretend I don't. I'm just afraid."

"I don't blame you. I should have listened to you. You were right. About the farm and the bank and Dad. But everyone else was on the other side."

"We should always be on the same side. We have enough enemies without each other."

She came to sit beside him and he kissed her. It had been so long. She asked him to stay and he began to cry and she held him and stroked his hair and he felt like a child. They talked long into the night. They made love and slept in each other's arms for the first time in many months.

CHAPTER 4

The track Walt had plowed was filled with snow so Harry parked just off the highway and walked in. In the stillness of the valley the fragile snow fell straight down, glistened in a latticework that collapsed in sparkling craters with each step. Soft avalanches slipped from tree-limbs. One fall surprised a Stellar's Jay who squawked and shook off the powder in a swirl of blue sparks.

The river gurgled above the ice in spots. Where the ice was thin he could see large air bubbles move like white amoebas on the surface of the water beneath the ice. If he stood still and stared straight ahead, Harry felt as though the valley floor rose under him, carried him up into the snow-cloud.

He thought for a moment that he heard children's voices in the distance, laughter and shouts of joy. Then the sound faded and the stillness returned, broken only by the gentle flow of the water. He thought of the dream that had followed him since Viet Nam, the dark eyes of children dying in flames. He hadn't had the dream since the auction, had hoped it never would return. He wondered if these were the voices of those children.

He was anxious to see Walt and Frances. He had begun to think his brother Jack was right to call him a throwback. There didn't seem to be anyone younger than his grandparents' age that he really could relate to. Everyone his own age was caught up in a frantic rush to make up for the years they'd spent in Viet Nam or at home saving the world. And the younger generation didn't seem to have any purpose or direction at all.

Everything he wanted to learn was disappearing with a generation no one appreciated any longer. But as much as he respected those of his grandfather's generation, he knew that the old man had revered his own grandfather's time. The sociologists and psychologists said that was normal, an illusion of wisdom ascribed to elders who really were less knowledgeable than their descendants.

Harry no longer was sure that was true. He often thought of the old country saying, "If you're so smart, why ain't you rich?" and changed it to "If we're so smart, why aren't we happy?" There didn't seem to be an answer. He did not doubt that his grandparents had been far more satisfied with their lives than his parents with their time or his own generation with the present. The old folks had "settled for less," as Mom liked to say, but they had been so much more at home.

There was nothing like a trip to the city to remind him how out of synch his own life was. When he had been away for a while, he began to believe he could adjust, melt into the urban crowd and live a normal life. But once there he felt like some traveler in space or time dropped onto a penal planet to expiate some terrible sin. He was determined to stay here in this valley, grow roots and endure.

The old mare gazed at him across the fence and contentedly chewed her morning hay. He noticed that her ribs no longer showed and her back seemed straighter, as though she'd grown young in his absence.

Walt laughed when Harry mentioned it. "She's just a youngster," he said. "She could work another ten years if she's treated right. And give you four or five fine foals in the meantime."

Although it snowed still, Walt said that he expected breakup in about a month. The cottonwood buds were slightly swollen and already he'd seen warblers. The willows, he pointed out to Harry, were a brighter red.

Walt and Frances offered to let Harry stay with them while he built a cabin and insisted until he finally agreed. He had intended to set up a makeshift tent or sleep in his pickup and "rough-it" but the Davises convinced him that wasn't necessary. If he felt like he owed them something he could help Walt with the equipment and the stock.

"Believe it or not," Walt said, "I'm not as young as I once was. I could use the help."

Harry was grateful for the work. He also learned more than he had hoped about horses and horse-drawn equipment. Walt explained everything he did and named every piece of machinery and equipment as they inspected and repaired and oiled it. Often to Harry it was the old man's voice that recited the names.

Harry soon could harness a horse in a few minutes. It also was his grandfather he heard name off the parts of the harness, hame and trace and girth and bellyband, backband and crupper and breeching. It was so simple he wondered at the complaints he'd heard all his life from Dad's generation about the terrible trials of working horses. It took no longer to harness and hitch a horse to a wagon than it did for the same operation with a tractor. And Walt could control his horses with simple voice commands.

"Try that with a tractor," he said.

The old mare fidgeted and stamped her feet the first time Harry put the harness on her. He realized it was nearly ten years since she'd been worked. She was the old man's companion until he died and afterwards had been kept and fed because no one could imagine life without her. The harness Harry used was assembled from what he'd salvaged from the barn after the auction and he was sure it still smelled of the old man to the mare.

Soon she pulled the feed wagon for them, head up, neck arched with pride. The more Harry worked her, the closer they became. She whinnied softly to him whenever he came out of the house or returned from a trip out. He used her to plow the road again and brought his pickup to the house. He rarely started the pickup and began to understand why Walt and Frances still drove a thirty-year-old sedan whenever they had to go out. He checked the odometer on the old car and found that it had gone less than forty thousand miles.

He called Judith every few days from the store and she sounded happy to hear from him. DSHS had backed off for now and she waited for spring and the cabin. She always put both kids on the phone but Rebecca still had little to say to him.

Nathan came, as promised, the second week Harry was there. He had borrowed a one-ton truck and the back was loaded with lumber and miscellaneous doors and windows he'd found for the cabin. He had three days, he said, before he had to return the truck. Harry realized that he'd never been alone with Nathan before and half-expected the familiar sarcasm and rivalry to return, but Nathan took the role of old friend or distant relative and the two of them spent hours together, planned the cabin, or just simply talked. Walt and Frances were honored by a visit from a grandson of their old friends, the McTavishes, and treated Nathan with great respect.

The second morning he was there, after he'd helped Harry and Walt feed the stock, Nathan said he had something to show Harry. As they walked towards the truck, Nathan looked at him with an ironic grin.

"We talked to the sheriff. Joseph and me."

"That must have been fun," Harry said.

"I didn't know if we'd get out of there," Nathan said. "They kept us in that little room for about three hours. Before we left they were warning us that we might be charged with something. They didn't seem to know what."

"It must have been a big disappointment to them," Harry said, "when they found out I didn't do it."

"The fat one threw his notebook on the counter and started hollering," Nathan said. "Then they took us in the back. They wanted to know if we were related to your Indian wife and how long we'd known you. The young one said they wanted us to take a lie detector test but Joseph just laughed at them."

"I don't think Long Joe is afraid of anything," Harry said.

"Not white people, anyway," Nathan said. "They read us our rights and offered to get lawyers for us and everything. They had me worried."

"They probably checked for warrants on you," Harry said.

"Oh yeah, they knew every time I'd been arrested and that I spent a year in reform school. They said I wouldn't make a very good witness. But they couldn't find anything on Joseph."

"Not even his time in Western State?" Harry asked.

"They didn't mention it," Nathan said. "I think he used another name there."

"And they'd never dream that this little old Indian is smarter than they are," Harry said. "I wish I could handle the world as well as he does."

"Don't we all?" Nathan asked.

On the third day when Nathan headed back to Nespelem, Harry was sorry to see him go.

Harry had chosen a spot at the north end of the big meadow for the cabin and he anxiously watched the snow melt. Walt was right about breakup and before the first of April the warm days softened the ground and the valley became a bog. Willow and cottonwood buds were swollen to the bursting point and the bright tips of tamarack needles showed along the boughs.

Whitetail does led new fawns to water just down the river from the cabin site. Reject wanted to herd them as he'd often done with calves and Harry had to tie him or shut him up in the pickup until he learned to leave the deer alone. The dog would tremble as he watched them come and go and look at Harry for a sign to bring them to him.

Nathan knew someone who had some thirty-foot lodgepole house logs that had been down almost two years and were just right to build with. It would cost five hundred dollars for a log-truck load of them. Harry hesitated at first but it was such a good buy that he couldn't pass it up. His cash needs had gone down to almost nothing since he'd come back to the San Poil.

One morning Harry heard an air-horn blaring from the highway just after he and Walt had fed the stock. He went out to check and it was the driver with his load of logs. The driver looked familiar, then Harry realized it was the guy who'd impatiently waited for the pay phone that first day on the river. They nodded at each other with recognition. The driver backed the truck in as close to the building site as he dared in the mud.

"Had to get it done, today," the driver said. "Road restrictions go on tomorrow until breakup is over."

"Thanks," Harry said. "I can get started peeling these now."

They took three old logs Harry had found and laid them endways to the truck and pulled the stakes on that side. When the driver loosed the chains most of the logs rolled off. They pushed off the others and Harry took a good look at them. They were perfect. He paid the driver the five hundred dollars and watched him pull away.

He borrowed a large drawknife from Walt and started to peel the logs that afternoon. As dry as they were, they peeled easily. He loved the smell of the pine wood and knew that the cabin would smell that way for years. He couldn't wait to start laying logs. But first he needed a foundation.

He asked Walt how high he'd seen the river and Walt had said that at least twice he'd seen it just reach Harry's building site during spring runoff.

"It wouldn't take much of a mound to get you high enough," Walt said. "I've got an old wheel-scraper that would do the trick. You could dig yourself a pond while you're at it."

Harry liked that idea and spent some time deciding just where to put a pond. He planned to build up the old rock-dam Bill McTavish had used to raise the river enough to flow into his irrigation flume. If he located the pond right, he could gravity feed water into it. But he didn't want it too close to the house or the mosquitoes would be terrible. He figured that's why the McTavish house had been out along the highway. He'd thought of building there, but didn't want to be exposed to the highway traffic. When the McTavishes had built there it had been only a wagon track and almost no strangers traveled it.

He chose a spot for the pond about two hundred feet away and drove stakes to mark the corners. He hoped he didn't run into too many large rocks.

Walt grinned when Harry mentioned that.

"Don't worry," the old man said. "I've got the answer for boulders."

The snow was gone from the meadow in just a few days and the grass grew green. In the deep shade along the river patches of dirty white seeped their moisture into the earth. As the snow in the high-country melted the river rose and soon was a muddy torrent. They had to watch the bridge for logs and brush and other debris that caught there. Water came over the bank and flooded the lower end of the meadow.

Harry realized that it would be June before the cabin was up and roofed and if he started farming it would be even later. He did not want to wait that long for Judith and the kids to join him and each time he talked to her he could hear the depression in her voice. There was no room at the Davises' for the whole family and there was no place to rent in the valley. Especially without money.

Nathan visited him to see how the work was going and Harry told him how much he wanted his family there.

"No problem," Nathan said. "My Aunt has a tipi you could use. They won't need it until Stampede. It has a liner and floor and everything. Nice and warm."

"I don't know," Harry said as he thought of how other people would react to that. He could just see Mom or Jack and Diane, when they heard he lived in a tipi.

"I'll bring it," Nathan said. "We'll put it up and you'll see."

Nathan came in the one-ton again. The tipi poles stuck way out over the cab. Harry hadn't realized they would be so long and so big around; some of them were six inches at the butt. The cover was a large bundle of canvas stained with smoke. The day Nathan came the flood water nearly reached Harry's building site so they picked a spot for the tipi closer to the highway up on a little rise.

Nathan paced out an area and made marks on the ground with his boot heel. He laid out the three largest poles and lashed them together a few feet from the tips. Harry helped him walk the poles upright and Nathan set the bases on three of his marks.

"That's the tripod," Nathan said, "The rest is easy."

Already the frame was surprisingly strong.

He showed Harry how to lay the other poles onto the tripod and in less than half an hour the cone of poles was in place.

Harry noticed that the cone wasn't symmetrical but tipped towards the west and it wasn't round, but egg-shaped. Nathan took the loose end of the long rope he'd used to lash together the tripod and walked around the frame four times, snapping the rope into place to bind the apex of the cone tightly together.

One long pole and two shorter ones remained unused. They pushed the cover off the truck and Nathan unrolled it and folded it into a long triangle. He tied the tip of the triangle to the unused long pole at about the same distance from the tip as the point where the frame poles crossed. Nathan had Harry stand with his foot against the base of the pole as he started to raise it, then called for him to come and help him walk it up. The pole and cover were heavy but they soon had the pole vertical then tipped it towards the frame. Just before it fell into the gap at the top of the cone, Nathan turned it so the top of the cover was on the outside.

It took only a few minutes to unfold the cover and lay it around the frame. It hung loosely, not taut as Harry had seen before, but he waited to see what Nathan would do. Nathan got a ladder out of the truck and climbed to the top and used slender wooden pegs to fasten the cover together down as far as the doorway. Then he took a bag of wooden stakes and showed Harry how to twist them into loops of rope spaced every few inches around the bottom of the cover then drive them into the ground. They did one at the front, then one at the back, then one on each side so they would be even. Then they cut the quarters in half, then half again until the entire cover was staked down.

Nathan showed Harry how to move the bases of the poles against the cover and stretch the cover tight. They turned several curved poles so that the curve was outward. Nathan said these would straighten from the pressure of the cover. They dug holes about a foot deep for the bases of the three tripod poles and sunk them into the ground.

The two shorter poles fit into pockets on the flaps at the smoke-hole. Nathan showed Harry how to open and close the hole with the flaps and how to set them to shield the hole, depending on wind direction. The smoke-hole and the door faced east, a direction from which wind rarely came, but just right to catch the earliest sun.

It took almost as long to rake the earth and lay the canvas floor and to hang the liner that was suspended from the insides of the poles at about the height of Harry's head. Nathan made a hearth of river-rock in a hole in the center of the floor and then laid a fire of dry wood. Harry heard him whisper a brief chant before he lit the fire.

There was smoke inside for just a few minutes, then the fire began to draw air in between the liner and cover and out through the smoke-hole. Nathan adjusted the smoke-flaps a little to block the southerly breeze and the tipi soon was warm and pleasant.

"Here's your new home," Nathan said with a grin. "You'll have to be careful. In the old days a woman could divorce you just by throwing all your shit out of her tipi."

"I'll be careful," Harry said.

They sat on the floor and talked. Nathan told Harry about different tribes' styles of tipis, the difference between three-pole people and four-pole people. He described how they were set for different conditions or different purposes. Harry was surprised at how much Nathan knew and at how much there was to know.

As they talked they heard the roar of an engine and Harry looked out to see a bright red Ford Mustang park at the turnoff. Someone got out and put on a cowboy hat, started to walk towards the tipi.

"We've got company," Harry said. "Some cowboy in a red Mustang."

"Johnny Carlson," Nathan said. "Your neighbor. Bad news."

"I met his dad," Harry said. "Helped him pull a calf."

"He's bad news, too," Nathan said.

"I'll head him off," Harry said. He went outside and watched the young Carlson walk towards him.

"Howdy," Johnny said as he got within ten feet of Harry.

"Hello," Harry said. "You must be Johnny Carlson."

"How do you know that?" Johnny asked after a pause.

"Someone told me," Harry said.

"What you doin' with the wigwam?" Johnny asked.

"I'm going to store my hay in it," Harry said.

"I thought maybe you were an Indian," Johnny said. "I thought Indians owned this place."

"They do," Harry said. He felt Nathan come out of the tipi behind him.

Johnny looked at Nathan then back at Harry, said something below his breath.

"What did you say?" Nathan asked him.

"Nothin'" Johnny said. "Just thinkin'."

"You always think out loud?" Nathan asked.

Johnny glared at him. "Just keepin' an eye on things. Too many hippies and shit movin' in around here. We don't like squatters."

"What are you trying to say?" Harry asked him.

"Nothin'," Johnny said. "We've used this place for years, for fall pasture. We know the people that own it."

"You mean my family?" Nathan asked him. "We put horses in here almost every spring."

"Those're your horses?" Johnny asked. "Damned fine horses. Some of 'em."

"All our horses are fine," Nathan said.

"Well, there'll be cows all over here in the fall," Johnny said.

"Not this fall," Harry said. "I'm going to farm it."

"This ain't no farm," Johnny said. "This is cow country. We need this pasture."

"It's not for sale," Nathan said.

"Well, we'll see about this," Johnny said as he stomped away.

"I told you he was bad news," Nathan said.

When Harry called Judith to tell her that the tipi was ready, she was excited, then Harry heard her voice become more guarded, her energy drop. He knew it was his fault and he hated it. He was determined to show her that he could be trusted, could be relied on. It would take time.

He told her he would be over in two days to get them. Judith worried about Rebecca having to change schools.

"She has friends, here," Judith said. "Over there she will be alone."

"She will have her family here," Harry said.

"Friends are important at her age," Judith said.
"Then we'll find her friends," Harry said.

Walt and Frances told Harry that his family could eat with them until the cabin was finished or Judith could cook there. But Harry wanted to be as independent as possible. He appreciated what the Davises had done for him, but he wanted to do it on his own. It seemed like all his life he'd depended on someone who always let him down.

He made a run to Uncle Paul's, got all the cooking utensils and other stuff that seemed useful in a tipi. He took bedding and dishes and more of his clothes. He reluctantly told Paul of his plan.

Paul said it sounded like a great adventure.

"At least you will all be together," Paul said. "That's the most important thing. And if you need anything, just give me a holler."

Paul told Harry a Sheriff's deputy had been out to see him. "He said some Indians had been in to see them, said that they saw your Dad go in the old man's place then heard a gunshot. He wanted to know if I saw any Indians at the auction. I told him I knew that two Indians had bought some horses. That seemed to piss him off good."

Harry told him what he knew of Long Joe and Nathan's encounter with the Sheriff's Department.

"Maybe now they'll accept the truth."

"Not if they can help it," Paul said. "I know
they're still holdin' up the insurance. Your Mom called the other day bitchin' that she still didn't have any money. I don't think things are goin' that well with her and Jack and Diane." He grinned. "Seems to me like they're well-matched."

Harry grinned back.

"It'll give them all somethin' to do."

Harry practiced with the fire and the smoke flaps, soon could keep the tipi warm with ease. He borrowed Walt's chainsaw and cut more wood and stacked it nearby. He drove to Republic for groceries but not sure what Judith would want, did the best he could. Walt and Frances assured him that they would help with anything they needed.

As he left one morning just after dawn to get his family, Harry looked back from the road at the tipi and smiled to himself. It wasn't what he had intended but it could serve as home for now.

CHAPTER 5

Judith had everything packed and Harry could see she was anxious to go. She kissed him and gave him a hint of her old smile. Little Joe, too, could not wait, jumped into Harry's arms and said, "Daddy, I miss you, let's go home."

Rebecca just looked at him when he smiled and said "hello" to her and she silently helped carry things down to the pickup. When she was out of earshot, Judith said, "She made the mistake of telling one of her girlfriends that she was going to live in a tipi. They've been teasing her. She didn't even go to school yesterday."

A few of the women Judith had gotten to know came to tell her good-bye.

Valerie looked at Harry and shook her head. "You're makin' a mistake, girlfriend," Harry heard her tell Judith. "I wouldn't want to be up in the mountains all alone with him." She glanced at Harry and he knew she intended for him to hear. "Don't forget. Tony will be here waitin' for you." She winked for Harry's benefit.

They were on the road in the early afternoon. It was full-blown spring on the coast, everything green and flowers in bloom. Flocks of ducks and geese circled over Lake Washington as they crossed the Floating Bridge. Harry left I-90, drove north to Highway 2 so they could go over Stevens' Pass. He and Judith often had gone that way when they first were together and in later years as they prepared to move to the farm. Maybe the old familiar surroundings would help ease the tension.

They were crowded on the pickup seat and Little Joe squirmed and chattered. Harry didn't mind, enjoyed the contact and hoped they'd spend many hours close together. Rebecca remained silent and he realized he had a lot of work to do with his daughter. He smiled whenever he saw her look at him and he made sure to include her in anything he said.

They stopped at a good fish-and-chips place Harry remembered in Wenatchee and Little Joe ate with abandon. Judith had saved some money from her last welfare check and insisted that she pay. She had notified DSHS about the move and her caseworker said that if she went back to her husband that would automatically disqualify her for any further assistance. Harry assured her that they wouldn't need it.

Harry watched Judith's face soften as they neared her home. They left Highway 2 at Coulee City and drove up the east side of Banks Lake. The big irrigation reservoir was low and a wide band of white alkali-stained rocks showed above the water along the shore. He never could drive through the Grand Coulee, past Dry Falls and Steamboat Rock, and not think of the cataclysmic flood that had ripped through the area in prehistoric times when an ice dam on the Clark Fork River in Montana had broken and released the huge lake that had built up behind it.

They were to spend the night with Judith's family in Electric City at the north end of the lake. Little Joe could hardly contain his excitement. He loved to spend time with his grandfather, Matt, and his grandmother, Helen, was his favorite person in the world. Rebecca began to smile and chatter to Judith about her eagerness to see her grandparents.

Harry was apprehensive about how his in-laws would treat him after all the problems, but they welcomed him warmly and Helen offered him coffee and a piece of cake as soon as they sat down. He told Helen she still was the best cook he knew. She had more lines around her eyes than when he first had met her, but still she was a beautiful woman, a darker version of Judith with the same eyes, same smile.

Judith's sister Rachel was there on a visit with her infant son. She had married a local boy who owned a small construction company. She drove to Moses Lake two evenings a week to take college classes. Sara, two years older than Rachel, was in medical school in St. Louis and wanted to come back when she finished and work with the tribe. Their brother, Joseph, had graduated from law school at Stanford and worked in legal services for the Navajo tribe in Arizona, but he, too wanted to return home when he could.

Harry always was struck by the incongruity of Matt Adams, large-boned, blond, ruddy complexion, with his dark, Native family. Harry identified strongly with Matt and hoped he could do as well with his family as Matt had done.

The three women soon had dinner on and it was as good as usual. Helen was the complete wife and mother, spotless house, great food, happy, successful children. Harry hoped the old saw about looking at your mother-in-law to see your wife in twenty years held true. After dinner they all talked while the children played.

Rachel left for home and Helen noticed how tired Harry was.

"You kids need to get some rest. Your room is made-up, Judith."

They slept in Judith's old basement room which opened out into the garden, the room where Harry and Judith first had made love many years before.

"Remember?" Judith asked him and smiled that familiar smile. "You were scared to death of me."

"I was not," Harry lied.

The children soon were asleep on the trundle bed Helen had made up for them. Harry and Judith quietly made love.

Rebecca groaned when she saw the tipi.

"It will be fine," Judith said. "And it's just for a little while."

"Where do I go to school?" Rebecca asked.

"We're in the Wilbur District, but you could go to Republic if we take you up the river to the bus-stop every day. I think you would like Republic better. Wilbur is all wheat-farmers and cowboys."

"What's wrong with wheat-farmers and cowboys?" Harry asked her.

"Nothing if you have blonde hair and blue eyes," Judith answered.

When Rebecca went for a walk along the river Judith told Harry that she had decided to keep her out of school for the remainder of the year.

"She's having enough trouble," Judith said. "She doesn't need a whole new school to adjust to right now."

When they went in the tipi, Judith said, "I know this tipi. It belongs to my Aunt Lucy. See that cut." She showed Harry where the canvas had been mended with fine hand-stitches. "That happened at the Stampede in Omak the year Nathan came in third in the Suicide Race. A white man cut it to get inside, some tourist. Nathan and my cousin, Lucky, caught him and nearly beat him up but a deputy heard him yell and rescued him. He told the deputy that someone said that was all he had to do to get an Indian girl, he called it 'tipi creeping.'"

Harry showed her the building site and the logs and the pile of lumber and doors and windows Nathan had brought.

"I'm so glad you and Nathan get along," she said. "I knew you had a lot in common. That's why I like both of you."

Harry wondered what she meant by that.

The road was very muddy near the bridge so they walked in to the Davises'. Walt and Frances greeted Judith as though she were a long-lost relative and remarked on how much she and the kids looked like her family.

"It's almost like Bill and Martha reincarnated," Walt said. "No offense."

They all laughed.

Judith was impressed with the condition of the old mare.

"The old man would be so proud of her," she said wistfully. "I miss him, Harry."

"He talks to me every day," Harry said.

Walt and Frances offered to let them stay with them the first night but Judith wanted to get things arranged in the tipi. Harry lit a fire, set the smoke-flaps so it drew nicely. Little Joe played outside with his dump truck while they moved things in. Judith left her nicer things in the pickup and Harry said he would run down to Uncle Paul's and put them in storage with their other stuff.

Several times that first night Harry awakened and lay in the darkness, listened to Judith and the children as they slept. He could hardly believe they were all together again. Rebecca was restless, talked in her sleep and rolled about. He wanted to reach out and comfort her but knew that he dare not, not yet.

Judith wanted a sweat. She chose a site down-river from the tipi, just below the spot where Harry planned to put a pond. It was a shelf barely above the high-water line, screened by bushes from every direction. She cut tall, thin chokecherry and saskatoon saplings and sunk their butts into the earth in a circle, bent the tops over to form a dome and tied the tips together. She covered it with a tarp, left a flap for the door.

She dug a shallow hole and used stones from the river to build a fire-pit nearby. When it was ready she built a fire and let it burn down to coals then piled on more river-rock to heat. She used two short, stout sticks to move hot stones into a depression in the center of the shelter. As it began to heat she called the children and had them strip to their underwear and sit on blankets inside. She talked Harry into joining them.

The first round of rocks cooled and she moved in more, built up the fire and put more on to heat. She brought two buckets of water and set them near the hot stones. She put in a third round of hot rocks and came inside, closed the flap and stripped. It became very hot and soon they all were sweating profusely. From time to time she dipped a can of water from a bucket and threw it on the stones for steam.

In about twenty minutes she had Little Joe and Rebecca follow her outside and Harry heard them yell and then laugh as she took them into the river. When she had dried them off and had them dress she sent them to the tipi and rejoined Harry in the sweat. She dipped more water and heated the little dome until Harry could barely stand it.

"I've missed this so much," she said. "It's the worst thing about the city."

When it was so hot Harry thought he would have to escape she took his hand. "Come on. Into the river."

He was reluctant at first, but she insisted. After the first instant, the water did not feel cold. She had him immerse his head and when he bobbed up she floated beside him, smiled up at him.

"We'll all feel better, now. It will wash the city out of us."

Harry called Uncle Paul to see what he knew about the sheriff and the coroner and the insurance money. Paul said that all he knew was that the coroner had finally signed the death certificate, cause of death "self-inflicted gunshot wound."

"I ran into Jack in town and he said your Mom was leavin' for California the first of July so she must think she'll have her money by then." Paul paused. "I think there's some money there belongs to you, Harry. Jack was sayin' that when he got his share he was goin' to invest it in this new subdivision the banker is puttin' together. Seems to me your share of the partnership comes before any inheritance."

"I don't care about the money," Harry said. "Not that I couldn't use it. But it's just blood money to me. If Jack wants it, he can have it. Meg'll be around too, with her asshole husband. All I want is a fresh start."

"I know what you're sayin'," Paul said. "But you busted your ass on that place. You oughta get somethin' out of it."

"I got an education," Harry said. "That's all I can expect."

"Well, good luck Harry. You take care of yourself. And your family. I'm gonna come up there and have a look at that place one of these days."

"We'd love to see you, Paul," Harry said.

Harry was anxious to get on with the cabin and the farming. Walt helped him hook up the old mare to a one-bottom riding plow and Harry soon could plow a straight furrow with ease. He plowed about a half-acre of the upper meadow and used a section of spiketooth harrow to level it down. He made a run to Republic for seeds and found a decent selection at Anderson's store. He bought peas and cabbage and curly kale and some other early-season vegetables. Prices were high and he decided to write away for some seed catalogs.

Walt told him that Bill McTavish had grown tomatoes and peppers and even watermelons on the place and Harry wanted to try a little bit of everything the first year. He had decided to plant a few acres to alfalfa for hay for the horses and some oats for grain. He estimated that there was about forty acres of good cropland along the river. Across the river where the place bordered the Davises' was mostly timber and some good grazing that would need to be fenced.

The real question was what to do for a cash crop. With such a small area and markets so far away he would have to be very careful. He needed something of more value than hay or grain. Sweet corn would do well but it would be ready for harvest right in the middle of the commercial season when prices were low. He was afraid to commit to tomatoes and other hot-weather stuff because of the labor involved and his uncertainty about the best varieties. This would be a test year for those crops.

He told Uncle Paul about his problem when he took Judith's stuff down for storage.

"Funny you should mention that," Paul said. "There was a guy through here less than a month ago tryin' to find someone to grow carrots for his juice company. Carrots would work up there. And he was offerin' as high as a dollar a pound. Had to be done without chemicals. He said the best carrots he'd been able to find was over here east of the mountains because of the volcanic soil. He'd been all over but nobody wanted to mess with it. He needs a thousand pounds or so a week and they have to be fresh, no more than twenty-four hours from the field."

"I could do that," Harry said. "Even if I had to haul them. A thousand pounds at a dollar a pound would make the trip look pretty good."

"Carrots are a lot of work," Paul said. "You'd have to do several acres. That's a lot of weedin' and diggin'."

"I've got lots of time," Harry said. "Just no money."

"He even had the seeds," Paul said. "He knew exactly what he wanted."

"How do I get hold of this guy?" Harry asked.

"He left me a card," Paul said, "in case I ran into someone. Let me find it." He rummaged around in a drawer and came up with the card.

"High Mountain Juice," it said and there was a line drawing of Mount Rainier with fields of vegetables on the lower slopes. There was a name, Richard Rosen, and a phone number.

"Use my phone," Paul said. "May as well find out now."

Richard Rosen was out when he called but expected back any time. Harry told the girl on the phone why he had called and left Paul's number. He decided to wait for a while.

In less than half an hour the phone rang and Paul handed it to Harry.

"This is Harry Isaacson."

"Rick Rosen," the man said. "Barbara says you could grow some carrots for us."

"I've got a little place up on the San Poil River," Harry said. "I'm looking for a cash crop."

"How little?" Rosen asked. "I'd need at least ten acres."

"I've got forty acres of farm ground," Harry said.

"That doesn't sound little to me," Rosen said. "When can you come see me?"

"That might be a problem," Harry said. "I don't want to leave the place right now."

"We would have to have a contract," Rosen said. "I need to be sure the thing is handled."

"I don't know about a contract," Harry said. "This is my first year on the place."

"Do you know what you're doing?" Rosen asked. "Have you ever farmed before?"

"All my life," Harry said. "Except for a few years in college."

"We need to talk about this," Rosen said. "Where is this San Poil River?"

"Just a little ways east of Grand Coulee Dam," Harry told him, "then north a few miles."

"That's the Colville Reservation," Rosen said. "I didn't think anyone farmed up there."

"There's a few of us," Harry said. "Come take a look."

"I may do that," Rosen said. "I can get away next week. Tell me how to get there."

Harry gave directions, arranged to meet him at the store the next Tuesday. He didn't want to tell him to look for a tipi.

Harry decided to plow as much of the upper meadow as he could before Rosen came so that he could see that it was possible to farm there. He was concerned about the reaction he would get anyway, living in a tipi and farming with horses. He told Walt about it and Walt said to bring the guy in to their place if he had any doubts about horse farming.

Walt brought over his big team and a two-bottom plow to help and they plowed most of the meadow in two days. Harry thought it was about twenty-five acres. The soil was beautiful. There were a few rocks but nothing serious. Harry loved being able to work the ground without the roar of a tractor. He could listen to the birds sing and the splash of the river. He understood, now, why the old man had hated tractors.

He harrowed down the plowed ground in another day. Then he planted vegetables in the garden plot near the building site. He asked Walt about the old irrigation system and Walt said he wouldn't need any water until the end of June. By then the river would be down and it would be easy to build up the old rock dam. He had a ditcher Harry could use although the old wooden flume that was rotted away would require a lot of work.

Nathan came by for part of a day. Harry told him about the carrot contract.

Nathan asked him when he would have the building site ready and Harry said he would work on it as soon as he had the time. He showed Nathan the old irrigation flume, barely visible, which ran along the river bank from just below the bridge and once had carried water across the meadow where it could run into laterals and water most of the farm ground.

Nathan said that to rebuild the wooden flume could take all summer. He remembered that some road culverts were being replaced where the tribe planned to do some logging. He said he would see if he could get the old culverts. If they could get them cut in half they would make a good replacement for the flume.

Judith insisted that Nathan stay for dinner. She was good at cooking over the open fire and served up a great meal of beans, potatoes and some pork-chops Frances had given her. They sat around after they ate and Nathan and Judith reminisced about all the crazy times they'd seen in this very tipi at the Stampede. Rebecca laughed hard at some of the stories and seemed happier than she had since the move.

Rick Rosen was almost an hour late. When he did get there mud was spattered up both sides of his new black Volvo Turbo and he was not in a good mood.

"That Manila Creek Road is a mess. There are washouts all over the place and no guard rails. A god-damned log truck almost ran over me, passed me on a hair-pin and threw mud all over my car."

"That's normal," Harry said, "We hardly notice."

"You don't look Indian," Rosen said to him.

"You can never tell," Harry said.

"So you think you can grow a bunch of organic carrots for me?" Rosen asked him.

"If I decide to," Harry said. He wasn't sure if it was such a good idea.

"Hey, man, I really need the carrots," Rosen said. "I can sell all the fresh carrot juice I can make. I'm willing to sign a contract."

"What kind of a contract?" Harry asked him.

"You commit to a thousand pounds a week and I pay eighty cents a pound."

"What if I don't have a thousand pounds some week?" Harry asked.

"There would have to be some kind of penalty," Rosen said. "It would be a major hassle for me."

"No thanks," Harry said. "Too many variables. You get what you get."

"Well," Rosen said, "I could agree to buy up to a thousand pounds a week. But the price would vary according to the market."

"That won't work," Harry said. "I need a stable price. Besides, eighty cents is too low. I'd say a dollar twenty-five."

Rosen was shocked. "I can get them shipped from California cheaper than that."

"In twenty-four hours?"

Rosen looked at him. "They would have to be completely organic. Certified."

"I don't use any chemicals," Harry said. "I don't know about certification."

"They have to be certified," Rosen said. "My labels say 'certified organic'. And you would have to deliver them."

"No problem," Harry said. "I can haul a thousand pounds in my pickup."

Rosen looked at the old International. "Is it reliable?" he asked.

"It makes that Manila Creek drive without a hitch," Harry said.

Rosen wanted to see the farm so Harry led the way down the river. Rosen parked on the shoulder of the highway and walked in. He wanted to know about equipment and when Harry told him he farmed with a horse, Rosen was very skeptical. Harry took him into Walt's place and Rosen clearly was amazed by what he saw.

"I didn't know there were any places like this left."

He asked Walt if he wanted to grow some stuff for him. He still needed beets and cabbage and some other produce.

"Naw," Walt said. "I'm too old for that. I just piddle around, grow what we need. And feed for the stock."

Before he left, Rosen said that he would send Harry a contract. "Just for the banker," he said. "I won't commit you to anything you can't do. But you need to get certified."

"That Jew came by our place," Johnny Carlson said when he stopped by one morning as Harry worked in the field. "The one in the black Volvo. He tried to talk my dad into growin' shit for him, cabbage and beets and stuff. Dad sent him packin' quick. We don't need a bunch of Jews up here. He said he had a contract with you."

"Not yet," Harry said. "But I may grow some carrots for him."

"Dad won't like that," Johnny said. "Next thing you know there'll be Jews and niggers all over the valley. There's already a couple of niggers up by Curlew."

"You mean Black people?" Harry asked.

"We call 'em niggers here," Johnny said. "And we don't want 'em. Indians are bad enough."

"This is the reservation," Harry said.

"Yeah, well, my dad says we'll put an end to that one of these days, too. This is America. No one should have special privileges."

"Some privilege," Harry said.

The State Organic inspector was a hippie woman in a state truck with a clipboard and a friendly smile. She looked around the place and asked a few questions about when it last was farmed and if any chemicals were used. She signed the certificate and gave Harry his copy.

"This is a beautiful place," she said. "How did you find it."

"It belongs to my wife's family," Harry told her.

"Some people have all the luck."

The contract came from High Mountain Juice and it was close to what Harry had expected. He lined out some language about default penalties, signed it and sent it back.

There was a handwritten note from Rick Rosen.

"I met your neighbor, John Carlson. What an asshole. I will send you sixty pounds of carrot seed when I get this contract back. Good luck, Rick."

The seed came by UPS. The driver parked on the highway and walked in. "The directions said look for the tipi," he said. He had Harry sign for the package then brought it to the back of the van with a hand-truck. Harry picked it up and threw it on his shoulder.

"Be careful," the driver said. "That's heavy."

The early vegetables were up along with a solid carpet of weeds. Judith helped Harry do the hand-weeding and got Rebecca to do a little. He wasn't sure how to plant the carrots. If he broadcast them weeds might overwhelm them and there would be no way to weed them except by hand. Walt had a cultivator that could be adapted to cut the weeds between rows but he didn't have a planter that would handle such small seeds.

Harry saw an ad for a hand-pushed planter in one of the seed catalogs and called about it. They told him it would plant carrots fine but would take three weeks to get to him. He couldn't wait that long. He called around and finally found a similar machine at the feed store in Ephrata and drove down to get it. He hated to spend the sixty dollars but if it solved the problem it would be well worth it.

It did plant the carrot seed although thicker than he wanted. He set up stakes so his rows were straight. Walt said he would need forty-inch middles for a horse to walk in so Harry settled on double rows forty inches apart. It took him three days of steady work to get the carrots planted. He had marked out ten-acres near the river, which should be easy to run water to if he didn't get the whole irrigation system up.

He plowed another ten acres right along the river on the lower meadow as soon as it was dry enough and broadcast alfalfa seed there by hand. Uncle Paul had given him the seed, extra, he said, but Harry thought Paul was just helping out. He bought three bags of barley at the feed store and broadcast it with the alfalfa as a cover crop. Then he borrowed Walt's little offset disk and used it to bury the seed.

Walt had seed oats he had saved from the last year and told Harry he could replace them when his crop came. He planted ten acres on the high side of the meadow along the highway to oats. They would make a crop even if he wasn't able to water them.

He wanted to try tomatoes and peppers and eggplant but he needed seedlings. He finally found a nursery in Moses Lake that had what he needed but they were very expensive. He reserved as many flats for the first week in June as he thought he could afford, but he had to cut back his plans. He needed to build a greenhouse before next Spring.

He got several varieties of watermelon and cantaloupe seeds and a few honeydews. Walt said he should wait until the last week in May to plant the melons. He had two varieties of sweet corn, an early and a late, and put in several rows of each. He decided to plant the balance of his garden ground to pumpkins and winter squash. They wouldn't require much effort and also would make something even without irrigation.

There were several frosts in mid-April but they didn't hurt the peas or cabbage or other early crops. Some of the sweet corn had broken the ground and got nipped, but it would come back fine. The carrots sprouted slowly in the cold ground but by the end of the month they had begun to show.

Harry had wanted work and he got his wish. There was something to do every waking minute and when he went to bed his mental list was longer than it had been in the morning. There was no time to work on the cabin site but he knew he had to have it up before winter. Tipis were fine in warm weather.

The barley and alfalfa and oats were up, and most of the carrots, when he made the run to Moses Lake for his seedlings. While he was there he bought twenty white plastic buckets from a restaurant for fifty cents each. He borrowed Walt's wagon and hauled buckets of water and some aged manure to transplant his tomatoes and peppers and eggplant. The work was slow but Judith helped and he loved to work with her.

By the time his transplants were in the ground the weeds had overtaken the carrots and sweet corn. Walt helped him set up the cultivator with sweeps and duck-feet and pulled it over with his smaller team. Harry had trouble at first keeping the cultivator straight so it cut weeds and not carrots but as he got used to the team and they to him the work became easier and faster.

Three days later when he'd finished the cultivating, the melons and squash already showed green. There were several hot days in a row and his new transplants wilted and he was afraid he would lose them but two days of rain followed and they soon stood straight and began to show new leaves.

Nathan came for a visit and Harry barely had time to talk to him. Judith spent several hours with the kids and Nathan, walked the far side of the river and visited Walt and Frances. Harry was surprised that he didn't feel jealous.

Harry realized that spring had come all around him and he'd hardly noticed. All he could see was the soil and his crops and the wrong end of the horses. Most of the people he knew would think he had a hellish existence, but he could not remember when he'd been happier.

CHAPTER 6

It was the second week in July before the work slacked off at all. By then Harry's fields of barley and alfalfa and oats were green, the carrots stood tall in nearly weed free rows and the garden plants thrived. There had been enough rain to maintain the momentum but if it was as dry as usual through July and August he would need irrigation water.

Nathan had managed to talk his way into a truckload of the discarded culverts and Harry borrowed Uncle Paul's truck so they could haul them. Nathan had a friend with a log loader who agreed to load the culverts for them for the cost of his fuel.

Altogether they had over four hundred feet of the metal tubes and once they were cut in two they would make eight hundred feet of flume. That was more than enough.

The log-trucker who had delivered the house logs, Eric Brown, also had a cutting torch. Nathan knew him from high school and convinced him to cut the culverts for ten dollars an hour. Harry and Nathan marked them with chalk and it took Eric all of one day to cut them in half.

Most of the ridge where McTavish's flume had run was still intact. Harry used Walt's wheel-scraper and lots of shovel-work to fill in the gaps. He and Nathan tore out the old wooden flume, salvaged a little good lumber and burned the rest.

The old mare dragged the sections of half-culvert into place and they fastened the ends together with bolts, used tar to seal the joints. They had checked the grade with a hand-level fastened to a ten-foot two-by-four, but Harry wished he'd had a transit to make sure the water would flow.

The first section of the flume was less than two feet above the level of the pool where the river backed up behind the remnants of the old dam. Harry thought they could raise the water that much with no problem. They hauled rocks in Walt's wagon and carried them out into the river. It took more rocks than Harry had expected but on the third day a trickle of water flowed into his flume. He watched it flow along to the "Y" then one branch continued parallel with the river and the other out across the meadow. There were just a few places where they had to adjust the level by using rocks or blocks of lumber or sections of tree branches to raise the flume or dig out under it to lower it.

When it all flowed to Harry's satisfaction, they carried more rocks out onto the dam and raised the water level a few inches more and the flume flowed half-full. He used lengths of flexible sewer pipe he'd found at a salvage store in Ephrata to siphon water over the edge of the flume into head-ditches he'd made with Walt's ditcher.

When he had cultivated the carrots and sweet corn he'd replaced the duck-feet that ran in the middles with corrugating shovels which left small ditches for irrigation. Now if the rows were angled properly to get the right slope it all would work.

There were a few low spots where he had to build-up the banks of his corrugations to force the water through. He would mark those and fill them before the next season. But, in general, old McTavish had done his work well and Harry was grateful. He watered the carrots and sweet corn and the garden.

Harry got a letter from Rick Rosen. Rosen said he was anxiously awaiting the first load of carrots, which he expected in late July. Harry was worried that they wouldn't be ready in time. They still were not much larger than a pencil although they were long and straight and grew fast. He wished he had been able to get manure onto the fields before he planted. Next year he would.

A leak in one of his culvert joints caused a washout which let a section of the flume break loose and he spent most of two days repairing that. He inspected the whole system again and was liberal with tar wherever another leak might occur.

The river level dropped lower and he had to build up the dam to maintain his flow. Walt told him that McTavish had not been able to get water into his system when the river was too low, but that usually was in September and the crops were made by then anyway.

Harry noticed that cars would drive by very slowly or even stop on the highway to watch him work with the horses or whatever he happened to be doing. Sometimes he would see the red Mustang that belonged to Johnny Carlson sit on the road for fifteen or twenty minutes.

There was another regular visitor, a gray Range Rover that would cruise the road in both directions, obviously looking at his place. One day he saw the same rig in Anderson's parking lot in Republic so he waited to see who drove it. It was Eliot. He wondered at Eliot's interest in his farm.

He noticed that the hippies who lived in the A-frame had returned. He recognized the van that he'd seen in the winter and saw that they had planted a tiny garden that soon was overrun with weeds. He saw the van cruise by his place slowly a couple of times but they never stopped.

Judith made a trip with Nathan and the kids to visit her grandmother, Hattie. She also wanted to see Shadow and the colt, maybe ride Shadow if she got a chance. She returned two days later with a lot of perennial herbs the old woman had given her. She planted them along the riverbank in places they would do well without much care. She also had several paper grocery bags full of dried herbs, which she carefully stored in canning jars she borrowed from Frances.

Judith had begun to spend a lot of time with Frances and sometimes the whole family would go there for dinner or to spend a Sunday afternoon. The Davises' children and grandchildren visited occasionally from Boise or Spokane and they would stop in their cars to stare at the tipi and the crops, but they never had anything to say. Whenever Walt's son, Franklin, was there, if Harry came around he would go in the house and not come out until Harry was gone.

Harry got another letter from Rick Rosen alternately demanding and begging for a load of carrots. Harry checked and decided that he probably could get several hundred pounds of thinnings, which would be better than nothing.

Judith helped him pull the small carrots and they left the tops on so the roots wouldn't wilt. They piled them in the shade along the river and covered them with wet burlap bags. When they had all they could pull in their spare time in two days they cut the tops short and bagged them. They had eleven large burlap bags full and Harry guessed the bags weighed at least sixty pounds each. They loaded them in the back of the pickup and wet the bags down again then covered them with a wet blanket.

Harry left before dawn. The trip to the coast was smooth and he drove through the late morning rush-hour traffic on the Eastside. High Mountain Juice was in Redmond. Harry found the address in an industrial park near Lake Sammamish. Rick Rosen was on the telephone, stared at Harry without recognition at first, then smiled and brought his call to an end.

"You have carrots for me?"

"Sure do."

Rick followed him out to the pickup. Harry pulled back the blanket and opened a bag, pulled out a handful of carrots.

Rick frowned. "They're awfully small."

"Does that matter, for juice?"

"Well, I guess not." Rosen took a carrot from Harry. "They all have the tops on?"

"That keeps them from wilting," Harry said. "I can cut them off, but they travel better this way. Taste one."

Rick wiped off the carrot, took a bite and chewed. "They are good. Nice and sweet."

"They'll be bigger next time. These are thinnings."

Rick stared at him. "How many are there?"

"A bunch. This didn't touch the main crop. Two more weeks I could bring twice this many every week. Probably until frost."

"All right," Rick said. "This is going to work!"

Rick had one of his employees help Harry unload the bags and weigh them. It was seven hundred and twenty-eight pounds. Rick gave him a check for nine hundred and ten dollars.

"More where that came from. Hope I see you again soon."

"The end of next week," Harry said.

He took the check to Rosen's bank and cashed it. It was the most money he'd seen in a while. He could hardly believe that the fifteen hundred dollars left from last year on the farm and the three hundred Judith had brought with her had lasted. They had gotten very good at not spending money.

He called Ron at his apartment, got the machine. He called Radford Retirement Environments and the receptionist said Ron was out for the day on business.

Right, Harry thought. He had no reason to stay longer so he headed back, crossed Stevens Pass just after noon. He stopped at a mall in Wenatchee to find presents for the kids. He knew Little Joe longed for miniature horses and he tried to find some that looked like draft horses but they all were rodeo and race horses. He got two of them and a play set with a barn and some fence sections. He got Rebecca a doll with braids and a buckskin dress, hoped she liked it. He found some nice wool and cotton yarn and some crochet hooks for Judith. He knew that she missed her loom, but there was no room for it in the tipi. She had borrowed some crochet hooks from Frances and spent her evenings doing beautiful work.

He was on the Manila Creek summit before five o'clock.

The next load of carrots was just short of a thousand pounds. Rosen said that the juice from Harry's first load had been the best he ever had put out. He told Harry to bring as many carrots as he could as often as possible. They would be better even after three weeks in cold storage than what he usually had available.

Harry had called Ron ahead of time and met him for lunch. He told Ron about his success with carrots. Ron wanted to know how much money he'd made and when Harry told him a little over two thousand dollars, Ron laughed. "That's a two-week check for me. After taxes."

"But you have to live here."

Walt took a look at Harry's oats and said that if he was going to cut them for hay he'd better do it soon. Harry wasn't sure how he would handle the hay. He had no barn to store it in loose and he didn't know if anyone would come in with a baler to do just ten acres. But then he didn't know what he'd do if he let them make grain. He had that problem with his barley, too. He would have to find a small combine or someone who would custom-cut it for him.

He saw Johnny Carlson at the store but he said his dad probably wouldn't help and he didn't know anyone else with a baler or a combine. He called Uncle Paul and Paul said he should take a look in Capital Press, the farm newspaper out of Salem, Oregon. Harry couldn't find anyone who carried it so he called and had them send out a copy of the paper.

When the paper came Harry was amazed at the huge classified section full of used machinery. A lot of the prices were very good but most of it was in Western Oregon. There were ads from machinery dealers all over Washington, Oregon and Idaho so Harry began to call them. Finally one dealer in Pasco said that he had an old John Deere 55 combine. He had planned to scrap it but if someone had a use for it he would sell it for a hundred dollars.

"It's a little beat," he said, "but they're pretty rugged and there's parts available."

Harry asked the dealer to hold it for him. He borrowed Uncle Paul's truck and headed for Pasco. The combine was in better shape than he had expected. The little Wisconsin engine ran fine and other than belts and chains everything seemed to be in working order. He spent almost two hundred dollars on belts and chain links and some spare sprockets and pulleys the dealer had.

He unloaded the combine using the road for a dock and parked it by the tipi. When he wasn't watering or weeding or digging carrots he worked on the old machine. Harry had first run a 55 that belonged to the old man when they first moved to Washington and he knew it backwards and forwards. Soon he had it running smoothly.

He could see that he never would have time to fill his building site with Walt's wheel-scraper. He asked Nathan if he knew anyone with a small dozer that would be interested in a day's work. Nathan said that Eric usually could borrow his father's D-4. He called Eric from the store and Eric agreed to do the job for forty dollars an hour and a fifty-dollar move charge. It seemed like a bargain to Harry.

Eric began to doze out the pond, pushed the dirt up onto the cabin site. About two feet down he ran into a large boulder. He dug around it on all sides but could not budge it. He got off the Cat and came over to talk to Harry.

"We could leave it there, but it would kind of mess up the pond."

"I'd sure like to get it out of there. How big you think it is?"

"No idea," Eric said. "Could be big as a house."

"Got any ideas?"

"You know old Walt Davis?"

"Sure do."

"He could take care of it quick," Eric said. "He did the blasting for the highway when they put it through. All the old timers say he's the best."

"I'll go talk to him."

Walt was working on his mower when Harry found him. He told Walt about the problem.

"I can fix it," Walt said. He put away his tools and unlocked a heavy cabinet in the back of his shop. Harry saw that it held about half a case of dynamite sticks and assorted blasting caps and fuses. Walt took a stick, broke it in half and selected a cap and a roll of wire and a small dry-cell battery. He relocked the cabinet.

Nearby were several bags of nitrogen fertilizer. He opened one and dumped about half of it in a bucket, poured in some diesel from a fuel can and mixed it in with a stick. "Grab that, would you?" he said to Harry, pointed at the bucket.

Harry picked it up and followed Walt.

Walt spent some time examining the exposed edge of the boulder, dug around with a shovel and talked to himself. He picked a spot and dug down more than two feet. He had Harry pour the fertilizer in the hole then he stamped it down. He dug a hole in it with a screwdriver large enough to wedge in the half-stick of dynamite and tamped the pasty nitrogen around it. He attached the cap and the wires and unreeled the roll about a hundred feet.

"Everybody clear-out. Cover your ears."

Eric had moved the dozer up to the road and Harry and Nathan walked to the tipi. Harry went inside and told Judith and the kids to put their hands over their ears. He went back outside and called "Ready," to Walt.

Walt lay on the ground and Harry could see he had the bare ends of the wire in his hands. He touched the wires to the battery terminals and there was a split-second delay, then a great roar as dust and rocks and gravel boiled out of the hole, some high into the air. The concussion hurt Harry's ears even with them covered. Small pieces of rock rained down, some as far as the tipi. The dust cloud hovered high above.

When the dust had partly cleared and rocks stopped falling, Walt got up and walked over to the hole.

"That should do it."

Harry walked over and saw that the hole where the dynamite and fertilizer had been was now a crater about six feet deep and ten across. A large chunk of the boulder lay in the bottom. The exposed side of the main rock showed numerous cracks.

Walt rolled up his wire and grinned at Harry. "I told you I knew what to do with boulders."

Johnny Carlson came roaring in a few minutes after the blast. He jumped out of his car and ran towards them.

"What the hell was that?" He demanded.

"What was what?" Harry asked.

"That noise. Some kind of blast. Scared my mom half to death."

Walt chuckled. "That was my gravel-maker."

"You have to have a license and a permit to do any blasting," Johnny said. "My dad's going to call the sheriff."

"I've been licensed since before your dad was born," Walt said.

"Well my mom has bad nerves," Johnny said. "You should have warned us."

"I know all about your mom's bad nerves," Walt said.

Johnny glared at him. No one said anything else so he turned and stomped towards his car. He looked back, as if to say something, then got in and roared away.

"Dynamite isn't his mom's problem," Walt said. "His dad is."

"What do you mean?" Harry asked him.

"He treats her the way he treats livestock," Walt said. "Keeps her penned up in that house. Beats on her if she gets out of line."

"Why does she stay?" Harry asked him.

"She took off once," Walt said, "Not long after that kid was born. She was just a kid then, herself. John found her down in Wenatchee, called the cops and they committed her to Medical Lake for more than a year. Since she got out I don't think she ever comes out of that house. And nobody goes in."

The dozing job cost almost five hundred dollars but now they could start to build. While the dozer was there Harry had Eric cut a trench about a hundred feet long and four feet deep on the upper end of the garden. He had an idea for a dugout greenhouse for next spring.

Harry bought plywood to form footings for a concrete floor for the cabin. He lined the forms with salvaged plastic he'd gotten from Rick Rosen on his last carrot run so the plywood wouldn't be ruined. He'd also gotten some short pieces of re-bar from a construction site in Seattle, the foreman said they'd just be hauled to the dump.

Nathan came the day he poured the footings. The ready-mix truck came from Grand Coulee, charged an extra fifty dollars for the distance. The pour went easily. Three days later they poured the floor. It took a few hours to trowel it smooth, but it would be a fine floor.

Then it was time to haul another load of carrots. When he got back the oats were ready and he ran the first field-test with his combine. It worked well although for the first day something broke every little while. He had most of the parts he needed and managed to improvise others. He kept a list of spares to search for in the winter.

He had found an apple shed near Wenatchee that let him have old apple bins for two dollars each and he borrowed Paul's truck to haul two loads of the four-foot square wooden boxes. He bought plastic liners for a dollar each and set up a long line of bins near the road to hold the oats. He knew that mice eventually would chew their way in, but the loss would not be great.

As he ran the combine in the oat field he saw Eliot's gray Range Rover pull into the road. Eliot parked and came towards him. Harry shut down the machine and climbed down.

"Those are some good-looking oats," Eliot said.

"Not bad," Harry replied.

"You want to sell some?" Eliot asked him. "I need oats for my horses. I usually haul over from Okanogan."

"I could sell some," Harry said. "If you have a way to haul them."

"That trick with the bins is pretty slick," Eliot said. "You want to sell some of those, too?"

"I could let you have some for five dollars each," Harry said. "And two dollars for the liners."

"I've been paying eight cents a pound in Okanogan," Eliot said.

"These are organic," Harry said. "Certified. There's a cereal company in Bellingham that will pay twenty-five cents."

Eliot shook his head. "But then you have to haul them."

"I can borrow my uncle's truck," Harry said. "I can haul quite a ways for seventeen cents a pound."

"I'll pay you fifteen cents and pick them up right here," Eliot said. "I can park my truck here and you can load right onto it."

"I could let you have six bins," Harry said. That's about a hundred and eighty bushels," he paused, "Five thousand, seven hundred and sixty pounds. Eight hundred and sixty four dollars. Plus forty-two for the bins and liners. I'll make it an even nine hundred dollars."

Eliot pulled out a small notebook and a silver pen and did the math. "Nine hundred dollars," he said. "I'll have my truck here this afternoon."

Eliot's hired man brought the truck and Eliot picked him up. Harry loaded the bins on, put in the liners and started filling them. He finished the next morning.

Eliot stopped by to see if it was ready then came back with his hired man. When the truck was gone he handed Harry nine crisp, new hundred-dollar bills.

"Let's just keep this between you and me."

Harry filled eight more bins with oats besides what he'd sold Eliot. He wouldn't need that much for his horses, but the price was likely to go up, not down. He checked the barley but the kernels still were soft so he knew he had at least a week before he needed to cut it. He made another carrot run, almost fourteen hundred pounds, and stopped at a big machinery dealer in Quincy to get some parts for the combine.

He wanted to build a corral and some kind of shelter so Judith could bring her horses down from Cache Creek, but it didn't look like he would have time. He told Walt about it and Walt said he had plenty of room for two more. Harry told

Judith and she was excited. Nathan borrowed a horse-trailer and Harry went to Nespelem to get it. Judith and the kids went along and they visited Hattie for a while, then loaded the horses.

The colt nearly was as tall as Shadow and didn't want to load into the trailer. Judith calmed him down and finally tied a scarf over his eyes. With the blindfold on he let them guide him into the trailer. When Judith uncovered his eyes he panicked and struggled against the tie for a few minutes. When they unloaded him into Walt's corral he ran and bucked and snorted at them. Everyone agreed that he was a beautiful animal.

The barley produced nearly five hundred bushels and he stored it in bins beside the oats. There was a good stand of alfalfa left when the barley was cut. Next year they would have their own hay. The old mare obviously had been bred by Walt's Belgian stud and would give them a foal next Spring.

There was a flood of produce from the garden. Tomatoes and peppers and eggplant began to ripen and all the early stuff was at its peak. The sweet corn was ready and the melons soon would be. Harry had little time for anything but harvest. Judith spent a lot of time with Frances, canned and pickled and dried as much of the harvest as she could. Harry raided the thrift stores for canning jars on his trips.

On his next carrot run he loaded a selection of the other produce on top of the bags of carrots. He stopped at several small markets he remembered and soon sold it all at prices he could hardly believe. He saved some of each for the little Italian market near the rooming house where he'd lived before he and Judith moved in together. The proprietor remembered him and happily bought his remaining produce. When Harry told him that he soon would have melons the proprietor smiled and Harry remembered the fine melons he'd bought there.

"It's very different here, now," the proprietor said and shook his head sadly.

Harry took back over three thousand dollars even after he bought new tires for the pickup.

They laid house logs whenever they could find spare time. Nathan helped, as promised, and so did Walt. Soon the walls were in place. One of Nathan's friends, who made his living cutting firewood, cut them some poles the size of tipi poles for rafters. Harry bought galvanized steel roofing and felt great relief when the roof was on. Now, even if the fall rains came early the place would be dry.

A building inspector stopped to see if Harry had a permit for the cabin. Harry told him it was Indian land, outside the inspector's jurisdiction. He started to question Harry, but then Judith appeared and he backed off.

"Well, I hope you know what you're doing," he said.

Harry had planned to use caulking to chink the cracks between the logs, but Judith said she wanted to do it the traditional way. She dug clay from a deposit she'd found along the river and soon had the logs airtight. She did agree that they should insulate the roof and Harry brought Fiberglas batts on one of his Seattle trips. He nailed plywood to the undersides of the rafters and built a loft over two-thirds of the main floor with a ladder for access.

He bought a sink and cabinets and bathroom fixtures from a salvage place. He ordered a small pump, a well-point and some pipe and drove a household well just outside the cabin. He had all the water the little pump could handle less than forty feet down. He got a used propane hot-water heater and a little propane cook-top for whenever they didn't want to use the wood cookstove. He used Walt's big team to plow a ditch as deep as possible for a drain-field then dug it a little deeper by hand. He laid in perforated pipe and hauled a septic tank from Grand Coulee.

Harry brought the cookstove and Judith's loom from Uncle Paul's and soon the cabin began to look like home. He wanted to cover the concrete floor, but Judith said she didn't want linoleum or anything synthetic. He spent some time on the coast looking at tile and hardwood, but it all was too expensive. Finally he found a small company in Woodinville that made concrete tiles, similar to Mexican clay tiles, and he bought enough for half the main floor.

He searched for a wood heater but there was nothing under five hundred dollars that would produce enough heat. He finally found a steel steam cleaner housing in a junkyard and got a welding shop to adapt it for a stovepipe and to make a door. He had his woodstove for just over fifty dollars.

They took down the tipi and Harry was sorry to see it go. It had become his home. It was hard to believe it was Stampede time already. They went to Omak for two of the days, watched the rodeo and visited a lot of Judith's relatives in the Indian camp.

Little Joe was very excited about the Suicide Race. When he heard that Nathan had once won the race, he said that he would win it when he grew up.

One day Johnny Carlson stopped by. He said his mother would like to buy some produce if they had any to spare. When Harry told him the prices he was surprised but bought almost fifty dollars worth. The hippies became regular customers and even Eliot would send his hired man to get vegetables. Other neighbors began to stop and even an occasional tourist.

When the melons were ripe they were as good as anyone ever had tasted and Harry realized he could have sold ten times as many. The tomatoes, too, were in great demand and the sweet corn. Any extra he hauled to the coast.

The middle of September the first frost came and all the hot weather stuff was gone. The cabbage and broccoli and other fall crops they had planted in late July began to thrive. The carrots still grew and some of them were over two inches in diameter. Rick Rosen bought all Harry would bring him.

They counted their money and had over fifteen thousand dollars even after what they'd spent on the cabin. They talked about putting it in a bank, but neither of them felt that was safe. It looked like a comfortable winter with all the produce Judith had preserved.

Rebecca started school in Republic. Judith drove her up the river to the bus stop every morning and picked her up in the afternoon. Little Joe could have started kindergarten, but they decided to hold him out for another year.

One morning Harry was awakened by the sound of cattle and Reject barking. He stumbled outside to see cows and calves all over his fields and garden. Some of them had gotten into his bins of grain and others trampled over his carrots. Almost half the late garden already had been eaten. He called Reject and they chased the cattle onto the road.

As they moved the last few, John Carlson showed up in his pickup and began to yell at Harry.

"This is open range country. My cows have the right to be anywhere that isn't fenced out. If I catch you chasin' them again, I'll sue for damages."

"Don't worry," Harry said. "There'll be a fence up by tonight." He knew he should have built the fence long before, should have expected this from Carlson.

He drove to Republic and bought two hundred steel fence posts and ten rolls of barbed wire. He wasn't sure if Walt had a post driver he could borrow so he bought one.

While Judith and the kids kept the cows out, he drove posts along the highway just off the right-of-way. By midafternoon he was stringing barbed wire. Carlson drove up and down the highway watching but said nothing more. Harry built a tight four-wire fence, turned it to the river on both ends of the property. The cows might get in across the river, but his farm-ground was safe.

Harry spent a week cutting wood on the far side of the river. There were a lot of dead tamaracks that cut and split easily.

Walt loaned him a chainsaw and he bought a splitting maul and some wedges. He stacked ten cords behind the cabin. It might not last until spring but with the horses it would be easy to cut more in the winter and he would be happy to have the work.

Uncle Paul came to visit for three days, brought a load of hay. He was very impressed with the little farm. He helped Harry put up some pole rafters for the greenhouse he hoped to have ready in the spring. He thought Harry's plan for a dugout was a great idea. He asked Harry how he was fixed for money and Harry told him they had enough to last until spring.

"The banker gave all the money left from your Dad's settlement to your mother," Paul told Harry. "I heard it was over two hundred thousand dollars. Half of that should have been yours as a partner."

"I don't care about it," Harry said. "She can have it."

Ron came for a couple of days. He couldn't believe all that Harry had done in just a year.

"It reminds me of my granddad," he said. "That old man could do more in a day than most people could in a week." He quit trying to convince Harry to move to the city. "You were right," he said. "For you. This is just what you said you wanted. I couldn't do it, though."

When the first light snow fell in late November Harry looked around the place and was satisfied. He hadn't been sure he would get this far the first year. His mind raced with plans for the winter, all the things he could do to make the next season even better.

They had a great Christmas with lots of presents for the kids. They spent two days in Electric City with Judith's parents and Rachel and Joseph both were there. Helen told Harry it made her happy to see them so happy.

There was a Christmas card from his mother when they got back home. She complained that Santa Barbara wasn't the same as she remembered at all. If things didn't get better she was going to move back and get an apartment near Jack and Diane.

There was a card from Jack, too, and a handwritten note in which he bragged about all the money he was making in real estate and how he was a partner in the new subdivision the banker had put together next to Desert Aire. They had named it Desert Mirage.

CHAPTER 7

It was a year exactly since the auction. Harry had been determined not to remember the day, but despite his best efforts his mind did a subconscious count. This year it fell on Sunday. The auction had been on a Saturday, the traditional day for farm sales. He knew that this time of year would be different for him forever.

He got a letter from Mom. "People are so mean here," she wrote. "Prices are terrible. It cost me almost $80 to have my hair done and it wasn't a good shop, either. I don't know how long my money will last. I'm sorry there was nothing left for you after the settlement, but the banker said I should take what was left. It wasn't that much. I have some new friends, we go to the mall together. I bought some new dishes and linens, for when I have company. Jack and Diane said they would come and visit me. Jack is doing very well, he made over $100,000 this year. Of course he works very hard. Meg has gotten a divorce. I don't know why she ever married that Bob. I knew he was a heel. He married his secretary. Sometimes I miss Washington. I haven't found a church here I like. Brother Hale wrote me, he said they all missed me very much. They are trying to raise money for a new addition to the church. I sent him a small check. Jack said I could visit them in the summer, but I don't want to be a bother. He said the sheriff decided you probably didn't kill your father.
I didn't think you did. Tell your children hello from grandma. Love, Your Mother."

Harry helped Walt with the machinery and the stock. Walt gave him a bill of sale on his small team of Belgians, an eight-year-old mare and a gelding a year older. The old mare would need a break when she dropped her foal in March or April. Harry used his new team to haul in more wood and to keep the road plowed.

He also spent a lot of time on the inside of the cabin. He trimmed the doors and windows, built shelves and closets and did a wood inlay over the plywood ceiling with some ancient silvered lumber Nathan got from a homestead someone tore down. He found some nice carpet for their bedroom and for the loft where the kids slept. He had hauled in a pile of river-rock before the snow came and he began to work with it, made a hearth for the wood-stove and a pebble mosaic for the entryway. He tiled the bath and built some storm windows.

Judith set up her loom and began to turn out beautiful pieces. She wanted to get some sheep and spin her own yarn. She got some new books on natural healing and collected herbs and bark and roots. Occasionally she would take Rebecca and Little Joe and spend a day with Hattie or with her mother.

Rebecca did well in school. Republic was her hometown, now, and she rarely talked about the friends she'd left behind in Seattle. Her teacher said her artwork was unusually good. She finally began to relax with Harry and sometimes would go with him when he fed the horses.

Little Joe followed Harry everywhere. He wanted to learn how to do everything Harry did. He was completely unafraid of the animals, especially the horses. Harry taught him how to drive the team and would let him drive the feed-wagon while he threw hay to the stock.

Harry and Judith talked through many long winter evenings while the kids slept. Judith would weave at the loom and Harry would work on the cabin or on some tool that needed maintenance. They grew closer than they ever had been in their shared existence. Plans and hopes and dreams meshed in their vision of the future.

Uncle Paul put Harry in contact with an organic dairy farmer who couldn't find enough certified feed for his cows. He offered Harry twenty-seven cents a pound for his barley and all the oats he would let go. He came all the way from Buckley to get the grain and wrote Harry a check for more than five thousand dollars. He told Harry he would buy all he had right out of the field next summer.

Harry researched greenhouses and decided that the best thing would be to put an inflatable cover on his dugout roof. That meant he needed electricity for the fans. He checked on battery powered motors and generators but decided that the only reasonable answer was to have the Public Utility District put in a power drop. It was a compromise he hadn't intended to make, but it would be nice to have electricity in the cabin for small appliances and an alternative to the kerosene lamps.

As soon as the ground thawed in late March he dug a hole and set a pole and had the state electrical inspector come. He told the inspector he would only use the power for the greenhouse so the inspection was simple. After the PUD energized his panel, Harry ran an underground line to the cabin.

He ordered seeds and started his seedlings as soon as he could keep the greenhouse above freezing. He bought two small space heaters for the coldest nights. The low profile and small air-volume made the greenhouse easy to heat. By the end of April he had more tomato and pepper and eggplant seedlings than he ever would need. He talked to Anderson's store in Republic and they said they would buy any extras he had.

He repaired Walt's old horse-drawn manure spreader and spread aged manure from Walt's corrals on his fields and garden ground. He disked up everything but the alfalfa, then deep-plowed the garden. He expanded the garden to grow even more for market.

He planned to split his ten-acre grain field, plant half to oats again for the horses but put the other half in buckwheat. Fairhaven mills in Bellingham had told him they would buy all the organic buckwheat they could find.

When he had some spare time he fenced the property across the river. It was over a hundred acres, much of it good range. He was determined to keep Carlson's cows off of it. He connected with Walt's back fence and together they had half a square mile protected. Carlson hired a surveyor to check the fence line and seemed surprised to find that it was right on the boundary. Harry didn't tell Carlson that he'd rented a transit to run the line.

Shadow had been bred while she ran free at Cache Creek and Judith wanted her close when her foaling time came. Harry built a pole corral between the cabin and the pond and set some large posts to build a shelter before the next winter. They moved Shadow and the old mare into the new corral but left the colt with Walt's horses. It was time to wean him and he would only be a problem when the foals came. Judith had decided to keep him a stud. He was a purebred Appaloosa and beautiful, black with white silver dollars on his rump. Judith named him Morningstar.

As he looked around the place that spring, Harry knew that the Old Man would have approved and that was the highest standard he knew.

Rick Rosen wrote Harry a letter, said they could dispense with the contract but he would buy all the carrots Harry could bring him. He also was interested in any other organic vegetables Harry wanted to sell. His juice business was booming and there was a market for many different blends.

Eliot came by when he returned from his winter in the south and tried to commit Harry to sell him all his oats but Harry said he would wait until harvest to make a decision. Eliot also was interested in any extra hay Harry might have. He made an effort to be friendly, admired the cabin and asked about Harry's family.

Johnny Carlson, too, was suddenly friendly. He hung around, bothered Harry while he tried to work and asked endless questions about how Harry did things. Harry was pretty sure Johnny's father had sent him to spy so he told him only what he wanted the older Carlson to know. Johnny began to confide in Harry about his problems at home, said his father would get drunk and terrorize his mother, sometimes hit her.

The hippies were back again. Judith befriended the woman, who called herself Wildrose. She was pregnant and fearful. They couldn't afford a doctor and didn't trust doctors anyway. Judith taught her about herbs and exercises and recommended that she find a midwife. Her boyfriend, Tamarack, tried to make friends with Harry, but Harry kept him at arm's length. He didn't care much for hippies since the way he'd been treated when he came back from Viet Nam. Most of them just seemed to be too lazy to work. And he hated their phony Indian names that they seemed to pick out of the air with no respect for the Native people.

In early April the old mare dropped her foal. It was a long-legged filly. She looked more Belgian than Percheron with her brown body and light mane and tail but there was a white roan-like frosting all over. Walt said she was a likely looking little thing, like all the foals his old stud sired. Her gangly gallop made Harry laugh as she followed her mother about the place. The old mare trusted Harry completely, let him handle the foal even when she nursed.

Two weeks later Shadow gave birth. Her foal, too, was a filly, red with a nice blanket and a large white blaze. Judith knew immediately which of the Cache Creek studs fathered her, a large red-dun with thoroughbred blood on one side. She soon had the little Appaloosa trained to lead. She would ride Shadow and let the foal trail behind them. Shadow was fiercely protective as she had been with her first foal and wouldn't let anyone but Judith and the kids close to her baby.

Late one morning as Harry drove the team Walt had given him, harrowed the ground where he would plant melons, he noticed a gray BMW drive slowly by. A few minutes later it came by in the other direction. It was gone for a while then he saw it park at the highway and someone walked towards him. As the man in a business suit came nearer he realized it was his brother Jack. He continued to follow the horses as Jack approached.

He turned at the end of the row and started back towards Jack, took his time. "Whoa," he called to the horses and tied the lines to the harrow's lift-lever. They stamped and watched him.

"Jesus Christ, you look just like the old man," Jack greeted him. "I couldn't believe it was you when I first drove by so I stopped at your neighbors'."

"It's me," Harry said.

"I need to talk to you, Harry."

"You're talkin' to me," Harry said.

"It's about the money. From Dad's insurance. The money left from the farm partnership."

"I heard Mom got all of that," Harry said. "I sure didn't see any of it."

"I thought you got yours," Jack said, looked at his feet. "I just found out you didn't."

"So you came to bring me my share?" Harry mocked him.

"Don't start that shit with me, Harry. I'm not a little kid anymore."

"No, I can see you're all grown up and wear a suit."

"I knew I shouldn't have come up here," Jack said. "But I had to try."

"Try what?" Harry asked him.

"It's about the money," Jack said. "Mom wants to invest it. In Desert Mirage. But she said it was half yours and she couldn't invest it without your approval."

"That's news to me," Harry said. "Sounds to me like she doesn't want to do it and used me for an excuse."

"She says she talked to a lawyer, in California, and he told her that if she spent all the money you could make a claim against her. Even for an investment. He said the banker didn't have the authority to give it all to her."

"Sounds like I could make a claim against him," Harry said. "I might enjoy that."

"You know he's the general partner in Desert Mirage," Jack said. "I don't need anyone to screw that up for me. I'm going to make a pile of money out of that. Mom could, too, if she'd invest. Everyone will make ten times their investment."

"Sounds a little too good to be true," Harry said. "Anyway, I don't know what that has to do with me. I don't have any money to invest and these horses are gettin' restless."

"I want you to give Mom authority to make the investment," Jack said.

"I can't give authority I don't have," Harry said. "Like I said, I didn't see any of that money."

"Well, will you at least sign a statement that you won't make a claim against her?" Jack pulled a neatly folded document out of an inside pocket. "I brought it with me. You would need to get it notarized."

"I'm not signing anything," Harry said. "If Mom or the banker owe me something then maybe I should collect it."

"It's just like you, Harry. You always fuck things up for other people. If you just want to be a dirt farmer that's your problem. Some of us want more."

"Yeah," Harry said. "More and more and more."

"Well, I won't forget this," Jack said as he stomped away. Harry heard the BMW roar and tires screech against pavement.

Ron wrote Harry a letter. He wanted to come visit for a couple of days in the middle of May. He had met someone he really cared for, he said, and would like Harry to meet her. Her name was Cynthia and she was an assistant project manager for Microsoft. He was sure Harry would like her.

Harry wrote back and told Ron to come any time but warned him that he was very busy and wouldn't be able to stop work to entertain company.

They came on a Friday morning. Ron said Cynthia had arranged a four-day weekend. He could get off whenever he wanted to.

"I still can't figure out what I'm supposed to do at work," he said.

Cynthia was dressed in expensive jeans and wore an Eddie Bauer parka despite the warm Spring weather. Her hair was cut short and she spoke in a clipped, rapid-fire manner that Harry was sure she had learned in business seminars. She had a tight-lipped smile for Judith and admired the cabin without enthusiasm.

Ron followed Harry out to the field where he transplanted tomato seedlings.

"What do you think of her?" he asked Harry. "I think she may be what I need. She really understands business. Shit, she has more investments than most retired people. Including a bunch of Microsoft stock. She knows Bill Gates. We went to a party that he was at."

"She seems nice," Harry said.

"She sure has straightened my act out," Ron said. "I go to work every day, stay late half the time. She has a plan to take the nursing homes public, start buying up little operations that are belly-up and turn it into a real chain. We could sell franchises in the small towns, cream ten or fifteen percent off the top."

"Sounds like a real genius," Harry said as he walked back to the end of the row for another flat of seedlings.

"There's still a job for you, if you want it. A good job. You could get your hands out of this mud."

"I don't mind mud," Harry said. "And it will be money by fall."

"It takes a lot of tomatoes to make what we bring in every week," Ron said. "Our main problem is how to spend it all."

"We all have our burdens," Harry said with a laugh.

"You could have it, too, Harry. It's beautiful up here, but what's the point if you're broke all the time?"

"I'm not broke," Harry said. "We did pretty well last year. And it doesn't cost much to live. We have all our own food and feed for the animals."

"You always said that's all you wanted," Ron said. "But I didn't ever believe you."

"Well, it's true," Harry said. "There isn't much I want that I don't have."

"I couldn't do it," Ron said. "I'd go into Costco and want one of everything they have."

"I stay out of Costco," Harry said. "Then I don't have the problem."

"You don't even have a television," Ron said. "Don't you miss it? Don't you want to know what's going on in the world?"

"Not really," Harry said. "It doesn't have much to do with me."

"I like being part of the mainstream," Ron said. "I don't want to be some throwback way out in the country. This is an exciting time to be alive."

"I agree," Harry said. "I'm excited every day."

"I figure in ten years I'll have enough money to retire if I want to," Ron said. "Then I can buy a place like this and hire someone to do the work. My dad's puttin' a lot of money in the stock-market."

"I don't want to retire," Harry said. "If I did, I'd just do the same things I do now."

"I know the war was hard on you, man," Ron said. "You've never been the same since you came back. But that was a long time ago. You need to forget about it like everyone else."

"It's not about the war," Harry said. "I'm just livin' like the old man did. I think he had things about right. That big dream out there could collapse any time. Even if it doesn't collapse for everyone at once, it can fall apart for anyone any time. This farm's goin' to be here."

"Well, I tried," Ron said. "Listen, Cynthia wants to see the laser show at Grand Coulee. Why don't you bring the family and drive over there with us."

"I don't know," Harry said. "We turn in pretty early. Besides, we see the laser show every time we come back from Judith's folks or go over to Grand Coulee to do some shopping."

Ron silently watched Harry work for a while. "So what do you think about Reagan's problems?" he asked finally.

"Which problems?" Harry asked him.

"That Iran-Contra thing," Ron said.

"To tell you the truth," Harry said, "I haven't heard that much about it."

"Well, it turns out that Reagan was sendin' weapons, sellin' 'em to Iran and usin' the money to support the Contras in Nicaragua. Because congress cut off the money. At least that's what the Democrats say. My dad doesn't believe it."

Harry remembered Jerry Maxwell trying to recruit him for some secret mission in Central America after the auction.

"It wouldn't surprise me. They're all liars. Reagan especially."

"Well, he's sure been good for business," Ron said. "Less taxes, less regulation."

"I'm not sure business is good for the country," Harry said.

"America is business," Ron said. "Business makes everything go."

"You can't eat money," Harry said.

"My Dad says there won't even be farmers in this country by the end of the century," Ron said. They'll grow all our food in Mexico and South America. The way the environmentalists want things you won't be able to farm here. No chemicals, no fertilizer. If they had their way the country would starve to death."

"I don't use any chemicals," Harry said. "And I get twice as much for my stuff as the chemical farmers."

"This organic thing is just a fad," Ron said. "It won't last. The scientists say it's just a bunch of bullshit. Like 'global warming.' Just somethin' to scare people. Reagan appointed a committee and they said there wasn't any global warming or ozone problem. Just communist propaganda."

"Either way, I'm okay," Harry said.

"I better check on Cynthia," Ron said and walked towards the cabin.

When Harry went in for lunch, Ron and Cynthia were leaving. "She wants to see Republic and Lake Curlew," Ron explained. "We'll be back in a couple of hours."

Harry was almost finished with his day's transplanting when Ron and Cynthia returned.

Ron walked out to the field. "We don't want to put you out, buddy," he said. "We'll stay in Grand Coulee. It'll be pretty late when the laser show is over anyway. We'll see you tomorrow morning."

They never did come back. Harry got a letter from Ron. He said that Cynthia had called her office and something came up. They'd come visit some other time.

Harry's tomato, pepper and eggplant transplants were all in when a late frost came and killed more than half of them. He had enough to replant, so all it cost him was the labor and the money Anderson's would have paid him for his extras. But instead of having a jump on the season he was late. The melons hadn't come up before the frost so they were okay. Walt said they often had light frosts until the middle of June and Harry decided he would have to find a way to get his tender crops in early anyway. He'd seen plastic tunnels advertised in one of the seed catalogs and decided to write away for some information.

The carrots survived the frost, as did the grain. The buckwheat was very hardy and grew like weeds. He had planted a large selection of vegetables for market and hoped to have peas and early broccoli ready by the end of June. He might even have some carrot thinnings by then for Rick Rosen.

He was near his south fence, checking the buckwheat's progress when he heard children's voices down-river. They were faint, distant, and he wondered what the kids were doing so far from the cabin. He climbed the fence and followed the sound. The kids knew they were not to leave the property and besides he was sure they couldn't have gotten past him unseen. One of them cried, then another. They must be someone else's children, lost and frightened.

He worked his way through heavy brush. The voices receded before him. Several children cried, now, and he hurried along, anxious to reach them. No matter how fast he moved they seemed no nearer. He nearly ran, felt frantic to save them. And the sound was gone, as it had come, faded in the morning stillness, and birds sang from the cottonwoods.

He sat on a downed log. It had been so real, he was sure of what he'd heard. Now it seemed foolish, impossible. Perhaps it was just the old dream from Viet Nam, come now in his waking hours. He remembered the eyes, the flames, the crying. He realized he was the one crying and shook himself.

It was two days before he could bring himself to tell Judith of the incident. When he did, she looked at him strangely.

"I'm not crazy. I heard them."

"I don't think you're crazy."

"Then what?" he asked her.

"Nothing," she said and would say no more.

"Harry, you son-of-a-bitch," someone yelled.

Harry turned from where he watched his pond slowly fill from the irrigation flume. Someone ran across the field towards him and he could see a new crew-cab four-wheel-drive pickup with a canopy and a rack of running lights on top parked at the highway.

As the figure neared him Harry recognized Jeff Lasker. Harry smiled and walked towards Jeff. They shook hands and looked at each other for a minute.

"You look like some old homesteader," Jeff said. "Reminds me of pictures of my granddad."

"You look like some city-slicker," Harry said. "You leave the mountains finally?"

"Hell no," Jeff said. "Still on the same place. Doin' the same thing. It just don't pay to look like a hippie any more in my business. This war on drugs is a pain in the ass. I just say no." He laughed. "How the fuck are you?"

"I'll make it," Harry said.

"So, did you finally decide to grow a real cash-crop?" Jeff asked him.

"Yep," Harry said. "Carrots."

Jeff laughed. "That's not what I meant."

"I know what you meant," Harry said. "I'm not ready to be an outlaw, yet."

"I was born one," Jeff said. "'Nam taught me the fine points. At this rate I'll have more money than God. I bought up three of my neighbors' places. They lost their nerve."

"You never had a problem with nerve," Harry said.

"Lisa's with me, and the kids," Jeff said.

"Bring them to the cabin," Harry said. "Judith will fix some lunch. How long you here for?"

"Couple of days," Jeff said. "Thought I'd come see how you were doin'. I've got two guys runnin' my operation. Less risk that way. I didn't know if I was goin' to find you. I went to your old place and there was someone new there, said you'd sold out. I finally found your brother. He's a regular asshole. Wouldn't tell me how to find you at first."

"We're not exactly close," Harry said.

"Your Mom was there," Jeff said. "She remembered me."

"I haven't seen any of them in a while," Harry said.

"Shit, I've only been back to Texas twice since 'Nam," Jeff said.

After lunch the kids all played outside and Lisa talked to Judith while Harry and Jeff went for a walk. Harry showed Jeff the gardens and fields and the twenty fruit trees he'd put in that spring.

"You own this place?" Jeff asked him.

Harry explained that it belonged to relatives of Judith's but that they could stay there as long as they wanted.

Jeff wanted to know how big it was. When Harry said a hundred and sixty acres, Jeff whistled.

"And I thought I had a place with forty. How far across the river does it run?"

Harry pointed out the far ridge that marked the boundary between his place and Walt's.

"And who's back there?" Jeff asked.

"An old timer. Friends of ours," Harry said.

"Jesus Christ," Jeff said. "Do you know how much money you could make here? Grow a thousand plants, just once, and you could retire. That'd be about three hundred pounds at as much as three thousand a pound. Think about it. I could set you up. And sell it."

"I don't think my nerves would stand it," Harry said.

"Shit, I saw your nerves in 'Nam," Jeff said. "You got no problem with nerve."

"Just dumb, I guess," Harry said.

"Well, if you decide to do it, just let me know. It's no harder than growin' tomatoes."

"I'll let you know," Harry said.

Jeff wanted to see some of the country so Harry decided to spend a day on a trip with him to the Kettle Valley then back through the Highlands and the Okanogan Valley. Judith and Lisa weren't interested in going, said they would stay with the kids and spend some time with the horses. Lisa had bought two horses and wanted to learn all she could.

They left just after daylight in Jeff's rig and drove north. They stopped for breakfast in Republic. Jeff said the little gold-rush town made him homesick, it was so much like the little towns in his area of Northern California. The food was plain and good and the waitress flirted with both of them, got the good tip she fished for.

Morning mist rose from Lake Curlew as they drove past and several whitetail does with fawns passed in front of them, made Jeff stop. The soft contours of the hills were a striking contrast to the sheer cliffs of the San Poil Valley. Jeff said it reminded him of Montana or Wyoming. They drove up the Kettle River to Danville and it was obvious Jeff had fallen in love. He began to ask Harry if he knew of any ranches for sale in the Kettle Valley and how much property there cost.

When Harry told him a lot of it, even riverfront, could be had in large parcels for less than a thousand dollars an acre, Jeff began to make plans.

They turned back at the Canadian border and stopped at the general store in the tiny town of Curlew so Jeff could ask if there was any property for sale. The storekeeper told him there was a ranch towards Toroda Creek to the west and Jeff wanted to go out that way. They found the "For Sale" sign and Jeff turned in but no one was home. He wrote down the phone number and asked Harry if he would investigate the place for him.

They followed Toroda Creek up to Wauconda, a crossroads store twenty miles from nowhere, stopped for a cup of coffee to go, then turned west. Tonasket was just a little cow-town like hundreds more and Harry told Jeff to go south on Highway 97 to Omak and Okanogan, twin towns along the Okanogan River, Omak on the reservation, and Okanogan, the County Seat, just off the Indian land.

"Well," Jeff said, "It's been a while since 'Nam. You all over it?"

"No," Harry said. "I don't think you ever get over it. I know my Dad's generation never did get over World War Two even after forty years. Sometimes they talk like they're still there."

"I still think about those kids," Jeff said. "Those two that used to follow you around, call you 'Daddy.' Sometimes I see their eyes. And the fire."

"Yeah," Harry said, "me, too. I thought I was over it, but lately I hear voices, like kids crying, but there's no one there."

"Sometimes that's what I remember most about 'Nam," Jeff said. "All the kids cryin'."

They drove on to Omak and Okanogan in silence.

It was midafternoon and they decided to have something to eat. There was a recently built motel along the highway called the Cedars Inn, which had a restaurant, so they went in there. While they waited for someone to seat them, Harry noticed a group of men at a back corner table. They were boisterous, obviously had been drinking. There were several men in business suits, not a common sight in the Okanogan. There were two white men dressed like ranchers in jeans and western shirts and one Indian dressed the same way. Everyone in the dining room seemed to be aware of the men.

As they followed the waitress to their table, Harry noticed that one of the men in jeans was Eliot. At the same time he saw Eliot look up and see him and Jeff. A look of astonishment crossed Eliot's face momentarily then he controlled it, looked away and made some loud joke to distract anyone at his table who might have noticed. Harry thought Jeff had reacted, too, at the sight of Eliot.

When they were seated and the waitress gone, Jeff leaned across the table and whispered, "I know that guy, the one with the loud shirt."

"Eliot," Harry said. "He's one of my neighbors."

"I know him as Eddie Tolman," Jeff said. "He carries some of the best blow on the West Coast. He trades with a couple of my neighbors, at least he did before they cut out. I sold him ten pounds one year. Some of the best shit I ever grew."

"I know he has race-horses," Harry said. "I heard he had family money."

Jeff chuckled. "Some kind of family. I always wondered where he lived. He likes to be mysterious."

Several times while they ate Eliot would look at them then look away when Harry noticed. He seemed very nervous. One of the men in a suit tried to sneak looks at them also, but he was very obvious. Harry had the distinct impression that he and Jeff were being talked about.

They drove out across the reservation, over Desautel Pass and down Cache Creek towards home. Jeff could not stop talking about how empty the country was. "California is beautiful," he said, "but in an area this big there'd be a couple hundred thousand people."

Harry told him that in Okanogan and Ferry counties together there were less than fifty thousand people including all the Indians on the Reservation.

"Maybe it's time I made a move," Jeff said.

CHAPTER 8

When Harry arrived at High Mountain Juice with a load of carrots there was a message for him to call Joseph and a phone number. After he cashed his check and bought a few things he called the number.

"Daybreak Star Center," a male voice answered, "General Custer speaking."

"Is Joseph there?" Harry asked.

"We've got all kinds of Josephs here," the voice said.

"Long Joe," Harry said.

"Will Short Joe do?" the voice asked. "A little dried-up Colville?"

There was a rustling noise on the phone then another voice. "This is Long Joe."

"Long Joe, this is Harry."

"Hello, Harry," Long Joe said. "Where are you?"

"Kirkland," Harry answered.

"I was wondering if you could give me a ride. To Nespelem."

"Sure," Harry said. "When can you be ready?"

"I'm as ready as I'll ever be," Long Joe said. "You know where the Daybreak Star Center is?"

"I've never been there," Harry said.

"Fort Lawton," Long Joe said. "At least it used to be until we took it back."

"I know," Harry said, "the back side of Magnolia, past the locks."

"That's it," Long Joe said. "I'll be here."

"I've got a few more things to get," Harry said, "then I'll be over."

Fort Lawton was a beautiful spot, the edge of a peninsula that jutted into Puget Sound just south of Shilshole Bay. Old shade trees, oaks and maples, lined the streets of the little army post that had been occupied by Native people when the military decided to abandon it. Now it was a park and a Native American Center serving the urban Indian population of Seattle.

Harry found the Daybreak Star Center and parked. Long Joe saw him and came out carrying a backpack and a suitcase, waved to Harry. Harry opened the canopy and helped Long Joe stow his bags.

They drove in silence. Harry took the Fremont Bridge and headed north then cut across to Lake City and drove towards Monroe and Highway 2. It was a bright early summer day and the intense green hills stood like cutouts against a bright, painted sky. It was the kind of day that almost made you forget the endless days of drizzle required to provide the water for the lush growth.

Harry watched the crews at work on a huge condominium project on the north end of Lake Washington, thought how he might be there if things had gone differently a few years before. He was glad to be going home.

After they passed Monroe and Sultan and Gold Bar and started the climb towards Stevens Pass, Long Joe finally spoke. "How is Judith?"

"Fine," Harry said. "She weaves a lot and has a lot of herbs planted. She spends a lot of time with Hattie."

"You two are happy together?"

"I've never been so happy," Harry said. "Judith and I are best friends again."

"How is the farm, Harry?" Long Joe asked.

"Great," Harry said. "You should see it. The cabin is finished and I put some fruit trees in. We made good money last year. I have a new team, Belgians, and the old mare had a filly." He laughed. "I guess you can see I love it there."

"So what is the shadow I see?" Long Joe asked. "Something bothers you."

Harry thought for a minute. "The place isn't mine. I don't own it. I might put in all this work, then lose it."

"You can stay there as long as you want to," Long Joe said. "We will not take it from you."

"No, that isn't it," Harry said. "I trust your family. It just isn't the same as if we owned it."

"Ownership is just an illusion," Long Joe said. "You cannot buy, or seize, and then defend a piece of the Earth. That is an absurd thought. First of all the lifetime of the Earth is millions of times longer than yours. How can you own something that both precedes and survives you? And the Earth is a living organism that must exist or not,as a whole. It is like staking your claim to a patch on the hide of a bison that is plunging over a cliff. In my way, you own only yourself, your body, your words and deeds. Everything else you only use for a while, for a moment or a lifetime. There is not much difference between the two from the Earth's point of view."

"But I want to be able to leave something for my children, "Harry said. "I want them to have something to start with, not struggle with nothing the way I have."

"You cannot determine the future," Long Joe said. "You cannot by will confer on your children freedom, or happiness, or success. You can only help them find the wisdom with which they can work out their own freedom, or happiness, or success."

"When you visited us in Seattle, at the project," Harry said, "you talked about broken covenants. I believe in the covenant between parents and children. I want to leave a legacy for my children. Not just ideas, but something real, something concrete to begin life with."

Long Joe looked at him for a while. "Harry, the white, what you call the Judeo-Christian, Covenant is between a man and his father, and it is about owning the Earth. It is a false Covenant. Our Covenant is much older and it is with our Mother, the Earth. She is the only one who can make a true Covenant. The Earth has never belonged to a man, to the Father. The father only inseminates the mother as the sun provides the seed of its warmth to stir the life in the Mother. The Earth is our Mother's body. How can it be ripped and plundered and divided into individual spoils without consequence? You have heard the story of the goose that laid the golden egg. Our Mother is the great blue goose that laid the egg of life that we feed on."

They both were silent again. Harry drove on over the pass and they descended towards Wenatchee. It was dry and hot east of the Cascades. Ravens rose from a road-killed deer and as they passed. Harry saw Long Joe's lips move as he whispered something.

"What a waste," Harry said.

"Death is never a waste," Long Joe said. "Just a change of status."

Harry had brought a lunch, offered Long Joe a sandwich, but he declined. It was early evening when they passed Wenatchee. It grew dark as Harry left Highway 2 at Coulee City and headed up the Grand Coulee. Steamboat Rock was just a gray shadow against the sky. A crowd of tourists gathered in the parking lot below Grand Coulee Dam to wait for the laser show that played every summer night upon the broken white water that plunged over the spillway. Harry crossed the bridge below the dam and drove towards Nespelem.

"It is good to be home," Long Joe said. "I have been gone a long time. Since last summer. I did seminars all over. You would be surprised how many white people will pay money to hear an old Indian talk."

"I'm not surprised," Harry said. "I'm just glad you don't charge me."

"The funny ones are the business groups," Long Joe said. "Their bosses make them go. They just sit there and stare and wonder what they are supposed to hear. Like there will be a test."

"I remember when I first heard you," Harry said. "In Denny Hall. The drum made me hallucinate. Or something. I thought I was going crazy."

"You dreamed," Long Joe said. "A dream you needed to dream."

"It didn't feel that way," Harry said. "It's a dream I hate."

"It only comes to you for a purpose," Long Joe said.

"I've had that dream again," Harry said, "or something like it. It is about some children I knew in Viet Nam. They were killed in a fire set by some soldiers. I hear them sometimes when I'm out working. Children's voices crying in the distance but if I follow them, no one is there."

"You mean at your place? On the San Poil?" Long Joe asked.

"Yes," Harry said. "Usually when I am at the south end of the big meadow where I planted grain."

"Very strange," Long Joe said and Harry felt the little man's eyes on him. "Very strange."

Wildrose could not find a licensed midwife who would come to the San Poil when she gave birth. Her DSHS caseworker had begun to ask questions, insisted that she see a doctor. When she told him that she intended to have a home-birth he became very upset and threatened to cut off her benefits. Tamarack drove her to Omak to see a doctor at the Farmworkers' Clinic and that seemed to satisfy the caseworker for now.

Judith encouraged her to go ahead with the home-birth. She said it was so much better than a hospital birth and that it was important that the mother be in control of the situation.

Wildrose said that the doctor had told her about all the problems that could happen if she gave birth outside of a hospital. Judith said he was just trying to scare her, that doctors were all threatened if they weren't in control.

Judith talked to the Indian midwife who had helped her with Joseph's birth and she agreed to come if they promised not to tell anyone. She said she had been getting hassles from the doctors, too.

"None of those men doctors ever had a baby," she told Wildrose, "so I don't know how they think they know so much."

Her name was Dorothy and she had attended many births out in the back-country of the reservation. She had been an OB nurse in Seattle and had studied midwifery at the University, but when she tried for her Master's degree the committee would never approve her thesis no matter how often it was rewritten or how well documented the research. She had returned to the reservation in disgust. But soon she had helped a cousin who wanted a home-birth, then someone else, and another, until now she had more than she could do.

She had gone to Hattie to learn about herbs and other natural healing methods and now was widely respected for her eclectic knowledge. Wildrose followed her instructions faithfully and soon had confidence that her baby would be healthy and happy.

Dorothy stopped by the cabin one morning to tell Judith that Tamarack had called her to say that Wildrose was in labor. Judith went with Dorothy, took Rebecca along. They did not return until late afternoon. Wildrose had given birth without incident to a healthy baby boy. Rebecca was very excited by what she had seen.

When next Wildrose went to Colville to get her food stamps she took her baby along. She returned very depressed. Her caseworker had refused to give her food stamps for the baby because she did not have a birth certificate for him. He also had told her that he would order an investigation of her eligibility and made it clear she was now on his bad list.

Dorothy had the answer for the birth certificate. The State had to accept a baptismal certificate the same as a regular birth certificate. She said that Saint Mary's Mission near Omak baptized home-born children all the time. At first Wildrose and Tamarack were reluctant because they were not Catholic or even Christian believers but Dorothy assured them it didn't matter.

They asked Harry and Judith to serve as Godparents and they all drove to the little mission above Omak for the baptism.

Father Bryan, the young Irish priest, was very friendly and asked no questions about the birth or marital status or religious background. He performed a brief ceremony, named the baby Cottonwood, and congratulated them all. Then he filled out the legal certificate. Wildrose was delighted. Tamarack thanked Harry several times on the drive back.

Johnny Carlson reminded Harry of an annoying little brother that he could not get rid of. He would follow Harry around while he worked, ask endless questions and expound his foolish opinions. If Harry told him to go away he acted hurt and confused.

When he discovered that Harry had a degree and had gone to graduate school and that he had worked as a superintendent on construction projects on the coast, Johnny could not understand why Harry was a farmer.

"Why do you spend your life followin' these shitters around," he asked. "No one lives way off out here by choice. My Dad says you must be hidin' from the law."

Harry laughed. "I'm really a drug kingpin. Farming is just my cover."

"Eliot is," Johnny said.

Harry looked at him. "Eliot is what?"

"A drug kingpin," Johnny said. "Or somethin' like that. Everybody knows it. Where do you think he got all his money?"

"Family money," Harry said. "That's what I heard."

"In new hundred dollar bills?" Johnny asked. "He never runs out of hundred dollar bills."

"Lots of people have hundred dollar bills," Harry said.

"You should see some of the people who visit him," Johnny said. "Old guys in suits drivin' Cadillacs. Colombians in vans with dark windows."

"How do you know they're Colombians?" Harry asked him.

"You can tell," Johnny said. "They're like Mexicans only different. They look like they would cut your balls off if you said 'boo.'"

"So you figure I'm hiding out up here, too," Harry said.

"There must be some reason," Johnny said. "No one wants to be a farmer anymore."

"So why is your father a farmer?" Harry asked him.

"He just got stuck," Johnny said, "But not for long. He's got big plans."

"What plans?"

"I can't tell anyone, not yet," Johnny said. "But we'll be rich in a couple of years. I'm not going to waste my life out here."

"People have to eat," Harry said. "There will always be farmers."

"Not here," Johnny said. "My dad says they won't even be growin' food in this country soon. Except in laboratories. All the farmin' will be done in Mexico and South America where they can use chemicals without the government messin' with 'em. That's all those people are good for anyway."

"The fewer farmers there are, the higher prices will be," Harry said. "Sounds like a good time to get into it."

"My dad says once they get the trade barriers down there will be such a flood of food you won't even be able to sell anything grown here. Reagan's got it all figured out."

"Well at least I'll always be able to feed my family," Harry said.

"They might pass a law against it," Johnny said. "Just like with alcohol. It might not even be legal to grow your own."

"That's why I'm hiding out here," Harry said with a laugh. "I'm a bootleg farmer."

Johnny glared at him.

Jeff wrote Harry a letter, a nearly illegible scrawl: "Dear buddy. Lisa and me liked the visut a lot. Youre wife and kids are great. Your qite a farmer. You all come see us. Remembur the farm on that river we saw. You said you wood check it out. I want 100 acurs or mor. I can pay cash. Need big bildings with elektrisity (ha ha). Right me what you find out. I can send muny. Jeff."

Harry decided to make it a family trip. They crowded into the pickup early one morning and drove up the river to Republic and stopped for some breakfast, then went on to the Kettle Valley. The "For Sale" sign still was up. He turned into the drive. It was a well-kept place with wheel-line sprinklers running on a hayfield and cattle grazing in a meadow along the river. There were several outbuildings including a long galvanized steel machine-shed or shop. The house was small but well maintained and flowerbeds bloomed along the driveway.

Harry walked to the house and knocked on the door. A woman answered, wiped her hands on her apron and smiled at him.

"I was interested in the place," Harry said. "Actually a friend of mine is. He asked me to check it out for him."

"Leland is somewhere around here," she said. "Look for his green pickup. He had a tractor broke down this mornin'." She looked out at Harry's truck. "You have people with you? Have them get out and come in."

"My wife and kids," Harry said. "They might like to stretch their legs."

He went to the pickup window; told Judith she was invited in. She and the kids got out and walked towards the house. Harry went towards the shop to see if he could find Leland.

He heard a hammer strike and turned that direction, found Leland at work on the tractor. He looked up, saw Harry and put down the hammer.

"What can I do for you?" he asked.

"A friend of mine saw your 'For Sale' sign when we drove by about a month ago," Harry said. "He asked me to check it out. There wasn't anyone here that day."

"Probably down to Wenatchee takin' Gladys to the doctor," Leland said. "She hasn't been well. We're gonna have to move down there, I guess."

"How much of a place do you have here?" Harry asked him.

"A hundred and forty acres," Leland said. "Forty-five irrigated here by the river then the balance there across the road and up into that stand of timber." He pointed towards a grove of pine trees. "Good grass and some trees about ready to cut. But I guess my turn at it's over."

"Mind if I take a look around?" Harry asked him.

"Be my guest," Leland said. "Long as you don't want a commission."

Harry laughed. "I'm a farmer not a real estate guy."

"This friend of yours a farmer?" Leland asked.

"Well, sort of," Harry said. "He lives down in Oregon, out in the hills, but he didn't grow up farmin'."

"Me neither," Leland said, "But I learned it. Well, have a look."

Harry looked around the buildings and was impressed with the good condition of everything. Fences were tight, corrals clean, weeds cut. He walked down to the river. Two twenty-horse pumps fed the irrigation line. The line was tight, no leaks. It was a beautiful little place.

Leland went in the house with him. Judith and the kids were drinking tea and Little Joe held up a cookie to show Harry. They talked about price and terms. They wanted two hundred thousand which Harry thought was a reasonable price given the improvements. He said his friend had cash and Leland raised his eyebrows.

"That's a lot of cash," he said. "More than I've saved in a lifetime. This some rich kid with family money?"

"I don't know where he gets his money," Harry said. "I know him from Viet Nam."

Leland and Gladys wanted to stay until late fall. They would let the equipment go with the place for an extra fifty thousand.

"You couldn't buy it for that," Leland said.

Harry wrote Jeff a letter with the details and got one back saying that Jeff and Lisa wanted the place. Jeff wanted Harry to handle the details for him. Harry called Leland and told him he had a deal. Leland said he knew an attorney in Republic who could draw up the papers.

"Somebody will need to get in here when we move. Otherwise the water will freeze up and everything will fall apart."

Jeff flew to Omak and Harry drove over to pick him up. He had brought cash, mostly hundred-dollar bills. Harry told him he should have gotten a cashier's check but Jeff said he didn't trust banks. "Money's money."

Harry could see that the lawyer in the Republic Title Company was very suspicious of Jeff's source of cash, but he didn't ask questions, counted it all and sent his secretary to the bank with it. He asked for Jeff's full name and said his wife would have to sign. Jeff said he would take the papers to Oregon for Lisa to sign then send them back by Federal Express.

Harry was glad when it all was over.

On the way back to Omak they drove up to the Kettle to look at the place again. Jeff was very pleased. He particularly liked the big machine-shed, windowless and tight.

"That's where I'll do my work."

Harry introduced Jeff to Leland and it was obvious Leland didn't like him. He didn't invite them in and didn't have much to say.

"Why don't you move up here, buddy," Jeff said to Harry as they drove away. "I'm no god-damned farmer. And we don't want to move up until next spring, at least. You can have all you can make off the place. All I want is that building. We'll have to build another house anyway. Lisa's got her mind set on a big, new house."

"I'm pretty committed where I am," Harry said. "But thanks." He didn't admit how tempted he was, but he did not want to get involved with Jeff's way of life.

Harry was weeding carrots when he saw the beige sedan pull into the road and stop at the cabin. A man went to the door and Judith let him in. Harry headed for the house. He saw that the sedan had a State of Washington license.

The man sat at the kitchen table with a clipboard, obviously interrogated Judith.

"Can I help you?" Harry interrupted.

The man looked at him. "I have a few questions. About your neighbors up the river."

"Who are you?" Harry asked him.

The man handed him a card. "Jeffrey Greene.
Department of Social and Health Services. Investigations Division."

"I'm here about Janice Woods."

"I don't recognize the name," Harry said.
From behind the investigator Judith mouthed "Wildrose."

"I think her alias is Rosebud or something like that. She lives in that A-frame up the river. We have some questions about her eligibility. I understand she has a husband?"

"I have no idea," Harry said.

"We know you are the Godparents for Ms. Woods baby," Greene said. "That could implicate you in any fraud being perpetrated."

"How would that be?" Harry asked him.

"If she is trying to conceal a husband, even a common-law husband, then she is receiving benefits fraudulently. Anyone who assists with that concealment could be an accessory."

"I understand Washington doesn't recognize common-law marriages," Harry said.

Greene looked at him sharply. "Just a technicality. If a recipient misrepresents the makeup of their household it could be fraud."

"I've only been there once," Harry said, "about two years ago. I have no idea who lives there."

"I've been there," Judith said. "Wildrose is my friend. The man, Tamarack, lives in a bus."

Greene frowned. "On the same property?"

"I don't know," Judith said. "But he doesn't live in the house."

"You're sure of that?" Greene asked her. "This could go to court and you'd be subject to perjury laws."

"I know she owns the A-frame and he owns the bus," Judith said.

"Sounds like a front to me," Greene said. He looked through the papers on his clipboard, then again at Judith. "You're Judith Isaacson?" he asked her.

"Yes," Judith said.

"We understand you delivered Ms. Woods' baby."

"No," Judith said. "I was there when the baby was born." "Was there a doctor there?" he asked. "Or a midwife?"

"Not that I know of," Judith said. "Just some friends."

"Who delivered the baby?"

"Wildrose did," Judith said. "It doesn't require a doctor to have a baby."

"It could be considered child abuse," Greene said. "There is a case on appeal right now."

"That's ridiculous," Judith said.

"It's time this reservation got civilized," Greene said. "We may not have jurisdiction over you people yet, but that could change."

Judith started to say something, restrained herself.

"I think we've helped you all we can," Harry said.

"So what is your source of income?" Greene asked.

"I'm a farmer," Harry said. "Take a look outside."

"Doesn't look like enough of a farm to support anyone," Greene said.

"We do all right," Harry said.

"Well I may be back," Greene said. "Something is very odd here."

Wildrose and Tamarack came the next morning.

"Thank you," Wildrose said. "I think he bought the story. We had moved a bunch of Tamarack's stuff into the bus."

"There really wasn't anything he could do," Judith said. "Unless he wants to hang around and see who sleeps where."

"I don't think he is through with us," Tamarack said. "I have a bad feeling about it."

"As long as you take their money," Judith said, "they will try to run your life."

"I hate being on welfare," Wildrose said. "I never thought I would have to live this way."

Tamarack looked at the floor.

"We wanted to farm," Wildrose said, "when we first came here. But we didn't know anything and no one would help us. John Carlson charged us three hundred dollars to plow up our field then all it grew was weeds."

"Everyone thinks farming is easy," Harry said. "Until they try it."

"I don't mind working," Tamarack said, "but I didn't know what I was doing."

"Eliot wanted us to grow weed," Wildrose said. "We planted some three years ago, but the National Guard found it. They wanted to arrest Tamarack but it wasn't on our property. We've been afraid to try it since."

"That isn't the answer," Judith said. "Why don't you grow your own food, at least. Harry could sell any extra you have."

"We don't have a way to even plow it, now," Tamarack said. "We never get enough money ahead to do anything."

"Harry could plow it for you," Judith said.

Harry looked at her in surprise.

"We couldn't pay," Wildrose said.

"We could use some help," Judith said. "We could trade."

Harry thought about it. "I could use some help around here. But it's hard work."

"I'd like some hard work," Tamarack said. "I would feel like I was doing something. I'm just wasting my life."

"There is still time to get fall crops in," Harry said. "When do you want to start."

"Now," Tamarack said.

Eliot pulled in just as Harry finished cultivating the carrots. The team stamped impatiently when Harry walked over to meet Eliot instead of taking them in.

"That's a good-looking team. Where'd you get them?"

"Walt Davis."

"I thought he never sold any horses. I tried to buy a team a few years back."

"I didn't buy them. We traded."

"I usually trade with money."

"I guess money can't buy everything."

"I saw you with Lasker," Eliot said. "In Okanogan. I didn't know you knew him."

"We were in Viet Nam together."

"I didn't know you were in Viet Nam, either."

"I guess you can't know everything," Harry said. "I don't advertise it."

"You see much of him since you've been back?"

"I've been down to his place a few times, and he's been up to see me."

"He seems to be doing pretty well," Eliot said. "One of his neighbors is a friend of mine."

"He mentioned that."

"He's made a lot of money in the last few years."

"I guess so. I stay out of other people's business. And they stay out of mine."

Eliot paused, looked at him. "I thought maybe you could use some extra money."

"I probably could, but I don't have extra time."

"It wouldn't take much time. Just a little nerve and a face nobody knows."

"I've got the right face," Harry said. "But what do you have in mind?"

"I need someone to pick up a package for me now and then. In LA. Then drop it off in the Bay Area or Seattle. Nothing to it. I could pay two thousand a trip. Plus expenses."

"You mean flying? I quit flying after Viet Nam, too. I like to keep my feet on the ground. Or at least my wheels."

"Well, if you change your mind," Eliot said, "You know where I am."

"Not likely."

"I'd appreciate it if you'd keep it quiet. About my knowing Jeff Lasker. And everything."

"I don't tell anyone anything."

"I've noticed that," Eliot said.

CHAPTER 9

Tamarack proved to be a willing worker. Harry was surprised at how little he knew. Things that Harry thought were instinctive, things that anyone must know, were a mystery to his new apprentice. Verbal instructions often confused him. The best way to teach him was to work alongside him, let him watch. Harry realized that he, too, had learned that way. It was just that he had been a small child following his father or grandfather around the farm.

Wildrose often came and brought the baby. Sometimes all four of them would weed carrots or pick peas while Rebecca watched Little Joe and Cottonwood. Reject loved the baby and would lie beside the carrier and guard him for hours. As they all worked together Harry thought of the farm in Kansas when he was a boy and the Old Man and Dad and Uncle Paul would work in the fields while the children followed them.

Harry drove the team and plow up the highway to Wildrose and Tamarack's place and plowed their small field. Then he hauled up a section of spike-tooth and harrowed it down. They planted cabbage and broccoli and peas and other crops that would make in the fall even after frost. Tamarack found a small used pump that he used to water the garden. When the plants began to come up he was very proud.

Judith began to teach Rebecca and Little Joe to ride. Shadow was patient and gentle. Both children were natural riders and listened carefully to their mother's instruction. Judith trained Morningstar for herself. All that Harry had heard about the dangers of stud horses seemed absurd as he watched the colt respond to Judith's gentle, firm persuasion. He was too young yet to carry heavy weights, she said, but by next year he would be her mount.

Wildrose wanted to learn to ride also. She'd had horses for a couple of years, but she knew nothing about them and no one would help her. They had gotten dangerously out of control and she finally had sold them. Judith soon had her on Shadow, riding as if she, too, had been born to it. When Nathan came for a visit Judith asked him to look for a couple of gentle saddle horses she could use for Wildrose and herself while the children rode Shadow.

She encouraged Harry to ride also, but he felt clumsy on horseback. He began to practice when no one was around and found that he enjoyed it. As much as the old man had loved horses, Harry could not remember seeing him ride. He must have ridden, as a young man in Kansas, working the ranch, but he had seen himself as a farmer, not a cowboy. Harry began to discover some cowboy in himself.

Each time he took a load of carrots to High Mountain Juice, Harry also hauled as much other produce as he could carry. He continued to sell to the small markets and Rick Rosen would buy any extra, but his prices were not as high. Harry was sure there was a better market. He had thought of setting up along the highway, as he'd seen others do, but did not want to spend the time away that would require.

On one trip after he had taken some produce to the Italian market on Ravenna he stopped for a sandwich at a tiny restaurant called "Siren Song." The food was fresh and good except for the tomatoes which were typical commercial quality, unripe and leathery. He remarked on the tomatoes to the owner when he paid his check.

"If you know where I can do better," he said sarcastically to Harry, "I'm all for it."

"You can do better than that in five minutes," Harry said and the owner stared at him.

Harry went out to his pickup and returned with a handful of his vine-ripened Fireball tomatoes and showed them to the owner.

The owner took one and cut it, tasted a slice. "Where did you get these?"

"I grew them," Harry said. "I bring produce over almost every week for High Mountain Juice." He looked in the cooler, saw High Mountain "Clearly Carrot." "See that carrot juice?" he asked. "That comes from my carrots."

"Everyone loves that juice," the owner said. "What do you have besides tomatoes and carrots?"

Harry named off a dozen vegetables that he grew, saw the excitement in the owner's eyes.

"Could you bring me produce? I would take a regular delivery."

"Sure," Harry said. "But it's expensive. It's organic, then I have to haul it over here."

"How expensive?"

Harry gave him some prices, made sure they were at least twenty percent higher than he'd been getting.

"I'll take it," the owner said. "When can you deliver?"

"I can let you have some off this load," Harry said. "I brought some extra."

They went out to the pickup and Harry saw the surprise as the owner looked at the boxes of tomatoes and peppers and cucumbers and eggplant. "I'll have melons in a couple of weeks," Harry said.

The owner took more than a hundred dollars worth and told Harry to be sure and come by the next week.

Harry stopped at several more small restaurants and more than half wanted regular deliveries. He had found his market.

A sharp burst of AK-47 fire rattled through the trees. Without thought Harry hit the ground, looked up to locate the shooter. Another burst and he ducked down, waited. One weapon, he calculated. He was a long way from his own guns.

He sat up, shook himself. The automatic fire sounded again from just down-river. He got to his feet and crossed the grain field to the highway. He could see someone in camouflage fire again into the woods. Harry started towards the figure. Some tourist, he assumed, who thought they were far from human habitation.

As he got closer he saw that the shooter was Johnny Carlson. "What the hell are you doing?" Harry called to him.

Johnny grinned, waved the rifle. "My birthday present. Cool, huh?"

"A good way to hurt someone," Harry said. "Do you know how far those rounds carry?"

"There ain't nothin' over there. Just old man Davis's cows. I was shootin' low."

"You need to be careful with that. I had lots of friends killed with AK-47s. Where did you get it anyway?"

"For my birthday. My dad got it for me. From Eliot. He said it was time I had a real gun instead of a twenty-two."

"That's definitely a real gun. You need to pay attention. Those rounds will carry a mile easy."

"I got to have some place to practice. A gun's no fun if you can't shoot it."

"I didn't know guns were supposed to be fun," Harry said. "Find a place with a bank behind, for a backstop."

"Take it easy," Johnny said. "I'm just goofin' around. I know how to handle guns. My dad taught me."

"Did he teach you that shooting from a Highway right-of-way is illegal?" Harry asked him.

"There's no cops out here. Those laws are for tourists."

"A law's a law," Harry said. "For everyone."

"There's too many laws," Johnny said. "Just because city people can't get along they pass all these laws then try to make it stick out here. It ain't goin' to work."

"Not much we can do about it."

"You might be surprised," Johnny said. "I know some people that think different about that."

Nathan came with a horse-trailer and two horses, a palomino mare and a big red gelding.

"They're a little antsy right now," he told Judith, "but they've been ridden a lot. By kids. They'll settle down. You know how to handle horses."

Judith looked at them, helped him unload them into the pole corral.

"I think they'll do. With a little work."

"They belong to Bernie Littlebear. He says you can keep them as long as you'll feed them."

Nathan stayed the day. He and Harry went to check the south fence across the river. If Johnny Carlson was going to be shooting into the woods, Harry wanted to make sure none of his stock wandered down that way. He told Nathan about Johnny's birthday present.

"There's trouble coming," Nathan said. "All the white people have been buying guns. Some of the Indians, too. Serious guns, not hunting rifles. I don't like it."

"What do they think they're going to do with them?" Harry asked.

"Lots of white people are talking about getting rid of the government," Nathan said. "This clean water act they just passed has a lot of them going crazy. They say loggers won't be able to work and that anyone who owns property on a creek or lake or river will have it confiscated."

"That's nonsense," Harry said.

"I think so, too," Nathan said, "But even some of the Tribal Business Council members believe it. They say we won't be able to cut a lot of our timber, or if we do it will cost so much to log it that it won't be worth anything. A lot of the ranchers think they'll lose their grazing leases."

"We can't just cut every tree and graze every blade of grass," Harry said. "There has to be some kind of control."

"A lot of people think that after the government gets rid of all the little guys then they'll turn it all over to the corporations," Nathan said. "It could happen. Just like they did with the railroad land. Or the way they took back the north half of the Colville Reservation when they discovered gold."

"These are different times," Harry said.

"It's the same people," Nathan said, "Their descendants, anyway. We're just a natural resource to them."

"If these fools think they can buy enough guns to take on the Federal Government, they're crazy," Harry said. "Do you know what an army division can do?"

"They wouldn't dare do it," Nathan said, "Not here."

"I don't think you understand the Federal Government," Harry said.

About two hundred yards from the river the fence was down. Harry found the clips that had held the barbed wire to the posts. They had been bent straight. It had to be done with pliers or wire cutters so it must be human work. He showed Nathan.

"Carlson," Nathan said. "Trying to steal the grass. He won't give up easy."

"Neither will I," Harry said.

Harry cultivated corn, was about to break for lunch when he saw the beige sedan pull into the yard. It looked like the one driven by the welfare investigator so he assumed there were more questions about Wildrose. Then he noticed that there were two people, a man and a woman.

He unhooked the cultivator and walked behind the team to the house, He watered them and gave them a little hay to occupy them until he was ready to go back. As he walked towards the house he could hear Judith's voice. She sounded angry.

When Harry opened the door the man turned quickly, kept his eyes on him. The woman stood nearby and talked to Judith.

"What's up?" Harry asked.

The woman handed him a card. "Child Protective Services—Marlene Crain," it said. He saw that Judith was very tense. It wasn't like her to lose it with authorities.

"There has been a complaint," Marlene said carefully. "Concerning alleged child abuse. Deputy Johnson," she indicated the man, "and I are here to investigate."

"You must have the wrong place," Harry said.

"You are Harry Isaacson?" the woman asked.

"Yes, I am," Harry answered.

"Then we have the right place. I was just asking your wife a few questions."

"Who made the complaint?" Harry asked.

"That's confidential," the woman said. She looked at the deputy. "Actually, I believe it was an anonymous call."

Deputy Johnson nodded.

"And that gives you the right to investigate us?" Harry asked her.

"It certainly does," she answered. "We take child abuse very seriously in Washington State."

"I don't abuse my children. And neither does anyone else."

"We'll determine that," the woman said. "We'll need to talk to the children. Privately."

"I would like to talk to an attorney first."

"This is an emergency situation," Marlene said. "There is no right to an attorney. Unless you want us to have a guardian ad litem appointed for the children."

"So we don't have any civil rights?" Judith asked. "Because of an anonymous call?"

"If you don't allow us to talk to the children here," Marlene said, "we have the authority to take them with us. Until a custody hearing."

"You can't take my children," Judith said. "We haven't done anything wrong. Anyone could have made that call."

"In a situation like this," Marlene explained, "when one of the parents has a history of mental instability and trouble with the law, we assume that there could be a problem."

Harry saw Little Joe's wide-eyed look from the loft. He felt his face flush and he trembled and he knew that the deputy noticed. He struggled to breathe evenly, unclenched his fists.

"We need to talk to the children, now," Deputy Johnson said. "If you would please step outside."

Harry and Judith went outside. Judith gripped his hand. He looked at her and saw she was crying. She led him away from the cabin.

"They can't take them," she said. "We have to do something."

"What can we do?"

"Take them and run. Hide in the mountains."

"We'd have to run all our lives. We need a lawyer."

"If they take them, I'll die," Judith said.

Harry put his arm around her and they waited.

It was almost half an hour before the cabin door opened and Marlene and the deputy came out with the children. The children obviously were very frightened. Harry felt Judith's hand tremble violently and he squeezed it hard, felt her steady.

Marlene approached them with a very tight face.

"We aren't going to take them right now," she said, "but we have some serious concerns. We will be watching this situation very closely."

"What are your concerns?" Judith asked.

"This whole situation, way off out here, is not healthy for children. Children need socialization. Rebecca says you kept her out of school one year."

"It was just a few weeks," Judith said. "When we first moved here."

"It always creates suspicion," Marlene said, "when parents don't want their children to have normal contact."

"They have lots of contact. I have family all over the reservation."

"I mean institutional contact. With school and church and other normal activities. Especially when we are dealing with a high-risk parent," she looked at Harry.

"Harry is a wonderful, loving father."

"Appearances can be deceiving. I'm sure you understand our job isn't easy. We are trained to spot problems very early."

"There aren't any problems here," Judith said.

"We'll make sure it stays that way," Marlene said. She turned to Rebecca. "Remember, if you have any problems you call the Sheriff's office. Or tell another adult. You don't have to be afraid."

"I'm not afraid," Rebecca said.

"And this business with the sweat or whatever you call it, everyone sitting around naked. I really disapprove of that."

"My people have always used sweats," Judith said. "It is very healing for the mind and the body."

"This isn't the dark ages," Marlene said. "Children need to learn propriety. I don't think Rebecca should be taught that it is okay to take her clothes off with a grown man around."

"He is her father."

"Fathers are often the worst," Marlene said with a look at Harry. "You should see the statistics."

Deputy Johnson watched them closely while Marlene got in the car. Then he backed carefully to the driver's side door and quickly got in. He gave Harry one more strong look as they drove away.

Little Joe ran to Harry and Harry picked him up. The boy whimpered against his shoulder, put his arms around Harry's neck. Judith stooped down to hug Rebecca.

"They asked us a bunch of silly questions," Rebecca said."

"Like what?" Judith asked.

"Like did Dad beat us and did he ever touch me where I don't want him to."

"They're going to take us away," Little Joe said. "What's a foster home?"

"They aren't going to take you away," Judith said. "We won't let them"

"They said you couldn't stop them," Rebecca said. "I was scared."

"Daddy doesn't hit me," Little Joe said.

"Why did they think Dad beat us?" Rebecca asked.

"Someone called them," Judith said, "and told them lies."

"Who called them?" Rebecca asked.

"We don't know," Judith said, "they won't tell us."

"How can they do that?" Rebecca asked, "just come and take your children away? That isn't right."

"No, it isn't," Judith said.

"They have dirty minds," Rebecca said. "They made us take off our shirts and pull down our pants."

Harry stared at her in disbelief. "They did what?"

"They did," Rebecca said. "Joe was crying. He thought they were going to hit him. They said they had to look for bruises."

"They gave us candy," Little Joe said.

"That's how they got him to stop crying," Rebecca said.

"They wanted to know if I wanted to go with them. They said there was a very nice foster home with lots of ice-cream and kids to play with."

"What did you tell them?" Judith asked her.

"I said the only place I wanted to be was with my parents."

"It will be okay," Judith said. "They know the truth now."

"I don't think they believed me," Rebecca said. "Marlene said sometimes parents threaten children not to tell things. I told her no one threatened me."

"You have to be very careful what you say to them," Judith said.

"I know," Rebecca said. "I could tell. I didn't like that man. The way he looked at me. I'm sorry I told them about the sweat but they asked me if Dad ever saw me naked."

"It's okay," Judith said. "You didn't know."

"If they ever come again, I won't tell them anything.

"That could be dangerous, too," Judith said. "It's hard to know what to do."

Harry put Little Joe down, patted him on the head.

Judith asked the children if they'd like to give the horses some carrots and they ran off happily to do it. When they were gone, Judith turned to Harry. "We have to leave here."

"We can't leave. Where would we go?"

"Anywhere. Where they can't take my kids."

"They can take your kids anywhere."

"What are we going to do, Harry?" We can't lose the kids. They're my life."

"They know that. That's why they do it."

"Now I know how they felt, when they used to take the kids away to boarding school. It must have been awful. They took all the children. Hattie went to boarding school until she ran away. Her family had to hide in the mountains to keep her."

"There is no place to hide, now. They would find us anywhere."

"What will we do?"

"We'll fight them," Harry said.

They left the children at Uncle Paul's while they drove into town to see the lawyer.

"Ed White," he said and put out his hand for Harry to shake. "What can I do for you folks? I understand it's a child-custody problem."

Harry described the visit from CPS.

"They have a lot of power," Ed White said. "It can be abused."

"What can we do about it?" Judith asked.

"Not much," Ed said. "The presumptions are all on their side. The argument is that it's to protect children. No one dares to take the other side on that one."

"It was just someone causing us trouble," Judith said. "None of it is true."

"All it takes is an anonymous call," Ed said. "People do it all the time. I know cases where people have lost their children because some neighbor had it in for them."

"There must be something we can do to protect ourselves," Harry said. "So it doesn't happen again."

"I don't know what," Ed said. "Except to be very careful and have lots of witnesses. Go to church, don't let them miss school too much. Get along with the neighbors. If they should come and take them, call me immediately. Don't go into a custody hearing without counsel. You'd lose for sure. With Harry's record and living way off out there. Now if you were tribe members it would be different. It's pretty hard to take an Indian kid, now. Not like it used to be. Why aren't you enrolled?" he asked Judith. You look like you're at least a quarter."

"Half," Judith said. "But I don't want to take from the tribe. They have enough problems."

"Well it would be some protection," Ed said. "And a nice little check twice a year, too."

"I don't want to do that," Judith said.

"Well take care of yourselves," Ed said. "Be careful. Let me know if there is anything I can do."

"Thanks," Harry said.

Harry was in the cabin on a lunch-break when he heard it. At first he thought it was some kind of flashback. He strained to hear, make sure it was real. It came closer and it definitely was a helicopter. He could tell by the echoes that it flew low. It came towards them from down the river.

He hurried outside to where he'd left the team, still in harness, with a little hay and buckets of water. They turned nervously towards the sound and the gelding took a step.

"Whoa," Harry said to him and went to their heads, took a bridle in each hand.

The helicopter came into sight just above the trees, flew straight up the river. In the corral the frightened saddle horses ran back and forth. Shadow reared and the new gelding crashed into the fence in panic. Harry yelled for Judith and she ran out of the cabin towards the corral.

The helicopter passed over them and about a quarter mile down-river turned back and swooped low over them again. The red gelding jumped into the fence, broke the top rail, backed up, jumped again and went over. The palomino mare followed him. They ran across the corner of the garden onto the road and headed for the highway. Harry looked that direction and saw two Broncos painted in camouflage drive slowly along. He could see several people in each and what he thought were gun barrels.

The draft horses panicked at the second fly-over and began to fight against Harry. He held on, talked to them as calmly as he could. Judith stood in the break in the corral and managed to keep the other saddle horses in. Shadow trembled and her eyes were wide. Morningstar stood close to her, sought his mother's comfort.

The helicopter made another pass on the far side of the river and a little higher. It stopped, hovered then moved on again. It made a wide turn over the Davis's place and came back towards them on a line parallel to the ridge that marked the back line. Harry saw that the Broncos had stopped on the road and someone stood beside the lead vehicle, looked at him with binoculars.

The helicopter circled twice then roared down the river once again and flew on to the north. The horses were in complete terror and it was all Harry could do to hold them. The Broncos disappeared up the highway. Harry led the team over to the corral and got them inside. There was no point trying to work them again that day. He tied them loosely to the top rail and went to get a pole to replace the broken one.

"What the hell was that?" he asked Judith as he put the new rail in place.

"The drug task force. They do it every summer. Looking for marijuana. I've heard about it but I've never seen it before."

"Those bastards," Harry said. "Somebody should sue them."

"You can't," Judith said. "They have immunity. Some people up on Cache Creek tried and the judge threw it out. Said they were just doing their job. They came in these people's house with machine-guns, lined them up against the wall and searched the place."

"That can't be legal," Harry said.

"It's the war on drugs," Judith said. "In a war you can do anything."

Harry thought how easy it would have been to bring the chopper down with one rifle shot. In a real war people shoot back. It reminded him of the "pacification" of villages in Viet Nam. No one there but farmers, women and children.

He pulled the harness off the team and turned them loose. "We'd better find the other two."

"I'll do it," Judith said. "They're used to me." She leaned against Harry. "I keep thinking what could have happened if the kids had been out riding when they came."

Johnny Carlson came by a little later. "Did you see that?" he asked Harry.

"You mean our brave men in uniform?"

"Yeah, they come every summer but they've never stayed here that long before. They must think you're a pot grower."

"I don't know why," Harry said.

"You're new, don't have a visible means of support," Johnny said. "That's all it takes."

"What do you mean, no visible means of support? It's pretty visible."

"Everyone knows you can't make a livin' off a little place like this," Johnny said. "Usually it's a front."

"It's an awful lot of work for a front."

"I was thinkin' what I could do to that chopper with my AK-47," Johnny said.

"Me, too," Harry said.

The day after the helicopter came Harry heard the children again. He was alone, walked through the grain to check it's progress. It took him only a few seconds to realize that it was the same voices he'd heard before, the same cries and sobs. He knew he would find nothing, but still was compelled to follow them.

He crossed the fence and walked through the trees. As always the voices seemed just ahead of him, just out of sight. He followed them further than he had before and despite himself could not help thinking that any second he would see them. He wondered if they could be some bird or animal that his mind altered. He wondered if they were the old dream from Viet Nam, somehow objectified as sound and projected here.

He continued to walk slowly along the river. The voices had become so familiar that there was a soothing quality in them, as though they belonged there, needed to be there. He stopped, listened carefully to judge the direction, but the sound was diffuse as though it came from the rocks, the river, the trees, and even the air.

He walked a few minutes more and felt that he had reached them. He was in a large old grove of Ponderosa Pines near the riverbank. Across the river tall black cottonwoods arched high. There was a deadfall log and he sat down on it. A sense of peace and well-being passed through him. The voices grew faint, seemed to be softly laughing. Then they were gone but the feeling of peace remained.

Harry sat there for some time, he was not sure how long. He thought of his life, his family, this beautiful Valley of the Cliffs where he had come almost by accident and now could not imagine being anywhere else. He knew that he had found what he so long had sought, a home and a life worth a fight if it came to that. He wanted to bring Little Joe to this place among the pines. It was a place for children.

Harry relaxed more than he had in a while. Sun filtered down through the pines and in the cottonwoods birds sang. A fish splashed in the river, drew his attention to the clear, soft music of it's flowing. He remembered waking, those many years ago, to see Judith naked in the river as though she were part of it or it part of her. He should have known then that this was their place.

CHAPTER 10

All the crops did well. Despite the late frost in the spring, when the hot-weather stuff came on it was plentiful. The water system worked smoothly and there was late rain in June which watered the grain just as the heads were filling. The buckwheat was nearly four feet tall and bent down under the weight of the seeds.

It took Harry a few tries to set the combine right for the buckwheat, but when he finally got it, the black grain poured into the bin in a flood. The reel and augers clogged often with the heavy stems but that was a small price to pay. He called Fairhaven Mills and they said they would take all he had and pay the commercial rate plus a dollar twenty-five a bushel premium because it was organic. He borrowed Uncle Paul's truck to haul it over the mountains to Bellingham.

He stored his oats in apple-bins as he had the year before. He used Walt's horse-drawn sickle-bar mower to cut the alfalfa and bought a used ground-drive side-delivery rake. Nathan knew an Indian farmer who had a baler and would come bale the hay for a share. Even after he paid for the baling he had eight tons out of the first cutting with at least two more cuttings to go. He drove to Okanogan for a pickup load of salvage pallets to stack the hay on and bought some large tarps. It would be at least another year before he had time and money for a hay-barn.

He did manage to build a shed for the horses, a post and beam structure with a galvanized steel roof. He split it into three stalls and one large open area. Judith was very pleased with it. It would be nice to have the horses close all winter.

Harry expanded his restaurant route and his coast trips took at least twelve hours, sometimes fourteen, and he returned each time exhausted. He finally had decided to open a bank account for all the small checks he got from the restaurants. He used a bank in Kirkland, far from home, where his account would be just one more number. He no longer was sure who could be trusted and who could not.

He bought a handgun at a gun shop in Monroe and picked it up on his next run after the waiting-period had elapsed. He was concerned that his arrests and commitment to Western State would be a problem, but the report came back clean. He wasn't sure why he wanted the little automatic, but it felt good to have it.

While he was at the shop, he looked at the large selection of assault rifles and asked to handle two of them. When the owner saw his ease with the guns, he asked, "Viet Nam?" Harry nodded.

He was tempted by a small-caliber, lightweight Colt rifle with a wire stock that had a deadly feel, but decided to wait.

"I can't keep those in stock," the gunshop owner told him. "They're dead easy to convert to full automatic."

There was a stack of magazines on the counter with a "free" sign. Harry picked one up. It was called The New American. It had a lot of John Birch Society propaganda and conspiracy theory stories, but Harry found himself in agreement with the sentiments about an intrusive government grown too large and predatory corporations. One editorial predicted a race-war to come. Harry found it hard to believe, but didn't reject it as easily as he once had.

He grew nervous whenever a police car followed him or when he drove through a speed trap along the road. Occasionally a sheriff's car would pass by on the San Poil Highway and he would tense until it passed out of sight. He kept a constant unconscious watch for beige sedans.

Judith wanted a root cellar. Harry was afraid to dig one near the cabin because it could flood in the spring. Walt told him that in the old days they would build-up a berm for food storage in the low-lying areas. Harry laid rocks for walls and hauled in dirt and banked it against the sides. Then he built a timber roof, caulked it good and covered it with three layers of plastic sheeting and buried it under four feet of soil. When he was finished it looked like a small hill with a door in it. It reminded him of the dugout soddies that the old man had told him their ancestors had lived in on the Kansas plains.

He lined the walls with shelves and built a heavy double-door filled with sawdust for insulation according to Walt's instructions. Judith filled the cellar with canned goods and dried vegetables, fruits and herbs, and she piled the floor with burlap bags of potatoes. She kept the carrots separate, said they would make the potatoes sprout. Harry built a cabinet against the north wall of the cabin where it always was cool and then filled it with the carrots.

Little Joe started school. He was surprised by the aggressiveness of the other boys and complained that they called him "redskin" and "bucky." Judith drove to Republic to talk to his teacher and afterwards the problems seemed less. He brought home a note one day that said he had gotten into a fight. He said the other boy had pushed him and called him a little savage.

Rebecca continued to get good grades but she often came home angry. She began to ask Judith about home-school. Judith made some calls from the store and found that Washington had recently eased up on home-school restrictions and the school districts had lost some of their power to compel attendance. Harry reminded her about what the lawyer had told them about CPS.

Little Joe came down with a sinus infection soon after school started. Every year there was a series of infections passed around the schools. Judith said that if someone wanted to design a way to spread epidemics a good answer would be to collect all the children together every day then send them home at night.

She made some Echinacea tea for Little Joe and wanted him to go in the sweat which usually burned out minor infections. She started a fire and put stones on to heat. When it was ready he refused to go in. She reminded him of how quickly he had gotten well previously but he was adamant. Harry had rarely seen him so obstinate.

"What's the matter, son. You know it would be good for you."

The boy's eyes welled with tears. "I know it's good for me. But then they will put me in a foster home."

They reassured him and told him he could keep all his clothes on if he wanted to. He reluctantly agreed but did not want Harry to go in with him. Judith put him in by himself and added the rocks and water when it was needed. By the next day he felt much better.

Jeff sent one of his friends up from Oregon to care-take the place on the Kettle until he and Lisa moved up in the spring. Harry led the guy up there and helped him get situated. He was a longhaired tough-guy with a Mexican girlfriend and lots of self-inflicted tattoos who called himself Gringo. Harry was sure his stay on the Kettle would be interesting.

The winter was mild and passed quickly. Harry ordered a one thousand-foot roll of slitted row-cover and wire hoops to hold it up. He also ordered a roll of polyester floating row-cover to try. He was concerned because he would not be able to cultivate the covered rows and the weeds would take over.

He decided to try plastic ground-cover under the tunnels to keep the weeds down. The catalog said it would increase soil temperatures also. He ordered some soil-heat cables and stapled them to his greenhouse tables. They heated the bottoms of the flats nicely and he was able to get seedlings up by late January. If it all worked he would have a real jump on spring. He ordered seeds and reserved more fruit trees from a nursery in Quincy. He also decided to try some filberts and hazelnuts.

With the row-cover he was able to transplant seedlings into the ground in early May. He first put down the ground-cover to warm the soil, then cut slits and transplanted into them. It took him a while to get the hang of setting the hoops and stretching the row-cover over them. With Tamarack's help he soon could cover a two hundred foot row in less than half an hour.

When he had the first row covered, he put his hand through one of the slits and was surprised at the difference in temperature even on a partly cloudy day. He got a thermometer and began to watch the temperature differential and found that on days in the low sixties his plants sweltered in a micro-climate near a hundred degrees. He could not believe how fast they grew.

There were several nights of heavy frost and he hurried out in the mornings to check his transplants and found that the temperature under the row-cover never was below forty degrees. Soil temperatures under the ground-cover stayed between fifty and seventy degrees. It was as if his plants were two thousand miles south in southern California.

It worked so well that he decided to plant his melons into ground-cover as well and he ordered two more rolls. On a trip to Seattle he found a wholesaler who carried all the material he was using for substantially less than he had paid through the catalogs. The supplier recommended the floating Reemay row-cover for the melons. It was much easier to lay out than it was to stretch the slitted row-cover over hoops. It didn't keep temperatures quite as high, but left lots of room for the melons to vine out.

Tamarack watched everything closely and bought some of the material for his own place. He had heard about a drip-irrigation system that used a flattened plastic tubing with slits every few inches. Harry found some of the drip-tape at the wholesaler and brought it back for Tamarack to try. It worked beautifully and allowed far more ground to be watered with the same amount of water. Harry began to think of getting a pump himself.

He had expected to remove the row-covers as soon as it got really warm in late June, but the ventilation from the slits kept temperatures from rising above a hundred and ten and his plants loved it. He pulled up one side to pick green peppers in late June then put the cover back on. Tomatoes were ripe when he finally took the cover off in mid-July. He had the earliest summer produce anyone had seen.

The restaurants loved it and Rick Rosen wanted more tomatoes and peppers for his juices. He even came up on his prices. Occasionally someone driving the highway would stop to see if there was anything for sale. Harry made a price-list and if he wasn't around, Judith dealt with the drop-in customers. Johnny Carlson's mother sent him regularly to buy produce and Eliot's hired-man came by often.

Money began to accumulate in Harry's bank account and he realized that it was the most money he'd ever had at one time. It scared him a little. He remembered Arne Olson telling him many years before, "Don't ever have anything, Harry. If you do, they'll just try to steal it from you."

Jeff and Lisa moved the end of July. They came to visit Harry and Judith and Jeff said they had stopped by to see Eliot.

"It's nice to have a connection up here," Jeff said. "I can't completely retire yet."

Lisa was very excited about the new house Jeff had promised to build. Jeff tried to get Harry to oversee it for him, offered to pay him well, but Harry decided it was too far away to do a good job while he kept his own place going.

Jeff offered again to let Harry farm his place, move into the old house when the new one was finished.

"The equipment's all there. You could forget this horse-farmin' shit and do some real farmin'. You could grow a bunch of vegetables up there with all this row-cover and stuff you're doin."

Harry said he'd think about it for next year. He didn't want to close off an opportunity, but he knew he didn't want to leave the San Poil.

Uncle Paul told Harry that Mom had returned from California and moved in with Jack and Diane.

"They made a deal," Paul said. "If she would invest the money she had left in that Mirage project, she could stay with them. Your money."

Harry laughed. "Maybe they'll make me a bundle. I can retire."

"Your Mom was tellin' me I should retire," Paul said. "That's all she seems to think about. Everybody retirin'. I don't know who's gonna feed us all."

"Mexicans or somebody that doesn't know any better accordin' to her," Harry said.

"She's goin' back to her old church," Paul said. "I think Preacher Hale is up to his neck in that real estate project, too. I heard it wasn't goin' so good. They're about out of money and they still don't have any lots ready to sell. I heard somebody skimmed off a bunch of money. Probably you-know-who."

"Far as I can see they all deserve each other," Harry said. "If that money they owe me keeps them away from me, it's money well-spent."

"I tried to tell your Mom," Paul said, "about what I heard. But she told me she knew Jack wouldn't lie to her."

"Not unless it would make him some money," Harry said.

The summer passed. With his growing experience and Tamarack's help, Harry had more time to read an occasional newspaper or magazine. He bought a small radio and listened to the news almost every day. He was surprised at how out of touch he was and how little it seemed to matter. The US Navy shot down an Iranian airliner over the Persian Gulf then claimed that the airliner was acting in a threatening manner. There was a lot of talk about a new form of cocaine they called "crack" which was popular in the Black areas. Judith said that a lot of the people in Holly Point used it.

Despite the Iran-Contra scandal and the stock-market crash the fall before, it looked like George Bush would be elected president and the Republicans would continue to turn the country over to the corporations. Michael Dukakis seemed to be a ridiculous candidate who had no idea why he should be president.

Harry was amused by the downfall of Jimmy Swaggart. He was one of Mom's favorites and it must give her fits that he had been caught with a prostitute and admitted he'd been doing it for a while. He wondered if Mom ever would see through the lies they told her in church. He doubted it.

Little Joe did not want to go back to school. Harry finally promised him that if he would give it a try and things did not go well he would take him out for home-school. Rebecca was feeling a little better about school but she said that if Joe was going to stay home, she was too. Judith thought home-school would be a good idea, but Harry still was concerned about the authorities.

They got no more visits from either CPS or the welfare investigator. Wildrose had voluntarily dropped her benefits, even food stamps, and was very relieved not to have to deal with DSHS. She said she realized that the process had kept her depressed. They had stayed through the winter and had done well considering their meager resources. Harry and Judith shared their stored food with them and Tamarack was hard at work on his own root-cellar which he was determined to have full by the time the snow came.

Harry decided finally to build a hayshed next to the horse barn. He spent the money for some treated posts and bought a load of poles for framing from Eric Brown.

"This has turned into quite a place," Eric said. "I didn't know if you were goin' to make it when I brought those house logs and dozed your pond. Figured you were one more hippie with a dream. Doesn't look like a hippie place anymore."

"I'm a farmer," Harry said. "Always have been."

"I can see that, now," Eric said. "I wish I knew how to grow all this stuff. All I know how to do is cut timber and make it into boards. Now they may not let us do that anymore."

"The timber will run out some day, anyway," Harry said.

"Yeah, I know," Eric said. "My Dad and all these old-timers keep sayin' we'll never run out of timber, but I see how much less there is than when I was a kid."

"That's why I like dependin' on somethin' that comes up every year," Harry said.

"Maybe next year you can show me how to grow some of this stuff," Eric said. "I've got a little place up Cache Creek a ways. I've got water and stuff. I saw those plastic tunnels you had this spring. I think that could work where I am."

"Be glad to show you," Harry said. "Let me know."

He had some material left after he built the hayshed so Harry decided to build a pig shed and pen. Uncle Paul had been offering to sell him some weaner pigs for a couple of years and he decided he would take him up on it. He built it a couple of hundred feet from the house, not far from the river where he could easily get water to them. It was small, but he could fatten half a dozen hogs and that would be more than they ever could eat. He figured he could sell any extra pork.

He got four weaner pigs for a start. He had enough extra oats to give them grain. Walt said if you soaked the oats they made great hog-feed, high-protein which made for good, lean pork. Harry had a large pile of cull potatoes and there always were lots of carrots left at the end of the year. He'd never told Rick Rosen how many he left in the ground when he got tired of hauling them.

When the frost came he fed the frozen melons and cucumbers to the pigs and always had aphid infested cabbages or beets with wire worm that he could give them. They thrived and soon greeted him happily whenever he came around the pen.

Some friends of Wildrose and Tamarack gave them four goats after they had to bailout of their high-country place when the snow came. Wildrose didn't really want them but had not been able to say no. She asked Judith if she wanted them and Judith said yes, she had been wishing for goat's milk anyway and one of them was a milking doe. She rigged a pen on one side of the hayshed where they could get inside out of the weather later on when some of the hay was gone.

Frances Davis got sick late that fall and Harry watched their place while Walt stayed in Spokane where the doctor in Republic sent her. The doctors never did diagnose exactly what was wrong with her but she gradually got better and they let her come home. Walt wanted to pay Harry for his time but Harry told him he never would get even for the help Walt had given him.

Judith spent some time with Frances, recommended some herbs that would help her. Frances said they made her feel better than the medicine the doctors gave her.

"I don't know how they knew what to give me anyway. They admitted they didn't really know what was wrong other than a little high blood pressure and some arthritis."

Judith laughed. "They have to give you something. Or you might not believe they know everything."

"Well I know for sure I don't want to go back to a hospital," Frances said. "If I'm going to die, I want to do it right here at home."

"You're not going to die any time soon," Judith said.

Harry went to the University Book Store on one of his last produce runs and spent over two hundred dollars on books. He got several nice ones on spinning and weaving for Judith and another on sheep raising. He wanted finally to get her some sheep in the spring so she would have her own wool. He also bought himself several recent books on archaeology and other subjects he'd once studied. It was time he caught up again.

With the books and several other projects he'd wanted to complete, Harry thought the winter was too short. Before he knew it, he was plowing again and preparing for another crop-year. He understood what the Old Man had meant when he always had said that the years went by too quickly. Harry loved the turning of the seasons, but it would be nice if they'd slow down a little.

In the early Spring Long Joe came for a visit. He'd spent the winter in the Southwest conducting seminars and speaking to groups. He had made some money and had nice Navajo silver and turquoise jewelry for Judith and Rebecca. He brought a braided leather bridle with silver conchos for Little Joe. For Harry he had a hat, a soft, pearl gray Stetson and a band finely beaded with turquoise and quartz beads in a rattlesnake motif with real rattles dangling from each end of the tie.

Harry put it on and whenever he moved his head there was a soft rattle. Little Joe thought it was great.

"I thought you could use a little snake-medicine, Harry," Long Joe said. "Just put this on whenever they come around to bother you. White people are afraid of rattlers."

"I think I need to sharpen my fangs a little," Harry said.

Long Joe had brought a bedroll and slept outside. They tried to talk him into sleeping in the cabin, but he refused.

"The best thing about the Southwest," he told them, "is that it's always warm enough to sleep outside. I don't like a roof between me and the sky."

Long Joe asked Judith if he could use her sweat and she happily agreed. Harry heard him chant long into the night as he performed his cleansing ceremony and returned to the world of the San Poil.

One day Long Joe and Judith took the kids for a long ride on the far side of the river.

Little Joe came back very excited. "We saw an eagle," he told Harry, "and lots of deer. There were some bear tracks, too, but we couldn't find it. Joseph says we can go back again if it's all right with you."

"It's fine with me," Harry said.

One night after dinner when they all sat outside watching the spring sky Long Joe began to chant. Although Harry could not understand the words, the chant made him feel as if he floated there under the brilliant sky. He remembered the drumbeat that had caught him unawares and made him dream in the basement of Denny Hall years before when he'd first heard Long Joe speak. It was the dream about the children and he thought of the children's voices he often heard down the river.

When Long Joe grew silent and Harry was sure he had finished, he said, "I still hear those children, down the river. I think the voices come from that Ponderosa stand about a quarter-mile down."

"It is a blessing," Long Joe said. "I have never known a white person who could hear them."

"What are they? "re they spirits?"

"Everything is spirit. But these children you hear are special." He paused and Harry knew that a story would come.

"Many years ago," Long Joe began, "When white people first came to the Valley of the Cliffs, they saw that it was very beautiful and fertile and they coveted it for themselves. They had learned that the best way to take Indian land was to provoke a fight. When the Indians fought back, then the army would come and take the Indians away to Oklahoma or Florida or some other terrible place and the white people could homestead the land.

"The people who lived in the Valley of the Cliffs, the San Poil Band white people called them, were a very peaceful, happy people. There was much food and shelter from the winter winds below the cliffs. Salmon and black eels filled the river and camas grew in great abundance in the meadows. In summer, on the high ridges, great banks of huckleberries waited for them. In the fall a profusion of saskatoons and chokecherries, wild plums and elderberries lined the creeks. Great herds of deer and antelope gave winter meat.

"The San Poils traded with migratory tribes of Nez Perce and Salish people who passed through the valley and with their cousins, the Nespelems and Okanogans. Willow baskets and smoked salmon, warm robes and pemmican passed from hand to hand. Sometimes a member of the wanderers would fall in love with the valley and stay. The San Poils welcomed them, adopted them. No one was their enemy and there was no reason to fight.

"The white men who wanted the valley waited until the San Poil men were away then they attacked the village, ran the horses away and killed some of the women and children. They caught some of the small children and tied them with leather thongs and put them on salmon racks over the fires to die. They were sure when the San Poil men saw this they would fight and lose their land.

"But a wise old chief persuaded the men not to fight. He told them that fighting would not bring back the children but would cause them to lose their land. They had a great ceremony for the spirits of the dead children and they did not fight. And they never have lost their land. Of all the bands and tribes on this reservation only the San Poils and Nespelems and Okanogans have stayed on their own land.

"Ever since that time people have said that they hear the spirits of the children crying or laughing at play just down the river from where we are now. That is the children you have heard."

"That's a beautiful story," Harry said. "But how could I really hear children who have been dead for a hundred years. I'm not sure I believe in spirits or ghosts."

"So you believe only in what you can see?" Long Joe asked him.

Harry was sure it was a trap so he answered carefully. "Yes, in things I can perceive."

"So you didn't perceive these voices?"

"I'm not sure," Harry said. "Maybe they were just in my mind."

"Everything is just in your mind," Long Joe said. "Where else could it be?"

"But it isn't like a normal perception," Harry said. "I hear them but I can't see them."

"So you must hear and see everything? Must you smell it, too?" Long Joe asked him. "How about these stars? You see them but you don't hear them. Are they real?"

"We know they are real," Harry said. "Because of telescopes and other instruments."

"How about the stars we can't see?" Long Joe asked. "The ones that are too dim or too far away? And far-off galaxies. Are they real?"

"We know those things are real," Harry said.

"Have you ever seen them?" Long Joe asked. "You mean that you believe in them, not that you perceive them. Someone told you they are there."

"But scientists have ways of knowing and checking," Harry said.

"So you believe in what scientists tell you?" Long Joe asked.

"Yes," Harry said, "most of it."

"Your mother believes what the preacher tells her. Is that real?"

"That's religion," Harry said. "Science is different."

"I read somewhere," Long Joe said, "that religion is faith in someone else's belief. It sounds like you are talking about religion, not science. Or maybe they're the same thing."

"Science is based on knowledge," Harry said, "not faith."

"Your scientists know there are other dimensions because they can calculate that it must be so," Long Joe said. "We have long known that there are other dimensions, because we visit some of them. That is the difference in our two ways of knowledge. I do not need a map to a place I have been, or a scientist to tell me that it is there. Your scientists cannot find ninety percent of the matter that they calculate has to be in the Universe. But they will not consider that it is in the parallel worlds that you can visit, even though they have also calculated that parallel worlds must exist. There are many worlds in the same place at the same time like a hologram. The difference between them is just a point of view. Your physicists will tell you this must be true if the rest of what you believe about the world is true. Sometimes we get a glimpse of these parallel worlds."

"So how do we know what is real?" Harry asked.

"Everything is real," Long Joe said, "Or not real depending on your point of view."

"You must drive people crazy," Harry said, "In your seminars."

"No, I drive them sane," Long Joe said, "Although most of them think it's crazy. I went through this stuff about parallel worlds in a big church in Los Angeles where lots of rich people go. When I finished, I told them, 'So your science agrees with my religion, but it does not agree with yours.' I thought I would have to sneak out the back door they got so mad."

Long Joe stayed for several days, told them many stories of the old days, of the Dreamers, Smohalla of the Wanapums, and Skolaskin, the San Poil prophet whose village had been just a few miles south of them where the river joins the Columbia at Whitestone. The children listened with fascination and would follow Long Joe all day to ask questions. Harry let them miss two days of school to spend time with him.

When Nathan came for Long Joe they were sorry to see him go, made him promise to come for another visit soon.

CHAPTER II

A few days after Long Joe left, Harry turned on the radio to listen to the morning news. There had been an oil-spill in Alaska, in Prince William Sound. Reports conflicted, some said it was huge. Exxon, whose tanker, the Exxon Valdez, had run aground, assured everyone that it was minor and would harm nothing. In any case the corporation would take care of everything. The Alaska Governor also reassured everyone that all was under control.

Harry was sure that it was far worse than the reports admitted, worse, probably, than ever would be known. The corporate executives and politicians talked in the evasive language of spin control. Truth was not a consideration.

As he harnessed the horses for the day's plowing, Harry realized that there no longer was anywhere far enough away to escape. If even Prince William Sound, in remote Northern Alaska, could be fouled and lied about, probably ruined, for the profit of a wealthy few, then there was no escape.

He always had known that all the suffering in Viet Nam was not for freedom or democracy because he had seen the war cost everyone there both freedom and self-determination. If the South Vietnam Government and the US did not run the lives of the people then the Viet Cong did. It was only after he was home again that he learned the real reason he had been forced to kill people he did not hate. It was for profit.

Now this mindless greed permeated the entire planet. The privileged few were willing to risk everything to feed their wants. Not their needs, those who profited always had far more than they needed. And here in the San Poil Valley, one of the last tiny pieces of the continent left to the Native people, he could feel the forces of profit and greed at work.

He felt that some day it would come to a fight. He did not fear the fight for himself. He almost welcomed it, a chance to strike back, get even.

But he knew what fighting did to families, women and children and the old folks. Always they suffered while the men fought. He had to find a way to stay out of the fight when it came, but a way that did not mean losing everything. He knew it was a very old problem he faced, a seemingly inescapable fact of human existence. And now there was no place to run.

Harry started transplanting seedlings in April. The groundcover and row-cover system had worked so well that he planted almost everything that way. It required less labor, fewer times over the ground with equipment and produced a better result. It wasn't traditional, but he knew that the old man would have loved it. He hadn't been against progress or technology, just against innovations that helped the rich and hurt the poor.

The old man never really had been poor himself, although during the depression, Harry knew, the family had very little money. But they always had food and shelter and heat in the winter. But his grandfather always had identified with the less fortunate, had said that a country was only as rich as it's poorest citizens.

Everyone helped everyone back then and the fortunes of a community rose or fell together. Hungry children were not only the problem of the parents but a judgment on the whole community. Everyone understood then that things sometimes were beyond a person's individual control, that the group must cooperate for the good of all. A hungry family would find baskets of food on the porch. Delinquent mortgages mysteriously were paid.

Now, it was as if hardship were the fault of the victim or God's judgment on the wicked. "I've got mine, screw you," was the prevalent attitude. The only place to turn if you needed help was the government where the bureaucrats controlled and degraded those who came to them.

Harry thought about his bank account on the coast, the most money he ever had saved, yet he knew that any day it could be gone. IRS could seize it and discuss it later; an illness could deplete it in no time; an accident or lawsuit could wipe it out. In any case it was not enough to take care of the family for long if they were not on the farm. No amount of money was real security, no place was safe.

Eric Brown showed up one day and asked Harry if he could watch them lay row-cover and ground-cover. Like most country people Eric found it hard to watch someone else work and he soon pitched-in with Harry and Tamarack and the work went faster than ever. He came back the next day and brought his wife, Barbara, who obviously was part Indian. She and Judith and Wildrose decided to make a sumptuous dinner for them all and it turned into a spontaneous party. It amused Harry to watch Eric and Tamarack become friends after years of living near each other but believing they were on different sides.

Eric wanted to buy ground-cover and row-cover and drip-tape so Harry ordered more from the wholesaler and had it shipped out by UPS. He hauled it up to Eric when it came and took a look at Eric's garden. It was a nice spot, about two acres, nearly flat with a southwest exposure and a high ridge to the northwest for wind protection. Harry gave him some advice on how to lay it out and assured him that it would work nicely.

Eric had bought a hand tiller and worked down most of the ground. He showed Harry where a spring up above had been diverted into a concrete tank then piped down to the house. There was good pressure and he said that the spring never had gone dry on them. He wanted to know if Harry could sell any extra produce he had and Harry said that he would give it a try.

Harry hauled his first load of carrots in mid-June. Rick Rosen followed him out to the pickup, warned him that he might have to cut back on his business. Several large corporations had seen the profit in the juice business and started to move in. Rosen still could deliver better juice, fresher, at a lower price. But at least one of the distributors had started to threaten the stores, force them to choose between High Mountain and their products. If it was only juice, it would be easy to compete, but the distributors also delivered other products the small markets depended on. And they offered better credit than Rosen could afford. Harry saw that he was very worried.

The restaurant business thrived and Harry could not keep up with the demand. Some complained that he had only those items that were in season, not the full line that the distributors bragged about, but his quality was so good that they couldn't resist it. He picked up a couple of new places, didn't lose any of the old ones.

He banked his checks and some of the cash. He bought supplies and groceries and gifts for Judith and the kids. He looked at pickups at the used dealers. The faithful old International was not running well and he did not want to put more money into it. It soon would be twenty years old. He was surprised at what it would cost him to get anything reliable. His bank account didn't seem as large as it had.

On the way out he stopped in Monroe at the gun shop and bought the Colt assault rifle he had looked at the year before.

The dealer said, "I can't advise you to do it, it's illegal, but if you ever need to convert to full automatic the parts are available from this guy." He handed Harry a business card with a Snohomish address.

Harry took the card and bought ten boxes of shells to get the discount.

The organic inspector came again. She was friendly as before although she had more forms to complete and the fee was higher. She was impressed by the changes to the little farm in the last two years. Judith invited her in for a cup of coffee and she stayed much of the morning. She said the number of certified farmers was growing rapidly. Even some of the big farmers in the Columbia Basin had converted although she suspected that some of them cheated when no inspectors were around. The higher prices for certified organic produce were a powerful temptation.

Several more chemicals had now been declared "organic" by the State and others were under development. She said there also were more approved fertilizers and soil amendments.

"So 'organic' doesn't mean organic any more?" Harry asked her.

She shook her head sadly. "It's changing. The chemical companies and corporate farmers put a lot of pressure on the State to let them into the market. They have the money to get it done. We fought for years to get the State to do organic certification, now the people that fought against us are going to take it over."

"The government redefines the word and everyone qualifies," Harry said. "It reminds me of how they rewrite the SATs to make them easier, then brag that scores have gone up."

Harry began to work the old mare again, used her to pull the wagon for fencing jobs and to haul seed and seedlings. She seemed to enjoy it. Her foal already was as tall as a saddle horse, would be larger than her mother. Harry trained her to lead and would let her follow her mother when she worked. Walt said that was the best way to get them used to the idea. Harry planned to breed the old mare again in the coming winter.

Judith began to ride Morningstar. He was fast and fearless, loved to run the trails on the far side of the river. Little Joe could handle Shadow and Judith trusted Rebecca with any of the saddle horses. Sometimes the two kids would ride together and come back with flowers for Judith or some treasure they'd found. Little Joe liked to drive the team whenever Harry would let him.

Harry bought two cheap fishing rods and some tackle and taught the children to fish. Whenever Judith wanted trout for dinner they were happy to provide them. They found a good swimming-hole beside the lower meadow and Harry built a diving board for them.

Harry constructed a poultry-house near the pond with one side for chickens and the other for ducks and geese. For the waterfowl he put a low fence around the edge of the pond and on the other side of the little building he built a run for chickens with a cover to protect them from hawks. He ran power and bought an electric brooder.

Anderson's store had chicks, ducklings and goslings and he bought fifty chicks and a dozen each of the others. He lost a few in the first week but they began to get their permanent feathers and grew quickly. Frances offered them six of her older laying hens and a young rooster so Harry split the chicken area and built four nests. Frances told them to watch for signs of broodiness in the hens and if one wanted to set she would give them more fertile eggs for the hen to hatch.

In just a few weeks they had fryers ready from the commercial chicks and one of the hens had a clutch of fifteen eggs ready to hatch. Harry still had oats from the season before and fed them greens from garden thinnings and weeds.

He bought six more weaner pigs from Uncle Paul and decided to slaughter two of the hogs he'd fed through the winter. He'd seen Hogs butchered, long ago in Kansas, but couldn't remember the whole process. Walt offered to help. He had an old scalding-tank he hadn't used in years and Harry hauled it over to his place.

When they were ready Harry led the largest hog out and used his hunting-rifle to shoot it. As much as he had prepared himself for it, it was a difficult thing to do. When the hog fell, Walt moved quickly to cut its throat. Harry had grown attached to the hogs and the butchering process also was a mourning. He remembered Long Joe saying that death was just a change of status.

Harry built a small smokehouse and hung his hams and bacon and some of the chops inside to cure. The fresh meat was more of a problem and he took most of it down to Uncle Paul's to put in his freezer. Finally he spent the money on a used chest-freezer he found on one of his coast runs. It soon was full of pork and chickens and produce. He began to look for another.

It was August when Washington First National made the news. Harry heard it on the local business report from the Spokane NPR station. An audit had turned up irregularities. Further investigation had determined that huge losses were inevitable, wrongdoing likely. A panic by depositors triggered a suspension of operations. The Feds took over.

There was no more radio news for a couple of days so Harry bought a Spokesman-Review to read the details. The newspaper article he found also was vague, referred to "questionable real estate investments," and "irregularities in record-keeping practices."

"Some officers of the institution may have committed acts which could be determined to be illegal," it said, but no charges had yet been filed. All the information was attributed to "unnamed but usually reliable sources."

Two days later Harry found a small article that said that the license for Farmlands Real Estate had been temporarily suspended because of trust account irregularities and a further audit was ordered. So Jack was out of a job. And Mom's money probably was gone. So much for Jack's dreams of millions. Harry thought of all the times Jack had ridiculed him for his lack of money and grand ambitions. The little farm on the San Poil didn't look that bad.

The other big news that season was the collapse of the Communist system in Eastern Europe. The conservative commentators were sure it was the final victory of the great Reagan Revolution as though, like Joshua, by standing at the enemy wall and spouting brave words, Reagan had caused God to strike it down. Harry had long felt that if Communism was as bad as it seemed the people would eventually get rid of it.

In Viet Nam he had seen that the Communist ideology had been almost accidental and the war had been about expelling the foreigners and any belief system the Western powers hated would have been attractive to the people. Mostly they just had wanted to get on with life without interference from anyone.

No one seemed to remember that all the evils of the Communist Empire, the powerful oligarchy supported by the bureaucrats and the police, harassment of ordinary people based on anonymous accusations, and a non-responsive government that used a bloated military to interfere in the affairs of other nations, were now a part of everyday life in the United States. Harry envied the peaceful revolutionaries in Poland and Czechoslovakia and East Germany for their belief in freedom and better times ahead. He was not sure the same was true in his homeland.

Jeff Lasker came to see Harry one day and asked him to come up to his place to give him some advice on electrical work. Later in the week Harry had a free afternoon so he took Judith and the kids and drove to the Kettle. The place did not look as well-kept as it had when Leland was there, but there was a huge new house nearly completed in the middle of the hayfield between the old house and the road. It had ended the usefulness of the twenty acres of prime hay because there would be no way to move the wheel-line sprinklers across it. It obviously had not been watered and the alfalfa was yellow and dying while wild mustard had taken hold in many places.

Jeff came out of the old house to greet them. "Lisa and the kids aren't here," he explained to Judith. "They went to stay with our old friends in California until I get the new place finished. She says she's sick of tryin' to keep this old dump clean. Myself, I think she's spoiled."

Judith took Little Joe and Rebecca for a walk while Harry followed Jeff to the new house. The electrical work was in good shape and nearly finished. There was a four-hundred-amp service and double circuits everywhere with lots of capacity left on the panel. The inspection tag already was signed-off.

"Looks good to me," he said to Jeff. "You don't need my help."

Jeff laughed. "Not here. I want to show you something."

He led Harry to the shop. What had been a high, open building had a new, low ceiling not more than seven feet from the floor. Jeff went to a back corner and opened a small panel and worked a latch. A folding stairway dropped from the ceiling.

Jeff grinned. "My new place of business."

Harry followed him up the stairway into a large, open attic. Jeff flipped on a light-switch. The roof had been heavily insulated and sheeted inside with plywood that was covered with a bright, white plastic. The walls, also, were covered with the reflective material. Several large, suspended ducts ran to a bank of fans on one end. A grid of white plastic pipe studded with mist-heads was below the ducts. There was a large stack of boxes along one side and in front of them several large, hooded lights, which Harry recognized as halides.

"Professional, huh?" Jeff asked. "My only problem is power. There is a hundred-amp service for the shop but that isn't enough and even if it was they'd wonder why I suddenly used ten times as much power as the old-timer did."

"So what's the question," Harry asked him.

"I want to run a big line down from the house. They won't have any history on how much the house should use. But I don't know how to do it and I can't call an electrician. It would be worth ten-grand to get it done."

"I don't know," Harry said. "I don't want to get involved in anything."

"You wouldn't be involved. There won't be anything illegal here until long after you're gone."

"Let me think about it. When do you need it done?"

"Yesterday."

"You'll need a long piece of heavy cable," Harry said. "You can't buy that locally without someone asking questions."

"Just tell me what you need. If you can pick it up on the coast, I'll send the money with you."

"I probably could, but it makes me a little nervous."

"Hey, man, I'm just hiring you to do a job. You don't know what's going on."

Judith advised against it. "We shouldn't take any chances."

"Ten-thousand dollars. That's a lot of money. It won't take me three days and there's nothing there now that's illegal."

"Someone must know about Jeff. With all that money and the way he looks. I don't think he's fooling anyone."

"I have to do it," Harry said, "for the money. I'll be careful."

He went back up to Jeff's the next day and measured for the cable. Jeff had a plow that would make enough of a trench to bury the line but it would be visible for a while. Jeff said he would take care of that by plowing up the whole area. "Lisa wants to landscape this old hayfield anyway," he said.

Harry made a couple of calls and got prices on a thousand feet of cable that would carry the load. Jeff wanted to run forty lights at a thousand watts each. Then there would be the loss from the long run. He had decided that they could tap the shop panel for the pumps and fans.

Jeff gave him the money for the cable and panels and other hardware he would need and paid him his ten thousand in advance.

"Wait until I'm finished," Harry said.

"I'm not worried. I know I can trust you."

Harry made a produce run and picked up the electrical equipment. He put the ten thousand in his bank account. He had decided to buy a new truck on his next trip.

They laid the cable at night. Gringo helped them, then continued to plow that end of the field. Harry agreed that it was a good plan. Soon he had trouble locating the cable run himself. He tapped the house panel as unobtrusively as he could, but a close inspection would certainly cause question. He told Jeff that if anyone ever noticed he should say that he powered some irrigation pumps off the mysterious line.

They ran the cable up to the shop attic through an innocent looking pipe and Harry installed a double panel and ran cable through conduit to two-hundred-forty-volt outlets spaced every few feet along the floor. He stayed over one night and finished the following morning. Harry engaged the main breaker and Jeff was very pleased.

"Thanks. It was a bargain. I'll be even for all this with one crop."

Harry traded the International for a two-year-old Ford four-wheel drive three-quarter ton with dual wheels, heavy suspension and a towing package. The dealer gave him a decent trade-in and he paid cash for the balance.

He wanted to find a fifth-wheel trailer for the produce runs. He had more than he could haul and both Tamarack and Eric had stuff they wanted to sell. He had about decided to find out what he could back-haul to the San Poil. There were a lot of things he could pick up at Costco or Fred Meyer, mark-up and still sell cheaper than local stores. He would be able to deliver grain wherever he found a market and buy machinery or livestock to take home.

He stopped before he drove away and took a last look at the old International. It had served him well for so long. He had retired it once, before the auction, then went back to it when the bank took everything. It had seen his good times and his bad times. He had spent so many hours in it, probably more than any other place he ever had been. It had moved him and Judith twice, first from Seattle to the farm in Block

88, then to the San Poil. The children had ridden in it hundreds of times. The new rig never would feel quite the same.

Fall came suddenly to the San Poil. Harry sensed the approach of frost and spent two days covering his melons with Reemay and putting slitted row-cover back on the peppers and tomatoes. He managed to extend the season slightly, but moisture from the mature plants collected underneath and they soon began to mold.

He pulled up the covers, picked what was ripe, then gathered green tomatoes and peppers and laid them out in flats in his greenhouse with the heated tables turned on. That system worked well and he still had tomatoes ripening the week before Thanksgiving.

Judith, Frances, Wildrose and Barbara made many gallons of tomato sauces, pickles and preserves. They dried tomatoes and peppers and apples. The root cellar was so full it was hard to find anything in it. Tamarack had his root cellar complete and Eric was hard at work on one of his own.

Nathan came by with whole salmon for sale for ten dollars each and he and Judith showed everyone how to build racks to smoke them.

Walt offered to trade one of his fat calves for two of Harry's hogs and Tamarack and Eric bought one to split. They spent most of one week butchering and cutting meat. Judith and the other women dressed-out chickens and ducks and geese. Harry expanded his smokehouse and they cured some of the waterfowl as well as pork. Walt showed them how to cut thin strips of beef for jerky and they hung several racks to dry.

Harry bought another large freezer and soon it, too, was full. His obsession with their food supply was to the point that when he calculated their reserves he realized they could not possibly eat everything they had stored in a year. He began to look for trades.

Uncle Paul had several neighbors who were happy to get clean, homegrown food and Harry began to take a load down every two weeks or so. He traded for old horse-drawn equipment and saddles and tack. He accepted good hand-tools, interesting artwork and antiques and just about anything he thought he might have a use for or could trade again. He had more than he could store so Uncle Paul let him use part of his storage building.

One guy was a gun-collector and offered to trade every kind of weapon from a Frontier-style derringer to black-powder rifles to Ouzis. Harry spent some time talking to him about the gun business and realized why Eliot was involved. There was a lot of money in it. He finally traded some hams and a slab of bacon for a Sharp's fifty-caliber Buffalo gun like the one the old man said his grandfather had used to feed the family when they first were in Kansas.

Uncle Paul told Harry that Jack had been sued by the investors in Desert Mirage along with the banker, Washington First and two other Realtors who had pre-sold the nonexistent lots. The investor group was headed by Reverend Hale who had given several self-righteous interviews to the newspapers and Spokane television. All the Desert Mirage assets had been seized pending the outcome of the suit.

"They're still in that big house and so's your Mom," Paul said, "but I don't know how they plan to pay for it. I understand there's a pretty hefty mortgage against it. I did hear that Diane went to work, back at the Wak 'n Yak."

"Jack could always find a way to steal money," Harry said. "He's probably running another scam already. Besides, half the politicians in the County were in on that mess. They'll bail him out."

"I don't think that's goin' to work this time," Paul said. "I heard all the Real Estate Licenses were suspended and there's a court-order against any of them doin' any business. The Feds are involved and I don't think they're goin' to play games."

"I don't know," Harry said, "Jack's always been able to slip out of any trouble he got into. He's not bothered by havin' to tell the truth or take responsibility or any of that. Shit, he's probably figured out how it's all my fault."

Paul chuckled and the scar across his eyebrow made that eye seem to wink. "Well, he comes by it honestly. When your Dad and me were kids everything was always my fault."

Harry made a trip to the Kettle to see Jeff and took along a selection of meat and canned goods as a gift. Lisa was very happy to get the food. She said she drove all the way to Omak every week just to buy groceries and even then it was nothing like the selection she was used to in California. She had learned to cook from scratch more than ever before.

The new house was finished and reminded Harry of a gymnasium or a mausoleum. It had to be one of the largest houses in the county and it appeared that mostly they lived in the kitchen.

When Harry rang the bell at the front door it was several minutes before Jeff appeared. "Next time, come around back," he told Harry. "We don't use this door much."

Jeff wanted to show Harry his "business." Harry refused at first, but Jeff insisted and it didn't seem like it could do any harm. As far as anyone knew, the building was just Leland's old shop.

The smell was apparent before they reached the building, a sweet skunk-smell that Harry knew immediately. A large Rottweiler was tied near the shop door and another ran loose inside. Jeff quieted the dogs and led Harry to the stairway.

Harry was amazed at the number of plants inside the shop attic. There were several stages from newly potted cuttings to mature plants heavy with buds and almost ready for harvest, all in ten-gallon black pots. Harry began to get a headache from the smell and the brightness of the lights. Jeff showed him different varieties, some feathery Sativa plants and some stocky, broad-leaf Indica. There was a cutting area screened off with light-curtains and lit with banks of fluorescent tubes. There were many stages of cuttings from tiny two-leaf starts to six-inch plants ready for transplant. Another long, reflective curtain divided plants in bloom from those in accelerated vegetative growth.

Jeff had built a drying-room on one end with two large squirrel-cage fans ducted outside. It was hung full of cut plants drying.

"This is where most of the smell comes from," Jeff said. "I have a remote radio switch at the house to turn these fans off when anyone is around."

"It's quite an operation," Harry said. "But I'd be too paranoid. How do you sleep."

"Like a baby," Jeff said. "I figure if somethin' happens, it happens. I've got enough money to hire the best dope lawyers there are. And if that doesn't work I can take off to Costa Rica or somewhere. We've got fake passports and everything. Besides, I have a friend that knows the right people in the County. Shit, man, I make enough every three months to pay for this place."

"How do you get it out of here?" Harry asked him.

"Load it in my truck and head for the coast," Jeff said. "I put on my cowboy hat and boots and play farmer. Nobody really wants to stop it. It's the biggest cash-crop in the country." He laughed and slapped Harry on the back. "Shit, buddy, I'm just a good capitalist. This country depends on people like me."

CHAPTER 12

When Harry stopped at the store to get the mail there was an official-looking envelope among the Christmas cards. The return address was the Federal Building in Spokane. He tore it open in the truck. The address on the letter included his Social Security Number.

He read:

"Dear Mr. Isaacson: This office is charged with the responsibility of investigating the circumstances surrounding the failure of the real estate development known as Desert Mirage. As an unindemnified stockholder in Mirage Enterprises, General Partner of Desert Development, developer and General Contractor for the subject property, it may be determined that you have incurred some liability. In order to determine the possible liability you may bear to the Federal Government, Resolution Trust Corporation, or to those investors in Desert Development who may have been defrauded by actions of the General Partner, Mirage Enterprises, you must complete and return the enclosed questionnaire within ten calendar days from the date of receipt hereof. You will be notified of your obligation to cooperate with further procedures concerning this investigation in the near future. Sincerely, John W. Burchard, Auditor."

There was a six-page questionnaire attached that started with name, date of birth and marital status and continued on to ask for details of his entire life. They wanted bank account numbers, business records and a list of all property owned. They asked for the dates of arrests and any prison terms or psychiatric commitments. There was a notary block below the signature line.

Harry hurried home and showed the letter to Judith.

"You don't own any stock," she said. "It must be a mistake."

"Maybe they have me confused with Jack," Harry said. "But they have my Social Security number."

"You need to talk to a lawyer."

"I'll go call Ed White. He seemed okay."

"He's from Ephrata, too. How do you know you can trust him? He might even be on the other side."

"How do I know who I can trust?"

"Find someone on the coast, someone who doesn't have any connection."

"I don't know any lawyers. Who can I ask?"

"Joseph! My brother. He might know someone. At least he would know who to ask."

"We can try. Do you have his phone number?"

"No, but my mother does. I need to go call her."

Harry stayed with the kids while Judith went to the store to make the call. When she came back she smiled at him.

"I'm supposed to call him again tomorrow morning," she said. "He has a classmate who is in a law firm in Seattle. He'll see if he can talk to us. He said if we had any money in the bank to get it out."

"I'll leave now," Harry said. "I've been worried about that money. I'll call from Seattle."

"Okay. I can ride Shadow to the store. Go, Harry. Hurry."

Road conditions were terrible on Stevens Pass and the drive took three hours longer than usual. It was evening and the bank was closed when he got to the Eastside. Waves broke over the Evergreen Point Bridge as he crossed Lake Washington and gusts of wind blew the truck sideways. Rain beat against the windshield.

He went into the Greek cafe in the University District for something to eat. There were Christmas decorations hung on the walls and fake frost on the windows. He ordered a Feta cheese omelet and Greek fries and watched the other patrons. As always in this place that was so familiar he felt more alienated than in some place he never had been. It wasn't the superficial differences in the appearance of students and professors, but something to do with how life, here, had gone on without him.

He wasn't sure why it mattered. He wouldn't come back here to the academic world if they begged him to, and his life on the San Poil was what he always had wanted. Yet something here always disturbed him although he could not seem to stay away. Maybe it was just that the U. District changes marked the passage of time for him.

He almost could see the ghost of a young Harry Isaacson, bearded and bitter, just back from the war, brooding in his field jacket in the corner of the cafe. And there was another ghost, a young Native woman, arresting in her beauty, a serious seeker of knowledge, who had fallen in love with that other, unhappy ghost. He still sometimes could not believe it had happened.

He finished his food and paid his check. He and Judith had agreed to leave messages with Uncle Paul, if necessary, so he called, but Paul had not heard from her. He needed to find a place to stay. Ron's place was out. He did not need an evening with the Dragon Lady. He didn't want to see anyone, just find a bed to collapse in.

He crossed back to the Eastside to be near the bank when it opened. He found a room in a new, cold motel near Totem Lake, could not believe how much it cost. He called Uncle Paul again, gave him the number to pass along to Judith if Paul heard from her. He flopped on the bed and used the remote to turn on the television, searched for CNN.

A commercial faded, was replaced by the breaking news theme followed by footage of military action somewhere. Helicopters flew and fired; tracked, armored vehicles clattered down a street. The green light of a flare floated across the landscape, cast grotesque shadows. Small arms fire chattered in the background.

"You are watching live events in Panama City where United States military elements have landed, reportedly in an attempt to enforce the indictment of Panamanian President General Manuel Noriega on drug-trafficking charges. It is not known if the general has been apprehended or even located. Some elements of the Panamanian Military are putting up a stiff resistance. The White House and Pentagon released a statement calling this a limited action and in no way an invasion of the sovereign nation of Panama."

There was a shot of several military officers in battle-gear conferring, then a cut to the night sky where several jets could be seen in a fast fly-over. A hand-held camera jiggled, showed a shot of several personnel carriers roaring by. A soldier shouted and gave the camera a thumb's up. There was static as the satellite feed was lost, then the smiling face of the announcer.

"We are waiting to bring you a live news-briefing from the Pentagon. Again, earlier this evening advance elements of an American strike-force landed in Panama in an attempt to arrest Panamanian President Noriega on drug-trafficking charges. We are told this is not an invasion, but a limited action directed at enforcing the drug laws of the United States of America."

Harry sat stunned on the bed. He had known about the Noriega indictment but never had believed that the military would be used to enforce it. And all this business about a limited action sounded too much like what they told the people at home about Viet Nam. War never was limited. He could imagine the terrified Panamanians behind the walls of the buildings in the television pictures. There must be many bodies in the streets and children already orphaned by this "limited action."

Harry had thought when the last few Americans left Viet Nam in humiliation, escaping from the roof of the embassy, that the country would be more cautious about sending the military to enforce US values around the world. Now with Grenada and Panama and shadows looming in the Persian Gulf, it seemed that Viet Nam had just whetted the appetite of the government and the military for the blood of those who disagreed with them.

He turned off the television and lay on the top of the bed with his clothes on. He did not sleep well and the eyes of children dying in flames haunted his dreams.

He awakened early and went out at six-thirty, found an espresso stand open at an Arco station and stood in the drizzle while his coffee was made. He drove by the bank and the sign said they did not open until ten. He bought a newspaper and went back to the motel. The front page was full of glowing accounts of the brave mission to Panama. He thought that it must have sounded the same on the streets of Rome when news came back that Jerusalem had been burned to the ground to punish the Zealots or that the intrepid soldiers of the tenth legion had conducted a mass crucifixion to prevent the downfall of the empire.

Inside were several stories of the Savings and Loan Crisis. One story gave a list of banks taken over by the Government. On the list was Washington First National Savings Bank. Harry wondered how many people were caught in the mess as he seemed to be.

He turned on the television. The network morning news ended with a video collage of the action in Panama and a voice-over praising the bravery of the young men and women who risked their lives to keep America safe. The local news began with a similar tape then cut to an interview with a woman in Auburn whose son had called her from Panama. She was so proud that her son could help protect America from drugs.

Local stories were interrupted to show a statement from President Bush in which he explained that the use of troops was only to protect America's children from the corrupt and evil foreigners who sent drugs to poison our cities. This action would send a message around the world that America was not going to sacrifice a generation for the profits of drug-kingpins and international terrorists.

Just before nine the phone rang and it was Judith. She had talked again to Joseph and he had given her the phone number of his classmate from Stanford, Jerry Steinman, who was a junior partner in a big downtown law firm. He had told Joseph that he would be happy to help.

Harry put in a call and the receptionist said that Mr. Steinman was due in around ten. It was a wonder that anything at all got done in the city.

He was restless, checked out and drove around. He went down to Redmond, past the house he had built for him and Judith. It had been re-painted and the yard changed. The garden was gone, replaced by a swimming pool, empty now, dead leaves collecting in the bottom. Some of the tall firs at the back of the lot had been cut to make way for an ugly gazebo. Christmas lights blinked from the branches of one of the Spruce trees Harry had planted by the walk. It gave him the same eerie, empty feeling as the University District.

It was nearly ten so he drove up the hill to Kirkland and parked in the bank lot. He watched until a woman unlocked the door and he went inside. The teller frowned when he didn't stand behind the rope to be called forward. He showed her a check and told her that he wanted to close out the account. She punched the number into the terminal and he saw her eyes widen. She carried the check to a woman officer who sat at a desk behind a barrier.

The officer followed the teller back to the station and held the check.

"You are Mr. Isaacson?"

"Yes, I am."

"Could I see some identification?" she asked tightly.

He pulled his driver's license from his wallet and handed it to her.

She frowned at it, looked up at him then down again. "And you want to completely close the account?"

"Yes."

"We'll have to hold some balance to cover any outstanding checks."

"I haven't written a check in over a month," Harry said.

She punched some numbers, looked at the screen.

"I see you don't write many checks on this account. Would you wait a moment, please?" She disappeared through an office door.

The teller forced a smile at Harry. He didn't bother to return it.

The woman officer returned followed by a man. He had a fake holly pin with plastic berries on his lapel. He held the driver's license, looked at Harry. "Is there a problem?" he asked.

"No," Harry said, "No problem. I just want to close out the account."

"If it's our service," the man said, "We offer several options. With this much money you could be drawing quite a little interest from a combined account."

"I just want my money," Harry said.

"You realize that we must report withdrawals over ten thousand dollars to the authorities."

Harry hadn't thought of that but he wasn't going to turn back now.

"That's fine. It's my money."

"Yes, of course," the man said. He looked again at the terminal. "I see you are married. Is this a joint account?"

"No, it's not."

"Some kind of family emergency?" the man asked, waited.

"Yes."

"I'm sure you'll want a cashier's check."

"No," Harry said. "I want cash."

"That's a lot of money to carry."

Harry noticed a security guard watch him from the far side of the lobby.

"I can handle it."

"Would you write this check out for cash, then," the man said, handed it to Harry.

"I'll need to know the balance," Harry said.

The man looked at the terminal, hesitated.

"Thirty-eight thousand, four-hundred seventy-two dollars and 44 cents."

Harry wrote the check and signed it, handed it to the man. He carried it to a card-file, checked the signature against the signature card. He looked again at the driver's license, then Harry. He scribbled his initials on the check and handed it to the teller. The woman officer frowned one last time at Harry and went back to her desk.

While the teller opened her cash-drawer with a key the man looked at Harry. He handed back the driver's license.

"I'm sure you understand," he said. "This early in the morning, and the way you're dressed, we have to be careful."

"Sure," Harry said.

The teller counted out the money to him, watched suspiciously as he stuffed the pile in his jacket pocket.

"Thanks," Harry said.

She didn't respond.

He called the attorney's office from a phone booth. The receptionist passed the call to Jerry Steinman's assistant.

"This is Kelley. Mr. Steinman had to go to the courthouse," she said. "He asked me to see if you could come in at one o'clock for a conference."

"I had hoped to see him earlier," Harry said.

"I'm sorry," she sing-songed, "Mr. Steinman won't be available until one."

"Okay," Harry said. "That will work."

"Thank you, Mr. Isaacson," Kelley said. "We'll see you at one. And Mr. Steinman asked that you bring any documents with you."

"Okay. I'll be there."

He didn't want another scene like the bank so he decided to get some city clothes. His boots, jeans, sweatshirt and parka didn't seem to give the right impression. For years as a graduate student and teaching assistant and again when he worked for United Homes he had worn slacks and sports-jacket every day, suits for important meetings. He had forgotten that in the city clothes were the person.

He wondered where to go, thought momentarily about spending the money for a three-piece pin-stripe and some expensive shoes but knew that would be ridiculous. Besides he would need a haircut and beard-trim for that look. He hated to spend any money at all on useless clothes.

He remembered a Shop n' Save thrift store in Bridle Trails and went up there to see what he could find. He found a gray Harris Tweed sport-coat like he would have worn at the University and some black slacks that would fit. There weren't any decent shoes his size but he bought three dress shirts. Altogether his bill was seventeen dollars.

There was a Payless nearby so he got some shoe polish and a brush. He spent a few minutes to clean up his boots and smeared on the polish with a paper napkin he found in the glove box. He buffed the boots until they shone.

He stopped at a Burger King and carried in the clothes in their paper sack, changed in a bathroom stall and combed his hair and beard. He looked in the mirror and laughed. It had been a while since he looked like that.

Steinman's office was in Pioneer Square. Harry found a Diamond lot nearby and parked the truck, fed the cash-box six dollars. He started to lock-up then remembered he'd stuck the money in the glove box. He got it out, split it up into several pockets. He took the manila folder with the letter from RTC and a couple of newspaper clippings about the case.

On the elevator a businessman in a suit said hello. The receptionist seemed surprised when he gave her his name and asked him if he would like coffee while he waited. He didn't take the chance on office coffee.

Jerry Steinman was an affable young man dressed in jeans and jacket, no tie. His hair was longish and curly. He shook Harry's hand and showed him into his office.

"So you're Joseph's brother-in-law. I've heard quite a lot about you and Judith. How is she?"

"She's fine."

"Joseph is quite a guy," Jerry said. "A real force. He could have gone into just about any law firm he chose."

"The family is very proud of Joseph," Harry said.

"So," Jerry looked at him seriously, "You have a problem with the Feds. Something to do with a fraudulent real estate development."

"I don't know," Harry said. "I got this in the mail." He handed Jerry the letter.

Jerry frowned as he read. He put the letter down.

"So how much stock do you hold in this Mirage Enterprises?"

"None," Harry said. "I wouldn't have invested in it at gun-point. My brother is involved in it and I think my mother may be. I heard she was."

"But you didn't put any money into it? Is this your Social Security number?"

"Yes, but I didn't invest a penny in it."

"You're sure?" Jerry pressed. "I don't mean to question you, but this is a very strange story."

"It sure was a surprise to me."

"I'd better make some calls," Jerry said. "I hate to bring it up, but I would at least need to cover my expenses."

"How much do you need?"

"A thousand dollars for a start." He spread his hands and shrugged. "I'm sorry. This sort of thing can be expensive."

Harry took out one of the bundles of money and counted off ten hundred-dollar bills and handed them over. He saw Jerry's eyes widen.

"I just closed out my bank account," Harry said. "Joseph told Judith we should do that."

"Good advice," Jerry said. "But I wouldn't let anyone see that wad."

"Don't worry. I won't."

"Where can I reach you? After I make some calls and find out what's going on."

"I hadn't planned to stay over here," Harry said. "And we don't have a phone at home."

"Joseph said you lived way out on the reservation. Can you call me?"

"Sure. When?"

"Tomorrow. Afternoon. I should know something by then."

"Thanks," Harry said.

"Glad to be of service," Jerry said. "If you need any other legal advice give me a call. I really think a lot of Joseph and I'm happy to help out his family." Jerry handed him several business cards. "Just give one of these to anyone who has questions."

"I'll remember that."

"Happy to help," Jerry said. "Say hello to Joseph for me."

"Sure thing.

Harry left a message with Uncle Paul for Judith that he was on the way home. He decided to buy some Christmas gifts. He stopped at the University Book Store and got books for everyone in the family. He was surprised at how much they cost. He bought a tape player and several tapes he knew Rebecca would like.

He wanted to buy Little Joe something other than toys, couldn't find anything at first. He went into a western store on the way out of town and bought him Tony Lama boots and a real Stetson hat. He found a Navajo saddle blanket there for Judith and also bought her a pair of saddlebags he knew she wanted. He decided to keep the theme and got Rebecca a fine woven serape from Mexico and a pair of moccasins.

He stopped at a Safeway store and spent over a hundred dollars on fresh fruit and nuts. He went to a Starbucks store for five pounds of good coffee and bought some fine chocolate as well. At a gallery in Gold Bar he got some beautiful mineral crystals he knew Judith would like.

As he drove over the pass just after dusk with all the presents in the back and Christmas music on the radio he felt a little like Santa Claus.

Jerry Steinman wasn't in when Harry first called. He went back to the store an hour later and finally got hold of him.

"Interesting story," Jerry said. "You are listed as a stockholder by Desert Mirage, but the auditor admits they don't have anything signed by you. As far as I can determine, someone bought stock in your name and used your Social Security number. I assume that would be your mother or your brother. It was worth over fifty thousand dollars when they bought it. Of course, it's a liability now."

"It must have been my mother," Harry said. "My brother came to see me almost two years ago, tried to get me to sign a release so my mother could invest in that mess."

"Why would she have needed a release from you?"

"Some of her money was supposed to go to me," Harry said. "When they settled the farm partnership the banker gave all the money to her. My Dad and I were partners in the farm."

"Would this be the same banker that was the managing partner for Desert Mirage?"

"That's him," Harry said.

"He could be in some real trouble," Jerry said. "You could file suit against him. And your mother, as far as that goes."

"No," Harry said, "I just want them all to go away."

"Well there probably won't be anything left when this is all done anyway," Jerry said. "RTC seems to think they can hang them all. Especially the banker."

"He'll weasel out of it," Harry said. "Along with my brother."

"They're really getting tough on this, finally," Jerry said. "It's been too embarrassing politically."

"I'll believe it when I see it," Harry said. "So how about this letter I got?"

"Well, the auditor wouldn't actually admit that they couldn't come after you, but, frankly, I don't see how they could. If anything you are among the people who were defrauded by this group. I suppose your mother could claim it was a secret gift or something, but I still don't see how you could be liable if you didn't even know about it. And obviously you didn't make or concur in any decisions."

"So what do I do?" Harry asked. "Just wait? I don't like having something like this hanging over my head."

"I can write them a letter," Jerry said. "I'll just lay out the facts and deny any liability, maybe make some noise about filing suit ourselves. That will probably back them off although I wouldn't count on any outright admission from them. Technically they could open it back up any time."

"So how about this questionnaire?" Harry asked.

"Don't return it," Jerry said. "They might try to get an injunction to force it out of you which we could fight at the time."

"So any way I go, I lose," Harry said.

"I guess you could say that," Jerry said. "There really isn't any way to make it all go away. I'll keep the cost as low as I can."

"I appreciate your help," Harry said. "Let me know if there is anything else I should do."

CHAPTER 13

It was another mild winter. Harry put the old mare in with Walt's Belgian stud to be bred again and Judith decided to breed Shadow to Morningstar. The palomino mare that Nathan had brought to them dropped a fine colt in March who looked just like his mother.

Harry got in his seeds and supplies and also ordered what Tamarack and Eric needed and some extra just in case someone wanted to buy it. Each year there was more traffic on the San Poil Highway and he had decided to see how much produce he could sell just by putting up a sign. Prices in the stores were higher than ever and quality worse.

He got a letter from Rick Rosen which said that Harry should call him each time he came over to make sure that he wanted a delivery. There was a large new organic farm in the Skagit Valley and he had contracted with them. High Mountain Juice was expanding to counter the competition from the large companies and he needed to be able to have daily deliveries so that he could operate around the clock. He appreciated what Harry had done for him and would buy as much as he could.

Harry realized that his relationship with High Mountain probably was over. He planted fewer carrots and expanded his hot-weather crops. He needed to rotate his fields more often but without irrigation water for part of the grain fields he could not include them in the rotation. He thought about drilling a well and pumping the water, but decided to wait at least one more year to save the money.

He had bought a small safe to hold the cash he'd withdrawn from the bank and built a hidden compartment in the back of his closet for it, but he still did not like holding the cash. He wished that he could invest it, but couldn't think of any investment he would trust.

Walt offered to let Harry farm his fifty acres of cropland on shares. It was not irrigated so it would not work for produce, but Harry had done well enough on grain. Walt would take most of his share in hay for his livestock and also would take produce in trade so that he and Frances could cut back on their garden. He would throw in the use of his big team and all the equipment.

"In the old days," Walt said, "I would turn the place over to one of the kids and take it easy. But I can't imagine Franklin with manure on his boots or dirt on his hands. And his sister's husband is too good to work at all. They've been livin' on her wages for ten years."

"It's funny," Harry said. "When I had a good job in Seattle, all I wanted was a chance to farm."

"I'm afraid," Walt said, "That when Frances and I pass on those kids will sell this place to some developer and there'll be vacation cabins on every five acres. I know a fella can't own somethin' after he's gone but I hate the thought of this place not bein' a farm. Sometimes I think I'll give it back to the Indians."

"You could put it in the Farmlands Preservation Trust," Harry said. "Then whoever gets it can't use it for anything but agriculture"

"That would make the kids madder than hell," Walt said. "I'll have to think about that."

Tamarack could handle Harry's team pretty well, so Harry began to drive Walt's big team. Together the two teams could do about as much work as a good-sized tractor for a lot less outlay in money, with a lot less pollution and a lot less noise. And the net result was the employment of one more person. It seemed like a sensible approach to Harry.

The two teams working in tandem became a regular tourist attraction and it was a rare day when someone did not stop on the highway to watch them at work. Harry was anxious to get his produce sign up and take advantage of the traffic.

Johnny Carlson came by one day when Harry was laying groundcover. Harry hadn't seen him all winter. He drove a new four-wheel-drive Toyota pickup and wore a wide-brimmed Stetson and shiny boots.

"Howdy."

"Good morning," Harry replied.

"Still got your hands in the dirt," Johnny said.

"Better than havin' your head in the clouds," Harry said.

Johnny stuck his thumbs into a wide leather belt with a garish buckle.

"I just come back from Texas. Dad sent me down to stay the winter with my Uncle Don. He's a retired rodeo rider. Third place National in saddle broncs his last year."

"Good for him," Harry said, continued to work.

"I been thinkin about rodeoin'. A guy can make pretty good money. And girls love riders."

"A guy can break his back and not be able to do anything with the girls."

"My uncle says he'll teach me. And Dad says he'll pay for the school if I do any good."

"You know how to ride? Your dad doesn't have any horses."

"Well, I rode quite a bit in Texas. Besides, Uncle Don says a good rider never spends more than ten seconds at a time on a horse."

"You have to have a feel for the animal. Know how to predict what it'll do next."

"That's what they teach you in the school. Anyway, I wanted to see if I could borrow a horse from you, do a little ridin'. Just for practice."

"The saddle-horses are Judith's. You'd have to ask her. But she's pretty particular about who rides them."

"She lets that Nathan ride them," Johnny said, "And he's a Suicide rider."

"He doesn't ride like that here."

"Dad says he'll buy me a horse if I show him I can ride. I just need a chance."

"Judith's up at the house. Go ask her."

"She scares me. I don't know how to talk to Indians. It's like they're always laughin' at you."

"They're always laughin' at almost everything," Harry said. "Go on, she won't bite you."

Judith agreed to let Johnny ride if he let her teach him. He grumbled, but agreed. He came almost every morning for his lesson. She decided to start him on the red gelding. For the first week she wouldn't let him take the horse out of the corral. She made him brush his horse before and after he rode and pick the hooves clean. She had him work the gelding on a lunge-line and with the bridle from the ground. She made him sit in the saddle without moving for long periods.

"How's he doing?" Harry asked her after a couple of weeks.

"He's learned a lot of patience and respect for horses," she said with a grin. "I don't know if he'll ever ride in a rodeo, but he's not afraid of them anymore."

When she let Johnny ride outside the corral she would ride with him and keep up a running commentary on his posture, his hand position, his rhythm. They rode only at a walk. He wanted to trot and gallop and all the daring things that real cowboys did, but Judith refused. He blew up at her one day and yelled about "pussy ridin'" and "fuckin' smart-ass women." She laughed at him and told him not to come back for a week. When he did come back he had a tight rein on his temper.

Eliot drove up while Harry was at the store getting mail. He came over to the truck and said, "Hello, neighbor. Haven't seen you in a while."

"I'm right where I've always been," Harry said. "Nose to the grindstone."

"I heard you were farming Walt Davis's place too. You don't know when to quit."

"I never did."

"Nice rig," Eliot said, patted the truck's fender.

"The old one was about to die."

"Well, you must be doing all right," Eliot said. "I know what these cost."

"It was used. I couldn't afford anything new."

"I talked to John Carlson the other day," Eliot said. "He's losing his grazing lease. Some Indian wants it and they have precedence on the reservation."

"I hadn't heard."

"He tried to lease my place for the grass. I'm surprised he hasn't approached you and Walt."

"He knows what the answer would be."

Eliot lowered his voice. "Lasker tells me he offered to let you farm that place of his. That's a pretty nice place, lots of water."

"I don't need the risk."

"You mean his cash-crop? You don't have to worry about that. It's handled. I know some people in the County who don't want to mess with the business. They bust a little guy now and then to keep the Feds happy, but they don't want to cut their own throats by driving money out of the County."

"I have enough to worry about."

"It occurred to me," Eliot said, "That John Carlson would be willing to pay a good price if he could put together enough land to keep his cows eating. He would be in pretty good shape if he had yours and Walt's and mine and the hippies'. And there's some other pieces for sale, like that eighty south of you with all the timber. It might be the time to make a move."

"I can't sell my place anyway. It belongs to Judith's family."

"They could probably use the money. And you could take a cut for putting the deal together."

"Thanks, but no thanks. I like things the way they are."

"Things never stay the way they are," Eliot said.

Harry was transplanting tomatoes when he saw the beige sedan come in the driveway and park beside the truck. His chest tightened and his heart raced. He watched Marlene from CPS get out and approach the cabin. She wore a dowdy dark blue suit with a bright scarf at the neck and high-heels. There was a different deputy with her, in uniform this time, hand resting on his gun. Harry threw a little more hay to the old mare that was hitched to the wagon, made sure the wheel-brake was on.

They still were at the door when Harry came up behind them. They had not seen him and the deputy whirled around, ready to draw his gun.

Marlene forced a smile. "Just a friendly visit," she said. "May we come in?"

Harry and Judith looked at each other. "No," Harry said. "We can talk here."

Marlene frowned. The deputy started to say something, stopped himself.

Finally Marlene cleared her throat. "We just like to check back with families who have been referred to us. Just to make sure everything is all right. Especially when events have occurred which might produce stress on the family."

"What event was that?" Harry asked her.

Marlene smiled sweetly. "Your problems with the Federal Government. The fraud charges."

"If you're talking about the mess with Desert Mirage," Harry said. "That was the government's mistake. It's all been cleared up."

"Our report said the case was pending," Marlene said.

"Just a minute," Harry said. He went into the cabin and came out with one of Jerry Steinman's business cards. He handed it to Marlene. "This is the attorney who represents me."

He could see her react with surprise. "You won't mind if I call him, then?"

"No, please do," Harry said. "I'm sure he can explain it all to you."

Marlene handed the card to the deputy who scrutinized it. "Pretty expensive attorney."

"He's a friend of my brother's," Judith said. "They went to Stanford Law School together."

"Your brother is an attorney?" Marlene blurted out.

"Yes," Judith said. "Does that surprise you?"

"No, of course not. I just thought..." her voice trailed off.

Judith smiled at her. "My family places a high value on education. My father is a lead engineer at Grand Coulee. I met Harry when he was in graduate school and I was at the University."

Marlene obviously was off-balance. Harry decided to help.

"I taught Anthropology at the University of Washington," Harry said. "I was kind of a protege of Dr. Houck."

"I know him," Marlene said. "I mean I've heard of him. Wasn't he the Department Chairman? Why did you leave the UW?"

"I took a job as superintendent for United Homes," Harry said. "They made me an offer I couldn't refuse."

"But, why...?" Marlene was confused. The deputy backed up a few steps, looked away.

"Is there anything else you need?" Judith asked her. "I'm quite busy."

"No. I don't think so. I just wanted to say hello."

"Well, hello, then," Judith said with a wide smile. "Come see us any time."

"Sorry to bother you, sir," the deputy said to Harry.

"Thank you," Marlene said as she walked towards the car.

"You're very welcome," Judith said, winked at Harry.

Jeff showed up one day about noon.

"Had to take care of some business with your neighbor. How you been, buddy?"

"I'll make it," Harry said. "I sure don't run out of something to do."

"I hear you're a big-time farmer, now."

"News sure gets around up here."

"I suppose I can forget talkin' you into farmin' that place of mine."

"I guess I'm stuck right here."

"Gringo isn't worth a shit as a farmer," Jeff said. "He planted a bunch of grain last year and couldn't keep the water on it, let it all burn up. It was all full of weeds, anyway. Made the neighbors wonder how we support ourselves."

"There should be someone up there that would lease your farm ground or farm it on shares."

"I can't have just anyone hangin' around the place. They might stumble into the shop at the wrong time. I need to find someone I can trust that knows how to farm."

"Not that many farmers left," Harry said.

"Well if you think of someone, let me know. I'll kick Gringo's ass out and let them have the old house."

"If I run into someone I'll let you know."

There was a letter from Jack in the mailbox:

"Dear Harry, I'm sure you've heard about our trouble. We lost our house and Mom lost almost all her money. The Government is talking about pressing fraud charges against me. I guess the banker cheated us all. There is a lot of money missing and I think he took it. Some people think I got some of it, too, but I didn't. If I did I wouldn't be broke. He has a good lawyer from Seattle and I heard that they are going to settle with him for a fine. Ed White is my lawyer. He says he knows you. I guess I'm sorry for the way I've treated you sometimes. I sure do need your help now. I hear you're doing very well up there and I wanted to know if I could borrow some money. A few thousand would sure help. Mom may have to go into HUD housing. We're living in the Radfords' trailer park, now, but if I don't get a job soon we'll have to move. It's hard getting a job with something like this hanging over your head. I may have to sell my car. Ed White says it will probably take years to settle it all. If you know of any jobs I would be interested in just about anything, even farming. If you need any help there on your place I would work for laborer's wages. I guess I understand better how it was for you when Dad lost the farm, with the kids and all. I wish we still had that place, I drive by it almost every day. Well, let me know if you can help. Take care of yourself. Your brother, Jack"

Harry knew that he should have sympathy for family members in trouble but realized that he didn't feel much at all. It wasn't fair that Jack should take the rap and the banker walk, but that was how things usually went. Jack probably had signed things he shouldn't have and been set up to take the fall. As for Mom, she'd gotten out of the collapse of the farm with a bunch of money from Dad's insurance and now she'd wasted that. It wasn't his fault they made bad decisions.

He thought momentarily about sending Jack to Jeff, but quickly decided against that. Jeff never had liked Jack and Harry wasn't sure Jack could be trusted with any kind of secret. As for hiring him, Harry could only remember how much Jack always had hated farming and how lazy and useless he'd been. It was too bad, brothers should help each other.

He showed the letter to Judith and her first thought was for the children.

"We should take them some food. We have more than enough."

"Diane would just throw it out," Harry said. "She wouldn't know how to cook it. She thinks organic food is dangerous."

"Well, I wish there was something we could do for the kids. It's not their fault and they're your blood."

"Some people can't be helped. If we loaned Jack money he would just waste it living high. He could sell that BMW for enough to buy a small place. Or live on for a year."

"Well, all I know," Judith said, "Is that if families don't help each other we're all in serious trouble."

The corn was in full tassel and the grain was a lighter green as it began the change to ripened gold. Tomato plants pressed against the row-cover and pink fruit showed here and there. Harry already had opened the row-cover on the peppers for an early picking. There had been cabbage and peas and broccoli and cauliflower ready for more than a month.

Harry's sign worked well and every day several cars stopped and people came in to buy produce. He had made one run to High Mountain Juice with a load of carrots and had delivered early produce to his restaurants. He always saved some for the Italian market on Ravenna, mostly as an excuse to see the proprietor.

Rick Rosen was under great pressure with his expansion. He had rented two more bays in the industrial park and brought in bigger machinery. He told Harry that he didn't enjoy the business any more and would sell if he got the right offer. Harry saw some of the carrots from the Skagit Valley farm and they were pale and limp compared to his.

Harry, too, felt harried and hassled. He probably would make more money that year than he ever had on the San Poil, but he had no time for himself or even for the family. He took Little Joe with him whenever he could and made sure he always was home for dinner. Walt's place took a lot of time and Tamarack was farming nearly five acres and couldn't work for Harry as much as he had. Eric had a big trucking job, hauled logs to a mill in Kettle Falls from before dawn until after dark. Barbara tried to keep up with their garden.

John Carlson bought Johnny a horse, a flashy paint gelding. He would gallop by occasionally, waving his hat and yelling like a cowboy. Carlson hadn't been able to replace his lost range lease and had sold nearly half his cows for slaughter. Even then he had to buy hay that summer to keep them fed. Beef prices had slumped with the recession and it was rumored that Carlson wanted to sell out.

Eliot's business didn't seem to suffer from bad economic times. He bought several new racehorses and tried to hire Judith to work them, but she refused. He traded his Range Rover for a new one and added a wing to his house. He had a woman living with him, reputed to be an actress he'd met in Hollywood, but she was seldom seen except from a distance. His two teenage sons from a previous marriage came for a few weeks and Harry saw them out riding with Johnny Carlson a few times.

Some new people moved in upriver from Wildrose and Tamarack. Johnny Carlson said the man's name was Chet Weston and he was a survivalist. They cut a road back into a grove of cottonwoods along the river and built a cabin that couldn't be seen. Harry wondered if they knew they had built below the spring high-water line. There was a steel gate at the highway and signs that said, "No Trespassing" and "Free America for Free People" and "Beware of Dog."

Harry stayed so busy he had little time to enjoy the place. He loved the work and the feeling that he was building a future for his family, but life seemed to fly by him. He thought of the Old Man's generation, a time when a small place was enough to support a family and if a man wanted to he could live a quiet, steady life without the need to do constantly more and more and more. He decided he would take some time every day just to appreciate where he was.

Early morning after he fed the stock was the best time to get away for a little while. The first morning he walked along the river to his south fence, admired the gardens and fields that had not been there three years before, not since McTavish had lived there. It was exactly the kind of place he had dreamed of most of his life. Even in Viet Nam, that alien world of mud and heat, he had been drawn to the farm villages and the people quietly living amidst the terrors of a high-tech war.

He felt the pull of the Ponderosa grove beside the river and crossed the fence. Birds sang from the nearby cottonwoods and the river gurgled and trout splashed. He sat on the deadfall log and absorbed the peace that flowed around him. Long Joe always said that there was spirit in everything and Harry could feel that spirit from the rocks and trees and grass and water.

He became just another creature, an outcropping of spirit in physical form, like all the others that had paused here on the riverbank for a moment or a thousand years.

He felt the voices of the San Poil children and remembered Long Joe's story. It was as though their spirits had flowed into pine saplings and grown into the tall trees that surrounded him. Death was just a change of status. Spirit endured.

Harry got back over the pass early on a produce run and decided to stop by Uncle Paul's. He was surprised to see Jack's BMW in the yard. Jack always had avoided Paul, agreed with Mom that Paul wasn't quite right. Since his injuries in World War Two, Paul had been an outcast, disfigured and a loner.

Harry knocked on the mobile home door and Paul opened it.

"Harry! Good to see you."

"Hi, Paul. I see the young Prince of Ephrata has come to call."

Paul grinned. "He's workin'. Really. I know it's hard to believe but I've been gettin' up to six hours a day out of him."

"Must be a miracle. You been followin' him around, make sure he actually does somethin'?"

"I did for the first few days. Don't worry, I know his habits. I'm just doin' what your Dad should have done with him a long time ago. If he wants to take off to town and have a beer with the boys, forget to come back, I don't say a thing. I just don't pay him. It didn't take him long to figure out that didn't work too well."

"I don't envy you the job," Harry said. "We never could figure out how to make him work."

"Somethin' happened back there after the war," Paul said. "They started raisin' kids like they was Roman Aristocracy or somethin', didn't have to learn how to work. I never did think it was goin' to do them any good."

"I don't know what happened to me," Harry said. "I always liked to work."

"You're a throwback. Sorry, but you seem more like my generation or even the old man's. You never could seem to get into the life of leisure."

"Seems like the leisure class gets all the money," Harry said.

"It may seem that way," Paul said. "But things even out. Some of them chickens are comin' home to roost right now."

"You mean the banker? And Jack? Jack wrote me a letter sayin' it looked like the banker was goin' to slip out of this with a fine. I figure in the end Jack will do the same."

"Even if they do, they have to live with themselves. You don't have to wake up every mornin' bein' Jack. I think you got the good end of it. I know your kids did."

"I hope you're right," Harry said, "But when I look around it seems like the lazier you are the better you do."

"Well I'll just keep on workin'" Paul said. "We know what's right."

"I'm not sure the rest of the world does."

"So what do you think of this mess in Kuwait?"

"It's time for another war. If you don't have a war every few years people get out of the habit, begin to think peace is normal. Especially with the Cold War over. Governments have to have enemies."

"You heard that most of the oil development in Kuwait was done by George Bush's father? They still own a lot of it."

"I didn't know that, but somehow it doesn't surprise me," Harry said. "As far as I know Kuwait is just the part of Iraq that the British didn't want to let go of when they gave Iraq independence. Because that's where the oil was."

"I think that's about right. But a lot of people I talk to are all gung-ho to go after Saddam Hussein. He's the bogey-man."

"Most of those gung-ho types never saw a real war. They think it's all a TV program. When it's all over everyone gets up and goes on."

"Well, I think it's goin' to come to a fight," Paul said. "I don't know how they can get out of it now. Once you get the country whipped-up for it, you got to fight."

One morning an official-looking pickup pulled into the driveway. Harry walked to the house and saw "State of Washington, Department of Ecology" on the door of the truck. A man talked to Judith.

"Can I help you?" Harry asked him.

The man turned. He was about Harry's age, dressed in jeans and a work-shirt. He smiled.

"Hi. I'm Lou Freestone, State Department of Ecology. I'm here to check on a possible illegal diversion of water from the San Poil River."

Harry frowned. "Who sent you?"

"Apparently one of the neighbors filed a complaint. I think the name was Carlson. We have to check it out. These new laws are pretty strict. They have our office all tied up. Basically we can't grant permits for irrigation at all right now. It's a real pain in the ass."

"Well, I use some river water for irrigation. But this place has used it for almost a hundred years."

"Do you know if anyone ever filed the water-right?" Lou asked. "A lot of the old-timers just thought it was useless paperwork."

"I don't know," Harry said. "I understood that if a place had been using water all along it was grandfathered in."

"There are a couple of court cases about that right now," Lou said. "It may be that anyone who didn't file before a certain point will lose their water. I think it's a bunch of crap. If I had my way we'd leave farmers alone. Developers are trying to grab all the water for subdivisions. I don't know what they think we'll do for food."

"I can't believe the little bit of water I use is a problem."

"Is someone trying to buy your place? Sometimes they file a complaint to put on the pressure to sell."

"That could be. Interesting suggestion."

"Anyway it isn't up to me," Lou said. "I write a report and the guys upstairs make the decision. I'll write it as favorably as I can, but you never know. If someone with money is pushing on it, it could go against you."

"So what do you need from me?"

"I need to look at the diversion." He got a camera from the pickup. "And any information you can give me about how long it's been used and what the purpose is. I'll research the filings and see if anyone ever did it."

Harry showed him the dam and flume.

"Nice," Lou said as he took some pictures. "Did you build this?"

"I rebuilt it," Harry said. "An old farmer named McTavish had this in here in the nineteen-twenties."

"Can you prove that? That sure would help."

"My neighbor back here worked for McTavish in the thirties. He's the one who showed me how it all worked."

"This McTavish an Indian?"

"He was married to one. One of my wife's relatives."

"That might help, too," Lou said. "They're a little more lenient with Indians. You must be part Indian," he suggested.

Harry grinned. "I could be."

"I'll mention that," Lou said. "And I should talk to this neighbor, get first-hand verification that it's been in use for more than sixty years."

They walked back to Walt's, found him working with one of the young horses.

He snorted in indignation when Harry told him what the problem was. "Why that's one of the oldest uses of water in this whole valley."

"These new laws are screwing up a lot of people," Lou said.

"Just more government interference," Walt said. "Sorry, but I think there's a lot more important things the government should be doin'."

"Personally, I agree," Lou said.

"How about if I drill a well?" Harry asked as they walked back.

"We can't approve irrigation wells," Lou said. "You can drill a domestic well without a permit. Technically that limits you to a half-acre of garden. But I don't know of anyone who has had a problem if they irrigate more. The Department isn't worried about that."

"So if I drill a big well, file on it as domestic, then use it for irrigation, you won't bother me?"

"That's pretty much it," Lou said. "At least for now. But don't quote me."

"So what happens next?" Harry asked.

"I write my report. I'll take as long as I can get away with. Then it goes upstairs for review and action. They'll send you a letter when they make a decision."

"I think I'll go ahead and drill a well just in case," Harry said.

"I would," Lou said.

Harry bought a fifth-wheel trailer and hauled his grain out to market. The buckwheat, most of the oats and some of the barley and wheat went to Fairhaven Mills. The dairyman in Buckley who'd bought from him two years before was happy to pay a premium to have feed delivered. He told Harry his was as fine as any grain he'd ever fed.

As fall came to the valley, the hay was securely stacked, the grain was dry and protected in Walt's granary, the freezers were full, the root-cellar was full and a great rick of firewood stretched nearly to the pond.

When Harry counted the money in his little safe there was more than when he'd taken it all out of the bank.

CHAPTER 14

Walt showed Harry an ad in Western Horseman for a piece of equipment called a fore-cart. Amish farmers built them in Pennsylvania. A fore-cart was a horse-drawn machine with two rubber-tired wheels and a seat for the driver. At the back of the cart was a drawbar and a standard three-point hitch for any kind of farm equipment. There was a small engine on-board which drove a hydraulic pump to raise and lower equipment or operate remote hydraulic systems. There was a power take-off for mowers or augers or any other implement that required power.

Harry was stunned. It was so obvious, so perfect, just like something the old man would have come up with. Why hadn't he thought of it? He wrote a letter for more information and mailed it that day. With a fore-cart he could use any small tractor-drawn equipment. The auctions were full of older machinery that would be perfect.

He asked Walt about a four-horse hitch, using both teams. Walt said it should work fine. He recommended that Harry start working with all four together to get them used to the idea.

Harry couldn't wait.

The information came. To get the fore-cart he wanted would cost several thousand dollars but the opportunities it opened up were tremendous. He studied the drawings and photographs and specifications and decided on a model that should do everything he needed and would be easy for a four-horse team to handle.

He drove to Moses Lake, where no one knew him, to buy a money order and sent it off to Pennsylvania. Delivery was to be in six to eight weeks. That would give him the winter to get used to the machine. He also would have time to go to some farm auctions and pick up inexpensive equipment before spring.

He had a well-driller come in November. He had waited until the big drill-rig was available so that he could sink a ten-inch hole. The tall derrick on the big pneumatic drill was a regular tourist attraction and half the cars driving on the highway slowed down or stopped to look. Harry noticed John Carlson's pickup stop several times.

The driller moved in about noon one day and before noon the next had hit more water than his test-pump could handle at less than a hundred feet. Harry filled out the papers to register it as a domestic well.

"You could water a couple of miles of this valley with the water in that hole," the driller told him.

The fore-cart came two weeks before Christmas. Harry picked it up from the freight dock in Ephrata. He hauled it in to Walt's shop and they spent most of two days assembling and testing it.

It was better even than Harry had expected.

"A guy could fall asleep in that seat," Walt said. "Almost seems sinful to be that comfortable behind a team."

"I think I can get used to it," Harry said. "Now if there was a steering wheel to handle the reins."

Walt laughed. "You don't want to forget there's horses out there ahead of you."

Harry hitched up the team the next morning and got them used to the fore-cart. Walt held the lead-horses' heads when Harry first started up the little engine. They didn't like the noise, but they soon got used to it.

Harry ran the hydraulics and the power take-off and was anxious to have some equipment to attach to it. He could use a swather now to cut hay and run a baler. New possibilities kept occurring to him.

Walt agreed to feed the horses and other stock and keep an eye on the place so they spent four days in Electric City with Judith's family at Christmas. Joseph came home for two weeks and they discussed the problem with Desert Mirage. He was confident that it had been handled and was sure that Jerry Steinman was as good as anyone they would find to represent them.

Helen and her three daughters put on a massive Christmas feast and everyone was happy to have the whole family together. Harry felt fortunate, as always, to be included. Rebecca pitched in and Matt proudly pointed to the three generations working side by side. Little Joe followed his Uncle Joseph around whenever he could and told Harry that when he grew up he would be a lawyer, too.

Harry watched the auction fliers that came every week. He looked for sales of older places with the small equipment he wanted for his fore-cart. He picked a Saturday sale near Wilson Creek. A farmer named Steve McLaughlin, a name he recognized from long ago, was ready to retire. The flier listed several things that Harry wanted. He got three thousand dollars out of his safe, hooked his trailer to the pickup and took Little Joe with him.

The snow was gone by the time they reached Coulee City and the dryland wheat was green, dripped with water condensed from the light fog. The little farm was up a side coulee, visible from nowhere. The house was typical for it's time, oriented, as always, towards the south. There was a spring-fed pond between the house and barn and pole corrals with fine Angus cows and several saddle horses. A black draft-horse team, two geldings, was hitched to an iron-wheeled feed-wagon piled with harness and other horse equipment.

The crowd was small, but it was early. There was not much of what would be considered modern machinery, the gigantic eight-wheeled tractors and similarly scaled implements now used on the dry land. This had been a mixed-farm with a range of crops and livestock. Harry immediately saw several things he would bid on. Little Joe ran to get a better look at the team.

Harry walked to the concession trailer. The same two women he remembered from his family's auction were at the service windows beneath the green and yellow awnings. A generator hummed from behind the trailer and steam floated up from a hot pot of coffee. Harry ordered a cup of coffee and the young woman smiled at him. He remembered her name was Sally.

"You look familiar. From a few years back."

"You sold us out," Harry said, "Five years ago, out in Block Eighty-eight. Isaacsons."

"Oh, I remember. Your father..." Her smile faded.

"My father shot himself, after the auction."

"I'm sorry. We all felt so bad."

"It wasn't your fault," Harry said. "It was no one's fault but his own."

She smiled again. "You look happier than you did then."

"I'd rather buy than sell."

"You farmin' again? I remember you still wanted to farm."

"Yep," Harry said. "Up on the San Poil River."

"That's beautiful country. I drove through there once goin' to Lake Curlew fishin'. With my ex. I thought that was all Indians."

"It's on the reservation," Harry said, "But there's private land, too."

"Must be nice up there."

Little Joe ran up to Harry. "Hey, Dad, there's a saddle just my size."

"We'll bid on it if it sells right. Go see if there are any canning jars or big kettles like your Mom wants."

"That your boy?" Sally asked as Little Joe ran off on his errand.

"Yeah. That's my kid."

"He's a cutie," Sally said. "We never had kids when I was married. And I didn't want to raise any without a Dad."

"It's hard on them. I was afraid that would happen to mine. Bein' their Dad is the most important job I have."

"You got any brothers?" Sally asked wryly. "I could use a man like that."

"The brother I've got you wouldn't want."

"Your wife Indian? I mean, your son looks it."

"She's half."

"I always wondered how that would work," Sally said. "They always tell you 'stay with your own kind,' but it seemed to me like if you fell in love with somebody it wouldn't matter what kind they are."

"That's how it was for me. I don't think of her as Indian any more than I think of myself as white. We're all just people."

"That's how I see it," Sally said. "We've got enough problems without hatin' each other for things we can't do nothin' about."

"I better see what he's up to," Harry said. "Nice seein' you again."

"I'll probably see you at lunch-time."

"You probably will," Harry said.

He saw several of the old neighbors from Block Eighty-eight. They nodded to him distantly, but had nothing to say. Just before the auction started up Harry noticed Uncle Paul's truck pull into the parking area and he went over to say hello.

"I thought you might be here," Paul said.

"I'm lookin' for some three-point equipment," Harry said. He told Paul about the fore-cart."

"Hell of an idea. I'm surprised the old man didn't invent it."

"He probably would have, if he was still around."

"I'll keep my eye out," Paul said. "That small stuff sells for nothin' nowadays."

"So how's your hired-man," Harry asked with a grin.

"A little restless, I think. He's over on the coast lookin' for a job. He's been tryin' to get his Real Estate license back. Looks like he may get it done."

"It figures," Harry said. "They make a big noise when somethin' happens, then when no one's payin' attention things go back the way they were."

"The banker left town," Paul said. "Good riddance, I say. I heard he was headin' some company down in Tri-cities that's buildin' a bunch of houses out on part of the Hanford Nuclear Reservation that the government doesn't want any more."

"They probably won't have to wire them for lights. They'll glow in the dark."

"The government says they're perfectly safe."

"That would make me feel better. They used to tell us Agent Orange was safe enough to eat."

"Now, Harry, they're just takin' care of us. That reminds me, you heard about this militia thing?"

"A little. I haven't paid much attention."

"There was a guy came by my place," Paul said. "They were havin' a meetin' at one of the neighbors. He said there was militias organizin' all over the country. He said the government was fixin' to take away everybody's guns. He gave me a bunch of literature."

"If they'd take away everybody's guns I might go along with it," Harry said. "But they'd have to start with the police. They're the only ones who've threatened me with a gun, lately."

"That's what this guy said, that when it was all over only the police and criminals would have guns and the rest of us would be caught in the middle."

"He might not be that far off," Harry said. "It's gettin' like a war zone every summer up where we are. The National Guard runs around in helicopters actin' like everyone is a criminal. Usin' drugs for an excuse."

"Two of my neighbors had their places searched just about a month ago," Paul said. "They were lookin' for pot and guns they said. They didn't find a thing but they tore both places up pretty good. Got a warrant based on some anonymous informant. They don't even have to tell you who the informant is anymore."

"Like you said, they're just takin care of us."

The auctioneer tested his microphone and started on some of the small stuff. Harry walked over to see if there were any bargains. Usually they sold hand-tools and miscellaneous items cheap at the start to get people interested.

Little Joe showed Harry several boxes of canning jars with lids and Harry bought them for a dollar each. He knew Judith would be happy with them. He also bought several boxes of miscellaneous tools and parts for nearly nothing. Sally wrote his name in her notebook and winked at him.

As the auctioneer moved down the line of household goods and hand-tools Harry saw a stack of curved, wedge-shaped, perforated metal pieces with several mechanical parts and an electronic box on top. He realized it was a satellite television system. He had been tempted for a while to get one because there was no television reception at all in the bottom of the San Poil Valley. But he had priced the systems and they were several thousand dollars, more than he wanted to spend.

When the auctioneer got to the satellite dish he asked, "This thing work, Steve?"

"Sure does," the farmer answered. "Works great. But where I'm goin' they got cable."

The auctioneer tried to start it at a thousand dollars, got no takers. At five hundred some of the people started to wander away.

"Okay. Somebody make me an offer. These systems cost three thousand dollars new and I don't think Steve has hardly used this one."

The crowd was silent. More people walked on.

"A hundred dollars," Harry said.

The auctioneer looked at him in mock-surprise. "A hundred dollars? Folks, we've got a bandit here today. Are we goin' to let him steal this fine satellite system?"

"Let him have it," someone in the crowd said. "Let's get this show movin'"

"Well, son," the auctioneer said, "You got yourself a bargain. Sold! To?"

"Harry Isaacson," Sally said.

The auctioneer, her father, looked at her. "Somethin' goin' on here I don't know about?" he asked.

There was a ripple of laughter from the crowd.

Harry bought a few more hand-tools but mostly was interested in a pull-type swather and a three-point offset disk but it didn't look like they would sell until after lunch. The saddle Little Joe liked would be sold just before the livestock at the end of the day.

He went to look at the team which stood patiently in harness. He wished he had brought more money, he probably could make a profit on the team. This crowd was all machinery-farmers and wouldn't have much interest in the horses. Eric wanted to get a team for horse logging. In some of the steeper and ecologically sensitive areas, that was the only way to log, now, except for helicopters.

Harry went over to Sally. "What if I buy somethin' I can't pay for today? How long do I have to get the money in?"

"Normal terms are forty-eight hours to come up with cash or cashier's check, personal check if the seller approves it. You're not supposed to move anything until it's paid for. But in your case, I think we could work something out." She smiled at him. "I know we can trust you."

"Thanks," Harry said. "I may try to buy that team."

"Aren't they fine horses? We sell a lot of horses, but those two are really nice."

"It would be my third team. I work four Belgians."

"A horse farmer. You are my kind of man."

"I'd better find my kid."

"Be sure and come by at lunch-time," Sally said.

Harry got a cup of coffee from Sally's mother and sat on the feed-wagon to drink it. Little Joe had found some other kids and they all ran around the place having a great time. Uncle Paul saw Harry and came over.

"Hey, Paul," Harry said. "If I get carried away and buy this team could you haul them for me?"

"Sure. Be happy to. But what do you need another team for? You a horse-trader now?"

"I'm thinkin' about it. I figure they'll sell cheap and I've got a neighbor that's been thinkin' about horse-loggin'."

"Well, you buy 'em, I'll haul 'em,"

Harry decided to beat the crowd to lunch so he found Little Joe and they got hamburgers and fries and cokes. Paul ate with them. The auctioneer finished the morning sales and Sally came over to help her mother, smiled at them and said, "Hi, guys."

A line formed at the lunch-wagon and several farmers stopped to say hello to Paul and Harry.

"Funny," Harry said. "None of them know me when you're not around."

"They just don't know what to say," Paul said. "They all knew your dad and the whole story. Nobody's got anything against you."

The auctioneer's skinny son showed up during the lunch break. He did a double take at Harry and glared as though he had some dim memory of him.

Paul laughed. "I think you made a friend."

Just after lunch they sold the swather and Harry managed to buy it for twelve hundred dollars. The little offset disk he got for three-fifty. He wasn't interested in the tractors and other bigger equipment so he went to look at the cattle. He had been thinking about raising some organic beef. There was a good market and he had enough hay and grain for a few head. There was over a hundred acres of grazing land that was unused since he'd fenced-out Carlson's cows. And that eighty south of him was for sale.

The auctioneer worked his way through the iron and came to the feed-wagon to sell the horse equipment. Harry paid a hundred and ten dollars for the youth saddle. It probably was too much, but he didn't want to disappoint Little Joe. The boy ran over and hugged the saddle which drew a laugh from some of the crowd.

Harry also bought a few miscellaneous pieces of harness.

When the tack was gone the auctioneer said, "Let's sell this team, harness and wagon all together. Somebody can start their own freight line."

Harry really hadn't wanted to buy the whole rig, but waited to see how it sold.

There were no openers at three thousand, or two thousand and Harry began to get excited.

"Well one thousand, then," the auctioneer said, "but that's just an opener."

"Come on, folks," Skinny said.

The crowd was restless.

"Well, Steve, I guess you take this rig to Arizona with you," the auctioneer joked.

Harry sensed his time. "A thousand."

"Sally's friend here, Mr. Isaacson, is goin' to help out and get us started," the auctioneer said. He started the chant, "I have a thousand, do I hear fifteen hundred, fifteen hundred, a thousand, now fifteen hundred? Twelve-fifty? Eleven hundred? A thousand, now eleven hundred." He paused. "Now, folks, this harness alone is worth a thousand. There must be someone here besides Mr. Isaacson that knows which end of a horse you put the bridle on. Do I hear eleven hundred?"

"Eleven hundred?" Skinny echoed.

"Yes," someone in the crowd said and Harry recognized Chuck Henry's voice. The bastard was just bidding against him; there was no way he wanted the rig. Well, let him think he'd just bought himself some draft horses.

"Eleven hundred now, twelve, eleven, now twelve," the auctioneer chanted, looked at Harry.

Skinny shook his whip in Harry's direction. "Twelve?"

Harry shook his head no.

"I guess we sold it," the auctioneer said, "Going once, twice..."

"Twelve," Harry said.

"I have twelve, now thirteen, twelve, thirteen." "Thirteen?" Skinny shook his whip at Chuck Henry.

"Fuck, no," Chuck said.

"Sold," the auctioneer said. "I don't know why these people are afraid to bid against you," he said to Harry, "but you've certainly had yourself a day."

"Just lucky," Harry said with a grin. He went over to Sally.

"I'm through. Can you give me a total?"

"Sure," she said and added up the sheet with his name on it. "Three thousand, two hundred seventy-eight dollars and thirty-seven cents," she said. She handed him the sheet. "You can pay my Mom."

Harry found Uncle Paul, asked him if he could borrow the balance over three thousand until Paul brought the horses up. Paul wrote a check. Harry took the check and his cash to the concession trailer and paid the auctioneer's wife. She wrote out the bills of sale and gave him a brand-inspection slip for the horses, then called Steve McLaughlin over to approve Paul's check.

Harry asked McLaughlin if he could use one of the tractors to load with and Steve said, "Sure."

Paul helped him and they got the swather on the trailer and the disk and miscellaneous stuff on the pickup. He would have to come back for the wagon. He unhitched the team, gave them a little time to get used to him. He led them over to a corral with a loading chute and Paul backed-in his truck. Harry gently took the harness off and carried it to his pickup.

Steve McLaughlin came over to help and the geldings loaded easily. Paul pulled away from the chute and Harry closed the truck-gate. He and Little Joe got in the pickup and the whole convoy headed for the San Poil.

Judith loved the big black geldings. Mostly Percheron, she guessed with some lighter breed mixed in a few generations back judging from their tall, slim profile. In the old days, she said, a lot of Indian horsemen liked to put a Percheron stud in with their saddle mares and breed for the tall, rangy mixed-breeds that were good for riding, working or packing.

Eric came to look at them. He thought they would be perfect for logging but was sure he couldn't afford them.

"I've priced teams. Those two are worth twenty-five hundred easy, maybe three."

"I'll make you a deal," Harry said. "I bought them right and I could lease them to you with an option if they work out. The harness would be included."

Eric was excited. "I'll trade my truck for a self-loader. And I can bid small jobs myself. But I'm not sure I can actually work a team. I'd need some training."

"No problem," Harry said. "You can help with the spring work and learn to drive at the same time."

"Great," Eric said. "Tell me when."

Harry went down to get the wagon. Steve McLaughlin was still there and came out to help load.

"You work horses?" he asked Harry.

"I've got a little farm up on the San Poil," Harry said. He told Steve about Walt and the fore-cart and his grandfather who'd always worked horses.

"Glad to hear someone's still at it," Steve said. "This farmin' with iron's okay, but now there are all these people in the city who don't have jobs. Seems to me they could all have jobs out here if we got rid of some of this iron. They'd get in less trouble, food would cost less, there'd be less pollution."

"That's too sensible," Harry said. "How would rich people make a profit off all that? People would get the idea they're self-sufficient and ADM stock would go in the toilet. You're startin' to sound like one of them radicals."

"I guess most everything my Dad believed is radical, now," Steve said. "We always took care of each other. We didn't need welfare and all this crap. If someone was hungry, we fed 'em. I don't remember any kids goin' hungry back then."

"If there isn't a threat that your kids will go hungry, you're not as easy to control," Harry said. "That doesn't work for the government."

"Now you're startin' to sound like a radical," Steve said. "I think you're sayin' the government benefits from hungry and homeless people."

"I never would say that," Harry said, "But it might be true."

"I know what you mean," Steve said. "A guy can't say half of what he thinks without someone makin' it into some kind of crime. Where I'm goin', down in Arizona, there's a lot of these militia people. I think they've got most of it about right. They say the cities are just concentration camps without fences. And someday soon there'll be fences, too."

"They don't need wire fences," Harry said. "The fences are in people's heads."

"You got that right," Steve said. "Those people wouldn't know how to take care of themselves if you gave them a hundred and sixty acres and the tools."

"My Granddad always said that all the great-grandchildren of the people who ran to the cities for the big money and easy life in the twenties and thirties would one day be back beggin' the ones of us who stayed behind to feed 'em," Harry said. "He said it would take four generations for them to lose all the knowledge and be completely dependent on the government and the corporations."

"He hit it just about right," Steve said. "Those old-timers weren't stupid."

"They've spent sixty years makin' jokes about 'dumb farmers'," Harry said. "Most of the people in the city believe it."

"I'd like to have 'em out here for about a week. Let them follow one of us around and see if they keep up."

"They have to go to the gym to get any exercise at all. Otherwise they'd just turn into vegetables. And thinkin' how to do things is somethin' you pay an engineer to do. No one can do that for themselves."

"It was the wars," Steve said. "After the first war and the second war all the boys comin' back wanted to stay in the city. They was used to bein' run around in gangs and told what to do. And havin' the government give them whatever they needed. It was like they forgot how to be individual people."

"Viet Nam was different, that way," Harry said. "Half the veterans I know are hidden away in the hills somewhere, tryin' to make it on their own."

"That was a bad war," Steve said. "Not that any of 'em are good, but Viet Nam just tore everything apart. Over nothin'. We lost, but I don't see no Vietnamese marchin' through the country. They just wanted us out."

"The government didn't like the way they lived," Harry said. "They were just a bunch of dumb farmers, too. We went there to teach 'em modern ways. And take their oil for pay."

"I guess it's up to our government to tell everyone how to live, now," Steve said. "Like we was Rome, or somethin'. It's like this mess with Iraq. I'm not sure it's our business."

"I heard George Bush's family owns a lot of the oil business in Kuwait," Harry said, "We've got to protect rich people's interests. That's all over the world, now."

"I was watchin' the bombin' last week before we took down the satellite dish," Steve said. "The announcers was talkin' like it was all some game, like a movie or somethin' with no one really gettin' hurt."

"All these politicians ought to serve a tour in a war," Harry said. "They might vote differently."

"They might, at that," Steve said. "I suppose they don't care what we think anyway."

"Well, I better get on down the road with this wagon," Harry said. "We'll take good care of it. It won't get turned into a planter."

"Say," Steve said, "I've got some other stuff around here I don't need to take to Arizona. There's a packsaddle and some more harness. And I've got a big old anvil I was goin' to take in for scrap, weighs almost a hundred pounds. It's perfect for shoein'. Let's take a little look around."

"I didn't bring much money with me."

"I ain't talkin' about money," Steve said. "I'd like to know some of this stuff was still bein' used. By someone who understands. Shit, son, I'd've given this place to some young guy who didn't want to subdivide it or dump chemicals all over it."

They spent half an hour finding and loading miscellaneous tack and tools. Much of it reminded Harry of the old man's stuff that had been sold at his family's auction five years before. As he pulled out of the coulee and headed home he knew he carried both a legacy and a duty. He was indeed a throwback.

CHAPTER 15

Harry assembled the satellite dish, mounted it on a sturdy post and installed the dish-mover. Wildrose and Tamarack had an old portable television and they brought it down to test the dish. There was an instruction book and Harry set the angle and got the receiver working. He moved the dish until he found a live channel and waited until it identified itself. He wrote down the numbers from the dish-mover and the channel ID. He kept searching and wrote down as many channels as he could find. A lot of channels were scrambled, but even so there were quite a few in the clear. He was happy to find two PBS channels.

Tamarack said they could keep the television until they bought one. Harry sat down that evening to watch the news. It was full of videotape from the gun-cameras of US planes on raids over Iraq and interviews with American soldiers anxious to fight the Republican Guards. The announcers did voice-over commentary as if it were a sporting event. Before his eyes buildings exploded and vehicles were obliterated. He could think only of the people who died there.

War-fever ran rampant as the country prepared for massive casualties. All the talk was of challenge and dare and lessons for evil aggressors. Whenever someone attempted a rational justification, all that seemed to be at stake was a few cents per gallon on the price of gasoline. It was hard to paint the Emir of Kuwait as a good guy. Historically Kuwait seemed to be only the oil-rich part of Iraq the British were unwilling to give up when forced to grant independence. What was constantly described as an allied action, except for a few token troops, obviously was a US operation.

Harry turned off the television and stared into the fire through the open door of the stove. The dark eyes of Iraqi children floated before him, died in the flames.

Harry warmed up the greenhouse and planted flats. First were peppers with their need for a long season. He had learned that tomatoes started too early were set back as they lost momentum before transplant. He planted lettuce and spinach and other quick-growing greens for family use and to sell to early drop-in customers.

He spent time with the four-horse team and fore-cart and soon could maneuver it almost as well as a tractor. Eric came to work with the new team and Harry enjoyed teaching him. Tamarack, too, came almost every day to help or watch or just to talk. Often the families came as well and the women would combine talents to provide wonderful meals. Judith taught the others to ride and weave and Wildrose brought her beautiful quilts to work on.

Barbara was pregnant and Judith and Wildrose coached her, encouraged her to have a home-birth. Often the women went to see Frances who was ill again. They all admired her delicate crochet work and when she felt well enough they would sit in a circle while she taught them.

Walt seemed indestructible, rarely had a bad day. The arthritis in his hands and elbows bothered him in the mornings, but Judith recommended a tea of comfrey and willow-bark that gave him much relief. He showed Harry and the others how to work with various kinds of metal in the forge. Harry set up the old man's forge and Steve McLaughlin's anvil in a small shelter he built off his barn and both Tamarack and Eric spent a lot of time there. Eric discovered a talent for sculpture and made small figurines and miniature farm machinery for Little Joe and Cottonwood.

It appeared for a few days that the problem in Kuwait would be handled without further combat, but the United States rejected an Iraqi offer to withdraw and launched the ground attack. Television news was full of interviews with American generals who bragged they would cut the head off the Iraqi snake and bomb Saddam Hussein in his bed. There were charts and animations and experts to explain the intricacies of high-tech war.

Harry didn't want to watch but couldn't help himself. It was all very impersonal and antiseptic, no talk of human beings killed, just of tanks destroyed and units neutralized. There were no close-ups, just panoramas. Everyone was assured that only Iraqi soldiers were being harmed, and after all, they deserved it. When reporters demanded estimates of Iraqi casualties the spokesman was evasive.

Combat was suspended the end of February with all the oil wells in Kuwait on fire and much of Iraq destroyed. Plans were announced for heroic victory parades to welcome the soldiers home. That was better, Harry supposed, than being spat upon as many of his fellow-soldiers had been after Viet Nam, but that would not make the effects of the war any less. It was one more nightmare for the country to carry.

The letter from the Department of Ecology came. The Review Board had determined that that Harry's diversion of water from the San Poil River was an illegal, unregistered use of water and must not continue. There were citations from The Revised Code of Washington laying out civil and criminal penalties. There was a procedure to appeal the determination. Harry filed the letter in his safe and began to look for a pump to use in the well.

Long Joe came the middle of March. He had spent another winter in the Southwest, was tanned and healthy. Nathan brought him and stayed for two days. Little Joe was delighted with the visit. Harry wanted their neighbors to meet Long Joe so they had a dinner and invited Wildrose and Tamarack and Eric and Barbara. Walt and Frances came as well.

After dinner the talk turned inevitably to war. Tamarack argued that the war had been fought to protect the petroleum industry and take Iraq out as a competitor. It was just business. Eric blamed Saddam Hussein and repeated George Bush's charge that he was another Hitler. He wasn't sure just what the parallel was. Walt said that if you keep a large standing army eventually you have to use it or the people won't continue to pay the bill. Nathan said it was just American racism at work.

Judith insisted that the society was in collapse and that the war was a diversion, a means to delay the end. Barbara said she would not give them her baby to fight any war. Wildrose watched Cottonwood and Little Joe at play on the cabin floor and agreed with Barbara that whatever the reason she would not send her son off to fight. Frances said it made her sick to think of all the fine young men she'd known who'd died in wars in her lifetime.

Long Joe waited until the conversation lulled then said, "Every one of you is right. But beneath it all is the so-called Nation-State. Years ago Harry tried to convince me that there was a need for National Governments. I told him then that there was only one thing that National Governments did well and that was war.

"Tonight, eighty thousand children will go to bed hungry, just in Washington State, so I don't think this huge government is good at feeding children. There are homeless people all over the country, many of them veterans of the last war, so I don't think the government is good at providing shelter or honoring veterans. Everywhere the strong exploit the weak and crime fills the streets, so I don't think the government provides justice and equality.

"Our roads and bridges and railroads fall apart and airplanes fall out of the sky and the government does nothing. Prices go up, quality goes down. Half of all marriages end in divorce; soon, most children will grow up without a father. Women are beaten and raped; the planet is poisoned. Species go extinct at the rate of a hundred a day. All this is under the leadership of the great Nation-States. As your politicians love to say, 'This is the greatest Nation the world has ever known.' But they don't seem to do much well.

"Ah, but in war they excel. Bombs can be targeted through a bathroom window; airplanes can fly halfway around the world to kill. Cruise missiles with brains fly over enemy territory seeking targets. Laser-guided shells and heat-seeking missiles can destroy with unprecedented precision. So what if the missiles each cost enough to feed all the hungry children in this state for weeks? So what if the Gulf War cost enough to build houses for all the homeless?

"Did you ever notice that if there is a problem the government always responds by declaring war? We have a War on Poverty, a War on Crime, a War on Cancer and a War on Drugs. Even in politics we choose up two sides and make war on each other.

The government knows that war is the only real means it has to cope with problems.

"And the larger the government, the better it performs it's true task. The larger the group, the more the people will go along with inequalities and atrocities. Nothing affects them personally. In the small group, if someone takes more than their share it hurts someone they know, someone they probably are related to. It is harder to cheat and steal and kill when you have to watch the victim suffer. The way the white man fights wars, one man makes the bomb, another loads it in the plane, another man gives the order and yet another drops it. Who's to blame? If we are to have war, it needs to be hand-to-hand. When you kill an enemy, you should hear him scream, feel his hot blood on your hands."

There was silence in the cabin broken only by the voices of the children.

Finally Harry said, "I won't take the other side of that argument any more."

"Now if I could convince the rest of the world," Long Joe said.

"I'm sure you try," Frances said. "Someone should."

"We all must do it," Long Joe said. "We all must find a new way. Historians call the European countries and their colonies 'the gunpowder empires,' because that's all that distinguished them, gunpowder and the will to use it ruthlessly. When Columbus sailed, Tenochtitlan and Teotihuacan and other American cities were larger, cleaner and more beautiful than Rome or Paris or London. The people had developed a way of life that was in balance with the Earth. But what they did not have was the means to kill large numbers of people at a distance. That is what defines European civilization. Civilization in that sense was a wrong turn excused by a bunch of mystical nonsense. When a species takes a wrong turn then either there will be a re-turn or extinction. It takes a much more radical turn to correct the mistake than was the mistake itself. And it happens much more quickly."

"Those that survive will be those furthest from the direction of the doomed. So maybe I'm right. Maybe it will be my children or their children's children who have the answer. None now living will ever know. We each must pass on that which we think can help the most. The wisest man sees only seven generations ahead. That is why true wisdom is in dreams. Wisdom drawn from material things is a passing fancy, shaped as much by its discoverer as by reality.

"But we can't all just be farmers anymore," Eric said. "The world has changed."

"The world has not changed," Long Joe said. "WE have changed. And we could all be farmers. That doesn't mean we couldn't all be many other things also. Look at this group here. In just a couple of years by working together you almost have become independent. Really, you produce much more food than you need and Harry hauls it to the coast and trades it for money.

Then you buy trucks and televisions and other things you don't need. I'm glad Harry bought a truck because he will give me a ride in it, but it is not truly a need.

"And even so, you all have time to do other things. Judith weaves and rides. Wildrose makes quilts. I have seen the beautiful things Eric makes from metal. You all have built your own homes.

"Look at your children, they are healthy and happy. Look at the elders here. They are not going to be sent to some nursing home to die in lonely desperation. If one of you needs something the others will provide it. I think you are more civilized than the United States. Why couldn't there be millions of groups like this or even ten or a hundred times as big? They could trade and build schools and all the things the government pretends to do. In the end, all we have is the Earth, the Ancestors and the Children."

"But how could rich people exploit us all then?" Walt said. "Sounds radical to me."

"Eliot would have a hard time in a system like that," Tamarack said. "He would have to work!"

"And John Carlson wouldn't be able to use his money to push everyone around," Eric said.

"It's just a dream," Wildrose said.

"There is power in dreams," Long Joe said.

Breakup, as usual, was a muddy mess. As soon as the ground was dry enough Harry began his spring work. He had found a two—bottom three-point plow in Quincy and tried it on the fore-cart. It was faster than the old riding-plow of Walt's that he'd used, and when he got to the end of the row he could raise it quickly and make his turns with ease. The offset disk worked great and he found a small spring-tooth harrow that broke up clods quicker than anything he'd used.

UPS brought his ground-cover and other material, and he got some peas and broccoli planted in early April. Eric borrowed a bucket-loader and they cleaned all the corrals and sheds, spread manure heavily on all the fields except where he planned potatoes. Harry had found a potato seed grower in Idaho who did all his work with horses and had many heirloom varieties of potatoes that included fingerling varieties grown on the Washington coast by Native people for a long time.

Historians said the ancestors of these potatoes had been brought to the Northwest from Peru by the Spanish in the seventeenth century. Long Joe had told Harry that the Native people had grown potatoes for thousands of years and that it was one more example of white chauvinism to believe that such an important crop could not have come the short distance from South America until white people got here to do it. Even archaeologists admitted that there was a lot of pre-Columbian trade up and down the Pacific coast.

The Idaho seed-grower had Jerusalem artichokes and comfrey and Harry ordered several pounds of each to get a start. He found a small nursery with several varieties of raspberries and currants and a currant-gooseberry hybrid called Josta berries and he bought several dozen of each. The fruit trees he'd planted over the last two years were growing strong and he expected his first small crop of cherries and plums and apricots in early summer.

Harry wanted to get in as many perennials as possible. Once planted they produced more for less effort and provided cuttings or tubers that could be planted or sold. He bought a book on grafting and began to practice with prunings from the orchard.

The greenhouse filled with seedlings and he had plenty of grain for seed. He was pleased with the local sales and looked forward to the time when he didn't have to haul any of his produce to the coast. Long Joe always said that the healthiest food was that grown closest to where a person lived.

Eric continued to work with the black team and soon had their trust. Walt showed him how to rig for skidding small logs and they thinned a small tamarack stand across the river for practice. Harry wanted the poles to frame a shop building. Eric found an old self-loader truck to trade for and put in bids on small logging jobs. He began to talk of buying a portable sawmill so he could saw lumber to sell or trade.

Tamarack drove the small team when Harry wasn't using them in a four-horse hitch and he developed into a reliable teamster. He told Harry that if he saw another bargain on a team to get him one. Walt had a likely young gelding the same age as the old mare's first foal and he told Tamarack that if he helped train them he could use them whenever he wanted to. Harry and Walt agreed that they would give the team to Tamarack if he maintained his interest.

Dorothy came to help with Barbara's childbirth and she delivered a girl. They asked Harry and Judith to serve as Godparents and invited Tamarack and Wildrose to the christening at Saint Mary's where Father Bryan named the baby Hannah. Afterwards they had a celebratory dinner at Harry and Judith's cabin.

As Harry drove his four-horse team back from plowing Tamarack's field Johnny Carlson followed him for a while then passed with his horn blaring. Harry was pleased that the horses barely shied at the noise. When he got home Johnny waited for him.

"What kind of a rig is that?" he asked Harry, pointed to the fore-cart.

Harry showed him how it worked. Johnny was very impressed. He stood around while Harry unhitched the horses, fed and watered them.

"So how was rodeo school?" Harry asked Johnny when he finished.

"It was okay," Johnny said, looked down and scuffed his boot on the ground.

"So you ridin' in the Stampede this year?" Harry asked him. "I don't think so," Johnny said. "I'm not sure rodeoin' is that big a deal."

"I thought you were all gung-ho to be a rider," Harry said.

"That was last year," Johnny said. "I've grown up some since then."

"Did you flunk out," Harry asked.

Johnny glared at him. "No, I didn't flunk-out. I got my certificate."

"So what's the problem," Harry said.

"My Uncle Don says I don't really have what it takes," Johnny said. "He says they just passed me because I was his nephew. He says I should have been ridin' since I was a kid."

"What are you goin' to do now?" Harry asked.

"I might go into the gun business," Johnny said. "My Uncle Don has a shop in Waco and he's makin' a bundle at the big shows in Dallas and Houston."

"What do you know about guns?" Harry asked. "Except how to blast away into the woods with that AK-47."

"My old man says I can work for him," Johnny said, "But he's told me himself there's no future in farmin'."

"I thought you were all goin' to be rich soon," Harry said.

"Don't worry," Johnny said, "We will be. But I can't talk about that."

"You discover gold over there or somethin'?" Harry asked.

"Just as good," Johnny said. "You'll see."

"Well, whatever it is should be on this side of the road, too," Harry said.

Johnny looked at him. "You should just sell this place".

"Why? We're doin' fine here".

"Not without water, you won't," Johnny said. "Wait until August comes."

"I've got plenty of water," Harry said.

"You can't use that well to irrigate," Johnny said. "It's just a domestic well. My dad checked. You can only water half an acre."

"I guess your dad knows just about everything," Harry said.

"He's not the only one watchin' you," Johnny said.

"Who else?" Harry asked.

"Well, Eliot says you messed things up gettin' all these people interested in farmin'."

"So how does that bother him?" Harry asked.

"This was a nice, quiet place until you came," Johnny said. "Now there's all these people stoppin' to buy vegetables and Indians comin' around. And that Jew friend of yours."

"Yeah," Harry said. "It's like Grand Central Station." "Well, my dad says you aren't nothin' but squatters, anyway.

You don't even own the property. He says somebody should buy it and kick you off."

"I don't think it's for sale," Harry said.

"Well, that could change, too," Johnny said. "Money talks."

Reject began to bark, looked towards the lower end of the meadow. Harry halted the horses and looked that direction. He saw a man there in a bright orange vest. Then he noticed a vehicle parked beside the highway with orange cones marking it.

He drove the horses to the barn, left them in harness and threw them some hay then whistled for Reject and walked to where he could see the man in the orange vest use a machete to cut away brush.

The man looked up as Harry and the dog approached.

"Mornin'. Just lookin' for a corner pin. Should be a quarter-corner right in here."

"Should be," Harry said, "but I've never actually seen it. Probably buried by high-water."

"Well I guess I'm in for some shovel work," the surveyor said.

"This a highway survey?"

"Nope, workin' for some guy named John Carlson. Subdivision application. Five acre tracts, I guess."

"How big a subdivision? Just that hayfield?"

"The whole place," the surveyor said. "Four-hundred acres less twenty with the house and buildings."

"How's he goin' to sell little pieces like that way off out here?"

"He's got a partner who's a Real Estate Broker up in Republic," the surveyor said. "They've been sellin' these five-acre 'ranchettes' like crazy. To people from Spokane and the coast. Everybody wants some place to get away to if things get really bad. You know, crime and so on. Or for retirement."

"But if they all come out here then they bring the crime and so on with them."

"Yeah. It doesn't make sense to me. I just run the lines and watch."

"I know it's just your job," Harry said, "But the last thing we need out here is a bunch of people who don't know how to live here."

"You might want to do the same thing and move on out," the surveyor said. "If this is your place, you could get a good price for it in small pieces. Go buy a place in Montana or somewhere."

"I'm a farmer, not a speculator."

"I know what you mean," the surveyor said, "I grew up farmin. Down by Colfax. But it's all changin'. I heard them talkin' about buyin' an eighty, must be just south of you here and there's some old-timer back in here somewhere they figure they can get to sell. They've got big plans."

"I don't want to wish you any bad luck," Harry said, "But I hope it doesn't work out."

"There's always surveyin' to do somewhere. It is a shame to screw up this little valley. But I guess you can't stop progress."

"Well, I'm goin' to give it a try," Harry said.

Walt said they hadn't talked to him yet but that he wasn't surprised at Carlson's plan.

"He's been determined to be a millionaire ever since he's been here," Walt said. "All those Korean War boys came back talkin' about bein' millionaires. I guess that's what they told them they were fightin' for. I always figured that if everybody got to be millionaires then it wouldn't be worth much."

"Sounds like my dad and his World War Two buddies. Who owns that eighty south of me? Everybody always says it's for sale but I never heard who owns it?"

"A guy from the coast named Gil Gilchrist. He bought it years ago, hopin' to retire there, then he got sick and had to stay near the doctors. It used to be part of a family allotment, a relative of Martha McTavish, but they got hard-up in the fifties and sold it."

"I wonder how much they want for it?"

"I don't know, now," Walt said, "But old Gil always told me if he sold it I'd have first crack. Seemed to be a man of his word. They used to bring their camper over and stay on vacations. He grew up on a ranch over by Saint Marys, Idaho and always wanted to get back. Maybe I should give him a call."

"I'd hate to see John Carlson get it," Harry said, "and subdivide it."

"There's a lot of timber on that piece," Walt said. "They'd probably cut it."

Harry thought of the Ponderosa grove and the voices of the San Poil children. "I'd sure appreciate it if you'd make that call."

Nathan came to warn them. "Some broker from Republic called my aunt," he told them. "Offered her a bunch of money for this place. Said he had a cash buyer."

"It's John Carlson," Harry said. "He's trying to do a big subdivision. Five acre tracts."

"My aunt told them 'no'," Nathan said, "But she's only one of six that has an interest in it. She says she has to tell them, have a family council."

"How do you think that will go?" Harry asked.

"I don't know," Nathan said. "A couple of them are pretty greedy. Especially my Uncle George. And they've all got kids who will want to sell."

"I need to be there," Judith said. "When is she going to tell them?"

"I'm not sure," Nathan said. "They usually get together at Easter for a big family picnic. Over by the Mission. I'll find out."

"I need to talk to them," Judith said.

"A lot of them will want the money," Nathan said.

"Well, then we'll buy it," Judith said.

"This broker is talking cash," Nathan said.

"We'll figure out something," Harry said.

Walt asked Harry to take him to the store to call Gilchrist. He was on the phone for quite a while. When he came back, he shook his head.

"I don't know. Gil's in the hospital. That was his wife I was talkin' to. He's pretty sick. She says nobody has talked to them yet, but they could use the money."

"Did you talk price?"

"She didn't know what they wanted. But if I know John Carlson, he'll try to steal it."

"Maybe I could make them a better offer," Harry said.

"Penny said I still had first crack," Walt said.

"Do you think they would take a contract with monthly payments?"

"I don't know," Walt said, "But at their age they probably need the cash."

"Well, I guess the cat's out of the bag," Johnny Carlson said. "The surveyor said he talked to you. My dad almost fired him. It was supposed to be a secret until it was done."

"Pretty hard to keep it a secret with survey flags and orange paint all over the place."

"So, I suppose you're goin' to fight it."

"I might."

"Well, it won't do you no good," Johnny said. "My dad's friends with all the commissioners. They'll do whatever he wants."

"I guess money can buy just about anything," Harry said.

"Money's the only thing that counts," Johnny said. "If you don't have money you may as well give up."

"So what's your dad goin' to do with all that money?" Harry asked.

"He wants to retire in a few years, move down to Texas where it's warmer. And he says I can go to college. He says enough money will buy my way in to any college I want."

"It won't buy you a pass on the entrance exams."

"It will buy me a tutor," Johnny said. "Anyone can pass with enough help. Shit, there's all kinds of Indians go to college."

"There's some pretty smart Indians."

"They get in because they got affirmative action," Johnny said.

"You've got some surprises comin'."

"No," Johnny said, "You're the one that's got surprises comin'."

CHAPTER 16

Easter dawned clear and bright. Harry fed the horses early and threw some extra scratch to the chickens and ducks. The goats bleated and begged before he could get to them with their hay.

Little Joe and Rebecca were excited about the picnic. Judith was in a somber mood, told Harry she worried about persuading her relatives not to sell the place or, at least, to sell it to them. Harry hoped that Long Joe would be there. If anyone could convince them it would be him.

They drove to Nespelem. Nathan met them at the junction and they followed him over Desautel Pass and down towards Omak. Above Saint Mary's Mission he turned off and followed a dirt track through sagebrush and small pines. About a mile in, the road went up and over a ridge and down into a small valley with a stream at the bottom.

Harry saw several cars and trucks parked there and children ran through the trees. A large tipi stood on a little bench above the creek. He waited until Nathan parked then he turned the truck and backed into a clear spot. Rebecca went to join a group of cousins she knew from her trips with Judith to see Hattie. Little Joe was shy, hung back near his parents until his mother called to one of the boys about his age and pushed Little Joe to join him.

Nathan came over to help them carry the food they'd brought. Judith had used as many of the things they grew as possible. She had potato salad, several roasted chickens, two large hams and a huge salad made from young Spring greens and baby carrots. She had made a casserole from frozen corn and dried peppers and two large cobblers, one cherry, one blueberry. There were murmurs of admiration as the three of them set the food on a long plank table.

Besides Judith's parents and sisters there were a number of people Harry remembered from their wedding and other contacts he'd had with Judith's family, but there were many more that he never had met. Judith and Nathan began to introduce him and he was sure he would not remember all the names. Most of them were friendly, although some of the young men had a challenge in their eyes. It reminded Harry of Nathan when he first had known him.

Long Joe sat in a lawn chair back under the pines, smoked with several men about his own age. He waved to Harry. Harry was relieved that he was there.

A large barbecue kettle smoked near the table and the smell of cooking meat drifted from it.

There was an open fire in a stone pit and various pans and pots were set around the edge to keep warm. Several people drank from cans or bottles of beer and Harry saw a barrel full of ice with chilled beer and soft drinks. A propane campstove on one end of the table held a steaming pot of coffee and another of boiling water for tea.

Judith went to join her mother and sisters and other women who sat on a collection of quilts and blankets. Harry went to the table to get a cup of coffee and Matt joined him.

"I guess we're the paleface section," Matt said.

Harry looked at the range of skin-tones and facial features. The people of the Colville Reservation were known for their easy acceptance of outsiders, even whites. Many "full-bloods" were light-skinned, sometimes freckle-faced, wore glasses and would not be noticed as different on any street in any white neighborhood. Others were very dark, nearly black, with coarse, straight hair and the bold plains-Indian noses that Harry had learned to see as beautiful.

He loved their easy familiarity and irrepressible humor. He thought of the last Isaacson family reunion he had attended, while still a child, on the Kansas plains. Their stiff, severe Calvinism and somber dress and manner made a stark contrast with the colorful clan gathered here in the highlands above the Okanogan Valley.

"We're just one end of this rainbow," Harry said.

"I remember the first one of these Easter gatherings I came to," Matt said. "I didn't know if they would scalp me or not. I knew that a lot of Helen's relatives weren't very excited about her marrying a white man, especially one who worked at the dam. And she had this cousin who'd always had his eye on her. They used to spend a lot of time out in the mountains on horseback and everybody in the family assumed they would end up together. Like Nathan and Judith. Then I came along and screwed it all up. I figured this guy would probably put a knife in me." Matt laughed and looked at the group of elders around Long Joe.

"That cousin was Joseph. I've never had a better friend. He has watched over all of us like a hawk. Like a Little Eagle. I always knew that if I messed up he would be there to step in. It used to bother me and I hated to see him come around. Finally I realized what a blessing he was."

Several of the women began to feed the children. Harry saw Little Joe eating with a group of boys. Rebecca sat with her Aunt Sara and talked seriously about something. Judith came over and took her father by the arm, led him to the ragged line that formed near the food. Harry followed.

Matt carried his plate to an empty lawn chair near Long Joe and Harry sat on the ground near him. There were many favorable comments about the food that Judith had brought. Long Joe made a point of telling everyone that most of it was grown on the San Poil place. Nathan, too, mentioned several times that Judith's food wasn't store-bought.

When everyone had eaten their fill, Sara and two other young women took most of the children on a hike. Some of the younger men and older boys formed two teams to play a rough and boisterous game of football. A shiny blue Volvo pulled into the parking area and a tall, striking young man got out. Harry was startled by a shriek from Judith.

"Joseph!" she shouted and ran to her brother, hugged him tightly. Helen was close behind her.

The football game stopped while the players gathered around Joseph, shook his hand or slapped him on the back. He broke loose to hug his father and shake hands with Harry. The football players tried to pull him into the game but he declined, went to sit with his mother.

After the excitement passed the adults began to collect at the long table. Long Joe and his group moved their lawn chairs close. Several people who had wandered away were called back. Harry realized that the discussion of their property was about to begin and he paced nervously beyond the far end of the table.

Long Joe caught his eye and motioned him over and Harry sat on the ground beside him. Initially the conversation was formless and leaderless. Small groups talked among themselves. Occasionally someone would hold everyone's attention for a few minutes then the general hubbub would return. Most of the talk was about the history of the property, who had rights to it and how it had been used over the years. Several of the elders remembered Bill and Martha McTavish as their own elders.

Long Joe and Hattie and Helen said nothing, waited patiently. Nathan and Joseph stood and talked quietly nearby. Matt sat beside Helen but did not participate. The football game stopped and several of the players came to join the discussion.

Finally one of the men near Long Joe took advantage of a general lull and said loudly, "My family thinks we should sell it. They offered a lot of money. We all need money."

There was a commotion of response, some positive, and some negative. Harry watched for Long Joe or Hattie or someone to take the other side, but they remained silent.

One of the older women looked at Helen for a minute, then said, "I am the closest descendant of Martha McTavish. In the courthouse they say I own the property. I always intended to give my share to my son, Nathan. If he showed some respect." Several people laughed.

The man who had spoken for selling it responded, "There is plenty of range for Nathan's horses. He'd be better off with his share of the money. He could buy a decent pickup."

Nathan took a step towards the table and said quietly, "My share belongs to Judith and her family. They have worked for it. No one cared about that property until they came."

"They can take the money and buy another farm," a young woman said.

A very old man who sat near Long Joe said, "Our land is not to be sold. If you want money, get a job." He looked at the man who had spoken in favor of selling. "George, you don't need the money. You can't count what you already have."

There was a ripple of laughter.

"I have a lot of grandchildren to feed," George said. "And a lot of horses."

"A lot of lazy grandchildren and fat horses," someone said, provoked laughter again.

"I need a new car," one of the young men who had been playing football said.

"You'd just wreck it like the last one," one of the women said. "Then we won't have land or money."

"I agree with Nathan," one of the young women said. "Judith has worked for the place. Let them keep it."

"She isn't even a tribe member," another young woman said. "She chose the white world. They should buy it."

Hattie spoke for the first time. "Judith is not a tribe member so that she doesn't burden the tribe. But she's more Indian than a lot of you. She knows the plants and ceremonies. She lives with the Earth. I say let them keep it. It will only be worth more."

"That white man wants it bad," George said. "He'll pay more than he offered."

"He wants to subdivide it," Nathan said.

"He's already subdividing his place," another young man said. "We can't stop it. But we can take advantage of it."

Long Joe stirred and commanded everyone's attention.

"The McTavish place fed a lot of us through many bad winters during the depression. The purpose of that place is to grow food. I know Judith and I know Harry. They are good people who grow food that feeds many others. Harry farms with horses when he could make more money with machines. I knew Harry's grandfather who also farmed with horses. It is not a hobby.

Harry works very hard and does not depend on others. And their children are our children. If the land is sold for money it will be gone in a year. Who will feed your children then if bad times come?"

One of the football players, who had gotten very drunk, said, "He's just a squaw-man. Judith should be with Nathan. Everyone knows it."

They all looked at Nathan.

"I have no claim on Judith," Nathan said. "And Harry is my friend. He is a good father to Judith's children."

"Then they should buy it," George said.

"It is not a fair price," Hattie said. "Not for farming."

"If your family gives them your share, then it will be a fair price," George said.

"Our share is the most," Nathan's mother said. "We will give it to them."

"Ours, too," Hattie said. "That only leaves a quarter, George."

"I don't care whose name it's in," Judith said. "It will always belong to all of us."

"George would rather have the money," Hattie said. "He should sign a paper to give it up."

"I don't know if we have even that much money," Judith said. "We could pay payments."

"The offer is cash," George said.

"We have the money," Matt said. "We'll pay George for his share."

"Only a fool believes he can sell the Earth," Long Joe said.

"A rich fool," George said.

"You can't eat money," Long Joe said. "If you sell, it's gone forever."

"He's right, Grandpa," one of the young men said. "We don't really need the money. I give my share to Judith."

George glared at him. "Your share isn't anything, Bill. Not as long as I'm alive."

"Then I'll give them back the money," Bill said.

"I agree," a young woman who appeared to be Bill's sister said, "We might need that food some day."

"If you have enough money there is always food," George said. "Just go to Safeway."

"I remember when you were hungry, George," Hattie said. "Your family had to eat commodities when you were little. We all did."

"Not ever again," George said. "I'll sell the whole reservation first."

"That isn't the answer," Long Joe said. "We need to have our own food, not Safeway food."

"We don't eat the food Judith grows," George said. "They sell it for money."

"You can go there anytime and get food," Nathan said. "I've seen them give food away. If someone needs it."

"We could pay you with food," Judith said. "So much a year."

"That's fair," several people said.

George was cornered. He muttered to himself, but finally said, "Okay. Any of my family that needs food can go there and get it. That comes first, before you sell any."

"Only those who really need it," Hattie said. "Not just because they're lazy or want to spend their money on beer."

"Who decides?" George asked.

"I will," Hattie said. "They can come to me and I'll write them a note."

"You know Hattie will be fair," Long Joe said. "It is her family also."

"That would have been a lot of money," George grumbled.

"You can't have all the money in the world," Hattie said.

"I can try," George said.

Everyone laughed.

"I guess I shouldn't have been so worried," Judith said as they drove home. "I was just afraid everyone would listen to George and decide on the money."

"They might have," Harry said, "If it hadn't been for Long Joe and Hattie and the others. And Nathan."

"They all really care about us," Judith said. "Even George. I've seen him argue all night about something. He didn't put up much of a fight."

"Do you think they'll want the food?" Harry asked.

"Some of them, probably," Judith said. "I hope so. I would like to see them eat better. Our food would be good for them."

"I wish we could just feed the people here in the valley," Harry said. "The way it used to be."

When Harry picked up Walt's mail, he saw an envelope with a return address in the name of Gilchrist. He felt a charge of excitement, mixed hope and fear. He didn't stop at the cabin but drove on in to Davises'. Walt was out fussing with a wheel on his feed-wagon. He smiled and tipped back his hat.

"This cussed thing still wants to wobble."

Harry handed him the mail. "I noticed a letter from Gilchrist," Harry said.

"Sure enough," Walt said and opened it, read silently. "Well, Carlson's real estate guy got to them, made them an offer," Walt said when he finished. "Too damned much, too, five-hundred an acre."

"That's low compared to prices I've been hearing," Harry said.

"Well, she says I still have first crack at it," Walt said, "But we'd have to match that offer. It's supposed to be cash."

"I don't have that much cash to spare," Harry said.

"Me, neither," Walt said. "Maybe we could pool our resources. I might come up with half of it."

"I probably could, too," Harry said. "I suppose John Carlson won't be too friendly afterwards."

"Now that breaks my heart," Walt said.

"We should set up an escrow and write a formal offer," Harry said. "Move fast before they find out and up the price."

"I wouldn't do anything in Republic," Walt said, "They're all in cahoots with Carlson."

"I'll go down to Moses Lake," Harry said, "I don't think his money reaches that far."

"You tell me what you need," Walt said. "I'll need to get to the bank in Wilbur."

Gilchrists accepted the offer and agreed to closing in thirty days. Harry drove back to Moses Lake with twenty thousand dollars in cash from his safe and a cashier's check from the Wilbur bank for Walt's half. The escrow agent seemed a little surprised at the amount of cash but said nothing. He told Harry that he needed instructions on how to have the deed drawn. Harry said he would talk to Walt and let him know.

Walt said that he and Frances wanted the deed to name them all tenants-in-common with the right of survivorship which meant that when he and Frances passed on the property would belong to Harry and Judith. Harry said that wasn't necessary but Walt would not hear it.

"I sure don't want Franklin or his sister to get their hands on it," Walt said. "He's as likely to cut that timber and subdivide it as John Carlson."

Harry sent a letter to the escrow agent.

When the closing date approached Walt asked Harry to bring the papers for him and Frances to sign, that they could drive to Republic to have them notarized. The escrow agent didn't like the idea but finally agreed. Harry was sure the resistance was because he couldn't pay himself the eight hundred dollar fee until everything was recorded.

Walt's eyes had begun to fail and he did not like to drive. He asked Harry to take him and Frances to Republic to sign the property transfer. They went into the Title Company and presented the file. The receptionist called the attorney out of his office to approve it before she would notarize it.

The attorney looked over the documents, paused at the deed. He carried it to a Forest Service map of the County on the wall and traced in township and range lines with his finger. He frowned and muttered something then walked back to them.

"Is this that eighty on the San Poil across from John Carlson?" he asked.

"That's the one," Walt said.

"I heard there was another deal on that property," the lawyer said. "I'll have to check it out."

"What is there to check out?" Walt asked him.

"There may already be a sale recorded on this parcel."

"We don't want title insurance," Harry said. "We just want these papers notarized."

The attorney looked at him sharply. "I'm not going to be party to some fraudulent sale."

"How would you be a party to anything?" Harry asked. "We just want your notary to verify the signatures."

The attorney studied the deed. "I assume you are Mr. Isaacson?"

Harry nodded.

"Tenants-in-common with right of survivorship," the attorney said. "So you have quite an interest in influencing the Davises to sign this. Maybe undue influence?"

"Nobody influenced me to do anything," Walt said. "This was my idea."

"That's a lot of money to give away," the attorney said. "They paid their half," Walt said. "Anyway I don't see how this is your business. I came in here to pay someone to put a notary stamp on it."

"We have to be careful," the attorney said. "Many times elderly people do things that aren't in their best interests."

"Just because my eyes are bad doesn't mean my brain quit working," Walt said.

"Harry and Judith are closer to us than our own children," Frances said. "If we want to buy property together that is our business."

"You'll have to go somewhere else," the attorney said.

"Let's go over to the bank," Walt said, "They'll do it."

As they left the office Harry saw the attorney pick up the telephone and dial a number.

A young woman officer at the bank happily notarized Walt and Frances' signatures. She was a local girl and recognized the names, began to chatter about people they knew in common.

Walt finally had to say, "Well, we better git," so that they could escape.

When they were back in the pickup Harry said, "There's no reason we can't record this right now. If we send it back to the escrow agent it might take a week. All he really needs is the recording number.

"The sooner the better," Walt said, "That attorney made me nervous. I'll bet he's workin' with John Carlson."

"I have that same feeling," Harry said.

The County Auditor's office said that they would have to have proof that the taxes were paid and the buyers would have to pay the transfer fees before they could record. It was over fifteen hundred dollars. Harry didn't have that much cash with him so they went back to the bank and Walt cashed a check to cover it.

When everything was in order, the clerk took a final look at the documents and said they would be recorded then next morning.

"We need to get a recording number now," Harry said, "If you wouldn't mind."

"I guess I could do that," the clerk said. She talked briefly to an older woman then smiled at them as she went into the back. She returned a few minutes later with a slip of paper with the number written on it.

"I'm sorry," Harry said. "Could we also have copies of the documents with the stamp on them."

"It will be a dollar a copy."

"No problem," Harry said.

"I'm sure glad you know what you're doin'," Frances said when they were back in the truck.

"I just didn't want to leave any room for trouble," Harry said.

When they got home John Carlson's white pickup was parked crossways in the drive. Harry stopped and Carlson got out, walked unsteadily towards them. He went to the passenger side window and the smell of alcohol was strong.

"If you bastards think you can stop me with these fuckin' games, you're badly fuckin' mistaken."

"It's no game, John," Walt said. "There was a piece of property for sale and we bought it."

"You knew I intended to buy it," Carlson said. "I don't like people sneakin' around behind my fuckin' back."

"No one sneaked," Walt said. "I agreed to buy that eighty more than twenty years ago. Besides, you never told me you wanted to buy it."

"None of your fuckin' business," Carlson said.

"It was all perfectly legal," Frances said. "You should be ashamed of yourself, John."

"I'm not ashamed of nothin'," he growled. "Well, I'm not through with this. I already called one of Gilchrist's sons and he's goin' to stop the sale. I offered sixty. I'll pay whatever I have to. A hundred."

"Money ain't everything, John," Walt said. "There are still some people who keep their word."

"Goddamned old fossils think you can stop progress."

"You're not that far from a fossil, yourself, John," Frances said. "You're just greedy for the money."

"Money's the only thing that ever did me any good," Carlson said.

"You never did yourself any good," Frances said. "That's where it starts."

"There's more than forty thousand in timber on that piece," Carlson said. "If you think I'm goin' to let you steal that..."

"It's too late, John," Frances said.

"Bullshit," Carlson said. "It's never too late. We'll block the recording. They can do an affidavit that old man Gilchrist is out of his mind and the County won't record it."

"We already recorded it," Harry said.

"The escrow agent does that," Carlson said, "Don't try to bullshit me."

"Well, we did it," Walt said.

"You better not get any funny ideas about cuttin' that timber or anything until this is settled," Carlson said.

"We don't want to cut the timber," Walt said.

"Don't tell me you didn't see dollar signs just like I did," Carlson said.

"There are other reasons to do things, John," Frances said. "The important things in life are what we share."

"Sharin' makes people weak," Carlson said, "I don't share nothin'."

"Sharing makes people strong," Frances said.

"Sharin' is what communists do," Carlson said. "These fuckin' Indians were just a bunch of communists. Look what happened to them. All this sharin' bullshit!"

CHAPTER 17

Harry drove to Moses Lake to look for an irrigation pump. He found a good, used five-horsepower jet-pump. The owner of the little shop remembered the old man, let Harry have the pump for three hundred seventy-five dollars. Harry knew it was a great buy.

He also bought some six-inch steel mainline pipe someone had hauled in for salvage. The junk-man threw in half a dozen risers with T's that just needed new gaskets. A big irrigation dealer had a large pile of old three and four-inch handline sections and Harry put together two long lines and a short one, made sure all the sprinklers worked. He still intended to use his ditches except for the grain and hay.

After he installed the pump he turned it on and watched the flow in his main flume. He could see that it would not be enough to replace what he'd gotten from the river. He decided that he would have to buy some drip-tape and convert at least part of the produce to drip irrigation.

When Harry had caught up with his spring work he went to walk the boundary on the new eighty acres. He sat for a while in the Ponderosa grove and felt the presence of the children. He was happy that they had stopped John Carlson from cutting the old trees.

He walked south along the highway. A sliver of the property lay across the right-of-way, made a small part of Carlson's big hayfield. It was easy to see the south line because of the survey markers on Carlson's side of the highway. He turned east, waded across the river and climbed the slope, looked back to stay on a straight line. It was too far and too rugged to keep track of distance by pacing so Harry looked for an old survey marker.

He was more than halfway up the ridge and knew that he had to be beyond the first forty-corner. He was not surprised that it was not marked, but he hoped that the quarter-corner at the southeast point of the eighty would have a flag or pin. The timber was heavy, had not been cut in a very long time, if at all. He topped the ridge, found a clearing and looked back one last time for landmarks to keep him on a line due east. He picked a light spot on a far ridge for a beacon, hoped he could see it as he descended the slope.

He thought he saw pink off to his right and went to investigate. Beyond that faded survey flag was another which led to a large pine with a yellow Forest Service survey plate which marked the quarter-corner a hundred and thirty-seven feet straight south of him. He turned north, made an attempt to guess the line but knew he would hit either Walt's back fence or his own.

There was a large spring surrounded by aspen trees just down the slope. The mud was deep and he detoured around the upper side of the aspen grove. It wouldn't take much to put in a pipe and tank for stock-water. He would talk to Walt about fencing the eighty for range.

On this northeast slope the trees were tightly packed. If Eric came in and cut a few and skidded them out with his team the remaining trees would grow faster and they could have lumber sawed from what they cut. Harry had thought for a while that he should build a produce stand along the highway. Rough-cut pine would be perfect.

When he reached the fence he was a few yards east of the actual line. He went to the mutual corner between his place and Walt's and sighted back up the slope along the boundary. There was a lot of timber. He began to realize that it probably was worth more than they had paid for the place just as John Carlson said.

Johnny Carlson became very hostile. Several times when Harry met him on the highway Johnny swerved into his lane. Frequently he could be heard shooting his AK-47 in the woods. Harry and Judith warned the children to stay away from him.

A sign appeared on Carlson's side of the highway, the formal notification that a subdivision application was pending. Harry talked to Walt and Walt said there would be a hearing where the neighbors could object to the project. Harry talked to Tamarack and Eric about it and they agreed that they should all go to the hearing and try to stop it. Eric said he had heard of one subdivision up by Republic that had been stopped because there was not enough water. Tamarack said he would call some old friends on the coast who were involved with environmental causes.

Eliot remained friendly, maybe even more so. Harry was sure he would repeat anything he learned to Carlson. Eliot laughed about how Harry and Walt had bested Carlson over the eighty acres, but something about it didn't ring true.

Harry made a trip to the coast to check out his markets before he planted everything. He was particularly concerned about High Mountain Juice, had not heard from Rick Rosen as he usually did in the spring. He also wanted to see how many of his restaurants and small markets still would buy from him. He asked Judith if she wanted to make it a family trip, but she said she didn't care if she ever saw Seattle again. She thought Little Joe would like to go so Harry asked him and the boy was delighted. They left just after dawn on a clear April morning.

The roads were clear and the drive easy. They pulled into Redmond almost an hour before noon. High Mountain Juice still was in the same location but the level of activity seemed low and the receptionist had a surly attitude. Rick came out of his office with a worried look, saw Harry and smiled.

"I was about to write you a letter. I think I have this mess sold. To one of the organic distributors. They're expanding into Oregon and Idaho and want to put out the juice under their own label. I told them about you and they want to talk to you.

They want to contract for a lot more than I ever bought. If you're interested in going big-time, this is your chance."

"I don't know about big-time," Harry said. "Doesn't suit my instincts."

"It's big-time or out as far as I can see," Rick said. "Little guys just can't compete. The whole organic food business is going corporate. Three distributors have almost all the business in this area, now."

"Well, I think I'll just stick with my little small-time approach," Harry said.

"I wish you luck," Rick said. "I sure appreciate the produce you've grown for me. If I could go back five years, I'd do it in a second."

"A hundred years would be better," Harry said.

He took Little Joe to Pagliacci Pizza for lunch. Afterwards he made the rounds of the restaurants and markets. The proprietor of the Italian market on Ravenna was happy to see him, said he would buy all the produce he could from Harry.

"These distributors come in and try to make us sign exclusive contracts. I don't like it. I'll stay independent or retire. I'm a businessman, not a stooge."

Most of the restaurants said they still wanted his produce, but several of the small markets said they had all they needed. Harry could tell from the way they talked that the distributors must have pressured them. He reminded them of his quality but they insisted that what they got from the regular deliveries was just fine.

One market owner asked him if he carried liability insurance. "On my produce?" Harry asked, incredulous.

"All the distributors insure it now," the man said. "What if someone chokes on a carrot or gets sick? I can't afford that kind of legal exposure."

"Have you ever heard of a suit like that?" Harry asked him. "Well, no," the man said, "But the distributors say it's bound to happen. Besides it doesn't cost me any more."

"So even if the quality is lower, it's more important to have liability insurance?" Harry asked him.

"I barely make a living as it is, with all these big stores moving in," the man said. "One lawsuit could wipe me out. I can't take the risk."

As he drove towards home Harry wondered if more trips to the coast would be worthwhile. He decided he would build his produce stand beside the San Poil highway and see what other alternatives there were. He would not miss the visits to the city.

When Harry had his crops in, he bought enough steel posts and barbed wire to fence the new eighty. He called the surveyor who had worked for Carlson and hired him to run the south and east lines for the fence. The surveyor already had found the main survey markers so it took him less than a day to flag the boundaries and he charged only two hundred fifty dollars.

Harry hired Tamarack and Eric to help build the fence and while they worked he showed Eric the stand of pines he wanted to thin. Eric was excited by the prospect. He had found a portable sawmill near Northport that he could buy for just over five thousand. He didn't have enough yet, but he offered Harry a good rate on the cutting if he would pay in advance. Harry couldn't see any way to lose on the deal.

Walt told them he had an old road into his corner below the pine stand so Eric could set up his mill just below and skid logs directly to it with the team. Walt said he wouldn't mind having some lumber stacked around for repairs and miscellaneous projects himself, so he also paid Eric in advance for some cutting. When they finished the fence, Harry pulled his fifth-wheel to Northport and helped Eric haul back the little mill.

Once the mill was set up and adjusted, Eric could skid logs in the morning and saw them in the afternoon. The one and two inch lumber he produced was fine. Tamarack worked-off some of what he owed Harry by stacking the lumber as Eric cut it. He "stickered it up" using two-by-two spacers so it could air-dry. They would haul it down later.

Harry noticed a movement and looked up. A white and black Sheriff's car drove up the road and turned in at the cabin. Harry left off weeding and walked towards it. He saw the deputy start towards the door, then turn and walk to meet him.

The deputy was a short man, soft and slow. He stopped, legs wide apart and his right hand on the butt of his gun. Harry stopped a few feet away.

"Good morning," Harry said,

"Yes," the deputy said, "You Harry Isaacson?" "Sure am," Harry said. "What can I do for you?"

"I understand you have an illegal irrigation well on this place," the deputy said.

"Not that I know of," Harry said.

"You have an irrigation permit?" the deputy asked.

"No, I don't," Harry said.

"Looks like you're irrigating," the deputy said.

"Sure am," Harry said.

"That's against the law," the deputy said. "I order you to stop it immediately!"

Harry chuckled. "Can't oblige you. I need to get back to work, now."

"This is not a joke," the deputy said. "I am the law, here."

"You, personally?"

"I'm a deputy sheriff," the deputy said, "Deputy John Miller."

"Glad to meet you," Harry said, "But I'm very busy this morning."

"I told you to shut off that pump!" Deputy Miller said, red faced and raising his voice.

"I'm afraid you don't have any jurisdiction over that," Harry said. "That's strictly a civil matter enforced by the Department of Ecology."

"We enforce all the laws," Deputy Miller said. "If you want trouble, you're not far from resisting arrest."

"I think you aren't far from false arrest," Harry said.

Deputy Miller took a step towards him, unsnapped the restraining strap on his revolver.

"Not only do you not have jurisdiction on DOE regulations," Harry said, "This is Indian land and you're trespassing."

"You don't look like an Indian," Deputy Miller said.

"You never know," Harry said. "Judith," he called towards the cabin, "Would you come out here for a minute."

Judith came out, puzzled.

"This is Deputy John Miller," Harry said. "He doesn't think we're Indians."

Judith smiled her dark smile. "My Grandmother is Hattie Antoine. Is that good enough."

Deputy Miller seemed to recognize the name. "I'll radio the shift-commander. He can make the decision."

He went to the car and they saw him talk on the radio for a while. Finally he came back.

"We've decided not to make the arrest right now. But don't think you've heard the end of this. Misappropriating public water is a crime. The prosecutor may charge you."

"Then he'll have to charge half the farmers in the County," Harry said.

"Well, you'll be seeing me again," Deputy Miller said, gave them a mean look and stomped to his car. He spun the tires, threw gravel against the cabin as he left.

By the time all the crops were in and the first cutting of hay put up it was the end of June. Harry went to check on the lumber and much of it was dry enough for his purpose. He had soaked the butts of twenty peeled poles in a non-toxic wood treatment he found in one of his catalogs. It was expensive and he hoped it worked.

He dug holes and set the posts on the site he had selected for the produce stand. The field was flat and firm there a hundred feet from the highway along the drive. He used long two—inch planks for stringers and joists and one-inch lumber for the flooring. He built simple trusses from two-by-sixes, sheeted them with one-inch and bought galvanized roofing. There were no walls. His design was a simple shed-roof with a lean-to porch on the front, faced towards the highway. The finished product was thoroughly Western with its bright pine posts and rough-sawed lumber. All he needed was a hitching-rail in front and a sign on the clerestory.

Harry used peeled logs to define a parking lot and fenced an area behind the building for storage. He searched the thrift-stores, salvage yards and used-equipment dealers for coolers and display cases. He bought a sheet of plywood and split it in two and Judith painted a sign. The name they decided on, out of many possibilities, was simply, "The Traders."

Harry called the courthouse and found out that all they needed from the bureaucrats was a ten-dollar County business license and a State Department of Revenue number. He drove to Republic for the County permit and sent in the paperwork for the State registration. The State sent back a package of forms and regulations and informed them they had to report and pay the State sales tax every month.

They decided to open on a Saturday in the second week of July. Judith cut some bright cloth streamers and hung them along the edge of the roof and from the tops of the posts. Wildrose and Tamarack and Eric and Barbara came to spend the day and Walt and Frances stayed for several hours. Quite a few tourist cars stopped as well as half-a-dozen locals.

They had a table display of Eric's metal sculptures and miniature machines and some dry arrangements Wildrose had assembled and mounted on silver-wood bases Tamarack made. Several of each sold. Judith hung some of her weavings and tagged them with what she thought were very high prices but two of them sold and two more people said they would be back to see what else she did.

Johnny Carlson stopped by and glared at everyone and everything, then left without saying a word. Eliot drove in, said a friendly hello to everyone, bought some early carrots and greens. Chet Weston and his wife and two of their kids stopped in, drank several cups of the free coffee and made an attempt to be neighborly. Their kids were loud and wild and everyone was happy to see them go.

At the end of the day when they counted the proceeds they had taken in over two hundred dollars and even after they paid Eric and Tamarack and Judith took her share on the weavings there was almost a hundred dollars net. It might not seem like much for a business in the city, but with their overhead and needs it showed serious promise.

In the middle of summer, some new people moved in on the Weston property, two families living in an old trailer. The men were as furtive as Weston and rarely showed themselves. When Harry did see them they inevitably were with Weston, all in camouflage fatigues and usually with guns. There often was the sound of gunfire from the property and Eric said that he'd heard they had built a shooting-range and claimed to train would-be security guards and militiamen. Occasionally Harry saw Johnny Carlson's pickup parked there.

Harry did not notice the sound of jets in the distance at first. When he did hear the faint roar, he assumed it was another airliner crossing the Columbia Basin to the south. But the sound did not fade, as usual, instead grew louder. Soon he saw them, side-by-side, wing tips only a few feet apart, headed up the valley several thousand feet above.

He went on with his cultivating, turned the team at the end of the row and started back. Halfway across the field he suddenly heard the jets again, flying back down the valley. He could tell they flew low. He stopped the team, jumped from the fore-cart seat and ran to hold the lead horses' heads. The planes were very low, maybe two hundred feet above the treetops on the valley floor, as though on a bombing run. The roar rolled through the valley, echoed from the cliffs and shook the earth. Panicked, the horses struggled, and he barely managed to keep them from bolting.

When the team had settled, he went back to the fore-cart and took the lines. He had just started when he heard the planes again, flying back up the valley. He went to the front and this time, even with his best efforts, the horses dragged the fore-cart about twenty feet off across several rows. As soon as the sound faded and the horses quieted he raised the cultivator bar then led the team up the field.

He nearly had reached the road when the planes made yet another low-level run. He recognized Navy markings. He could see that Judith was at the corral calming the other horses. He stood still and waited for the jets to pass. The horses were not so frightened by this time and he managed to keep them still. He quickly led them to the corral and put them inside before he pulled off the harness.

Judith was very angry. One of the foals had cut herself in the excitement and she asked Harry to hold the young horse's halter while she went to the house for iodine. As she disinfected the wound she muttered about "white men and their stupid macho games."

"Harry chuckled at her. "Present company excepted, I hope."

"You know what I mean. You aren't like them."

"I hope not," Harry said.

Later, Eric told them that he had heard that Air Force planes from Spokane and Navy jets from Whidbey Island had been cleared to use the area for practice bombing runs because it was similar terrain to Northern Iraq.

"They used to do it all the time," he told them, "but then they said it was like Southern Russia."

"Somebody should sue them," Judith said.

"They tried," Eric said, "but technically the reservation is Federal land so they can use it if they want to. Even the State can't stop them. Not that they would."

A letter came addressed to Harry and Judith and Walt and Frances as owners of the eighty acres. It was the notification of the hearing on John Carlson's subdivision sent out to all adjoining property owners. The hearing would be in just over thirty days. Walt said fighting it probably was useless but he thought they should try. Harry and Judith agreed.

Harry talked to Tamarack and Eric the next time he saw them. They, too, agreed that they should try to stop Carlson. Tamarack said his friend on the coast had told him that if there was not adequate water for a household on each lot then the subdivision could not be approved. His friend had sent a copy of the State law and they calculated how much water would be necessary for eighty five-acre lots and it was an enormous amount of water. The State law also required that the water be provided to each lot as well as access. Harry knew what kind of construction project that would require.

They all sent letters to notify the County that they wanted to testify at the hearing. Tamarack and Eric said that they would talk to some of the other people in the area about testifying as well. Harry mentioned the subdivision to Eliot when he stopped by the stand but Eliot was evasive, said he believed in individual property rights.

Two weeks before the hearing was scheduled they all received another letter saying that the hearing was delayed until December.

"John's up to something," Walt said.

One Sunday Nathan came to visit. Harry had taken the day off from fieldwork so he and Nathan and Judith watched the stand and talked. Traffic was good and several times Harry had to go over to the garden to pick produce to replace what had sold. Three of Judith's weavings found buyers as well as several of Eric's miniature farm machines and a couple of Wildrose and Tamarack's arrangements.

In the early afternoon Wildrose and Tamarack stopped in and a little while later Eric and Barbara came. Judith said they should have a picnic and Eric and Harry decided it was time to try a barbecue smoker kettle they had built from scrap steel and an old stainless oven rack. Harry hauled the contraption over to the stand and soon they had alder coals glowing fiercely. Judith went to the cabin to make a quick basting sauce and get some pork chops she had thawed for their dinner. She also brought a small ham. Rebecca led Little Joe and Cottonwood on a fishing expedition and they returned with eleven nice trout. Tamarack helped them clean the fish while Wildrose ran back to their place for a bottle of white wine. Harry got new potatoes and carrots and ripe tomatoes and green peppers and pulled some onions. Nathan cut willow boughs for skewers.

They set the rack high to cook the food slowly and put everything in but the trout and closed the kettle. The smell made them all ravenous as they sat and talked. Several people who stopped to buy produce asked if the barbecued food was for sale and were disappointed that it wasn't. Harry could see another opportunity to generate income.

As evening came on they opened the wine and sipped it while Judith cleared one of the display tables and set it with paper plates. They saw Johnny Carlson's truck stop on the highway then back up and turn towards the stand.

"It's the Prince of the San Poil," Tamarack said.

"Wonder what the hell he wants?" Eric asked.

"Probably smelled the food," Barbara said. "I think the only place he ever eats is the drive-in in Republic."

Johnny stopped and got out, came over to where they sat. "Looks like a party," he said and Harry could see that he was drunk.

"Private party," Harry said.

Johnny stopped, swayed as he looked at Harry. "You think you're pretty big stuff since you cheated my Dad out of that eighty."

"Nobody cheated your dad," Harry said.

"He's the one that does the cheating," Eric said.

Johnny turned to stare at Eric. "Your family ain't never been nothin' but gyppo loggers, Brown."

"Honest ones, at least," Eric said.

"He's just a kid," Tamarack said. "We can't blame him for what John does."

"I'm no kid anymore," Johnny said. "I'll have more money than any of you soon."

"Money doesn't make a man," Harry said.

"It sure don't hurt," Johnny said.

"You guys quit arguing and come eat," Judith called to them. Johnny stared uncertainly towards her.

"If you behave yourself you can have some, too," she said to him.

Harry started to object then stopped.

Judith set the extra place and motioned Johnny over.

Harry opened the barbecue kettle and began to pass skewers of the food around. He laid the trout carefully across the rack and they began to sizzle.

Even Johnny agreed that the food was wonderful. He asked for a glass of the wine but Judith said no. He grumbled but continued to eat with abandon.

Harry turned the trout and they curled as they finished cooking. He asked for plates and put one of the small fish on each.

"Too bad it isn't salmon," Nathan said.

"My granddad says they used to catch lots of salmon on the San Poil right along here before they built the dam," Eric said. "They used to smoke enough to last them all winter."

"Everyone used to go to Kettle Falls and get the big ones on the run to Canada," Nathan said. "We could all live on fish if they hadn't built the dams. Now they want to pay us a few thousand dollars each to give up our claims."

"We need electricity and irrigation water more than salmon," Johnny said. "The Columbia Basin would still be a desert."

"That would be okay with me," Barbara said. "I would rather have the salmon."

"The biologists say they would come back if there was a way around the dams," Tamarack said. "Fish ladders or something." "Grand Coulee's too high for that," Johnny said. "Face it, they're gone forever."

Nathan laughed. "When we were kids, we used to dream about the dams being gone. They told us in school that Grand Coulee was one of the top twenty Soviet targets if a war came. We always wondered what the flood would be like as it went down the gorge. It would take out Wenatchee and Tri-Cities and maybe even Portland. All the other dams would go. Remember, Judith?"

"We used to wonder how big a bomb it would take to start it all," Judith said. "I used to wish someone would do it. Then things would be like they used to be."

"That would take an awful big bomb," Johnny said.

CHAPTER 18

Uncle Paul came to visit and admired Harry's produce stand. "When I was a kid, back in the Arkansas Valley," he said, "There was a place like this every few miles."

"I didn't have a lot of choice," Harry said, told Paul about his market problems on the coast.

"They all live in a loony bin over there," Paul said. "They just don't know it."

"I think a lot of them know it," Harry said. "They just want to be King Loony."

"You may be right. Which reminds me, Jack wants to see you. He knows you used to stop by my place when you were haulin' to the coast. He's been callin' me every other day."

"What's he up to, now?"

"I don't know, for sure, but he's about to pull up stakes and move to the coast."

"He'll fit right in," Harry said. "But what does he need from me?"

"I think it's about your Mom. I don't think they're plannin' to take her along."

"She's out of money. What would they want with her now?"

"I think you hit it," Paul said.

On Saturday morning, Harry loaded up the family for the trip to Ephrata. After he talked to Jack and Mom he planned to go over to Moses Lake for some early back-to-school shopping. They stopped by Electric City to say a quick 'hello' to Judith's parents and could not get away until Helen had cooked them a late breakfast.

Jack and Diane's oldest daughter, Tiffany, answered the door, did not recognize them at first. She led them into the livingroom and disappeared into the back. In a few minutes Jack came out, greeted them with artificial cordiality.

"You should have called," he said to Harry. "Diane's workin' at the Wak 'n Yak again on weekends."

"Paul said you wanted to see me."

Jack lowered his voice and glanced towards the back of the big doublewide trailer.

"It's Mom. We're movin' to Renton. I get my license back the first of the year and I've already got a broker who'll hire me. Shit, they're sellin five-hundred-thousand-dollar houses every day. I should be able to make better than a hundred a year."

"What about Mom?"

"Yeah, well, we can't take her with us. I haven't told her yet, but we can't afford to support her over there, and all she has is Social Security."

"Too bad she made such bad investments," Harry said.

"I know. Everybody blames me, but I lost a bundle, too. Life is full of risks."

"It's just a little harder for her to start over," Harry said.

"Well, you haven't had to put up with her like I have," Jack said. "I think she's losin' it." He tapped his temple.

"So when are you plannin' to tell her?"

"When I figure out what to do with her. She'll freak-out."

"How about this trailer? She could stay here."

"Already sold. I've got to have some cash to make this move."

"So you're just droppin' her on me, without tellin' either one of us."

"She's your mother, too," Jack said.

"Let's do it now," Harry said. "We've got to be goin'."

"I can't tell her today," Jack said. "I'm meetin' with some people later. Business."

"I'm not plannin' to come back down here."

"Well, then, it's your fault," Jack said.

"It always is," Harry said.

When Mom came out she looked like she'd been crying. She was surprised to see Harry and Judith and couldn't remember the kid's names. She finally sat gingerly on the end of the sofa.

"I didn't expect to see you," she said to Harry. "I haven't been feeling well."

"Jack wanted me to come down."

Mom looked fearfully at Jack. Jack looked away.

"He has something he wants to tell you," Harry said.

"I... I, we're movin' to the coast," Jack said.

"I know that. Do you think I don't hear what's goin' on."

"Well, we never talked about it. I don't see how you can go with us."

"I figured that. Since all my money is gone. "And Harry's money."

"We have to find a place for you," Jack said.

"You mean a nursing home or something," Mom said. "I was afraid of that."

"We'll find some place nice. Harry will help."

"There aren't any nice places for old people. Unless you're rich. I wish we still had the farm."

"You never liked it when we were there," Jack said.

"I didn't know."

"What do you want to do?" Harry asked her.

"I just want to be left alone. No one wants me."

"That isn't it," Harry said. "We just have a decision to make."

"I can't afford to pay rent. And food is so expensive. I wish I had a garden."

"Maybe we can find a place where you can have a garden," Harry said.

"How would I plow it?" she asked, nearly in tears.

"You need to come live with us," Judith said.

Harry stared at her. "We don't have room."

"We will make room. She is your mother." Her voice reminded Harry of Long Joe.

He thought for a moment. "I could build another cabin. We've got all that lumber drying."

He saw a flash of gratitude in Mom's eyes.

"I couldn't ask you to do that."

"It would improve the property. It won't cost much. But it can't be very big," he told her.

"I would be happy with anything. Beggars can't be choosers."

"We're moving in six weeks," Jack said.

"You can rent her something if I'm not finished by then," Harry said.

Everyone pitched-in on the little cabin. It was only sixteen feet by thirty but very tight and warm. They found used fixtures for a small kitchen and the bathroom.

A store in Wenatchee closed out some carpet and Harry bought a piece large enough for the whole floor. He had plenty of windows and doors.

The rough-pine walls still oozed resin in places and Harry finally covered them all with sheet-rock and taped and painted it. With Tamarack and Eric to help, it took only a few weeks to build the place. Judith and the other women had a great time decorating and furnishing.

A week before Jack and Diane were due to leave, Harry pulled his trailer down and loaded Mom's stuff. There probably was more than she could keep in her new home, but he could build a storage for her. She continued to complain about her health and Jack's desertion, but Harry could see that she was excited about the move.

By late summer the traffic at the stand was so heavy that they hired Wildrose to watch it during the middle of the day and on weekends. People drove from as far away as Wilbur and Republic for the fresh produce and many customers said they had been sent by someone else who'd stopped there.

Several customers asked about the row-cover and other material that Harry used to grow produce and he could see that if he stocked some he could sell it. The drip-tape had worked even better than he expected and he planned to convert all of the produce to drip irrigation. Even with less water he would be able to grow more than he had and pick up some areas where the slope had been wrong for ditch irrigation.

As fall came on and early frosts knocked down the tender crops Harry was well satisfied with his new approach. Although they had not made as much overall as they had the last couple of years, the money saved from the endless trips to the coast made up the difference. He had more time, less stress and the feeling that he was at the beginning of something.

Mom had settled-in and spent some time with Frances. She baked cookies for the kids and told them stories she remembered from her younger days. She complained less about her aches and pains and sometimes offered to help Judith with her housework. She kept the little cabin spotless and added a lot of her own pictures and keepsakes to the decor.

When the first snow came they had plenty of firewood, cut from the logging waste. The freezers and cellar were full; there was a huge stack of hay. Walt's granary bulged with oats and barley and some wheat Harry had saved to grind into flour. They butchered six hogs and two young steers and everyone had all the meat they could use.

Harry had planted many flats of greens that he kept in the greenhouse. He could see that once again they never could eat their stored food before next year's came on.

The hearing on John Carlson's subdivision was at seven o'clock on a snowy Tuesday night a week before Christmas. Walt and Frances rode with Harry and Judith. Wildrose stayed home and watched all the kids and Tamarack went with Eric and

Barbara. As they drove up the river, Eliot's Range Rover caught and passed them.

The hearing room nearly was empty. Other than their group there were John and Johnny Carlson, the lawyer from the Title Company, two men with maps and charts who appeared to be planners and a clerk ready to take notes. Eliot sat alone in the far back. John Carlson turned to acknowledge him but Eliot just nodded distantly. Just before time to begin a short man in an expensive suit hurried in, conferred with Carlson in low tones then went to say "hello" to the planners.

The County Commissioners came in, two men in business suits and one dressed like a rancher. They sat at the table on the low platform in the front. The clerk took a seat at a small desk nearby. The planners set up their maps and charts on easels near the head table and gave each person a stack of paperwork stapled together. One of the commissioners called the hearing to order and asked for the applicant to step forward.

The title company lawyer stood and moved to the front, told them he represented the applicant. He launched into a long harangue on the benefits of the subdivision to the County. It would bring new taxpayers and consumers to swell the economic base and schoolchildren with their allotment of State education money. He praised John Carlson's long and faithful residency in the County, how he'd raised a fine son even with the extra burden of a disabled wife. The commissioners nodded and smiled when he hit the high points.

The lawyer introduced the man in the expensive suit who proved to be a consultant from Spokane who had studied the proposed subdivision and found it to be far more than adequate, even excellent. It was well within State law guidelines, he assured them, and there really was no basis on which they could deny the application. He thanked them for their kind attention and resumed his seat beside Carlson, patted John on the knee and said something reassuring.

One of the planners followed. He uncovered a large, colorful map of the project and with his long wooden pointer showed how it all had been laid out with a network of roads and water piped to each lot from several large wells. He pointed out that the lots had been drawn to take advantage of the natural terrain. As far as Harry could see it was just a rectangular grid taking no notice of several steep slopes, the boggy area along the road, or the deep ravine on the far side that would be totally inaccessible in winter.

When the planner finished, the cowboy commissioner asked if there was anyone present who wanted to testify against the application. Harry, Judith, Tamarack, Eric and Walt all raised their hands. The commissioner reacted with mock-surprise then a wink at John Carlson.

"Well, you-all can decide who goes first. You appear to be organized."

Harry stood and the commissioner indicated a chair, set like a witness chair in a court, on one side of the raised table. Harry sat there, waited.

"Well?" the commissioner asked.

"I have several objections to the project," he began.

"One at a time, please," the commissioner said and drew a laugh from the consultant and the lawyer.

"My main objection," Harry said, "isall of the exceptions and variances I see listed in your hand-out. This type of project is outside the zoning of the area that requires minimum lots of twenty acres. And this would allow the road and utility work to be done some time in the future by some "Owners Association" to be formed later."

The commissioners whispered among themselves. Finally, the cowboy said, "We're aware of the details of the application, Mr....uh...Isaacson. Was there anything else?"

"I just think the project should be made to comply with State Law," Harry said.

"Okay, thank you, Mr. Isaacson," one of the suited commissioners said. "We understand you don't like the project. Next," he said and looked to the audience.

Harry started to say something more, stopped.

Walt came forward and talked about the valley, some of the history, how it always had been the home of cattlemen and small farmers. He said the project should be limited to twenty-acre parcels to lessen the impact on the community and the environment. They listened politely and thanked him for his participation.

Eric followed and spoke rather incoherently about how he'd always lived in the valley and they didn't need a bunch more people. The cowboy cut him short and made a comment about how late it was getting.

Tamarack had his figures and his copy of the State Law. He quickly proved that to meet State water requirements would require as many as twenty wells which was more than the concentration allowed by the Department of Ecology. He also had some case histories in which similar projects had been defeated. He was well organized and read appropriate quotes from the statutes.

When he finished, one suited commissioner said, "We are quite impressed at how you've done your homework, Mr. Tamarack."

The clerk giggled at the name.

"We'll take all of this into consideration," the cowboy said. "Is there anyone else?"

Judith came forward, took the chair. They waited for her to speak. When she did, Harry was reminded again of Long Joe.

"Thousands of years before the cattlemen and farmers my people lived in the San Poil Valley. We took from it only what it gave. In only a hundred years it has almost been destroyed. It is one of the few places left with any semblance of the natural balance. And although it is Mr. Carlson's private property it is on the reservation, nearly surrounded by tribal land. This kind of project is an insult and affront to my people. If we are all to get along, then we must respect each other."

There was silence as she returned to sit beside Harry.

"Anyone else?" the cowboy asked, waited for a moment, then, "With all this negative testimony, I think it is only fair that the applicant be given a chance to rebut."

The lawyer immediately stepped forward, stood before the map and looked at the audience then to the commissioners.

"Rebuttal is quite easy. First of all, in regard to the concerns about exceptions and variances, as we all know, it is quite common to have such exceptions and variances on such a project. As far as the allowability of five-acre subdivisions, I will remind you that you already have approved two such subdivisions in the San Poil Valley. As far as the utility work, it would place a great hardship on Mr. Carlson to be required to do the work before sale due to the expense of the improvements. Besides the Homeowners Association will be able to do the work the way they choose.

"As to the concerns about the amount of water available, no one knows until a well is drilled. Our consultant assures us that there is a major aquifer in the area which will be more than adequate."

The consultant nodded from his seat, gave the commissioners a smile.

"As far as roads go," the lawyer continued, "We don't know where people will want to build their houses." He paused. "As far as the more general concerns raised, most of them are quite outside the scope of the statute. We all wish the past would return, but the truth is, it won't. Progress is an inescapable fact."

He paused again, looked at Judith. "As to Mrs. Isaacson's comments, I find them to be racist and ill-informed. We are all one people now, Americans, and differences of race and custom are irrelevant." He turned to the commissioners. "In fact, you are not allowed to consider such material," he reminded them. He turned again to Judith. "This is not a matter of race. Even your people can buy lots there."

When he had finished, the cowboy commissioner said, "Well that concludes our hearing. I want to assure all of you that your testimony will be considered for what it's worth in our final deliberations. You will be notified of our decision within thirty days by letter. Copies of the determination will also be available in the clerk's office."

Christmas passed and in mid-January the letter came from the commissioners. The subdivision had been approved, of course. The one bright spot was that they had found, in researching the law, that they had to require a bond from the applicant to guarantee the completion of utility work. The planners had set the bond at two hundred thousand dollars. It had to be posted before sales could begin.

John Carlson drove in the next day. He was very drunk and loud.

"You assholes think this will stop me? You think I can't raise this much money? My credit's good. I'll be a millionaire when this is over. It won't stop me, but you've made an enemy, now. You'll all live to regret this." He staggered back to his pickup and drove away.

Harry heard from Eliot that John had trouble raising the bond, eventually had sold all his equipment and cattle and mortgaged the twenty acres with the house and barns. Finally, in March, several "For Sale" signs appeared along the highway and occasionally Harry saw vehicles stopped there and real estate men in suits showed the property to clients. Harry hoped they had bad luck.

Breakup came suddenly; the river rose and nearly reached the cabin. Chet Weston's cabin and his followers' trailer were flooded and they set up a ragged camp along the highway on the only dry ground they had. Mom cooked them food and said that Jenny Carlson had sent them clothes and blankets. Walt said it was hard to have much sympathy for people who built below the flood line then were surprised when the water came.

Soon after the water receded another trailer appeared at Westons', a nearly new doublewide which they set on a concrete foundation on the high ground by the highway. Harry noticed a new Chrysler often parked there. Nearby they started construction on a frame building perched high on stilts. Mom told Harry that it was a church and that the new residents were a preacher, named Bobby Baker, and his wife, Brenda, who'd come from Montana. While they built the church they held Sunday services under a crude canvas shelter. For a floor, they covered the fresh mud with truckloads of wood-chips.

Harry was surprised at how many people attended. There were several vehicles there he recognized, but many more that were unfamiliar. Mom said people came from Republic and Kettle Falls and even from the Okanogan Valley to hear Bobby Baker's message of a New Covenant which would bring redemption to the people. Each Sunday she dressed in her finest and asked Harry to drop her off and she stayed the whole day. She asked Judith to let her take the children but Judith would not agree.

The Presidential campaign was in full swing by the time Harry finished the early plowing. Bill Clinton, the Governor of Arkansas, had surprised everyone by winning the New Hampshire primary and appeared to be the front-runner among the Democrats. He spoke often of a New Covenant for all the people. Harry was happy, at first, that someone just a few years older than he was could be the next president, but his good sense told him that Clinton was like the fraternity boys and law-students who ran the student government at the University when he was there,self-serving and arrogant. In any case almost everyone thought that George Bush was unbeatable after the great victory in the Gulf War.

Both the old mare and Shadow dropped foals that spring. Harry built more corrals and another horse-shelter. With the yearlings and the new foals, every pen he and Walt had was in use. Walt had traded Harry four cows and a young bull in exchange for work and produce and the cows all had calved in February. As soon as the calves were big enough Harry put all the cattle out on the new eighty and rode out to check on them every day.

Mom wanted a garden of her own so Harry plowed a small plot near her cabin and showed her how to use the ground-cover and drip-tape. She had lost some weight and was more active than she had been in years. She took walks along the river or over the bridge to see Frances. Once in a while she would ask Harry to take her down to Ephrata to do some shopping. She thought less about the past and lived more in the present.

They opened the stand in April, sold seedlings and early greens from the greenhouse and herbs from Judith's collection. Harry asked Mom to tend the stand for a couple of hours a day and she soon was eager for the job. It allowed her more social contact and soon several local women would stop just to talk to her. One of the women who frequently came was Chet Weston's wife, which made Harry uneasy.

One day he saw a woman he didn't recognize there talking to Mom. She was blonde, appeared to be a few years older than he was and obviously had been very pretty. She sat on a chair where she could not be seen from the highway and she seemed nervous when Harry came around. He asked Mom about her later and she said it was Jenny Carlson, that she had walked over to buy some produce and stayed to talk.

Rebecca developed an interest in photography. Harry bought her a thirty-five millimeter camera with a zoom lens and she soon took pictures of everything and everyone. Mom finally complained to Harry that every time she looked up she saw that camera. Harry tried to convince her that it was an honor, but she said she didn't want to be on display like some zoo animal.

There were many jet fly-overs that summer. Each provoked a sudden emergency and once, as she helped Judith train one of the yearlings, Rebecca was dragged into the corral fence and came away with cuts and bruises. Little Joe hated the planes and talked about shooting one of them down.

Someone brought in a small dozer on one of the lots in John Carlson's hayfield. They dozed a ragged driveway and a rough pad for a house or trailer. A family came in a motorhome for a few days and they built a small enclosed shed and drove a lot of stakes into the ground to mark some future project.

Occasionally a strange vehicle would drive into the timber on the slope beyond the hayfield to stay for a day or two. There were strange people at the store and occasionally one would stop at the stand. One man told Harry that as many as twenty of the lots already had sold.

"At two thousand an acre people can't pass them up," the man said. "There's nothing for that price where I come from. Even without timber and mineral rights it's a screaming bargain."

Harry didn't tell him that the going price in the valley was about five hundred an acre with timber and mineral rights.

Another time a young couple stopped in, nice people from Bothell who always had wanted a place in the country. The man's name was Mark Grant and his wife was Johanna. Johanna loved Judith's weavings and said that she, too, wanted time to create. Mark said he wanted to learn to farm. Harry asked him which lot they'd bought and Mark described one high in the timber above the ravine. Harry said it might be hard to farm up there but Mark said Johanna always had wanted a place with big trees. There were some huge scattered Ponderosas there on the southwest slope.

Late in August there was news of a standoff between ATF and FBI agents and a survivalist named Randy Weaver in northern Idaho less than two hundred miles away. The media painted Weaver as a desperate and dangerous gun-toting crazy who made his living selling machine-guns. News trickled out, first that Weaver's fourteen-year-old son had been shot dead. Then came the word that his wife, Vicki, also had been killed, reportedly as she prepared to shoot an agent.

Rumors soon came as well. The Westons had friends in that area and Mrs. Weston told Mom that the Weaver's neighbors said that there was an army of Federal Agents lurking in the woods and that both the boy and his mother had been shot without provocation or warning. It was the beginning, she told Mom, of the final war, Armageddon. The government would come to kill everyone who disagreed with them. It was a global conspiracy.

Some of the established news people began to ask questions about the handling of the Weaver case especially when it was admitted that Vicki had died with her baby in her arms as she looked out her kitchen door. There were discrepancies, too, in the reports about the boy's death.

The Weston's reported that Randy Weaver already had agreed to surrender to the marshals when the assault on his cabin began and that in any case the charge against him was a minor firearms offense that usually would be handled with a written summons.

Everyone who came to the stand talked about the case. They all had encountered the authorities, particularly the drug task force, and knew that the routine was to lie to make the case regardless of the truth and to cover your ass when you made a mistake. The rumors were easy to believe.

Finally news came that Weaver had surrendered and the excitement waned as he waited for trial. The government continued to "leak" information about Weaver's supposed violence and Racism.

The Westons brought a stack of leaflets with the Weaver's side of the situation written by one of the neighbors. While some of it seemed a little far-out, most of it could have happened in the San Poil Valley at any time.

The boy who had been killed was only a year older than Rebecca and according to the rumors had just been out walking his dog when he stumbled into the agents stalking Randy Weaver. They had shot him in the back as he ran to warn his father.

"When I think about Vicki Weaver," Judith said to Harry, "I can only think how easily it could have been me. Or any of us."

CHAPTER 19

The first week in September the helicopter came. It was accompanied by the usual caravan of foot-soldiers anxious to flush out the deadly weed. They flew many passes over Harry's place, seemed to concentrate on the new eighty. There was a rumor of arrests a few miles East into the wilderness where two hippies had camped-out to make their fortune. Mrs. Weston told Mom that the helicopter had spent much of one afternoon carefully searching every inch of their place. She was insulted that they would be taken for pot-growers. Harry was not sure that was the case.

A week after the National Guard invasion Harry rode out to check the cattle on a young half-draft mare he had decided to train for himself. She was winded and sweaty from the climb up the ridge on the new eighty and Harry led her down to the spring for water and rest. He tied her to a sapling where she could reach a small pool of water.

While she cooled, he walked back to the top of the ridge and looked out over the slope. In the distance he could see the tops of the Kettle River Range peaks between him and the Canadian border. A solid blanket of timber stretched away to the northeast and he knew that there was almost unbroken wild land from his ridge to the North Pole. A grizzly might leave his lair in the Yukon Territory and end up here on this ridge.

The mare whinnied and he cut across to her through a thicket of tall buckbrush and wild rose above the spring where some large aspens made an almost unbroken canopy. He tripped, caught himself and looked down, saw a thin, taut twine tied between aspen saplings. The twine was new. He had a momentary fear, remembered booby traps in Viet Nam. He stepped forward carefully, suddenly hyper-aware.

He noticed that the path seemed well worn and he wondered if squatters had wandered in on the eighty. He crept forward silently, ducked low to avoid the tangle of brush. After a few feet he encountered another twine set at trip-height. Ahead of him there was deep green which clashed with the semi-arid tones around him.

He moved forward, took a branch of the alien green thing and saw that it was tansy, taller than his head. He'd never seen tansy here, and every rancher in the area watched constantly for the deadly plant. It looked almost like it had been intentionally planted here in a large circle. Something caught his eye and he pushed through the tansy and saw a large bed of a different plant. It took a moment to realize the truth. He remembered Jeff's project and he was sure. He didn't know they grew so large.

He took a branch and examined the swollen buds.

He began to count the marijuana plants and soon passed a hundred. There probably were twice that many. His heart pounded and he stood transfixed. He was amazed that the task force hadn't seen it. Maybe they didn't want to. Maybe it was a trap. He looked around, listened.

He knew he had to do something immediately. If he were found there, no one would believe that the plantation wasn't his. He would report it. Then he thought of his encounters with the law and lawmen and knew that would be dangerous. Even if they didn't prosecute him they could seize and confiscate the property.

What if he pulled the plants and burned them? But it wouldn't burn green, would take a week or more to dry. And the smell of that much burned at once! Maybe if he had something to burn with it. He thought of the waste at Eric's mill a few hundred feet down the slope. He could drag or pack some up with horses, but it would take a lot. A fire that big would be hard to control and any fire would bring the smokejumpers in within minutes. Fire wouldn't work.

He backed out, used the same path. He circled well around the bright green patch and went to the mare. She was restless and he led her away from the mud and mounted. He took one last look and could not believe it hadn't been seen from the helicopter.

Judith's first fear was that it had been seen and that the Task Force was waiting to see who knew it was there. They talked quietly in the kitchen, considered alternatives. They thought of pulling it up and dumping it somewhere off the property but someone might find where it had grown and anyone in the area would be subject to arrest if it were found.

It was evening when Harry realized that Jeff probably would know what to do. Judith agreed reluctantly and Harry left for the Kettle before dark. He felt surges of adrenaline as he drove and opened the window, let the wind blow in his face.

Jeff agreed to come and look the next morning. He laughed at Harry's paranoia. "If they didn't find it with the chopper, they ain't goin' to find it, now. I'll bring my truck."

Harry was sure Walt would wonder if an unknown truck came through his yard, but there was no other road access to that side of the eighty. Harry hated to tell him what was up. The next morning early he walked in and found Walt with the horses. He told him what he'd found.

"Just get it out of there," Walt said. "But as far as callin' the sheriff, I think that would just be askin' for trouble."

Jeff came about ten and they parked the former U-Haul behind Harry's horse-barn while they walked up to take a look.

"Professional lookin' job," Jeff said. "Somebody's gonna be pissed. Anyway, buddy, you're rich."

"What do you mean?" Harry asked him.

"Finders keepers," Jeff said. "This patch is probably worth a quarter of a million. I'll split it with you."

"Not me," Harry said. "I don't want to take the risk. I just want it to go away."

"What risk?" Jeff asked. "I'll have it out of there by dark. Just keep an eye out today and then you won't have to worry about it no more."

"How about what's left?" Harry asked. "Leaves and stuff."

"I need some bed-sheets," Jeff said. "Ask Judith if I can use about ten if she's got 'em. I'll wrap it up and carry it out like Christmas presents. We can clean-up the rest."

Judith gave Jeff ten freshly folded sheets and he told Harry to drive the truck in to Walt's upper corner at four o'clock.

When the time came Jeff waited for him, leaned on the gate with a grin as Harry turned the truck around.

"Clean as a whistle," Jeff said. "There'll be a few feeder roots that didn't come up when I pulled 'em, but it would take a botanist to find them."

"I'll go pull up the tansy and pile it down here to burn," Harry said "Tell anyone that's all it was."

"That'll do it," Jeff said. "Well, I better be on the road, get this in the dryer before it molds."

Harry helped him load the fragrant bundles. Each was all a man could carry. Jeff dropped Harry at the cabin.

"I'll be in touch," he said, still grinning.

Two days later Johnny Carlson stopped at the stand while Harry was there.

"You seen anybody back in on that eighty you bought?" Johnny asked him.

"No strangers," Harry said. "Why?"

"I thought I saw someone up there," Johnny said.

"What are you doin' up there," Harry said.

"Nothin'," Johnny said. "I just ride up there once in a while. It's open range. You never know when our cows might wander over there."

"I keep the fence tight," Harry said. He watched Johnny fidget.

"I found a bunch of tansy up on the ridge," Harry said, watched Johnny start a little. "Looked like some asshole planted it."

"What did you do with it?" Johnny asked him. "I mean, you couldn't leave it there, your cows might eat it."

"I pulled it all up and burned it," Harry said. "It made a hell of a fire. Stunk, too."

Johnny looked at him, started to say something, stopped. "Some of it looked funny," Harry said. "I don't know what it was."

"You figured it out, didn't you?" Johnny asked him.

"Figured what out?" Harry asked.

"That I did it," Johnny said.

"You mean planting the tansy?" Harry asked him.

"And the other. You're just playin' dumb. Did you really burn it?"

"I burned everything I found," Harry said.

"I could have got out of here, finally," Johnny said.

"There a big market for tansy?" Harry asked.

"You know what I'm talkin' about," Johnny said. "Eliot said he could sell it for over a thousand dollars a pound."

"So he's the one that put you up to it," Harry said.

"A lot of people grow for him," Johnny said. "I've seen your friend Jeff there."

"Well, anyone that does it on my property is going to have trouble," Harry said. "I don't want my property confiscated so someone can get rich."

"It was supposed to be our property," Johnny said. "I planned it last year."

"It isn't yours," Harry said, "And I'll be watching."

"Well, it don't matter, anyway," Johnny said. "We're gonna have more money than we need, now. There's only eighteen lots left to sell and they've got deals on four of those. Chet Weston has a lot of friends that are buyin' them up so they can move out here."

It was three weeks before they heard from Jeff. He stopped by the stand and walked out to where Harry picked tomatoes.

"You oughta hire someone to do this," Jeff said. "Now that you're a rich man."

"Still not interested," Harry said.

"You can buy a lot of tomatoes for a hundred and eleven thousand dollars," Jeff said.

"I don't know if they sell tomatoes in jail," Harry said.

"For a little more than that you can buy the jail," Jeff said.

"Well, count me out," Harry said.

"I'll be back," Jeff said. "After I make the run. We'll settle-up then."

"We're settled," Harry said.

"That kid of yours takes pictures of everything that moves around here," Jeff said.

"She get you?" Harry asked.

"I think so," Jeff said, "but I ducked behind my rig when I saw her. I'm a little camera-shy."

"I'll tell her," Harry laughed. "But someone has to save all this. For posterity."

"I don't think posterity will want a picture of my ugly mug," Jeff said. "I got real good at duckin' cameras in 'Nam. Didn't seem like nothin' I'd want a picture of."

Eric found a steady stream of small logging jobs. Most of his clients were people who had just moved to the area or someone who wanted to build a new house or barn. The horses at work, skidding logs or hauling-out lumber were a great attraction and everywhere Eric worked he had an almost constant audience. Some of his customers had hassles with the building-inspector over the unstamped lumber, despite its obvious high quality. He began to advise people not to get a permit. No permit, no inspector.

Tamarack often worked with Eric for a share. He had grown three acres of produce and also helped Harry and Walt. Not much money changed hands, but a natural barter system kept things in balance. Everyone made something that was sold at the stand. Frances had recruited Mom to help her put out cinnamon rolls and other baked-goods. Judith's weavings continued to sell quickly. Many customers wanted pictures of Judith and her weavings.

Nathan was drawn to the place and spent a lot of time visiting or helping someone. Judith said he should move there and build a cabin, which made Harry a little anxious although he would enjoy having him close. Nathan still seemed not to have a serious interest in women and Harry occasionally wondered if he just bided his time. He knew Judith would think it ridiculous.

Long Joe hadn't come for his usual spring visit and wasn't at the family picnic. Nathan said he had been hired for a year as a visiting professor at a small college in Arizona. They laughed about him wearing suits and driving a Volvo.

Johnny Carlson hadn't gone to Texas for the summer. Harry saw him now and then on horseback or racing by in his pickup. His mother came sometimes to talk with Mom and Harry noticed that it was only when John was away all day. The Westons gathered yet another follower and added another trailer. Walt said they must have found the Ugly Trailer Sales. On several weekends a large number of cars were parked there and there was a lot of shooting in the woods along the river.

When school started Rebecca complained about not having a telephone. Most of her friends lived near Republic and she had no way to talk to them. Harry called the Telephone Company and they wanted him to pay for the line from the highway to the cabin and it had to be buried eighteen inches underground.

Harry refused at first, but Judith convinced him that it was important for the kids to have what was considered a normal social life. When Mom heard about it, she, too, wanted a telephone and offered to pay for part of the cost. Harry plowed a trench as deep as Walt's ditcher would go and Tamarack and Eric helped him deepen it to the eighteen inches required. The telephone man brought the cable and hooked it up to a new switching-box he installed in a gray vault beside the highway. It seemed strange not to have to drive to the store to call someone.

Wildrose gave birth to another boy and they called him Aspen. Father Bryan was gone and another, older priest with a severe face christened the baby. He repeated the name twice to make sure he had it right.

The christening feasts at Harry and Judith's had become a tradition. It was fall and food was plentiful so they all competed to make the best dish. The men agreed they were tired of being bested by the women and made a special effort at exotic cuisine. Harry was glad that Judith and the women stuck to the basics.

Mom became very active with the Perot for President movement and had meetings attended by a scattering of people from the valley. She said a lot of people who went to Bobby Baker's church were for Perot, said he was a true patriot. Harry read some of the literature Mom gave him and saw Perot on television a few times. Some of his rant sounded good, but there were those disconcerting flashes of absolute lunacy.

To almost everyone's surprise, Bill Clinton was elected President. George Bush retired to Texas to manage his son's careers. It didn't appear to Harry that much would change. The rich would get richer and the poor, poorer.

Jeff drove in a few days before Christmas with Lisa and two of their kids. After they talked for a while, Jeff went out and came back with a large box that he barely got through the door.

He set it down in the livingroom and pulled out a gift-wrapped box and handed it to Little Joe.

"I bet you didn't know I'd signed on as Santa Claus," Jeff said, stroked his graying beard and gave a "ho, ho, ho."

Little Joe tore off the paper and held up a miniature bulldozer, a detailed replica of a big machine. There was a whole compliment of machinery and attachments to go with it. Jeff handed another package to Rebecca and she unwrapped a very nice video camera with a dozen blank tapes and a tripod. Harry stared at Jeff.

"I always saw her takin' pictures," Jeff said, shrugged.

Judith was next and found a wide array of yarn and thread, skeins and bundles and spools and balls. Harry saw silk and fine wool and a rainbow of smooth cotton. He could only guess at the cost.

"Lisa picked most of it out of some catalogs we got," Jeff said. "I always liked those weavings."

Harry's was last, a large, gaudily wrapped square box. He peeled back the paper and opened the flaps. Inside were several smaller boxes, also wrapped. In the first was a top-of-the-line cordless drill. Each of the others held tools, enough to stock a shop. Harry knew it was several thousand dollars worth.

"There's another one," Jeff said. "Under that last box."

Harry lifted the box and under it lay a cashier's check for ten thousand dollars.

"What's this?" Harry asked.

"Interest on that debt I owe you," Jeff said.

"No," Harry said. "I can't take it."

"For Christ sakes, buddy," Jeff said. "That ain't nothin'. It'll make me feel better."

Harry folded the check and put it in his shirt pocket.

Bill Clinton made his inaugural speech. The theme was "Forcing the spring." Harry thought it typified the culture. Don't wait for spring and be ready when it comes, make it come now. It didn't seem like a very plausible plan. Clinton also talked again about a New Covenant which no one could quite understand. Harry remembered Long Joe's opinion of white man's covenants.

The end of February Harry awakened early and turned on CNN. The major news was of a bloody gun-battle near Waco, Texas between ATF agents and a group of religious nonconformists, the Branch Davidians, who were led by a man who called himself David Koresh. Koresh had been shot as he stood at the door. Four Federal agents were dead and an unknown number of the 'extremists.' There were calls for the FBI to take over.

Days of negotiation dragged by. The Federal agents insisted that they only wanted a peaceful resolution. Rumors from both sides saturated the country. One side said the agents had assaulted the compound, called Mount Carmel, without warning. The other responded that Koresh had sex with girls as young as ten. His defenders called him a holy man and the messiah. The justice department said he was a monster and a manipulator.

The story became a part of the background with routine up-dates and live bulletins. The authorities continued to maintain that the Davidians were an aggressive and dangerous band of revolutionaries and that the government only wanted to protect the children. They turned off the water and power. Rumors began to flow, reports that the charges against Koresh were false, that the FBI used high-intensity loudspeakers to play the screams of rabbits being slaughtered all night long. Harry wondered if that was to help the children sleep.

Koresh appeared on television with some of the children. They were stressed, but appeared normal, and he seemed a loving father. His religious ideas sounded a lot like those Mom always prattled about. The FBI responded with a cordon of tanks and riflemen. Harry looked at the flimsy frame buildings, no sturdier than the peasants' huts he'd seen obliterated in Viet Nam.

Attorney General Janet Reno produced what she claimed was proof that the children inside were being abused. She used that as a pretext for an ultimatum. The day their time ran out, Harry could not leave the television. Before his eyes tanks growled and rolled towards the farmhouse. Riflemen lay hidden with automatic weapons, ready to save the children. An armored vehicle with a long protruding pipe approached a wall, punched through. There was sporadic gunfire from both sides. The cameras focused on smoke, then flames, and fire raged through the wooden structure.

Fire trucks never came. Later the FBI admitted they had refused permission to fight the fire because they thought it was too dangerous. While agents and newspeople stood and watched, the compound burned to the ground. The reporter kept asking, "where are the children, why don't they come out," but they never did. Harry thought of the children he knew who had died in the fire set by soldiers in Viet Nam. He thought of the San Poil children roasted alive. Some people have a strange way of saving children.

Spring, as usual, was hectic. Harry realized that if he took on anything more he would not keep up without more help. Little Joe loved to help with anything around the farm but he was in school until late in the day and every year school seemed to run longer into the summer. He offered to stay home and help, said he could do a week's schoolwork in a day. Harry worried about CPS.

Rebecca worked hard in school, hoped to go to college early on a special program. She spent hours videotaping and had some spectacular footage of animals in their natural state. The spring on the eighty drew a large variety of wildlife and she spent hours there stalking the perfect shot. She also loved the river and had captured it in all its aspects. She hoped to study film production.

The Westons and Bobby Baker started a school at the Church of the New Covenant. Mom tried to convince Harry and Judith to send their kids.

"It's so much closer than Republic. And they teach real family values, not this New World Order stuff."

Judith said that if she took her kids out of school she would teach them herself.

Mark and Johanna Grant appeared one day and said that they had decided to move onto their property. They had paid it off and had the money to build a cabin and to live on for years if necessary. They both had quit good jobs but were confident in their decision.

"I just want some peace," Johanna told Judith. "We made a lot of money over there, but we never had time to enjoy it. I didn't want to spend my whole life running from one thing to another. I just want to build a little cabin up there in those big trees and learn to do some of the things I've always wanted to do."

Judith reminded her that the timber rights still belonged to John Carlson, but Johanna said the Real Estate Broker had told them that the property probably would not be logged for years and even then only a few of the big trees would be cut and they never would be missed.

The Grants had bought a large travel trailer to live in while they built. They hired a mobile-home mover to deliver it for them but he refused to pull it up to their property because there was no real road. Mark asked Harry for help. Harry went with him to look over the situation and found a circuitous route that he thought his truck would handle. They spent most of one day with Tamarack's help moving the trailer up to the ridge and onto the five-acre tract the Grants had bought.

It was a nice place if you mostly wanted a view, but Harry asked Mark about water and Mark said they would haul water in to fill the trailer's tanks until the water system was built. Harry asked how long he thought that would be and Mark said the broker had told them it should be built some time later in the year. Harry didn't have the heart to tell him he thought it might never be done. He also couldn't bring himself to tell them that he thought they probably would have to walk in most of the winter even though they had bought a new four-wheel-drive pickup for their adventure.

Harry added an enclosed extension to the stand and they stocked more miscellaneous tools and supplies. There was a constant demand from locals and visitors, especially for the food. Frequently someone was low on money and wanted to trade. Harry could see that barter business would be worth developing.

Walt and Judith had put together another young team and trained it to sell. Judith also had more saddle horses than she needed and decided to sell a couple of them. Eliot wanted to buy the team but Judith refused to sell it to him, at first. Finally she relented but made him agree that she could come see them any time, make sure they were handled right.

Nathan brought a young gelding for Judith to train. He was big and strong and fast and Nathan wanted to ride him in the suicide race in a couple of years. Judith told him he was too old for such nonsense and he said maybe he would help one of his younger cousins who wanted to ride.

Frances Davis got sick again in early Summer and nothing Judith could do for her seemed to help. Walt wanted to take her to the doctor in Republic but she adamantly refused.

"They'd want to take me to Spokane, again. Then I would be sick."

Whenever anyone came to visit she was cheerful, but Harry could see the lines on her face grow deeper and knew she must suffer more than she let anyone know. Walt was distracted and unhappy, told Harry he didn't know what he would do without her.

Mom tried to get Frances to go to church so Bobby Baker could pray for her. "He's performed some real miracles, before," Mom said. "You should hear the stories I've heard." But Frances said she was past miracles.

Judith asked Dorothy to come and see Frances. Dorothy said she thought it was a combination of things. "What they used to call old-age." Her prognosis was not good.

Judith and Wildrose and Barbara took turns visiting Frances and doing the housework. They also made sure there was food in the house. Harry took on the work in the vegetable garden and told Walt to spend as much time as he could with Frances. Judith took care of the horses.

Harry heard chainsaws, looked up to locate them. Trees crashed down and he heard an engine start, saw a skidder move beyond Carlson's hayfield. Diesel belched from the stack as the huge wheeled machine dragged a bundle of logs out onto the field. More trees fell and he heard shouts from the fallers as they directed the skidder to the next drag. Soon gashes into the earth stood out like bright scars against the hillside. Great piles of limbs and branches marked where each tree had fallen.

Before noon the wide pile of logs at the edge of the hayfield was higher than a man's head. A long flatbed brought a tracked grapple loader. A rotation of trucks hauled tall loads of logs southward. The fallers worked their way up the slope, cut everything but the smallest saplings as they went. John Carlson's white pickup appeared several times. A second skidder joined the first and the flow of trucks increased. The way they were going the whole job wouldn't take more than three days.

The next morning Harry watched John Carlson's cat doze a road, a series of tight switchbacks, up and over the ridge and down into the ravine beyond for truck access to the back slope and the tall trees below. He could hear distant saws and skidders at work and every twenty minutes or so another full load of logs came over the ridge, worked it's way slowly down the switchbacks, out to the highway and headed down river.

The slope that faced Harry now was a jumble of slash and torn earth. Scattered saplings stood tilted this way and that, tufts of needles on top like tattered battle flags. Many of the saplings bore scars scraped by skidder wheels and they would die within a year. Bright buckbrush and sharp Oregon grape were the only live vegetation that remained.

Within a few days of the logging, Eric told Harry that he had heard in town that a group of John Carlson's buyers had filed suit against him, claiming fraud. Eric said he'd seen it before. People never could imagine how different their property would look after it was logged. And the timber deeds always allowed the timber-owner to do whatever was necessary to take out the logs. And in twenty years they would be back to cut any trees that survived.

Some of the buyers probably would stop paying payments when they saw how their property had been destroyed, but they would lose their down payments and John Carlson would foreclose and sell the lots again. Eric said he knew of lots on other subdivisions that had been sold five or six times that way.

Mark and Johanna Grant came by the stand. They obviously were in shock. Johanna told Judith that she had tried to stop the loggers from cutting her beautiful trees. Finally when just a few were left she had stood bravely in front of one and offered to buy it but the fallers just laughed at her. She said there were only a few small trees remaining. Judith told her to get some tree-heal and paint over any scrapes and scars or they would die anyway.

By fall the logged-over ground was a mass of half-dry pine slash. The brown needles hung limp and the smell of pine resin carried on the wind. Dying vine-maple leaves turned sickly pink and yellow in a travesty of fall color. A heavy rain began to wash the gouges where logs had been dragged into miniature gullies that would grow with each downpour.

Eliot said that most of the big Ponderosa logs and been trucked all the way to Portland and loaded on a Japanese freighter for export. The price was more than double what the local sawmills would pay and the Asian market was voracious for clear pine lumber.

CHAPTER 20

One day as Jenny Carlson talked to Mom at the stand, Harry noticed that she had a black eye and other bruises on her face. She turned quickly away when she saw him look and she left a short while later. Harry asked Mom about it, but she said she hadn't noticed. He told Judith and she said she would talk to Jenny the next time she came.

The stand had become a kind of community center and it was a rare time when someone wasn't there, drinking coffee or tea and talking. Harry put up a bulletin board and anyone who wanted to advertise a service or something to sell put up a card there. The women from Chet Weston's group spent a lot of time there. Harry figured it was a way to get away from the men.

The next time he saw Jenny Carlson walk along the road and turn into the stand, Harry went to the cabin and told Judith. She immediately went to the stand. Later Harry saw Jenny with her head down as though crying while Judith comforted her. He hoped John didn't drive by and see it.

Judith told him Jenny admitted that John had been hitting her. She had hoped that when he got all the money from the lots and the logs he would feel better, but she told Judith he only had gotten worse. Judith had told her she should leave, no one deserved to be treated that way, but Jenny said she was bound by her marriage covenant and besides, she had no place to go. She told Judith about the time, long ago, when she'd tried to leave and John had found her in Wenatchee and the judge committed her to Eastern State. She was afraid it would happen again. Harry told Judith he knew how Jenny felt.

Judith was afraid Jenny wouldn't come back to the stand, but just two days later she was there and asked Harry if Judith was around. He told Judith and she dropped what she was doing to go talk to Jenny. Afterwards she told Harry she thought that if they could find a place where she would be safe Jenny was ready to leave. Harry said that would only bring John's anger down on them, but Judith said they had to help.

Judith made some calls, talked to women's shelters in the Seattle area and in Bellingham. She said it was very important to get Jenny beyond John's reach. Several shelters said they would take her if they had room at the time. She talked to Jenny again and told Harry that all Jenny needed was an opportunity and someone to take her away. Harry refused, at first, but Judith insisted and he finally agreed to drive Jenny to the coast.

The next time John left on one of his trips to Spokane, Jenny came to the stand and told Judith she was ready. Judith went with her to help her pack what she wanted to take with her. When it was ready, Judith drove the truck to Carlson's and helped her load. When she came back, Jenny sat on the passenger side and tears ran down her face. Mom saw her and came out to see what was going on. When Judith told her, Mom's face went pale.

"Her husband will blame us."

"The law will blame him," Judith told her.

Judith gave Harry the address and telephone number of a shelter in Lynnwood and another in Bothell in case the first had no room. Before they could leave, Johnny Carlson came dashing in and ran to Harry's truck.

"What are you doin' with my mom?" he demanded.

"She wants to go somewhere," Harry told him.

"Does my dad know?" Johnny asked. "I know he doesn't. He'll kill her. And you. She's not supposed to go anywhere."

"That's her business," Harry said.

"No it isn't," Johnny said. "She's sick. In the head. My dad has to make her decisions. She's not competent."

He went around to her side, tried to open the door. Harry hit the electric lock.

Jenny was crying and Johnny tried to force open the door. Harry started the truck and began to move. Johnny became frantic, stood in front of the truck to stop him. Harry quickly backed up and turned, accelerated and left Johnny standing in the drive shouting at them.

Before they reached the Manila Creek turn-off, Johnny's pickup came up behind them then tried to pass. Harry moved into the middle of the highway to block him. Johnny was very close, right on his bumper, blew his horn and bumped Harry's truck.

"I can't go," Jenny said between sobs. "I'll just get everyone in trouble."

"I'm afraid we're all in trouble, anyway," Harry said.

"Please take me back," Jenny said. "I've changed my mind."

Harry wondered if he should go back, but didn't want to explain to Judith. He was afraid Jenny would tell John she'd been kidnapped or something to save herself. Johnny continued to follow just behind and blow his horn. If he called the police, Harry knew they would be caught before they reached Seattle. He decided to go back and talk to Judith.

He used the turn-off to make a U-turn and sped back to the stand, Johnny close behind. Judith came to the truck with fire in her eyes.

"She says she changed her mind," Harry said. "I can't take her against her will."

"Let me talk to her," Judith said.

Harry got out and Judith sat in the driver's seat, reached over to comfort Jenny. Johnny rushed up to Harry, tried to hit him and Harry held his arm.

"Dad'll kill her," Johnny said. "She's my mom."

"She's a person," Harry said. "She doesn't have to put up with him beating her."

"He just gets mad sometimes," Johnny said. "We're used to it. It don't mean nothin'."

"It's assault," Harry said. "He could go to jail for it."

"Not in this County," Johnny said. "They're all his friends."

Harry let go of Johnny's arm, pushed him away.

"I'll call the cops," Johnny said. "They'll stop you."

"Your mother can go anywhere she wants to," Harry said.

"You'll be sorry," Johnny said. He ran to his pickup and tore off towards home.

Judith called Harry over.

"I'm going to take her. She really does want to go, she's just afraid."

"I don't blame her," Harry said. "Johnny went to call the police."

"I need to go quickly," Judith said. "Would you bring me my bag?"

Harry got the bag and handed it in to her.

"Call me from somewhere. Be careful."

About half an hour after they left, a County Sheriff's car flew past on the highway with lights and siren on. Harry hoped that Judith had enough of a head start.

She called two hours later from Wenatchee, said they had not encountered any trouble. Harry told her about the Sheriff's car.

"He may run that County," Judith said, "But I don't think he has enough money to run the whole State."

"How's Jenny?" Harry asked her.

"Much better, now that we're away from there," Judith said. "She's been chattering like a magpie."

Soon after the call, Harry saw a Sheriff's car pull into the parking area at the stand and he walked over. It was Deputy John Miller and he glared at Harry as he approached.

"Can I help you?" Harry asked him.

"Have you seen Mrs. Carlson today," Deputy Miller asked.

"She was by here earlier," Harry said. "Why?"

"We have a report that she's in some kind of trouble," Deputy Miller said. "She's sick, you know." He lowered his voice. "She's a nut-case."

"I didn't know," Harry said. "She always seemed normal to me."

"We have information that you and your wife are involved in a conspiracy to help her escape," Deputy Miller said. "That could lead to serious charges, even kidnapping."

"I didn't know she was a prisoner," Harry said.

"Don't get smart," Deputy Miller said. "With your record you better be very careful." He fiddled with the butt of his gun. "Is your wife home?"

"No," Harry said. "She's on a business trip."

"What kind of business would that be?" Deputy Miller asked.

"Sorry," Harry said. "Proprietary information."

Deputy Miller frowned. "We need to talk to her."

"Sorry," Harry said. "Can't help you. I'll let her know when I see her."

"Well, I'll be back," Deputy Miller said and stalked to his car.

Judith called again from Lynnwood after she had dropped Jenny at the shelter.

"How's she doing?" Harry asked.

"She's confused and frightened," Judith said. "But she'll be okay. At least she's safe."

"Don't count on it," Harry said. He told Judith about Deputy Miller's visit.

"I warned them here that her husband was very dangerous," Judith said.

"I hope they understand," Harry said.

"I'm pretty tired," Judith said. "I think I better stay over and come back tomorrow. I'd like to see Jenny again before I leave."

"We're fine, here," Harry said. "Don't worry."

Some time after midnight Harry awakened to the sound of someone pounding on the cabin door. He pulled on his jeans and stuck his .380 automatic in the back pocket. When he opened the door, John Carlson tried to push his way in.

"Where is she?" he demanded.

"Who would that be?" Harry asked.

"You know who," John said. "Jenny. I know you helped her run away again."

"She's an adult," Harry said. "She can go where she wants."

"Not her," John said. "She's not right in the head. I'm her guardian."

"Well, she's not here," Harry said.

"I'll find her," John said, "And when I do, there'll be hell to pay."

John made a motion as if to grab Harry. Harry stepped back, drew the gun from his pocket.

"You're trespassing," he said to John

"You bastard," John said. "You'll regret this. I'm not someone you want for an enemy. Not in this County."

"I'm not your enemy, John."

"Well, I sure as hell don't need friends like you," Carlson said. "You will hear about this."

Harry heard John's pickup drive away and turn onto the highway at a high rate of speed.

Judith's trip home was uneventful. Deputy Miller came to take a statement from her. He was very polite and cautious. Harry knew they were trying to create some kind of case against them. Judith called Jenny at the shelter every day and reported that she sounded relieved but depressed.

"What can you expect," Judith said. "It's like someone coming out of a concentration camp."

A few days later, when Judith called for Jenny, the shelter told her that Jenny no longer was there, that she had gone back home. Judith was angry and asked the woman why they let that happen. The woman told her that they couldn't do anything because Jenny had been declared incompetent and her husband was her legal guardian.

Judith drove to Carlson's and tried to see Jenny. She said John had cursed at her for a while and threatened to shoot her. He told her he was going to file suit and take everything they had.

Little Joe begged them not to make him go to school that year. He promised that he would study hard and help with the farm work. Harry made some calls about home-school courses and found several he liked the sound of, but when they sent out information most of them were very religiously oriented and not strong on academics. He called the school district and they didn't like the idea, came up with all the reasons it wouldn't work. None of their reasons were very convincing and Harry knew the several thousand dollars they got for each student was their main incentive.

Finally he went on a trip to the coast and took Little Joe along. There was a home-school center near the University District and Harry was impressed with the wide range of assistance they could provide. They also knew the law and Harry discovered that the school district had to allow students to go part-time for any classes they wanted to take and that the authorities no longer could compel attendance.

He called Judith and she said that if he thought it was okay he should get whatever they needed and give home-school a try.

The man who ran the home-school center strongly recommended a computer and Harry spent several hours looking at the options at several computer stores. The systems they pitched ran into the thousands of dollars and each one assured him that their particular system was just what he needed.

Finally, out of frustration, he went into a small storefront shop in the Wallingford District that advertised used computer components. The guy who owned the shop was very knowledgeable and spent some time showing Harry various systems and components. Harry began to see that computers were no different from other machines and soon understood what he needed. The shop owner helped him assemble a good used system and select the best software for his purposes. The entire package was just over twelve hundred dollars and included an agreement to trade-up at the purchase price. Harry was happy and Little Joe was excited.

They bought several workbooks and textbooks at the University Book Store and found some more software. By the time they had everything they needed it was late evening and Harry decided they should stay over and go home the next day. Harry got them a room on the Eastside so they could avoid the commuter traffic in the morning and they ate dinner at Pagliacci. Little Joe seemed very relieved.

A flier appeared on Harry's bulletin board announcing the formation of "The San Poil Militia." It was a roughly written call to arms with references to the Randy Weaver case and the fiery debacle in Waco. A meeting was to be held at The Church of the New Covenant on a Saturday in late September. At first Harry thought it was ridiculous, but finally decided that he would go just so he would know what was happening.

There was a large crowd by local standards, mostly men, some dressed in fatigues and carrying weapons. Many of them seemed already to know each other. Eric was there and Johnny Carlson and a number of people Harry recognized from the stand. They all milled around outside until finally Chet Weston went around to tell everyone that it was time to start.

Bobby Baker spoke first, said a brief prayer and welcomed everyone. He quoted the Book of Revelations concerning the last days and the trials and tribulations to be visited on the Elect. He assured them that the good people there in his church were exactly who Saint John had seen in his visions as the righteous who would live at the end of days. He said that America was under assault from without and within and that it was up to the true Christians to defend her, even unto death. God's covenant, he said, promised everlasting life to the faithful.

Chet Weston followed the preacher. His message was full of thinly veiled racism although several times he made it clear that he did not include the Native People in his list of the dark forces that threatened civilization. Harry looked around at the number of Colville's and mixed-race people and could understand why he made the exception.

Drugs, Weston said, were a tool of the devil sent to seduce the children away from the true path of salvation. One of the great tasks of a militia was to find and destroy drugs and the minions of the devil who trafficked in them. The Federal Government was in league with the international drug cartels and could no longer be trusted to deal with the problem. The people must rise up and take back the power.

He took his seat on the platform to a rousing round of applause. Harry looked around and noticed Eliot standing in the back of the church in sunglasses and a military-style hat. All the seats were full and not much standing room remained.

An NRA man spoke next about the right to bear arms and the plans the government had to confiscate all guns. A chorus of boos greeted this information. He told them membership applications would be available after the meeting.

A "Colonel" from a militia in Montana spoke briefly, assured them all that not only was a militia legal, it was specifically required by the constitution. It was the Federal military that was illegal and violated the constitution. He was followed by a "General" from Colorado who talked about the necessity of communication and coordination on a national scale. When the great final war came, all the true patriots must do battle for the glory of God.

Weston returned and asked for a voice vote on a resolution to form the San Poil Militia. There was a loud shout of yes. No one dared vote no. Weston quickly was elected commander by the same process and he then appointed several of his friends to staff posts such as Director of Communications and Intelligence, Weapons Acquisition and Security Chief. He then announced another meeting to be held in two weeks.

Weston started to leave the microphone, then returned. "Oh, by the way, our good friend John Carlson has a nice subdivision just down the road with five-acre lots available for real good prices. Any of you from other areas who would like to come share our life here in God's Valley can contact Jim White who is here with us today or call his office in Republic."

As the meeting broke up a long line formed at the card-table where the NRA man helped people fill out applications. Harry saw a group of people surround Jim White to look at a map of John Carlson's subdivision.

Two white and black Sheriff's cars sped along the highway, lights flashing, and turned in at Carlson's. In a short while an ambulance followed. About an hour later all three vehicles left together, drove slowly upriver towards Republic. Harry had a sick feeling in the pit of his stomach. He walked to the cabin and told Judith what he'd seen.

"He killed her," Judith said. "She knew he would."

"It's something bad," Harry said. "I can feel it."

"He'll get away with it, too," Judith said. "He has too many friends."

"You mean his money has too many friends," Harry said.

Mom heard the news first when someone stopped at the stand to tell her. She sent Little Joe to get Harry.

"Jenny Carlson committed suicide," she said as soon as Harry was within earshot. "I knew you should have left her alone."

"How do you know that John didn't kill her?"

"He wouldn't do that. He's a Christian man."

"So beating on her was a good Christian act, I suppose."

"Well, your wife needs to learn to stay out of other people's business."

"Like when she invited you to come live with us?" Harry asked her.

"That was different. We're family."

"Jenny doesn't have a family," Harry said. "Now she doesn't have anyone."

"Well, I feel sorry for John. I'm going to make him a casserole or something. Everyone at the church will want to help."

"I think they need to investigate," Harry said.

"They already did. The Sheriff already announced that it was a self-inflicted gunshot."

"How do you know that already?" Harry asked her.

"Brenda Baker was in Republic. Everyone was talking about it."

John had the funeral at The Church of the New Covenant just four days after Jenny's death. Everyone in the valley was invited except for Harry and Judith and their friends.

Mom asked Judith if she could use her oven to bake some bread while she made a casserole in her own. There was to be a big potluck at the church after the funeral.

"John wanted me to tell you not to come," Mom said to Harry. "He blames you for Jenny's problems. I told him I would give you the message."

"It sounds like you and John are getting pretty friendly."

"What do you mean by that?" Mom asked him.

Harry didn't go to another militia meeting, but Eric continued to go and reported to him. Over a hundred people had signed up for the militia and the women's auxiliary group. They held maneuvers in the woods across the river from Westons' on tribal land. None of the Indians had joined and Eric said that they now made it clear their racist views included the Native People whom many of the militiamen referred to as "Red Niggers."

Eric said they had a lot of illegal weapons, fully automatic rifles and even some machine guns. He'd heard some of them talk about small mortars and recoilless rifles but he never had seen those. Someone had given them a lot of money. Eric thought it was John Carlson and maybe Eliot. Johnny Carlson had made a trip to Texas with several of them and they had come back with more weapons.

Several of the new members already had bought lots on Carlson's subdivision and they had organized a letter-writing campaign to bring more people of like mind to the valley.

Eric brought Harry some of their literature. It told of a great global conspiracy, centuries old, which involved groups such as the Illuminati and the Freemasons and included the Council on Foreign Relations and the Trilateral Commission. Many members of congress belonged as well as administration members and corporate heavyweights. They traced Bill Clinton's career as a conspirator from his Fullbright Fellowship to his current CFR membership. It was the Devil's Covenant at work in the minds of men.

Harry found some of their message hard to argue against. Everywhere the strong exploit the weak, justice is for sale and truth is hidden beneath a mountain of lies. Surely the corporations and the government have joined forces to enslave the people. Obviously the rich and powerful live lives far removed from the struggles of everyday people, a gap larger than that between Lords and Serfs in the dark ages.

But Harry remembered the old man saying that the best conspiracies are the unspoken conspiracies driven by self-interest and greed. There need not be secret meetings and clandestine operations. All that is necessary is that those with power work together to perpetuate that power. All concentrations of power are conspiracies, all elites criminal cartels.

"Don't let them fool you, Harry," the old man had said, "Rich men don't sit in the Country Club figurin' out ways to share their money."

Long Joe came to visit just before Christmas. He had gifts for everyone and the kids kept him up most of the first night he was there. Little Joe showed him how to use the computer and Long Joe became very absorbed in it. He told Harry he had decided to write a book, but was no good with a typewriter and no one could read his handwriting. A computer might be just the thing. Harry told him about the notebook-size machines he'd seen and gave Long Joe a card for the used computer place.

The next morning when Harry got up to feed the stock, Long Joe already sat at the kitchen table with several folders of handwritten notes spread out. He grinned at Harry.

"The author at work."

When Harry returned to the cabin he made coffee and sat down across from Long Joe. "Life seems to be treating you okay."

"Maybe it is that I am treating life better," Long Joe said. He told Harry he had several offers for stints as Visiting Professor as well as a national lecture tour if he wanted it. He said it felt very strange to be honored and sought after for saying the same things that had led to his commitment to Western State twenty years earlier.

"I haven't changed. Except that I don't go hungry for lack of money any more. And now I have to worry about taxes."

Harry laughed. "Maybe the Republicans will pass a big tax-cut. Newt Gingrich says that's what we all need."

"White people are great thinkers," Long Joe said. "They spend twenty years living it up on the National Deficit Credit Card, then when the bill comes due they all want lower taxes."

"It's a strange world, Long Joe," Harry said. "The same people who ran around saying 'America, Love it or Leave it' during the Viet Nam War now are buying weapons to fight the government. It seems to me that if there is a conspiracy that's been going on for two hundred years, then it was the force behind the war, too."

"The common thread," Long Joe said, "Is the fighting. A lot of people, especially idle men, look for any reason to fight. If no enemy presents himself, they will pick one. The problem, in a sense, is the same one we had before the whites came. There is not enough to do. It no longer requires everyone's work for survival. And it will require fewer people all the time. There have to be other things for people to do, things that are valued and regarded even though they may not add more money to the pot. They say Reagan won the Cold War, yet within a few years of this great victory, the government he headed has become the replacement enemy for many of the people who supported him. If there are no Communists then there must be global conspiracies or drug lords or atheists to hate."

"Wise people always have known that the energies of men, especially young men, must be channeled and guided. The urge to fight and protect easily becomes mindless killing and hatred. I have read things from Ancient Greece, from Rome, from the Middle Ages, from anthropologists who study primitive cultures and all of them struggled with the problem of male energy. In this culture we deny that it exists."

"Newt Gingrich says that through social evolution we have become the greatest Nation the World has ever known," Harry said. "We are the very apex of civilization."

"I believe in evolution," Long Joe said. "There is a Spirit that evolves through us, through everything, the trees and rocks and rivers. Your scientists dream about imaginary structures called 'genes' which they admit are not real. These genes, they say, are made up of even smaller particles called atoms and even smaller particles called electrons and protons and gluons and putons. All of which, they say are not really real because the stuff turns out to be as much energy as matter. I call that substance 'Spirit.' And I see it evolve through us, leaving us each a dry, withered husk to be plowed again into the soil. But I cannot believe that it is all a 'glorious accident.' That is a nonsensical idea. What is an accident? Something you can't predict ahead of time or understand the cause for. So we can't predict our own beginning or end. That's news! Neither does a rat predict the spring of the trap."

"But it's science," Harry said. "How can you argue with science? If a scientist says it, it must be true. After all, they have replaced God."

"Now you're just trying to provoke me," Long Joe said. "Good scientists are at least trying to see. Most of the white culture tries very hard not to see. Your anthropologists almost understand. They are able to trace the path of the Great Spirit through the physical remains. Their mistake is that most of them believe that is all there is. But to study the physical remains is to study the dry and broken chrysalis after the butterfly has flown.

"All these wonderful discoveries, that we are not conscious of much that we do, that language is usually a way to excuse something, that young men tend to be violent, that old men and women are wiser than young ones. The surprise is that there was a race that did not know these things. All the primitive cultures know them. That is why they go to great pains to make their people conscious, to help them see through the mask of language, to channel young men's energies, to honor and heed the elders. Most 'new knowledge' is something we threw away a few generations ago, then when we stumble upon it again we congratulate ourselves on our 'discovery.'"

"If you were so damned smart, why weren't you rich?" Harry asked with a grin.

"Oh, we were rich," Long Joe said. "No white man ever saw this 'New World' as it was before the white man came. Your disasters, the diseases and dislocations, ran ahead of you like the bow wave on a canoe, an effect that precedes its cause. But we were rich in a truly human sense. From the time we were really awake, after the dark times, my people tried to see through the mask, to the animal within, then created human institutions which cancelled the bad and strengthened the good.

"If one human problem is greed and another is lust for status then surely it does not make sense to confer higher status on the more greedy as the white culture does. That way each problem reinforces the other. My people worked one problem against the other. It was simple, grant high status to those who give-away. Greed will be balanced by the desire for status. What a neat trick. But it can only be done by people who see through the mask."

"But if you see through the mask," Harry said, "Then you have to admit problems, maybe we aren't the greatest civilization the universe has ever known. What will our children think of us, then?"

"They will think that you have grown up, become elders," Long Joe said. "Only the immature allow things to just happen to them, are surprised by each new day. Now your wise men say that we cannot escape our animal beginnings. Some of us knew that long ago. There are stages in any recovery. The white culture is still in the phase they themselves have labeled 'denial.' I call that the 'baby' phase. Many of the Earth's peoples long ago found ways to deal with those shadows of the past. You balance greed against status and call it 'potlatch,' or you allow them to run rampant hand-in-hand and call it 'capitalism'. War can be a game of courage and daring, or it can be genocidal slaughter. Mating can be love or rape. Is there any doubt which way is better for the people and the planet? Of course there is always greed and power and war and lust. That is the challenge. If you ignore them, they become the monsters outside your door or under your bed. We brought them alive in masks and dance and stories. We feared them and made fun of them and conquered them in lonely visions. And we loved each other more in our struggle."

"You need to write that book, Long Joe," Harry said.

CHAPTER 21

A clear January morning followed two days of light snow. The valley was still but for the soft sounds of the livestock at their morning feed and the distant yelp of a coyote. Smoke drifted from the cabin chimney and steam pulsed from the nostrils of the horses as they chewed. Harry admired the massive muscles on the big team that had been Walt's. Hooves the size of dinner plates left giant tracks in the fresh snow.

Reject licked Harry's hand and the warm tongue startled him. The dog looked towards the bridge, drew his attention there. He saw Walt walk slowly towards him, his own dog by his side. As they neared, the dog ran to greet Reject and the two of them frolicked in the unmarked snowfall. Harry noticed that Walt's face was wet as though he cried and his eyes were bright as he looked up.

"Frances is gone," Walt said in a hoarse whisper. "Before dawn this morning she woke me to say goodbye." Fresh tears trickled down his face and he wiped at them impatiently. "We both knew her time was soon, but..." He shrugged.

Harry put his arm around Walt's shoulders and felt his own tears spring. "I'm sorry. We all loved her."

"She knew you did. She was so happy when you moved here. She said that God sent you so she could be a real grandma before she passed on." His breathing was labored. "I knew it would be hard," he said, "But I guess you just never realize..."

"What can we do for you?" Harry asked him.

"Just put up with an old man's sorrow," Walt said.

"It's everyone's sorrow. Can I call someone for you? The funeral home?"

"No. We talked about it. We agreed that whoever went first would bury the other right here on the place. It's where we belong. We never wanted to leave here."

"I'll help any way I can."

"Thanks. I may take you up on that. Is Joseph still here? I wanted to talk to him. He will know what to do."

"He's still here. Come in the cabin and we'll talk to him."

As they entered, Long Joe sat in his usual place on the floor near the woodstove. He looked up at Walt.

"I am sorry," he said. "The wheel turns."

Walt took a deep breath, steadied himself against the kitchen table.

"Joseph, I would like for you to do a ceremony, if you would. Frances always loved your people, wished she were one of you."

"She was," Long Joe said. "I would be honored to perform her ceremony."

Judith overheard from her place at the loom, came in and put her hand on Walt's shoulder.

"Frances was my other mother."

Rebecca came from her room where she was getting ready for school, immediately sensed something big had happened.

"Frances?" she asked.

Judith nodded and Harry saw that tears flowed from her eyes as well. He remembered Long Joe saying long before that tears were an offering for the dead.

"I'll tell my Joseph," Judith said and went towards the ladder to Little Joe's room.

"Could I borrow your telephone, Harry," Walt asked. "I should call Franklin, and his sister."

"Of course," Harry said.

While Walt made the calls, Judith made coffee and put water on for tea. When Walt hung up the phone, she smiled at him.

"Sit for a little while. Then I will go with you and help dress her."

Walt nodded and sat at the table, silently took the tea Judith offered. They sat quietly and Harry knew that they all thought of Frances, remembered her many kindnesses, her smile they would see no more. He felt sad but with a kind of excitement, an awe at the nearness of the great mystery. He remembered Long Joe saying death was just a change of status.

"Franklin is set on a regular funeral," Walt said.

"That is your choice," Judith said.

"He was pretty agitated when I told him what I was plannin' to do," Walt said. "Said he didn't want his mother buried like some savage."

"If being buried on the place she loved was what Frances wanted then I think that's what you should do," Judith said.

"I may need some help, Harry," Walt said, "digging a place."

"Whenever you need me," Harry said.

The place Walt and Frances had chosen was on a little rise overlooking the river. Walt had a miner's auger drill that he used to pierce the frozen soil down to about four feet. He dropped in a small dynamite charge and set it off. There was a dull thud and the earth shook and small cracks appeared where they had scraped off the snow.

"It's the same way Duke does it up at the Republic cemetery," Walt said. "I used to fill in when he couldn't get to it."

Harry used a pry-bar to lift out the large chunks down to the frost line and shoveled out the loose soil below. Walt offered to spell him, but Harry's body enjoyed the exercise. He told Walt to go to the house and help Judith. The grave was about eight feet long and half as wide and Harry dug until the surface was well over his head.

By evening everything was ready. Walt and Long Joe decided to have the ceremony early the next morning. Walt ate dinner with them, although he didn't eat much and was mostly silent. They all respectfully gave him his space. Harry was proud of Little Joe and Rebecca who did not forget the solemnity of the time but also were at ease with Walt.

After dinner there was a telephone call for Walt. Harry heard him say repeatedly, "It was what your mother wanted and what I want." It appeared that he was not getting through.

The gathering was small. Tamarack and Wildrose came with their boys; Eric and Barbara brought their daughter. Judith had reached Nathan and he drove over from Nespelem and brought Dorothy, the midwife, and Judith's grandmother, Hattie. Mom came at Harry's insistence but grumbled that they should have a normal Christian funeral at The Church of the New Covenant.

Frances was laid on the kitchen table on one of her handmade quilts. Judith had fixed her hair and used a little makeup. She had found some silk flowers that lay like a wreath around Frances' head. Her gingham dress and flowered apron were just as they all had known her as she bustled about the kitchen. Her face was relaxed, almost smiled at them.

Long Joe lit a smudge of sage and passed it over the body and addressed the four directions. Walt wept quietly while Long Joe spoke. He told of the valley, of the people who had lived there and loved it. He talked of the farmers who came, the McTavishes and Davises, who fed the people and loved the soil. He spoke of friendship and neighbors and continuity. He reminded the children that each of them carried a part of Frances with them and a duty to remember. He described the great circle of birth and life and death and beyond, the web of spirit that connects all existence.

Harry thought of the last Remembrance Day he'd gone to in Kansas, how the old man had held his hand and told him that remembrance was for the living, not the dead. He took Little Joe's hand in his and smiled down at him.

When he had finished, Long Joe asked each of them to say something. The comments ranged from Judith's eloquent remembrance of all she had learned from Frances to Cottonwood's tearful "I loved Grandma Frances very much."

When everyone had spoken they sat for a while in silence. Sage smoke permeated the room. At last Long Joe nodded to Harry and he rose with Judith to wrap Frances in her quilt covered by a soft piece of white canvas. Judith tied the bundle with a long braided cord made of green and red and blue cotton. When they had finished Nathan and Tamarack and Eric joined Harry. Each took a corner of the shroud and with their arms underneath carried Frances gently to the grave Harry had dug. The others followed.

They lowered her into the Earth with two ropes looped underneath her and again they all were silent.

Long Joe picked up a handful of the soft soil and placed it in Walt's hand. Walt hesitated, then poured it slowly into the grave and the sound of it striking the canvas carried a finality that took Harry's breath away. Next Long Joe sprinkled a handful and indicated to the others that they should do the same. When they all had done their part Long Joe led them back to the house, left Harry and Nathan to fill the grave.

Everyone stayed for most of the day at Harry and Judith's. Not long after noon the telephone rang and Judith answered. Her eyes met Harry's as she talked and he knew there was a problem. When she finished she unobtrusively signaled Harry and went outside, he followed.

"That was the Funeral Home in Republic. They wanted Walt. I told them he wasn't here. They said Franklin had called them and said they should pick up his mother's body. I said I didn't know anything about it. They said they would talk to the sheriff if they didn't hear from Walt."

"I'll talk to him."

He found Walt with the horses, talking softly to them. Harry went over and put his arm around Walt's shoulders.

"Judith just got a call from the funeral home. They said Franklin called them."

"I don't need no funeral home," Walt said.

"They said they would call the sheriff if they didn't hear back from you."

"I guess they won't leave us alone even after we're dead. I'll call them tomorrow morning. I'd like to have one day of peace."

Two Sheriff's cars appeared while Harry did his morning chores. Deputy John Miller got out of one car and two other deputies came from the other. Miller swaggered up to Harry and took his usual wide-legged stance.

"Seems like every time we get a call down here you're involved."

"Seems like every call you get down here turns into nothing," Harry said.

"We'll get something on you sooner or later," Deputy Miller said. His compatriots came up close behind him for backup.

"So what do you imagine I did this time?" Harry asked.

"I wouldn't take that attitude if I were you," the taller of the two backup deputies said. "Disposing of human bodies is a serious offense."

"Brady, you stay with this one," Deputy Miller said. "Wilson and I'll go get the old man. If his wife shows herself, detain her. Our information is that she was involved. The old Indian, too."

Harry moved to continue his chores.

"Just stay right here," Deputy Brady said.

"Am I under arrest?"

"Not at this time," Deputy Brady said, "Just detention for questioning."

"Then I'll finish feeding while you think up some questions."

Deputy Brady followed closely while Harry threw hay to the horses and other stock. Harry took the sloppiest, most manure-filled routes. Deputy Brady tried to tiptoe behind him in his shiny cowboy boots, nearly fell and caught himself against the rail fence. Harry struggled not to laugh.

In a few minutes the other two deputies returned with Walt between them. Walt looked angry. He came over to Harry and turned on the deputies.

"This is none of your business. Frances is buried where she always wanted to be. And I'll be buried right beside her."

"That isn't legal," Deputy Miller said, "Unless you have a cemetery permit. And secretly burying someone raises questions about how they died. It isn't normal."

"The way you're acting isn't normal," Walt said. "What if it was your wife or mother?"

"Then I'd expect to have them buried in a civilized Christian manner," Deputy Miller said. "And I wouldn't be afraid of having someone else see the body."

"Everyone here saw her body," Walt said. "Nobody hid anything."

"It sounds very suspicious to me," Deputy Wilson said. "Were you and your wife having trouble?" He looked at Deputy Miller. "Do you know of any domestic violence calls down here?"

"I don't remember any," Deputy Miller said, "But they are way out in the woods."

"The only domestic violence problems down here were over at John Carlson's," Harry said. "Until he killed her."

Deputy Miller spun around. "What do you mean killed her? That was ruled a suicide."

"No one around here believes that," Harry said.

"Well, if you know something and haven't made a report you could be arrested for that," Deputy Brady said. "You can't just throw accusations like that around."

"Seems to me that's what you're doin'," Walt said.

"You better watch your mouth, old man," Deputy Wilson said. "You're under suspicion of murder."

Harry saw Deputy Miller shoot Deputy Wilson a look of disapproval.

Long Joe appeared from behind the barn and approached them. Harry wondered how long he'd watched.

"Can I be of assistance?" Long Joe asked.

The deputies looked at each other and John Miller nodded. "Who would you be?" Deputy Brady asked Long Joe.

"Just myself," Long Joe answered.

"Your name!" Deputy Wilson snapped.

Long Joe looked at them steadily until one by one they averted their eyes.

"I am Joseph."

"Joseph who?" Deputy Wilson asked, pulled out an aluminum-covered note-pad.

Long Joe looked at them each again, finally addressed Deputy Wilson.

"Joseph, Little Eagle," he said. Deputy Wilson wrote down something.

"Where do you live?" he asked Long Joe.

"Oh, I'm alive wherever I am," Long Joe answered.

"Place of residence," Deputy Miller said.

"For now, here," Long Joe said. "Tomorrow, who knows?"

"If you don't straighten out your attitude, we may provide your residence tomorrow," Deputy Wilson said.

"Are you threatening me?" Long Joe asked.

Deputy Wilson frowned. Deputy Miller stepped in.

"We are conducting an investigation concerning the disappearance of Frances Davis," Deputy Miller said.

"No mystery," Long Joe said. "She died."

"Her body is missing," Deputy Miller said.

"Wrong again," Long Joe said. "She was buried by her family and friends."

"What cemetery was she buried in?" Deputy Wilson asked.

"A traditional Native burial ground," Long Joe said. "She was one of my people."

The deputies all looked at each other in surprise.

"Looks like you're outside your jurisdiction again," Harry said. "Maybe you should turn it over to the tribal police."

Deputy Miller glared at him. Deputy Wilson started to say something, stopped himself.

"We still are in the traditional mourning period," Long Joe said. "We prefer not to be disturbed."

Deputy Wilson no longer could restrain himself. "You fuckin' Indians always pull this shit," he said angrily. "It's time we did away with this reservation bullshit. You're just one more group with special privileges."

"You've bothered us long enough," Harry said.

The deputies looked at each other. None of them wanted to speak next. Deputy Wilson turned and went to his car, made sure they could see he was on the radio. Deputy Miller shifted his weight from one foot to the other and back, seemed to be furiously trying to think of something to say. Deputy Brady followed Deputy Wilson and sat on the car seat with his door open and glared at them.

Deputy Wilson signaled to Deputy Miller and he walked over to stand by the car and the two of them talked in low tones. Harry and Long Joe moved towards the cabin.

"Don't take off anywhere just yet," Deputy Miller called to them, "We're not through with you."

Walt waved as if to dismiss them and followed Harry and Long Joe.

"Thank you, Joseph," he said in a low voice.

"I am just helping them find the truth," Long Joe said.

As they reached the cabin, Harry heard the Sheriff's cars start and back, one after the other, towards the highway.

Just before dark Deputy Miller returned. He came to the cabin door with a sheaf of papers. Reject barked at his heels. Harry opened the door and Deputy Miller handed him a several page document headed, "Emergency Injunction and Restraining Order."

"Where could I find Walter Davis?" Deputy Miller asked.

"At his place, I guess," Harry said.

Deputy Miller looked at the snow-covered road across the bridge.

"Can I drive in there?"

"I wouldn't," Harry said.

"Would you give this to him?" Deputy Miller asked, held out another of the documents.

"Don't know when I'll be seeing him," Harry said.

"Well, shit," Deputy Miller said.

He went back to his car, locked and tested the doors, shot Harry a mean look and headed for Walt's, waded the foot-deep snow in his precarious boots. When he had crossed the bridge and disappeared into the trees, Harry followed him.

When Harry came out of the trees close to Walt's corrals he could see Deputy Miller approach Walt near the barn. As he drew closer he could see that Walt was very upset.

"You won't get away with this," Walt said loudly.

Deputy Miller said something Harry couldn't hear. "I don't care if a judge did sign it," Walt said.

Deputy Miller saw Harry. "I thought you weren't comin' over here."

"Changed my mind. I forgot I needed to see Walt."

Walt looked at Harry. "Did you read this thing?" he asked.

"Not yet."

"It says they're going to dig Frances' body up for an autopsy."

"Court order," Deputy Miller said with a smirk. "I guess we weren't out of our jurisdiction."

"We'll see about that," Harry said, looked through the papers in his hand. "When is the hearing?"

"No hearing," Deputy Miller said. "It's an emergency. The backhoe is on its way."

Harry could see that Walt was at the edge of his self-control.

"Come with me, Walt. We need to make a call."

"If you think you can get a lawyer into this, it's a little late," Deputy Miller said. "It's after business hours and by morning it will be all over."

"Come on, Walt," Harry said and took the old man by the arm.

Deputy Miller followed along behind them as they walked back over the bridge to Harry's cabin. Judith waited for them. Harry told her what was happening.

"Block the road," she said as they watched Deputy Miller climb in his car and drive away.

"I'll shoot someone if they try to dig her up," Walt said. Judith patted his shoulder. "We'll get it taken care of," she said.

Long Joe appeared and spoke softly to Walt, led him into the cabin.

"I'm going to call Jerry Steinman," Harry said.

Steinman's office was closed but the voice-mail message included an emergency beeper number and Harry dialed it, gave his name and phone number.

He considered Judith's suggestion about blocking the road and decided it was a good idea. While he waited for Steinman to call back he hooked his fifth-wheel trailer to the truck and backed it onto the bridge. He wanted to make sure they couldn't use the backhoe to drag it off so he unhitched it and let the air out of all four tires. He loaded the truck with bales of hay from the hay-barn and moved them onto the trailer. When he was nearly finished Judith called him to say that Jerry Steinman was on the telephone.

"Hello, Harry," Steinman said. "What can I do for you?"

Harry gave him a quick version of events since Frances' death.

Steinman thought for a minute. Not much we can do this evening," he said. "If you can stall them until morning, I may be able to get a stay on the order and a hearing."

"They really don't like any of us," Harry told him, "And as far as I can see, they're all crooked. And Walt's threatened to shoot anyone that tries to dig his wife up."

"Sounds like I'd better get over there. I've got a status conference in the morning and a couple of appointments. I can get someone to cover for me. You better give me some directions I can follow in the dark."

Harry gave him directions for the drive, said he would have someone meet him at Grand Coulee and lead him over Manila Creek.

Not long after he got off the phone, Harry heard a truck turn onto the drive and went out, saw a dump truck with a flatbed trailer carrying a backhoe. The truck stopped beside the cabin and Harry went to the driver's side. It was a young man he'd seen around Republic.

"Howdy. Lookin' for the Davises'."

"You can't get there right now," Harry said.

"How's that?"

"The bridge is blocked."

"Well, we better unblock it," the man said. "We have a court order."

"Can't do it."

"Listen, buddy, this is just a job to me. But the Sheriff is on his way, and the coroner. I wouldn't buck it if I was you. They're expectin' trouble."

"If that was your grandma over there in that grave, would you want them diggin' her up with a backhoe?"

"I suppose not. But it ain't my business. The Sheriff said he thinks the old man killed her."

"That's ridiculous. She's been sick for a couple of years. We all saw her body at the funeral. My wife helped dress her."

"That's kind of a different story than they told me. By the way, I'm Frank Connor. I see you up in Republic now and then."

"Yeah," Harry said. "I thought I recognized you. Listen, I've got a lawyer comin' over from the coast to take care of this. If we could just hold off until mornin' I'd sure appreciate it."

"Let's take a look at that bridge," Frank said. He grabbed a flashlight and followed Harry to the bridge. "Not bad," he said. "It'd be a hell of a job to get that off there. Any other way in?"

"Nope. It's the only bridge in ten miles."

"Well, I guess we're stuck until mornin'."

As they walked back to the cabin three sets of headlights turned onto the drive. Deputy Miller's car led the way. He stopped behind the backhoe.

"Well, let's get this show on the road," he said to Frank.

"Can't get over there," Frank said. "Bridge is blocked."

"Blocked?" Deputy Miller said. "How?"

"Somebody's hay trailer," Frank said. "Doesn't seem to be any way around it."

Deputy Miller headed for the bridge. He shined his flashlight on the trailer.

"Your trailer, I suppose," he said to Harry.

Harry didn't reply. The other two deputies who'd been with Miller earlier came up behind them followed by a man in a suit and overcoat. Harry assumed it was the coroner.

"Well, drag that piece of shit off of there," Deputy Miller said.

"I'm not touchin' another man's property without his agreement," Frank said.

"Son-of-a-bitch," Deputy Miller said.

"I'm not going to stay here all night," the coroner said. "I've got surgery tomorrow morning. If she's dead, she'll still be dead tomorrow."

"The judge wanted this done immediately," Deputy Wilson said. "He won't like it."

"Then he can get me a raise so I can do this full-time," the coroner said.

"We can move that trailer," Deputy Miller said. "Come on, Brady. We'll throw that hay off of there and drag it off with the squad-car."

"I don't think so," Frank said. "All four tires are flat."

Deputy Miller looked at Harry. "You bastard."

"Well, I'm going on back to town," the coroner said. "When you get this sorted out give me a call."

"I can't leave my rig sittin' here all night," Frank said. "If you fellas would move your cars, I'll have to back out to the highway."

The deputies looked at each other. Finally Deputy Miller shrugged.

"It'll all be here in the mornin'. At least it had better be."

As the procession backed towards the highway, Harry went in to tell the others what had happened.

It was after one AM when Jerry called from Coulee City to say he would be in Grand Coulee in less than an hour. Judith left to lead him over Manila Creek and Harry stayed with Walt and Long Joe and the kids.

Walt napped on the sofa and Long Joe nodded by the fire. Harry went to the bedroom to get a little sleep. Judith woke him to say that Jerry was there. Harry glanced at the clock and it was after four.

Judith had coffee on and Jerry sat at the kitchen table in jeans and a parka. He smiled at Harry.

"I hear you held them off."

"Just temporarily," Harry said.

"I need to be at the court-house when they open," Jerry said. "Judith says it's about an hour drive. Someone will have to take me up there. I left my car in Grand Coulee."

"I didn't think he should bring it over Manila Creek," Judith said.

"I see what you meant, now," Jerry said.

Walt was awake and came over. Jerry introduced himself.

"I don't know if you can stop them," Walt said. "They're used to having their way."

"They're still under the laws of the State of Washington," Jerry said. "I brought some material with me. I need to read a little, if you don't mind."

"Be my guest," Walt said.

Harry went out to feed the stock. He thought he saw a car parked on the highway near the turn-off but couldn't be sure in the dim moonlight. When he'd finished with the stock he went for a walk, south along the river. Almost unconsciously he found himself in the children's grove and brushed the snow from the deadfall and sat there. Reject sat beside him, ears alert, looked one way then the other.

As soon as his breathing was regular, Harry could hear the faint voices. The sound was a murmur, just below the threshold of his hearing and he strained to listen. He could not determine even the language they spoke, but the feeling was of happiness and peace. As he concentrated he heard a new voice, older, a woman, and the hair along his neck rose as he recognized Frances' soft lullaby.

Dawn came, a faint lightening in the eastern sky above the mountains and the stars faded with the voices.

Harry and Walt and Jerry left for Republic a little before seven. The courthouse was not yet open and they drank coffee at the hotel while they waited. Jerry continued to read from several law-books and photocopied extracts. At eight-thirty he put it all in his briefcase and they drove back up the hill.

Harry and Walt waited on a bench in the hallway while Jerry talked to the court-clerk. He came out to say he had a meeting with the judge in chambers and would be right back. It was about forty-five minutes before he reappeared. His face was grim.

"I have them stalled for now. But I don't know how long it will last. You may be right about them all being crooked. I think we better affidavit this judge off the case and have it heard before a visiting judge. I don't think he was telling me the straight story. Anyway, we have a preliminary hearing on the exhumation order tomorrow. We need any witnesses who saw the body and knew Walt and Frances. I guess you're stuck with me overnight."

"I don't know how I can pay for all of this," Walt said. "We'll worry about that later," Jerry said. "We have a certain amount of pro bono time and I can prevail on the firm to discount the fee and give you some time."

Tamarack came with his van to help with transportation and Judith and Long Joe and the kids rode with him and Wildrose.

Eric and Barbara said they would meet them at the courthouse. Judith couldn't reach Nathan and Jerry said that wouldn't be a problem, that they already had enough witnesses.

The three deputies sat in the back of the court-room, whispered among themselves and cast mean looks at them. Harry saw Franklin Davis, dressed in a suit, talking to another man whom he thought was the prosecutor. He told Walt and Jerry.

"That kid is up to no good," Walt said. "He wants our place, him and his sister."

They sat through several other minor cases before State of Washington versus Walter Davis was called. The judge went to chambers and a visiting judge from Okanogan County took the bench. Jerry and Walt sat at the counsel table. The prosecutor argued that the State had a vital interest in determining the circumstance of Frances' death. He also pointed out that burial on private property without a permit was illegal and the body would have to be moved anyway.

Jerry argued that the circumstances of the death could be determined without exhuming the body and that Walt had agreed to apply for the cemetery permit and hadn't known that it was needed. The judge asked Walt a few questions and clearly was sympathetic. He asked Jerry if he had witnesses who could testify to the circumstances of the death and Jerry gave him a list of those who had come with him.

The prosecutor called Franklin to his table and they held a whispered conference. The prosecutor stood and addressed the judge. "Your honor, it has come to my attention that there may be reason to question Mr. Davis's mental competency. The State moves for a continuance pending the resolution of the competency matter."

Jerry argued that it was too late to interject the question of competency and that it was irrelevant in determining the cause of Frances' death. Walt glared at Franklin who could not meet his eyes.

The judge ordered a ten-minute recess while he considered the matter and retired to chambers. Jerry came back to talk to Walt. Franklin went outside with the prosecutor.

The bailiff called the court back to order and the judge gave his ruling. He granted a competency hearing, set for two weeks from that day. As to the circumstances of Frances' death he said that he saw no clear evidence that there was any reason to suspect foul play and therefore he would bar the exhumation and give Walt sixty days to obtain a permit.

Jerry said they hadn't done too badly considering that it seemed to be stacked against them. He promised to return for the competency hearing and asked them all some of the kinds of questions they could expect. Walt was indignant at the whole idea and Jerry cautioned him to be careful not to lose his temper in court no matter what they tried.

Walt asked Jerry to go outside for a few minutes and they talked in the sun on the south side of the barn for a while. When they were finished, Judith left to take Jerry back over to Grand Coulee.

"I've got just the medicine for Franklin and his sister," Walt said to Harry.

"What's that?" Harry asked him.

Walt grinned. "You'll see soon enough."

CHAPTER 22

On the day of Walt's competency hearing they all drove to Republic together. Jerry had come the day before and stayed overnight at Walt's. The courtroom was half full. Harry saw Franklin talking to John Carlson and the title company attorney who now represented him. Harry also saw that Eliot was there, sitting in the far back. He wondered if Eliot would testify against Walt.

He didn't, but John Carlson did, rambled on under the attorney's questioning about things he had heard and guessed and wondered about. The judge repeatedly told him to limit his testimony to things he knew first-hand. That wasn't much.

Franklin testified next and he also had little first-hand knowledge. When Jerry cross-examined him, Franklin admitted that he had seen his father only three times in the past five years and then only for a few hours each time. When Jerry asked his main reason for believing his father was incompetent he said it was burying his mother on the place instead of in a cemetery. He couldn't say why, just that it didn't seem normal.

The surprise witness was Chet Weston. He told the story of how Walt had threatened to shoot him and several other men when they "accidentally wandered onto his property." Jerry asked him for more of the details and got him to admit that he and several other militia members had been in camouflage uniform, heavily armed and "conducting training maneuvers" at the time and that they had knowingly crossed Walt's fence. He never actually had seen Walt with a gun and he couldn't remember the exact words Walt had used to threaten them.

Jerry called Harry and Judith to testify about their association with the Davises. Franklin's attorney tried to trip them up with questions about memory lapses and "unusual behavior" on Walt's part and was very exasperated by their calm, truthful answers.

Last Jerry called Walt to the stand. He remembered Jerry's admonitions and did not wander or repeat himself in his answers. When Jerry asked why he thought the action had been brought, Walt said, "They want the place, to subdivide it. But they aren't ever going to get it."

Franklin's attorney tried to get Walt angry, asked questions about Frances' death and whether he had abused or neglected her. Walt maintained his composure and drew a laugh even from the judge when he said, "Son, Frances and I worked out the few differences we had long before you were born."

Then Franklin's attorney stumbled through a meandering closing argument and tried to use Walt's decision to bury Frances on their place as a major indication of the old man's mental problems. Jerry pointed out that the burial matter already had been settled and the permit legalizing it would be ready within a couple of weeks.

The judge ruled within a few minutes, dismissed the competency action and admonished Franklin's attorney against becoming involved in personal disputes that did not meet the test of legal action.

Franklin and John Carlson left together. Eliot quietly disappeared. Walt asked Harry and Judith to wait for a few minutes while he went to the auditor's office. He returned with a grin on his face and handed Harry a newly recorded document headed "Statutory Warranty Deed."

It was a few minutes before Harry realized what it was. The document gave Walt's property to Harry and Judith free and clear. A second sheet was a bill of sale for all of Walt's cattle and horses in return for "love and affection."

"I had Jerry bring these with him," Walt said. "Frances and I decided a couple of years ago that it's what we wanted to do. Jerry says Franklin and his sister may try to cause a fuss about it and claim they should have part of their mother's share as her heirs."

"They could never make it stick," Jerry said, "But they could make you spend some money defending it. I don't know if they are that vindictive. Besides, if they don't check the County records they may not know about it for years."

"Are you sure about this?" Judith asked Walt. "We didn't expect anything like this. That isn't why we've been good to you."

"If I thought it was, you'd never get it," Walt said.

"I can assure you it's what he wants to do," Jerry said. "I asked him every question I could think of."

"You two are the kids Frances and I should have had," Walt said.

"And you're the father I never had," Harry said.

About the time that breakup started, Mom told Harry that Chet Weston was running for County Commissioner. Bobby Baker was his campaign manager and the National Rifle Association and the Christian Coalition had promised them support. Mom had volunteered to help and they put her in charge of recruiting other volunteers.

"It's a chance to get involved on the right side of things," she told Harry. "You should think about it. Your reputation around here could use some fixing."

"I'm not sure that's the kind of fixing I need," Harry said.

"I know you're not a Christian, Harry," Mom said, "But at least for your kids' sake I hope you see the light and accept Jesus. When all the good Christians take back the power, it's going to go hard on this generation of vipers that has turned their backs on the Lord. It's bound to happen. Christians are going to run this country again."

"You mean Christians like the banker and Preacher Hale who took all of your money?" Harry asked her.

"They didn't take my money," Mom said. "They were victims just like me. It was the government and the Jewish bankers. They created that whole Savings and Loan thing so they could steal money from good Christian people. Their Day of Judgment will come."

There are a lot of Christians who shouldn't be too anxious for the Day of Judgment," Harry said.

"I don't know why you can't see the handwriting on the wall, Harry," Mom said. "John Carlson already gave Chet a thousand dollars. And your friend Eliot did, too."

"Eliot isn't exactly my friend," Harry said.

"Well, he seems like a nice young man to me," Mom said.

"Did you ever wonder what he does for a living?" Harry asked her.

"He has family money," Mom said. "He comes from very wealthy people back east."

"Not everyone believes that," Harry said.

"Well, I don't know what you're trying to say," Mom said. "Good breeding shows."

On the anniversary of the massacre at the Branch Davidian Compound in Waco, Bobby Baker held a memorial service at The Church of the New Covenant. Mom tried to get Harry and Judith to go with her.

"It's for the children. The government burned those children alive. No matter what their parents might have done those were innocent children. It could have been any of us."

Harry agreed with her that the FBI and ATF had been no better than the SS or the KGB both in Waco and at Ruby Ridge.

"It's a fine old tradition," he said to her. "White men roasted Indian children alive down on that eighty Walt and I bought."

"I don't believe that," Mom said, "You're making that up. Christian men wouldn't do that."

"Oh, I'm sure they thought it was for the children's own good," Harry said.

There was a large crowd at the service when Harry dropped Mom off, vehicles parked all over the river-bottom and a large tent was pitched beyond the church to handle the overflow. While he did not care much for Bobby Baker or Chet Weston he was happy to see that people in the country had not forgotten.

By the end of April the weather was hot and the spring rains barely wet the ground. Harry had to use irrigation water to germinate his crops and bought a booster pump to get a little water onto the high ground to bring up the grain. Walt said it had a bad feel to it and he wouldn't be surprised if there was a drought that lasted all summer.

Judith reported that her Elder relatives also were worried and likened it to summers in the thirties and fifties when great tracts of forest had burned and animals died of thirst. The snow-pack had been below normal and the spring flood on the San Poil was barely noticeable. Even Chet Weston and his followers stayed dry. Mom assured Harry it was the Good Lord's blessing on Chet's political ambitions.

Jeff Lasker came to visit and reported that the Kettle River, too, barely had risen and he'd heard of some wells that already were dry. He tried again to lure Harry to his place. When Harry told him about Walt's gift and the eighty they had bought, Jeff was very impressed.

"Shit, buddy, looks like you'll soon be as rich as I am."

"Mainly it looks like more work to me," Harry told him. "If I'm not farmin', I'm doctorin' cows or pullin' calves or tryin' to get the stand ready for the season."

"You need to hire some help and quit tryin' to do it all yourself," Jeff said. "We're not a young as we used to be."

"I'm not pullin' the old man thing yet," Harry said.

"I see those gray hairs," Jeff said.

There were only a few scattered showers through May and by June the grass on the exposed high spots was brown and dormant. There was good feed on the north slopes beyond the river but it wouldn't last through the season and Harry worried that he would run short of hay in the coming winter. He sold a few older cows and put up some cross-fences so that he could manage the range more closely.

Several new tents sprouted at the Weston property and there was a collection of travel trailers and pickup campers around Chet's cabin. Harry saw groups of strangers, most of them young men in military-style clothing, intruding where he knew they did not belong. Often ten or more of them would hang around the store and the owner complained to Harry that they ruined his business. They rarely came by the stand and when they did it was to talk to Mom and they didn't buy anything.

Wildrose said several of them had called her "hippie bitch" when she went for the mail and Barbara reported being harassed as a "red nigger." When Harry stopped for his mail they often would glare at him and block the door or stand in front of his pickup. He began to carry a rifle, visible in the gun-rack in his truck, and they backed off. He no longer let the kids ride their horses to the store for a cold drink or to get something for Judith.

Several of the militia members moved onto their lots on John Carlson's subdivision. They lived in makeshift camps or old travel trailers and a couple of them began work on crude cabins of unpeeled green logs. They bought an ancient water-tanker that lumbered around from camp to camp occasionally to deliver water. There was frequent gunfire from that side of the road and groups of them trained for Armageddon, reminded Harry of little boys playing war.

Mom put up some "Chet Weston - The People's Hope" posters at the stand and began to pass out fliers with his ten-point plan to save the County and Christian Civilization. Harry took down the posters and Mom said that some day he would regret choosing the wrong side.

Uncle Paul came to visit in mid-June. He said that parts of the Columbia Basin without irrigation water were dry as the Sahara and many of the dry-land farmers would lose most of their crops.

"I may have rocks a mile deep," Paul said. "But at least I have water. That old canal never looked so good."

He asked Harry if he had heard about Precision Farming. Harry said that he had seen some commercials on television, with some actor in overalls pretending to be a farmer, but he hadn't paid any attention.

"Well, I had a salesman come by my place," Paul said. "He told me he'd signed up more than a dozen neighbors. The deal is, they use these military spy satellites to make maps of your place. Costs a fortune to get them and you have to have a computer to use them right. He showed me how you could see if the ground was dry and whether your crops were wilted or had serious pest damage. Your computer analyzes it and gives you printouts with all these codes or colors you have to interpret. He says these satellites can read a license plate on a car from up in space. Anyway he finished this fifteen-minute spiel and I asked him what it could tell me that I couldn't tell myself just by takin' a walk around the place. I thought he was goin' to swallow his gum! I told him it sounded to me like the government was just tryin' to figure out how to get farmers to pay for their spy satellites. He left mad as hell."

"Well it might be a good thing for farmers that don't want to go outside," Harry said.

"Yeah," Paul said, "And the ones that can't tell if the ground is dry or not. He said that anyone who didn't use this new technology wouldn't be able to compete, would just be left behind."

"That's what the banker kept tellin' Dad," Harry said, "Until they foreclosed."

"I been thinkin'," Paul said. "My old tractor is about to give up the ghost and I'm not sure I want to invest in a new one. I was wonderin' if you knew where a guy could get a decent team. It's been a long time since I drove horses, but the old man taught me pretty good. And with one of them fore-carts I could use all my equipment."

"There's teams in Western Horseman all the time," Harry said. "They're not cheap anymore. We've got a couple of likely young geldings but they aren't trained yet. If you could get by until next Spring, Judith and Walt could turn them into a pretty good team. If you want to go with a four-horse hitch we might find a couple more young ones we could buy and train for you. You'd need a good strong harness which can cost a pretty penny and a fore-cart is a third the price of a good-sized tractor."

"I wouldn't care even if I spent a little more to begin with," Paul said. "I could save the difference easy on fuel and parts and aggravation."

"Horses can be aggravatin', too," Harry said, "But it's a better brand of aggravation."

"My thought exactly," Paul said.

"Well, if you're serious, we can sure help you get into it," Harry said.

"I'd appreciate it a bunch," Paul said.

There was a big Independence Day celebration at The Church of the New Covenant. Mom said there were speakers from all over the country. The County was to be Chosen Land, one of the High Places, which was to lead the way in the new Christian Civilization. She said Bobby Baker had given a great two-hour sermon on the Cleansing that was to come to the Chosen Lands and drive out all the Unbelievers. It was all in the Book of Revelation if you could read it. But, of course, Unbelievers couldn't read it. God had planned it that way.

She urged Harry again to accept Jesus and join the movement. She insisted that there was going to be a great uprising at the polls in November and even old reprobates like Tom Foley over in Spokane were headed for defeat. Newt Gingrich would lead a Conservative Christian Revolution that would renew America.

"I just wish your father could have lived to see it," she said.

"It seems to me," Harry said, "That the people who are paying for your great revolution are the same ones who killed him."

"You're wrong, Harry. This is a true Second American Revolution. You don't want to be on the wrong side. Remember what happened to the Tories. This is the future. I would like to see you be successful and happy. You spend all your life trying to bring back the past."

"Well if working hard, taking care of my family and not owing money to anyone is of the past, I'll take it."

"But you could lose it all, Harry. Brother Baker said that even the sons and daughters of some of us at the meeting would regret taking a stand against us. I know he was talking about you."

"So what are they going to do to me?"

"I don't know," Mom said, "But revolutions are dangerous if you're on the wrong side."

"Revolutions are dangerous on any side," Harry said.

Mom told Harry she had a letter from Jack and that he and Diane were coming to visit. Harry said he couldn't wait.

"I don't know why you hate Jack so much. I think you're just jealous because he's so successful."

The day they came Mom asked Judith if she would watch the stand so that she was free to spend time with Jack and Diane. "Jack has some big deal cookin'," she said, "and they may have to leave tomorrow."

They came in a new gray Mercedes that reminded Harry of the one the banker had driven years before. Jack apparently didn't want to take it on the gravel drive, parked it near the stand and he and Diane walked to Mom's cabin. Harry stayed in the field where he was working down some ground for a late crop of peas.

When he went to the house for lunch Jack came out to the corral as he watered the horses. He was dressed in slacks and an expensive looking knit shirt with crossed golf clubs on the pocket. He walked carefully in his gray leather loafers, tried to avoid the manure.

"Still at it?"

"You mean life?" Harry asked. "Doesn't seem to be much alternative."

"If you can call this life, way out here."

"I wouldn't trade with you," Harry said.

"You might think a little different if you saw my bank account. I've sold three houses over a half-million in the last sixty days. Got an eight-hundred-thousand deal ready to pop right now." He held up a cell-phone. "Can't be more than five minutes away."

"You can't get out of here with that thing," Harry said.

Jack switched it on, put it to his ear and frowned. "This really is the ass-end of the Earth."

"Mom's been tellin' me this is the Chosen Land," Harry said.

"You mean that religious bullshit?" Jack said. "No one with a brain believes that stuff. It's a good way to keep the dumb ones in line. It keeps the pressure on for the Republicans. I'm assistant chairman in my precinct over there. There's going to be a massacre in November."

"I stay out of politics," Harry said.

"I can't," Jack said. "For the business. Same with church. I've got to have all the contacts I can get. I spend half my time in some kind of meeting. It's really different living over there. Once you get a taste of it, though, you realize how much better it is."

"You forget I lived over there for more than fifteen years?" Harry asked. "I probably built some of those houses you're sellin'. I don't miss it a bit."

"Well, it's where I belong," Jack said. "I fit right in. Nice big house in Bellevue, good restaurants, golf courses everywhere. And my kids are all doin' great. The boys may be able to get into Lakeside. You can't get that kind of education out here. And Tiffany's in college, at the U-Dub. She wanted to go to that hippie school in Oregon, Reed, but we talked her out of it for this year."

"Looks like you've got it all under control," Harry said. "Until the economy takes a dive."

"I got to hand one thing to Clinton," Jack said. "Looks like this boom could be permanent. Now if the Republicans can just get in and keep it going. They better. With the monthly payments I've got, I can't stand a recession."

"I stay away from monthly payments, too," Harry said.

"How much real estate do you own, here," Jack asked.

"A little shy of four-hundred acres," Harry said and saw Jack's surprise.

"And you don't owe anything on it?" Jack asked.

"Not a dime," Harry said. "Just taxes."

"Do you know how much it's worth?" Jack asked. "If you subdivided this, you'd have... eighty five-acre pieces, at about thirty grand apiece if you had the right broker. Fuck, that's almost two and a half million. Are you shittin' me? You didn't have a pot to piss in when you came up here."

"Still don't," Harry said.

"And here you are still stompin' around in the horse shit," Jack said. "I never did understand you. Well, I better get back and see how Mom and Diane are doin'."

The weather remained dry and unusually hot. The fire danger was extreme and everyone in the valley watched for any slight wisp of smoke. Large Smokey the Bear posters at the store warned tourists about the danger of any open flame. Most private roads were closed and chained to prevent some four-wheeler from igniting a conflagration with a bad muffler or careless cigarette.

Harry moved his cattle every few days to allow the grass to recover. Even so he was afraid that before fall he would have to buy hay from the irrigated farmers in the Basin. Feed prices were high as the dry-land crops failed and everyone tried to stock up. Harry harvested a poor crop of grain and would get only three cuttings of hay at best and the yield might be half of normal.

Little Joe and Rebecca rode out every day to check on the stock and watch for any strangers who might cause a fire. One day as Harry worked on his swather in the yard the kids came galloping along the road and across the bridge. He could see something was wrong and hoped it wasn't fire.

"There's some men at Davises," Rebecca yelled as they came into the yard. "They said they would shoot us."

Judith heard them and came out of the cabin. Harry started in to get a gun.

"Who were they?" Judith asked Rebecca as the kids dismounted. "From the church," Little Joe said. "The ones that talk to Grandma."

"They were headed up to the eighty," Rebecca said. "They all have guns and those funny clothes."

Harry came out with his automatic clipped to his belt and told Judith to grab his saddle. He caught the red gelding and Judith threw the blanket and saddle on and cinched it down.

Harry slipped the hackamore over the gelding's ears, took the reins and mounted.

"Be careful, Harry," Judith said.

He walked the gelding to the bridge then nudged him into a trot, let him warm. He took Walt's old road towards the eighty. Off to his right he saw someone in camouflage duck behind a tree and turned that way. As he drew close the man stepped out then several others showed themselves.

Harry stopped the gelding and looked at them. "You guys must be lost."

"I don't think so," the first man Harry had seen said.

"We're just making sure this area is secure."

"This is my property," Harry said. "I'll worry about security here."

"This is a main approach to our command center," the man said. "We have a right to defend ourselves."

"Not on my property," Harry said.

"This is old man Davis's property anyway," another man said, a kid really, with too-big camouflage fatigues and a hat that almost covered his eyes.

"You're wrong, there," Harry said. "In any case you're trespassing."

"We're a patrol of the San Poil Militia," the first man said. "We're just guarding our territory. Most property owners appreciate what we do."

"I don't," Harry said. "Please leave or I'll call the sheriff."

The kid laughed. "That won't do any good. The sheriff is a member."

"Quiet," the first man said.

"He's just a squaw-man," the kid said. "We don't have to take this from him."

"He has a pop-gun," another man said and they all laughed.

"You're trespassing and I'm ordering you to leave," Harry said.

"We only take orders from our Commander," the first man said. "We'll leave this time, but don't think you've heard the last of this. There's a Landowners Association being organized and I'd advise you to join it."

"I'm not much of a joiner," Harry said.

"You better watch your back, asshole," the kid said and several others laughed.

Harry looked at them silently and they fidgeted until the first man said, "Fall in."

They formed a ragged double line behind him and they moved off the way they had come. Harry rode along behind them and they turned often to glare at him. He sat on the gelding while they climbed back through Walt's north fence. The kid turned to shake his fist at Harry before they were out of sight.

CHAPTER 23

Mom was determined to accept an invitation to visit Jack and Diane. Harry was sure she hoped they would ask her to come live with them. He hoped she was right but was sure they just wanted to impress her with their newfound wealth. She did not want to take the Greyhound and Jack was too busy to come get her. Harry finally agreed to drive her to Seattle the second week in August.

He didn't want to be gone longer than necessary so they left before dawn. Mom grumbled about leaving so early but became very excited as they neared Bellevue.

"What a beautiful place," she said when Harry found the address and pulled up in front. "I knew Jack would be back on top."

The house was a common design for the current fad in executive homes with a tall shake roof that made it seem imposing from the street. Harry knew there was as much volume in the attic as in the living area. Jack came out, still sleepy, and helped Harry carry in Mom's things. Clearly she had brought enough for a long stay.

"You need to come get her next week," Jack said when she was out of earshot. "This is really a bad time."

"It's your turn," Harry said. "I'm busy, too."

"Thanks a lot," Jack said.

Harry ate a late breakfast at a little Mexican place in Old Town and headed back. It was a beautiful day on the coast, bright and warm, and drier than Harry could remember. As he climbed the grade to Steven's Pass he noticed yellow leaves on the brush and trees and in places the grass was brown.

The east side of the Cascades was even drier and as he passed the Lake Wenatchee rest area he thought he smelled smoke. As he entered Tumwater Canyon he could see the smoke ahead and the strong smell of burned fir and pine was unmistakable. He hoped the highway wasn't blocked. The smoke grew thicker, the smell stronger and about halfway through the fifteen-mile canyon he could see flames on the top of the ridge to the south. The wind was stiff and the fire gained momentum, the smoke grew dense.

Cars in the canyon drove with their lights on and tourists stopped to stare at the burning trees. In places the fire had worked down the steep slope towards the river and half-burned trees fell, carried fire even further down into the narrow canyon.

Traffic slowed and crept towards Leavenworth. Forest Service fire crews raced towards the fire and as he came out of the mouth of the canyon Harry saw "Road Closed" signs blocking the westbound lane. He felt lucky to have gotten through.

The westerly wind carried the dark cloud of smoke out above him and the light was reddish and dim. As he skirted Wenatchee and headed out across the dryland, a Spokane radio station said that the Tumwater fire was out of control and there was another rapidly growing blaze near Chelan.

Harry looked to the northwest and could see the dark smudge of smoke from that fire. The announcer reported several smaller fires in Okanogan County with one about to break through the Forest Service fire lines at Thunder Mountain. There were no reports of fires in the San Poil area as yet.

Harry was glad to be home and to breathe smoke-free air. With the prevailing wind direction he knew that smoke from one or more of the fires to the west would reach the valley the next day.

By morning the smoke was a high, light-brown haze and the smell of burned pine permeated the valley. The west wind strengthened throughout the day and by evening the sun shone dimly and the sunset glowed a dull red above the hills. Even in the cabin their throats were dry and sore and Harry woke repeatedly throughout the night and went outside to make sure no fire was close to them.

In the days that followed there was a constant smoky overcast and everyone's eyes were red and watery. Judith kept the kids inside and when Harry went to Republic she had him buy some surgical masks to keep the worst of the smoke particles out of their lungs. It was hard to work with the masks in the heat and they soon became damp and clogged.

About a week after the first fires broke out Harry awakened with a start and realized that the smoke was much worse than it had been and it smelled fresh, close. He pulled on his jeans and ran outside to see flames creeping towards the cabin through the dry weeds beside the road. He looked at the highway and saw the stand engulfed in fire and as he watched the roof collapsed and flames shot up. He yelled for Judith and grabbed a shovel, ran to throw dirt on the fire along the road.

Judith came out and he pointed towards the stand. "Oh, my God."

She grabbed a hose and began to wet down the cabin and the low grass that surrounded it. The horses were agitated and churned about in the corral. She called to them and they settled a little. The fire along the road was enclosed by the irrigated garden on one side and the road on the other and Harry soon stopped it's progress and beat out the hot spots.

He told Judith to keep wetting down the cabin and then the barn. He had her soak several burlap bags and he ran with them and the shovel towards the stand. The building itself was hopeless, but the fire ran south beside the highway and Harry was afraid that if it got past the garden it would turn into the grain stubble and towards the timber.

As he began to fight the six-foot flames he saw Tamarack's van park across the highway. Tamarack had a shovel, joined Harry to battle the brush fire beside the highway. They were driven constantly backward by the heat from the wind-driven flames. Walt appeared and began to work with them. Despite their best efforts the fire reached the stubble field and grew to a twenty-foot high solid front as it raced towards the river and the small timber north of the children's grove.

Harry and Tamarack concentrated on the brush beyond the stubble, let the fire burn across the field and hoped that it could not jump the river. Walt joined them and they managed to stop any encroachment into the green brush on the edge of the timber. There was a flare-up as the stubble fire reached the riverbank and Walt said he would watch the smoking field so Harry and Tamarack could put out any wind-blown embers that crossed the river. Judith sent Little Joe and Rebecca with plastic jugs of cold water and they drank greedily.

The brush burned out and they used shovels to throw dirt on hot spots. It nearly was noon when they finally walked back to the cabin. Judith made sandwiches for them.

"I reckon we have our militia boys to thank for that," Walt said.

"That'd be my guess," Harry said. "They told me to watch my back."

"It could have burned the whole valley," Judith said. "I can't believe anyone would do that intentionally."

"I don't see how it could have been an accident," Harry said. "There wasn't much electricity at the stand and what was there was pretty tight. I checked it just a couple of days ago to make sure."

"It looked to me like it started in the brush by the highway and burned along your road into the stand," Tamarack said. "That brush was already burned when I got here."

"There's a sheriff's car up there," Judith said.

Harry looked towards the burned out stand, saw Deputy Miller staring at the smoking ruins.

"I'd better get up there." Tamarack followed him.

"I better go check on things," Walt said and headed for his place.

Deputy Miller frowned as they approached. "Not a good day for a fire."

"I didn't know there was a good day for this kind of fire," Harry said.

"Don't suppose you have any idea how it started," Deputy Miller said. "Looks like it could be electrical."

"I don't think so," Harry said. "I had it pretty tight."

Tamarack walked to the edge of the highway. "It started over here," he called to them.

They went over to where he stood.

"How do you know it started here?" Deputy Miller asked.

"Look," Tamarack said, "There's brush that isn't even burned, just the grass, and you can see where it fanned out from right over there." He walked over to the place he'd pointed to and squatted down. "Look at this," he said and pointed to a half-burned rag in the dirt.

Deputy Miller bent down and picked it up, sniffed it. "Gasoline," he said. He carried it carefully to his car and put it in a plastic evidence bag, wrote something on it with a felt pen. He turned to Harry. "Did you have insurance on this?"

"No," Harry said.

"Hmmm," Deputy Miller said. "How about on your cabin?"

"No," Harry said again.

"Crop insurance, or on the timber?"

"No," Harry repeated.

"Seems funny a person would have all this with no insurance," Deputy Miller said. "You're sure. We can find out, you know."

"Are you trying to imply that I started this fire?" Harry asked him. "Do you think I'd risk everything I have including a couple of hundred thousand dollars worth of timber for an insurance check? And then put it out after it started?"

"We have to check every angle," Deputy Miller said. "Everyone knows you're up to something down here."

Judith came towards them. "I was just listening to KOMW. They said there were thirteen fires set between here and Republic. They're all out now."

Harry looked at Deputy Miller. "You knew that," Harry said to him. "How does that fit with your little theory?"

"It could be for cover," Deputy Miller said. "It's happened."

"He thinks you set the fires?" Judith asked. "You must be crazy," she said to Deputy Miller.

"A lot of people wonder what's goin' on down here," Deputy Miller said. "Especially since you talked old man Davis out of his place."

"How do you know that?" Judith asked him.

"It's public record," Deputy Miller said. "You can't keep these things secret."

Another sheriff's car drove up and stopped across the highway. Harry recognized Deputies Brady and Wilson. Deputy Brady waved Deputy Miller over and they talked for a few minutes. Deputy Miller came back to his car.

"We'll get back to this later," he said to Harry.

The two sheriff's cars drove away and Harry saw that they turned in at John Carlson's driveway. A little while later he saw the two of them driving fast up the river. Someone was in the back of one of the cars.

Eric came by later in the day. He said that Johnny Carlson had been arrested for setting the fires. Someone had seen his pickup parked where one of the fires started and the gasoline-soaked rags matched an old shirt they found under his bed with pieces torn out of it.

Several deputies had been to Weston's compound to question militia members and the rumor was that there was some kind of conspiracy. People all through the valley were angry as they realized that a major fire had been prevented only by quick action by people around each of the fires.

"A hundred years ago they would have lynched him," Eric said.

"So why did he do it?" Harry asked him.

"Nobody seems to know," Eric said. "I've heard everything from him being depressed about his Mom dying to a militia conspiracy to burn down the valley so they could buy all the land cheap."

"Maybe he's just crazy," Harry said.

"I've heard that, too," Eric said.

"I have a bad feeling about it," Judith said. "I still think they will try to blame us somehow."

"How could they?" Eric asked. "They know who started the fires. And he's not exactly a friend of yours."

"I just have a really bad feeling," Judith said.

Over the next several days there were sheriff's cars up and down the valley often. Several times they turned in at John Carlson's. Twice Harry noticed a white and black car parked at the ruins of the stand but each time when he approached the car sped away. There were small stories in the Wenatchee and Spokane newspapers but very few details. The Wenatchee story did not even mention Johnny's name, referred to him as "a local youth."

Smoke from the fires to the west continued to hang over the valley. A fine soot clung to the leaves of the garden plants and they began to turn yellow and stop growing. Harry set sprinklers to wash them off and it seemed to help some, but clearly the crops would be damaged. He had trouble sleeping and frequently went outside at night to look and listen and smell the air.

Harry began to clean up the mess that had been the stand. Everything had been destroyed, coolers melted, agricultural supplies incinerated. With the poor crops and the oppressive smoke he could see that the season was blown. There would be enough to put up for themselves and to trade with friends, but he would have to dip into his savings and probably would end up buying feed for the winter.

Judith kept the kids close. Rebecca complained at not being able to take her video camera into the forest to photograph wildlife and Judith let her go out occasionally if she stayed near the river and did not leave the property. Harry rode out daily to check on the cattle and usually took Little Joe with him. The spring on the eighty was very low but still produced enough to water the stock although it was muddy and white mineral deposits encrusted the margin.

Harry was eating lunch when he heard Reject bark furiously. He was immediately alarmed. He looked outside to see several sheriff's cars and other vehicles leave the highway and drive fast towards the cabin. The first two cruisers went past the cabin and turned to block the road. Another parked crossways in the road between the cabin and the highway.

Deputies poured out of all the cars, several with drawn guns. Harry called Judith out and she brought Little Joe with her.

A deputy got out of an unmarked van, pulled a video camera out of a case and began to run here and there photographing the action.

"Hands in the clear, hands in the clear!" Deputy Wilson yelled at Harry and brandished an Uzi-style assault gun.

Harry kept his hands at shoulder level.

Little Joe burst into tears. "What are you doing to my dad?" he shouted and ran to Harry.

Reject barked angrily, ran at one of the deputies as if to bite him and the deputy kicked at him.

"Go," Harry commanded and pointed towards Walt's. The dog stopped and looked at him. "Go," Harry said again and Reject trotted towards the bridge.

"Watch that dog," Deputy Wilson called to the deputy in the car blocking the road. Reject circled well around and continued on, turned at the bridge to look back, then went on.

A woman deputy approached Judith, made her turn and lean against the cabin and patted her down. Deputy Wilson did the same with Harry then put handcuffs on him.

"You are under arrest for conspiracy to destroy Federal Property," Deputy Wilson said. "You have the right to remain silent. Anything you say can and will be used against you in a court of law. You have the right to an attorney. If you cannot afford one, the court will appoint one for you. Any questions?"
Harry remained silent.

Deputy Wilson showed Harry a search warrant signed by a US Magistrate in Spokane, but wouldn't let him read it.

Marlene from CPS was there, took Little Joe by the hand and tried to lead him away. He jerked away from her and ran back to Harry.

A deputy started towards him and Harry said, "Go with her, for now, son."

"What are they doing?" Little Joe asked him. "We didn't do anything."

"Just go along for now," Harry said. "We'll take care of it in court."

Little Joe turned reluctantly and followed Marlene to her beige sedan and sat in the front seat, still crying.

Marlene came back. "Where's Rebecca?" she asked Harry. Harry started to turn to her.

"Keep it right there," Deputy Wilson said and poked Harry with the barrel of his gun.

"I don't know," Harry said to Marlene.

"One of the kids is missing," Marlene said. A Deputy Harry didn't recognize, who seemed to be in charge, talked to a man beside him who was dressed in a rumpled gray suit. Then he called over two of the other deputies and began to give them directions to search for Rebecca.

"She went to her grandmother's house," Judith said.

Harry knew she was lying but the deputies seemed to believe her. He saw two deputies searching the cabin along with a man in civilian clothes. They soon came out with his guns and held up the Colt assault rifle as if it were some great prize.

"Tag everything," the boss deputy said. "Someone check out the barn."

Two deputies came out of the house with the computer system, wires dangling and put it in the back of a van with the guns.

"Shall I transport?" Deputy Wilson asked the boss.

"May as well," the boss said. "This is going to take a while."

"What are you looking for?" Harry asked him.

"You'll find that out at the trial," Deputy Wilson said. Deputy Miller came over and grinned at Harry. "I told you it was just a matter of time. We always get our man."

The woman deputy took Judith to one of the cars and put her in the back. Deputy Wilson followed with Harry and put him in another car. "Let's roll."

The car blocking the road moved to let them through. Deputy Wilson waved to the driver with a wide smile. At the highway Deputy Wilson turned south instead of north towards Republic.

"Where are we going?" Harry asked him.

"Okanogan County Jail," Deputy Wilson said. "There isn't room in Republic for all of you."

"Who else?" Harry asked him.

"You'll find out," Deputy Wilson said. "Do you want to make a statement now? It might go easier on you if you just spilled it all."

"What am I supposed to spill?" Harry asked him.

"You can play it that way if you want to," Deputy Wilson said, "But it will just go harder on you. They've got an Assistant US Attorney up in Republic running the whole show. You won't wiggle out of this one."

Deputy Wilson went over Manila Creek then north through Nespelem, took Desautel Pass into Okanogan. The car with Judith was close behind them. The drive took more than two hours. Occasionally a call would come for Deputy Wilson over the radio and he would report his location. There was other traffic on the radio but Harry could not make out much of it. There seemed to be a number of cars on the way to Okanogan.

Deputy Wilson pulled into a basement garage behind the Okanogan County Court House and led Harry to an elevator. When the doors opened they stood at the booking desk in the County Jail.

"Federal prisoner, Mike," Deputy Wilson said to an older deputy behind the desk.

"We're going to be full of Federal Prisoners before night shift," Mike said.

Wilson called the elevator back and when the doors opened Judith stepped out followed by the woman deputy. Mike unlocked the handcuffs and gave Harry a form to fill out then did the same with Judith. When Harry finished the form, Mike stood him against the wall to take a Polaroid picture and gave him a wire basket and told him to put his personal property in it. Then he handed Harry some red drawstring pants with a baggy pullover shirt and showed him where to change.

When Harry came out in his jail uniform, Judith was having her picture taken. "Call Jerry," he said to her.

"Quiet," the woman deputy said. "No talking between prisoners."

Judith winked at him and Harry grinned back. The woman deputy frowned.

"I need to make a phone call," Harry said to Mike.

"There's a telephone in the holding cell," Mike said. "Collect calls only."

Mike gave Harry a cot mattress and sheet and a flimsy blanket and led him down the hall, looked in a heavily barred window then unlocked the door. "This is home."

It was a large room with a few barred windows near the ceiling. There were ten double-bunks, all of them occupied and several mattresses on the floor along one wall.

There was a buzz of reaction from the prisoners and one of them yelled, "A new celly, who'd you murder?"

"There's a spot back there," another said and pointed to the far end.

Harry threw down the mattress next to a sleeping Indian who snored loudly.

"Don't bump the chief," someone said to him. "He'd scalp you before he got his eyes open."

"You a dope grower," someone else asked. "Half the people in here are dope growers. We been thinkin' about organizin' a union." There was general laughter.

Harry spread his sheet and blanket on the mattress and looked around for the telephone. It was mounted on the wall directly below the television that blared with afternoon cartoons. There was a steel plate etched with instructions for placing collect calls. Harry could not remember the number for Jerry Steinman and there was no way to reach directory assistance.

He sat on the mattress and racked his brain for a plan. He thought of Uncle Paul. He went to the telephone, dialed the number and held his hand over his ear so he could hear. Paul answered after several rings and the recording came on.

"You have a collect call from a County Jail. The charge will be two dollars and ninety-five cents for the first minute and fifty cents for each minute thereafter. To accept this call please dial one, to refuse the call please dial two for operator assistance..."

There was a tone as Paul accepted the call.

"Hello, Paul, it's Harry."

"What now, Harry."

"I don't even know. They won't tell me anything. They arrested Judith and me and took Little Joe somewhere. They said it was a Federal charge."

"Sounds serious. What can I do."

"Call our attorney. His name is Jerry Steinman. In Seattle. I can't remember the name of the firm but he would be listed in the yellow pages under attorneys. See if he can call me here."

"I sure will. Anything else I can do?"

"I don't know right now. Not until I find out what's going on."

"Well, be careful, Harry. I'll make that call right now."

In less than fifteen minutes a voice on the P.A. system said that Harry Isaacson should call Jerry Steinman and gave the number.

"A Jew lawyer in Seattle," someone said. "You must be big-time."

Harry made the call and Jerry came on the line. "What's up?"

Harry told him the story.

"And you don't have any idea what it's all about?" Jerry asked him.

"Not a clue," Harry said. "But the deputy said there was an Assistant US Attorney running the show and the warrant was signed by a Federal Magistrate in Spokane."

"I'll make some calls and get back to you," Jerry said. "My assistant just gave me a note that Judith's mother called for me."

"I'll be waiting," Harry said and heard Jerry chuckle.

"So, are you out of here?" one of the prisoners asked when Harry got off the telephone.

"Not yet," Harry said.

"Don't let the assholes get you down," someone else said.

About an hour later the door opened and Tamarack came in. He had on the same red uniform and carried a mattress. He reacted with surprise when he saw Harry and put his mattress down beside him.

They hadn't told him any more than they had Harry. He said they had searched their cabin and taken his guns and other "evidence" and arrested him and Wildrose and had taken Cottonwood and the baby away. He said they had found a little stash of marijuana that he kept and had acted like it was a major find.

Tamarack said he didn't have an attorney he could call or anyone else. Harry said he would ask Jerry if he would take Tamarack's case.

When the announcement came for Harry to call Jerry again the sun was low in the west, cast shadows on the ceiling, and the evening news from Spokane was on.

He called as before and Jerry came on. "They won't tell me much. They claim you're involved in a major conspiracy to blow up some kind of Federal property but they won't say what. You're supposed to be what they call a 'key figure'. And they are particularly interested in Judith for some reason. Are you sure you don't know what they're talking about?"

"I have no idea," Harry said. "I've just been living life as usual. The only thing I can think of is that the neighbor kid set a bunch of fires about a week ago and burned down our stand among other things. I just have a feeling this involves him."

"That might help," Jerry said. "What's his name?"

"Johnny Carlson," Harry said.

"I'll be on this first thing in the morning," Jerry said. "They're talking about moving you to Federal Detention in Spokane. I don't like that but I don't know if I can stop it. They'll have to file charges by day-after-tomorrow. We'll know more then. The magistrate sealed the warrant so they won't let me see that. I'm going to request a bail hearing but they say they have enough evidence to hold you without bail. They claim half a dozen conspirators are singing like meadowlarks."

"I don't know who that could be," Harry said.

"This is very strange," Jerry said.

Harry told him about Tamarack, asked him if he could take the case.

"I hate to bring this up," Jerry said, "But this is going to get expensive. Has this guy got anything? If drugs are involved they'll take his property."

"I don't think he has much money," Harry said.

"I'll see what I can do," Jerry said.

As Harry got off the phone there was a lot of excitement about a news story on television. He moved back so he could see the screen and saw shots that obviously were of the San Poil Valley and he heard the announcer say that more than a dozen arrests had been made by local sheriff's deputies working with an FBI militia task force along with the North Central Washington Drug Task Force and the Bureau of Alcohol, Tobacco and Firearms.

An FBI spokesman came on to say that dozens of illegal weapons had been confiscated along with several truckloads of other evidence and that the militiamen had been supported by drug money. Several of those arrested were cooperating with the investigation and more arrests were expected. He couldn't say yet what the target had been but assured the reporters that a major disaster had been averted.

There was much excitement among the reporters and anchor people that such a large story had broken in Spokane. The piece closed with a self-righteous commentary by the station manager about the evils of guns and drugs which obviously went hand in hand.

As he turned from the television Harry realized that the cell had grown quiet and that everyone was staring at him.

The dinner that two trustees wheeled in and served on plastic trays was unidentifiable and inedible. One of the prisoners saw that Harry wasn't going to eat his and asked if he could have it. Harry said, "Sure."

After they ate, one prisoner kept a lookout through the window in the door while several others huddled around the electrical outlet where the television plugged in. They had crude cigarettes rolled in various kinds of waste paper which had been hidden under mattresses or high on the back of window sills. When everyone was ready, a prisoner put a straightened out paper clip in each side of the open outlet and nudged the free ends together. When they arced, another man quickly lit a scrap of paper to pass around to light the cigarettes. From the smell Harry guessed that the tobacco came from butts collected here and there during exercise periods or clean-up details.

Throughout the evening the prisoners played cards, read or watched Spokane television. One noisy group had a Monopoly game with the board, money and cards made of notebook paper and pieces ranging from paper clips to raisins. There were many arguments over what the various property prices should be and exactly what the Chance and Community Chest cards said. They had one die which each player threw twice on each turn.

As he fell asleep Harry worried about Little Joe, somewhere in a foster home, and Rebecca who had been in the woods with her video camera when the police came.

CHAPTER 24

Harry awakened early and it was a few minutes before he could orient himself. He worried about the livestock, hoped that Walt had seen what happened and took care of them. He was sure that he had. He worried more about Little Joe and Rebecca, hoped that Rebecca had gone to Walt's and not home where they must have left a deputy or two.

He noticed that several more prisoners had been brought in during the night and there was no floor space left. He recognized two of the new prisoners from the militia patrol he'd confronted in the woods.

Soon after "breakfast" was served an announcement came for Harry to call Jerry Steinman. Someone was on the telephone so he waited, then made the call.

"I found out a little more," Jerry said. "You were right about the Carlson kid. I mentioned his name to the US Attorney and he got very excited. He wouldn't tell me what the deal was but it was obvious that he is the one who is giving them all the information. What exactly was your relationship with this kid?"

Harry told him a brief history of his contacts with the Carlson family.

"So you haven't seen him for a while?" Jerry asked.

"Not to talk to," Harry said. "I see him drive by on the highway now and then."

"How about these militia guys?" Jerry asked.

Harry told him about the confrontation in the woods.

"So they have a reason to hurt you if they can," Jerry said. "Sounds to me like they all are trying to lay whatever it is on you. But they'll have to have corroborating evidence."

"I don't know what they could have," Harry said. "I'm just a farmer."

"They mentioned your mother," Jerry said. "What could she have told them."

"She's staying with my brother in Bellevue," Harry said. "She was pretty close to the militia people and their church. They call it The Church of the New Covenant."

"I talked to Judith," Jerry said. "She says to tell you she loves you. She's worried about your kids. I told her I would see what I can find out. Oh, and one other thing. I talked to Joseph in Arizona, I just thought he should know. He's going to come up and give me a hand."

"That's good news," Harry said.

There was another message to call Jerry.

"Found out a little more," Jerry said. "I got them to release the Search Warrant Affidavit. They blocked out a bunch of stuff. It's all based on information from this Carlson kid and supposedly some surveillance, but they always lie about that. The part about what you were supposed to blow up is blacked out, but part of what they were looking for was ammonium nitrate, and diesel or gasoline or something to mix with it to make a bomb. You got anything like that?"

"There'd be a little gasoline around," Harry said, "But I'm an organic farmer, I don't use chemical fertilizer."

"Is that what that is?" Jerry asked him, "fertilizer."

"Plain old nitrogen fertilizer," Harry said.

"How about dynamite or blasting caps or anything like that?" Jerry asked. "They claim you had been known to do blasting at your place, supposedly practicing."

"Not me," Harry said. "Walt blasted a boulder for me a few years back. And he used some dynamite to loosen up the ground for Frances' grave. But he's got a license. He used to blast for the Highway Department."

"Apparently they searched his place, too," Jerry said, "But they couldn't take him in because of the license. Judith said her mother told her they came to their house with a warrant and tore it up pretty good. They took a bunch of your father-in-law's papers from work, blueprints and so forth."

"God, I have no idea what that could be about," Harry said.

"The warrant also covered drugs and paraphernalia," Jerry said. "Any problem there?"

"Not at my place," Harry said.

"They also claim they found a large amount of cash," Jerry said.

"We kept all our savings in a safe, in the cabin," Harry said. "I'm not fond of banks."

"Well I'm on it full-time," Jerry said. "I cleared everything else off my calendar which didn't make everyone here happy. Joseph is coming in at Sea-Tac this afternoon."

"I really appreciate this," Harry said. "We'll get you paid somehow."

"We'll worry about that later," Jerry said.

When Harry went back to his mattress the Indian they had called "Chief" stared at him. Finally he said, "I know you." Harry waited.

"Your wife," Chief said. "She's related to the Antoines. And Little Eagle."

"That's right."

"What'd you do?" Chief asked him.

"Nothing that I know of," Harry said. "They claim I wanted to blow something up."

"The dam," Chief said. "Grand Coulee. I heard about it."

Harry looked at him. "From who?"

"The guards," Chief said. "When they took me out to see the doctor for my prescription." He grinned, leaned close to Harry and whispered, "I'm crazy." He waited for the effect.

Harry shrugged. "Me, too."

Chief laughed. "Everyone's crazy," he said in a low voice. "Just some of them don't know it."

"I figured it out a long time ago," Harry said.

"Too bad you didn't do it," Chief said. "Then the salmon would come again and we wouldn't be hungry in the winter. We used to always talk about blowing up the dams. Somebody should do it."

"Not me," Harry said. "That's not my style."

"Give me a bomb," Chief said. "I'll do it."

The cell door opened and Harry looked up to see Jeff Lasker carry in a mattress. Jeff looked around, saw Harry, grinned and stepped across other mattresses to get to him.

"Hey, man, watch it," one prisoner growled at Jeff as he stepped across his mattress.

"Fuck you," Jeff said.

Chief slid his mattress over next to his neighbor and motioned for Harry to tighten up, make room for Jeff. Jeff slammed the mattress down and sat on it.

"Hey, buddy. Long time, no see."

"You don't seem surprised to see me here," Harry said.

"Shit, buddy, you're all they want to talk about. Mr. Kingpin. What'd we do?"

"I don't know what I did," Harry said.

"Whatever it is sure has them excited," Jeff said. "They took down my operation but they weren't even really interested. Just wanted to know how much money I'd given you for your 'criminal enterprise.' You sure had me fooled."

"I fooled myself, too."

"No shit? You don't know what it's about?"

"Just rumors. They won't even tell my attorney."

"Speaking of attorneys," Jeff said. "I better call one. Where's the phone?"

Harry pointed to the telephone bolted to the wall.

"Be right back," Jeff said.

"That guy your friend?" Chief asked.

"We were in Viet Nam together," Harry said.

"Me, too," Chief said. "I was in 'Nam. In Hue when they came. I lived in the jungle for a couple of weeks before the chopper found me. Lots of Indians in 'Nam."

"Lots of everyone," Harry said.

Jeff came back. "Well, my guy's on it. He says he can bail me, maybe even PR."

"They found everything?" Harry asked him.

"Yeah," Jeff said, "But enough money can fix just about anything. Eliot will help. He knows the judge here. Really well, if you know what I mean."

"This is Federal," Harry said.

"That's just one more step," Jeff said, "and a little more expensive."

Another call from Jerry came just before noon.

"I got a call from Fred Lewis," he told Harry. "He says he represents a friend of yours, Jeff Lasker. Same case."

"Jeff's a guy I know from Viet Nam," Harry said. "They brought him in this morning."

"Well, this Fred Lewis has less than a perfect reputation," Jerry said. "He and his brother do a lot of drug cases. They don't really care how they win. I would rather not work with him, but he thinks we could help each other. He does have some contacts with the Feds that might help."

"Use your judgment," Harry said. "I'm not sure I care how we win at this point."

"They've scheduled your arraignment for tomorrow afternoon," Jerry said. "They're going to bring a magistrate in from Spokane because of the number of cases. That's better than them taking you to Spokane as far as I'm concerned. They'll have a bail hearing at the same time. They'll try to hold you without bail or set it so high you can't make it. It always makes the jury think you're more dangerous if they keep you in jail. We'll argue the other way, of course, but we won't have much time to prepare. We won't really know what's up until the hearing."

"I may have found out something that will help," Harry said. "A guy in here told me that he heard the guards talking about a plot to blow up Grand Coulee Dam."

Jerry whistled. "No wonder they're excited. There'll be promotions for everyone if they can make it stick."

"So it's just a game and I'm a pawn," Harry said.

"That's about it," Jerry said. "I'm going to pick Joseph up at the airport and we're going to head over. We'll be in to see you tomorrow morning. If you need to get hold of me call here and they'll beep me. Oh, and Judith told me to tell you that she got hold of Nathan and he'll take care of the missing person and check on your place."

"Tell her I love her," Harry said.

The day crept slowly by. Groups of prisoners were taken out for court proceedings in the morning and again in the afternoon, but none of those involved with Harry's case were called out. He spent the time talking to Jeff and Chief and staring at the shadows on the wall.

He called Uncle Paul again and Paul was full of encouragement, offered to help any way he could. He said that Jack had called, trying to find out what was going on. Someone from the church had called Mom and told her some exaggerated story. Paul said he hadn't told Jack anything.

Harry still could not eat the food. Chief said he would have to eat sooner or later. Jeff ate his and said it wasn't that bad, better than "C" rations. Harry joked that it was time for him to lose some weight anyway and besides, he'd heard that your brain works better when you're fasting.

There were TV bulletins about the case twice an hour and each time they came on there was a chorus of boos because they interrupted the cartoons or game shows. Harry watched closely for any clue that would help him. Mostly they just repeated the vague and inflammatory generalizations he'd seen the night before. They promised that the next day after the arraignments there would be a special news program explaining the whole situation. By late afternoon they had begun to give a little information about The Church of the New Covenant and were calling the special report The Covenant Conspiracy: Terrorism Comes Home."

There was a loudspeaker message for Harry to call a number that he realized was Judith's parents'. He called and Matt answered.

"Just a minute, Harry," Matt said, "Someone wants to talk to you." There was a long pause and some clicks then he heard Judith's voice.

"Hello," she said.

"Where are you?"

"Down the hall from you. It's a conference call."

"Great idea. How are you doing?"

"I'm fine. I talked to Nathan and he was going to check things out at home. He will take care of any problems."

"I hope he finds everything," Harry said. "Especially the missing horse."

"He will," Judith said. "I told him where to look."

"How about Joe? He must be scared to death."

"My mother called them. They took him to Colville to some receiving home. She's going over to see him today. Jerry thinks they will give her temporary custody."

"That would be a relief," Harry said.

"I'll be glad when Joseph gets here. I think he will know what to do. He'll have to work through Jerry because he isn't licensed in Washington State."

"We need all the help we can get. Jeff's in here."

"I know. Lisa is here with me."

"Let's let them talk."

"Good idea. I love you Harry. We'll survive this. Little Eagle is coming."

"I'm very glad to hear that. I love you too."

He called Jeff to the phone and was pleased at his surprise when he heard Lisa. He left Jeff to talk in private.

Another message came for Harry to call Ron Radford. He dialed the number and Ron accepted the call.

"I heard about some trouble on the San Poil and tried to call you," Ron said. "Some asshole Deputy Sheriff tried to pretend he was you and find out who I was. I told him to go fuck himself."

Harry laughed. "They'll be after you, next."

"What the hell did you do?" Ron asked. "The news sounds like you were trying to start World War Three."

"Armageddon," Harry said. "The rumor is that we were trying to blow Grand Coulee."

"Well, I know you weren't involved in anything like that," Ron said.

"I'm glad someone does," Harry said.

"The reason I wanted to talk to you," Ron said, "Is that I figured you'd need some bail money. I might be able to help."

"It's going to be really high," Harry said.

"I can talk my dad into helping," Ron said. "He'll know you didn't do anything. And how about Jack? I ran into him and he was comin' on like Mr. Rockefeller. He oughta help."

"I wouldn't count on Jack," Harry said.

"Well, I'm going to call him and tell him he'd better," Ron said. "Who's your lawyer? I want to talk to him."

Harry gave Ron Jerry's name and phone number, said he probably was on the road.

"I think I'll just come over there," Ron said. "Cynthia has a couple of days off. We need a vacation."

"Thanks," Harry said. "I won't forget."

The evening news from Spokane ran a five-minute piece on The Church of the New Covenant narrated by a young investigative reporter who obviously smelled a great career step. He said he had discovered that church members had gone to Waco, Texas so obviously there was a connection with the Branch Davidians. Someone had told him that some Davidians who'd escaped were hiding out in the San Poil Valley. He hadn't actually found evidence of child abuse and molestation yet but obviously that was part of the pattern of these cults. Fortunately all the children had been taken away to good foster homes where they would receive decent care.

Most likely, he said, this Covenant Conspiracy was only the tip of the iceberg and probably was part of a great international web of terrorism that included the World Trade Center Bombers, Randy Weaver, the Branch Davidians, Friends of the Earth and perhaps even the Russian Mafia. He urged everyone to watch The Covenant Conspiracy: Terrorism Comes Home where he would name the names of these enemies of freedom and the American Way.

Harry slept fitfully. When dawn lightened the high, barred windows he took a shower and sat on his mattress to consider the day ahead. He hoped that Nathan had found Rebecca and that Little Joe was with his grandparents. He was anxious to see Jerry and Joseph and to find out what his true situation was. Chief woke up and sat cross-legged and murmured a song to greet the day. It gave Harry a sense of peace and he smiled and Chief smiled back. "Give 'em hell," Chief said.

There was a lot of noise from the street and one of the prisoners jumped up to grab the window bars and pulled himself up to look out. He reported several news vehicles outside including a large CNN satellite truck.

Not long after breakfast was served, a woman guard unlocked the door and called Harry. He went to her and she said he had visitors. She put handcuffs on him and led him down the hall and opened a door for him. Jerry and Joseph were there, stood to greet him.

"Can we get rid of those?" Jerry asked, pointed at the handcuffs.

"Sorry, against regulations."

When she closed the door Harry sat in an orange plastic chair across a battered steel table from the two attorneys.

"Well," Jerry said, "We don't know a lot more yet. They're supposed to have affidavits ready as soon as the clerk's office opens. They'll try to conceal as much as they can, just meet minimum standards to charge and hold you."

"How about bail?" Harry asked.

"They'll try to have you held without bail," Joseph said. "Jerry said they were talking about a million dollars if they had to grant bail."

"I talked to Ron Radford last night when we got here," Jerry said. "It sounds like he might be some serious help. If we can make them think there is no way you can make bail, they might go for a lower amount just to look good."

"Get Judith out first," Harry said. "I can survive."

"So tell us everything you can remember," Jerry said.

Harry told them the story as he knew it. There wasn't much to tell. Both attorneys agreed that Johnny Carlson was telling stories to avoid prosecution on the arson charges and that the militia members were going along with it to divert attention from themselves.

"But to even charge you they'll have to have other evidence. Hard evidence," Jerry said. "From what you are saying all I can see is the assault rifle which has not been converted to fully automatic so it's legal. And the money. But there's no law against keeping your own money in your possession. Have you paid your taxes."

Harry told them he was current on the State Sales Tax and had filed his IRS return on time.

"So how much cash was there?" Jerry asked.

"About forty thousand dollars," Harry said. "Maybe a little more."

"That is a bunch," Jerry said. "They'll try to make something out of it, drug money or something."

"No drugs at my place," Harry said.

"Don't count on it," Joseph said. "Drugs are easy to carry around and 'find' wherever you want to. I handled several cases of planted drugs on the Navajo Reservation. If they couldn't get someone any other way, that was the routine. Judith told me once that you had a friend who grew marijuana."

"He's in here," Harry said. "A guy I knew from Viet Nam."

"That's Lasker," Jerry said to Joseph, "The guy that hired Fred Lewis."

"That could be a problem," Joseph said. "You have any business with this guy."

Harry told them about wiring Jeff's shed and about the marijuana patch he'd found.

"Let's hope they can't prove any of that," Jerry said. "I'll go see if those affidavits are ready."

"Nathan found Rebecca," Joseph said to Harry. "She was hiding out at Walt Davis' place. He took her to Hattie's. I'll go see her after the arraignment."

"Tell her I love her and to be brave," Harry said.

"I will," Joseph promised.

Harry and Joseph went back over the details and Joseph took careful notes. Jerry returned with a stack of photocopies.

"Look over these affidavits. I'm going to handle the arraignment and bail hearing for this guy you call Tamarack. All they have on him is misdemeanor marijuana possession and I think I can get him PR'd.

"Ask him to keep an eye on our place," Harry said.

There were affidavits from Johnny Carlson, from an unnamed confidential informant, from some militia member named Allan Nicholson and from several members of the task force. Joseph handed Harry a felt pen.

"Mark anything we need to talk about."

Johnny Carlson's affidavit was written in language he never would use and Harry was sure that Johnny hadn't understood much of it. It claimed that Johnny had heard Harry and Judith and others talk of a plan to blow up Grand Coulee and start a great flood that would take out all the dams on the Columbia and destroy several cities in the process. The idea originally had been broached by Judith Isaacson. The plan was to build two huge nitrogen bombs, one on Harry's trailer and another hidden in the old tanker the militia owned and drive them onto the top of Grand Coulee Dam and detonate them.

The affidavit told of several meetings to further the plot and claimed that the plans for the bombs had been obtained off the Internet through Harry's computer system. They had somehow obtained blueprints of the dam and knew just where to place the bombs for maximum effect. They had practiced for the bombing by setting off large explosions in a field near the Isaacson cabin.

The plan was to be executed Labor Day weekend when the dam guards were distracted with all the tourist traffic. The money for the venture was provided by drug dealers who wanted to divert attention from their activities. Two of those providing money were Edward Tolman AKA Eliot and "someone named Jeff who owns a ranch in the Kettle Valley near Curlew." Johnny also had seen a large amount of marijuana being grown on Harry Isaacson's farm.

The affidavit further claimed that Harry and Judith had frequently been seen using drugs and that Johnny had bought both marijuana and cocaine from Harry. Furthermore Johnny suspected that Judith had given drugs to his mother which had caused her to commit suicide.

Eventually, Johnny claimed, he had grown so concerned about the plot that he had started the fires in an attempt to prevent it from being carried out. He now realized he should have gone to the authorities but he was afraid he would be killed because of previous death threats from Harry and other militia members.

Alan Nicholson's statement repeated much of what was in Johnny's. He claimed to have attended several meetings and to have been recruited to help build the bomb in the tanker. He never had actually been in a meeting where Harry was present, he said, but he had been told that Harry was a secret militia member, part of a terrorist cell called "The Sword of the Lord" whose members pretended to oppose the militia as part of their cover. There were several Indians involved but he didn't know their names. Harry's mother had been a courier for the group. He, too, feared violence from the defendants.

The confidential informant claimed to be a local man who had infiltrated the San Poil Militia at the request of the Sheriff's Department. He, too, claimed to have attended meetings where Harry and Judith's involvement was discussed and he knew of the plot to blow up the dams. He had not yet reported it to the Sheriff because of a blood pact vowing death to any informers. He told of a large supply of illegal weapons hidden at the militia "compound" and, he had been told, on Harry's farm.

The task force members' affidavits recited all their qualifications, what schools they'd been to, how many cases they'd worked and assured the magistrate that they had the necessary expertise to testify to various elements of the case.

An FBI Agent told of being called to interview Johnny Carlson when he'd started talking to a guard about the plot. From there he had conducted an extensive investigation to ascertain the connections between the various conspirators, to establish the trail of the money and to determine the danger to agents in making the arrests. He had proof of transfers of large amounts of money to Harry Isaacson from Jeff Lasker and Edward Tolman including a cashier's check for ten thousand dollars which had been cashed by Isaacson. There was a copy of the check with Harry's signature. There were bank reports of several large deposits and withdrawals of cash and it was known that Isaacson had paid cash for a large parcel of property and had a secret investment in a real estate project near Ephrata. There were signs in and around the residence of access to far more money than would be normal for such a small farm. The store run by the Isaacson's was probably used to launder illegal funds.

A Drug Task Force member who searched Harry's cabin claimed to have found "a plastic bag containing twenty-two grams of a white powder which appeared to be cocaine" and to having found "eight bags of a green plant substance appearing to be high-grade marijuana." He further said that he had found a well-hidden safe which when opened was found to contain seventeen thousand four hundred dollars in cash.

An agent from ATF said that he had found four illegal weapons in Harry's cabin including a fifty-caliber rifle, a fully automatic Colt assault rifle and a business card for a gun-dealer who was a known trafficker in illegal weapons with connections to several militias. In the Isaacson barn he had found just over three tons of ammonium nitrate, far more than could have been used on such a small farm but enough to build two very large bombs.

And near the fertilizer were, "a number of heavy wooden containers commonly known as apple bins which could have been used to mix and transport the explosive mixture."

Harry was angry. He told Joseph that most of it was lies and the rest distortions. Joseph told him to calm down, that they would handle it all in court. Jerry returned, said he had managed to get Tamarack out on his own recognizance and probably could plea-bargain the case to the one day served and maybe probation.

They went over the affidavits point by point and Harry explained the real situation with each item. He denied having any drugs or ammonium nitrate. Joseph was sure the drugs had been planted. As to the fertilizer, unless they could prove it was there maybe that would be a way to attack the whole thing.

They still were talking when the guard came to say it was time for the arraignment. She took Harry to the cell door and hooked his handcuffs onto a chain along with Jeff and several other prisoners including the militia members Harry had recognized. A male guard helped her get them all in line. It was impossible to walk without stepping on each other's feet or bumping into one another.

Harry could hear the noise in the hallway even before the guards unlocked the door. As the line of prisoners went through the door there was great excitement. There were shouts as television lights shone on them and still camera flashes blinked. It was several minutes before the guards and several deputies in the hallway could clear a path to the courtroom door just forty feet away. Questions were shouted at them and several reporters called out, "Which one is Isaacson?"

As they started through the courtroom door there was another wave of excitement and Harry looked up to see Judith and several other women prisoners on a similar chain being brought through the jammed hallway. Judith's head was high and her eyes flashed.

The courtroom was full and people stood in every available place. Many of them clearly were reporters with notebooks and mini-recorders. A bailiff stood in the front, called out, "No cameras, no tape recorders in here."

The prisoners were herded into an area that appeared to be the jury box and they all took seats. Reporters crowded around and tried to ask them questions. Several tried to get Harry to say something. He ignored them.

Jerry and Joseph came in, took seats among some other men in suits who appeared to be attorneys. Several of them said "hello" to Jerry.

The bailiff called, "Order in the court. Quiet it down. We have a lot of proceedings today."

When there was a semblance of order he knocked on the door to the judge's chambers and an elderly man in wire-rimmed glasses wearing a dark robe came out.

"All stand," the bailiff ordered and everyone shuffled to their feet.

"Be seated," the magistrate said as he took his own place. A court reporter fiddled with a computer at a table near him. "I am United States Magistrate Aldon Mitchell," he continued. "We are here today for the arraignments of several Federal prisoners on very serious charges. I caution everyone to maintain order and decorum as we proceed. Those charged with lesser offenses will be first. I ask all defense counsels to keep their presentations succinct and maybe we can get through all this in a timely manner."

They began with some of the militia women, most of whom had charges against them dropped and were released. The magistrate told them each to remain available for questioning and to otherwise cooperate with the police agencies involved. Two of them were to face minor firearms charges but were released on their own recognizance. Soon Judith was the only woman prisoner who remained.

Two of the militia men also had charges dropped in return for their cooperation with the investigation. Several others were held on bail ranging from a hundred thousand dollars to half a million on various drug and weapons charges and a charge of conspiring to destroy Federal property. When about half the men had been dealt with, the magistrate disappeared into chambers and the bailiff announced that there would be a one-hour recess for lunch. The two guards took the remaining prisoners back to their cells. Lunch already had been served and the guards asked them if they wanted some lunch brought up. Everyone but Harry said "yes."

After lunch there was the same scene in the hallway but by this time all the reporters knew who Harry and Judith were and concentrated their cameras, microphones and questions on them. Neither of them would respond. One reporter remarked that they were "good soldiers."

Jeff's case was just before Harry's. Fred Lewis argued that there was no proof of Jeff's involvement in any conspiracy and that any money transactions involved only business. The drug charges, he said, would more properly be State charges and the normal bail in such cases would be a hundred thousand dollars at most. Given that his client was a property owner and upstanding citizen he requested release on Personal Recognizance.

The Magistrate considered for a couple of minutes then said that since the conspiracy charges had not yet been dismissed he would set bail at a hundred thousand dollars. Jeff grinned and nodded his thanks.

Judith was unhooked from the chain, moved to the defense table and sat between Joseph and Jerry. She stood with them as the charges were read and said "yes" when asked if she understood the charges.

The Assistant US Attorney asked for bail of a million dollars, pointed out that as the source of such a heinous plan she was a clear danger to the community as well as a flight risk. Jerry argued that she had no knowledge of any conspiracy and that the only evidence against her was the testimony of those with a clear reason to transfer their own guilt to others. And since she was a mother with two minor children, her risk of flight was minimal and it was in the community's interests to keep mothers and children together.

The magistrate said that the charges were very serious and seemed well documented and that he had no choice but to hold her on bail of half a million dollars.

Silence gripped the courtroom as Harry stepped forward. He acknowledged that he understood the charges and sat between the attorneys. The Assistant US Attorney asked that he be held without bail and that he be moved immediately to Federal Detention because they had information that militia groups might try to break him out of the jail. He repeatedly referred to Harry as "The Principal Conspirator." He said that because of the drug charges the government had already instituted proceedings to seize and confiscate the real estate and personal property.

Jerry argued that there was no hard evidence of a conspiracy or intent to bomb anything, that there was reason to believe that the drug charges were fabricated and that in any case, reports of large amounts of ammonium nitrate at the farm were completely false.

The Assistant US Attorney smiled and asked the magistrate if he could submit a videotape as an exhibit and show it to the court. The Magistrate agreed. The court reporter and bailiff worked at a video player, got it on and working. The Assistant US Attorney handed the bailiff a tape and the bailiff put it in the machine, handed the remote to the attorney.

As the tape began, the attorney narrated. It showed the raid, Harry and Judith being arrested, a few seconds of Little Joe in Marlene's car. There was footage inside the cabin including the computer system, the supposed "finding" of the drugs, the safe being torn out of the wall. Then the tape showed the barn, walked through the door and focused on a large stack of paper bags of fertilizer, zoomed in to show the "ammonium nitrate" label. There was further footage of some barrels that supposedly contained diesel and the stack of apple bins along one wall.

The attorney turned off the tape and said, "As you can see, your honor, our case is very well documented and the charges by defense counsel are only a desperate attempt to get his client out of custody, probably never to be seen again."

The magistrate frowned, thought for a minute then set Harry's bail at a million dollars. He said he would consider the transfer to Federal Detention at a later time and hurriedly retired to chambers. The woman guard came to take Harry back to his cell.

He looked at Judith and saw that her face was very grim.

CHAPTER 25

As Harry entered the cell, the militia members who had been released on bail or had charges dropped stood in a line carrying their mattresses and blankets, ready to be released. Several of them laughed at Harry and one said, "We told you to watch your back, asshole. Have fun with the Feds." Harry ignored them.

Jeff had moved his mattress and Harry's onto a vacated double bunk and sat there waiting. "I'm out of here in the morning. A hundred grand is nothing."

Harry sat beside him. "I guess I'm here for the duration, like we used to say."

"Hey, buddy, I'm goin' to work on gettin' you out. I need to talk to your friend Ron. I think I can get Eliot to help."

"I don't see how you can raise a million dollars," Harry said.

"You'd be surprised," Jeff said. "A million ain't what it used to be. My property is worth that much if you get the right appraiser."

"Won't they confiscate it?" Harry asked.

"Naw," Jeff said. "Fred Lewis already got them to agree to let the State prosecute the drug charges and if someone pleads guilty to simple manufacture they won't go after the property. They just want some kind of a conviction. They're goin' to have to drop the conspiracy shit. They got no evidence. Fred told them that ten thousand was just a loan repayment. They can't prove any different. Besides, I'm goin' to offer Gringo a nice piece of change to take the whole rap. How was I supposed to know what he was doin' in my shop? He won't ever have to work again."

"Sounds like you're on top of it," Harry said.

"Cheer up, buddy," Jeff said. "I'm not leavin' you in here any more than I would have in 'Nam."

The "dinner" was brought in and once again Harry refused to eat.

One of the trusties winked at him. "You're a regular fuckin' celebrity. The staff is spendin' half their time tryin' to make sure some reporter doesn't sneak up here or get you on the phone." He looked around furtively and pulled a scrap of paper out of his pocket. "Here's a number you could call if you want to talk to a reporter," the trusty said. "If you do it, tell 'em Smoky hooked you up."

Harry put the scrap of paper in his waistband.

The promos for The Covenant Conspiracy: Terrorism Comes Home interrupted the programming about every ten minutes. One of the younger prisoners said, "Fuck this" and went to change the channel.

"Leave it," Jeff hissed at him and the kid went back to his bunk.

As soon as the national network news ended the special came on. It began with a series of explosions and an old hippie song "The Eve of Destruction" as a theme. The explosions were followed by an aerial view of Grand Coulee Dam on a peaceful summer day. The deep blue water of Lake Roosevelt trailed away to the north.

"This was the target," the reporter began. "This technological marvel, the source of power and irrigation water that makes the Inland Empire rich and green, the very heart of our economy. This evil plot by a small group of extremists would have cost us all dearly had not brilliant investigative work and lightning quick action by local and Federal authorities averted the nefarious plan."

The reporter looked deep into the camera. "Live-Wire News has attempted to interview officers involved in the dazzling investigation and daring raid that broke the back of this terrorist conspiracy but we have been told that the authorities do not want to make any comment this early in the judicial proceedings to avoid possible defense accusations of interfering with the defendants' right to a fair trial. They did tell us that they believe they have a nearly airtight case and expect to obtain convictions at least of the ringleaders.

"We also have been unable to contact the brave young man who first tried to stop the plot himself. Then when he was unable to do so told his story to authorities and set it all in motion. He is somewhere in protective custody and we wish him well. Perhaps this case will be instructive for other young people caught up in the nightmare of drugs and violence. We now continue with The Covenant Conspiracy: Terrorism Comes Home."

An aerial view of the San Poil Valley followed, then footage taken from the highway. "Such peaceful scenes belie the twisted plan that was born here on the Colville Indian Reservation just a few miles from the intended target."

There were shots of men in camouflage carrying assault rifles maneuvering through trees, dropping to the ground and firing. "Militia members similar to these seen in footage just obtained from Oregon hatched a deadly plan to destroy Grand Coulee Dam, in the hope that the ensuing flood would take out all the lower dams on the Columbia River, flooding several cities in the process and causing massive power shortages throughout the Western United States. The cost, according to officials, would have been many billions of dollars and thousands of innocent lives. It is hard to believe that any human being could plan such a disaster, but the leader of this group, a Viet Nam Veteran harboring a deep seated anger at America, and his Native American wife, allegedly spent years bringing the plot to fruition."

Next came videotape of the cabin and barn. "And this seemingly all-American scene was the nerve-center of the conspiracy. Dozens of illegal weapons, a small fortune in drugs and a large amount of untraceable cash were found in this log cabin. And here, in the barn, near peaceful horses and their innocent colts, was stored the mountain of high-explosives intended to obliterate one of the Seven Wonders of the Modern World. Authorities tell us that had the explosion been detonated here it would have incinerated the house and barn, killed all the animals and left a crater a hundred feet deep."

"Because of the drug charges the real estate and personal property will be immediately confiscated and sold at auction and the proceeds used to fund the War Against Drugs. A large part of the property apparently was put in the legal ownership of several Native American relatives of the wife, probably to protect it from possible confiscation. Officials say they are used to such maneuvers and recent court rulings should allow them to seize the property despite this ruse."

"This is the so called Church of the New Covenant just two miles from the home of the chief suspect. Although these terrorists claim to be Christian Patriots, their bizarre theology, similar to that of the Branch Davidian Cult, is a mixture of Right Wing conspiracy theory and Old Testament Wrath of God teachings. Reportedly the terrorist cell which was prepared to wreak such havoc on us all called themselves 'The Sword of the Lord,' a name sure to infuriate and disgust true Christian Believers."

"While most of those arrested were members of this church, the ring-leader apparently hid his connection to the congregation, using others as go-betweens. The pastor of the congregation, the Reverend Bobby Baker, has been questioned and released. Authorities say there is no evidence he had any direct knowledge of the conspiracy."

Last year's school picture of Little Joe flashed on the screen. "Many of these marginal people refuse to send their children to Public Schools, but rather 'home school' them, something child experts say is almost always a sign of maladjustment and dysfunction. Many of these children are abused, physically and sexually, and there is little hope that they will mature into contributing adults."

"We will take a break now for a message from our sponsors, but when we return with The Covenant Conspiracy: Terrorism Comes Home we will delve deeper into the aberrant psychology that could produce such a monstrous plot."

Harry's heart pounded and his throat was dry. He never had felt such rage.

Jeff looked at him and shook his head. "What a wonderful country."

The commercials ended and the reporter's face appeared on the screen. "As promised we will now take an in-depth look at the disturbed personalities that lead this war from within against America. As you will see it is not obvious on the surface who may be hiding such hatred for all of us. It could be your own neighbor or even a relative. The signs of disturbance are very small in the beginning, easy to overlook. We all must be watchful and report any signs of such aberrant behavior to the proper authorities.

"This is the reputed ringleader. His name is Harry Isaacson." There was a quick cut of Harry in jail uniform being led away from the courtroom. "Today in Okanogan County he was arraigned on Federal charges ranging from possession and sale of cocaine and marijuana to possession of illegal weapons to conspiracy to destroy Federal property. Conviction on all charges could lead to sentences totaling over four hundred years in Federal prison. Because the plot was not consummated the death penalty is not possible. Bail was set at a million dollars although the US

Attorney argued that Isaacson is such an extreme danger to the community that he should be held without bail."

"Plans are underway to transfer Isaacson to Federal Detention. There are reports that Isaacson has begun a hunger strike but authorities assure Live-Wire News that such antics will not influence their decisions."

"Isaacson grew up in Kansas and then Washington State after the family moved here in nineteen fifty-eight." There was footage of Columbia Basin farms, tractors plowing, combines harvesting.

"By all reports his childhood was uneventful, much like many farm boys. After two years at the University of Washington, Isaacson entered the US Army and was sent to Viet Nam. It is not known what events in Viet Nam may have triggered deep seated psychological problems perhaps growing out of an isolated childhood. In any case, within days after his discharge from the army began a long series of encounters with authorities."

"Here in this peaceful War Memorial Park Isaacson was arrested for vagrancy and drug use. Upon being sent to Harborview Hospital for psychiatric observation, Isaacson attacked and seriously injured a doctor and was subsequently committed to Western State Hospital for several months. Upon release from Western State, Isaacson returned to the University of Washington and even attended graduate school for several years although he never did obtain an advanced degree. During his time in graduate school Isaacson was arrested again, this time on suspicion of rape and assault although charges were eventually dropped for lack of evidence. An officer who remembers that incident tells us he believes the victim may have been intimidated into dropping charges."

There was a shot of the farm in Block Eighty-eight. "It was after returning to the family farm when he was unable to maintain steady employment that the suspect's condition apparently began to seriously deteriorate. After his assuming a partnership in the family farm, that business collapsed due to mismanagement which led eventually to the farm's sale at auction in nineteen eighty-six. Isaacson's father died from a gunshot wound within hours after the auction under very mysterious circumstances. Isaacson was held and questioned in the death, but again there was insufficient evidence to prosecute even though Isaacson was one of the beneficiaries of a very large life insurance policy."

"Other members of the Isaacson family seem normal and well adjusted. A brother who is a respected real estate professional lives in the Seattle area and his sister is a nurse in Spokane. The fact that he comes from such a fine American family leads one psychologist we contacted to speculate that Isaacson suffers from undiagnosed delayed stress syndrome. Be that as it may, it is hard to have sympathy for someone who apparently has never sought help for his condition."

The reporter smiled into the camera. "We must take another break, but when we return to The Covenant Conspiracy: Terrorism Comes Home we will share with you an exclusive interview obtained by Live-Wire News just this afternoon with someone who may be able to shed some light on the mystery of this strange journey from the heartland to terrorist leader."

Harry stared at the screen unable to speak. Jeff patted him on the shoulder. He could feel the eyes of the other prisoners on him.

The reporter was excited. "Welcome back to The Covenant Conspiracy: Terrorism Comes Home. I promised an exclusive interview and now I will deliver. This afternoon I flew with a Live-Wire News team to interview the suspect's mother at the home of his brother in the Seattle area. We will not show her face for obvious reasons and her voice has been altered. We think you will agree that this conversation provides information critical to an understanding of how this may have happened."

There was shot of Mom from the back sitting in Jack's livingroom. The reporter sat facing her, exuded gentleness and concern. "Mrs. Isaacson we are sorry to bother you at such a difficult moment. We hope you understand how important it is that our viewers gain some understanding of these recent events involving your son."

Mom nodded, heaved a dramatic sigh.

"Mrs. Isaacson, we understand that you knew nothing of the Covenant Conspiracy even though you were living near your son Harry at the time the alleged plot was conceived. Did you never suspect at all that something was not right?"

"Never," Mom said. Her voice sounded like Donald Duck. "Harry has always been so strange that it is hard to know what he's thinking."

"So then you would say that there have always been signs that he wasn't like other people."

"Harry always wanted to live in the past," Mom said. "He wanted to farm with horses when everyone else had tractors. When his father wanted to borrow money to modernize our farm, Harry was always against it. He said the way his grandfather did things was the right way."

"So you think maybe this plot he is alleged to have been involved with might have been a twisted way to try to bring back the past?"

"I guess that's possible," Mom said.

"Did you see this tendency to solve things with violence?"

"I know he always had guns around," Mom said. "And I remember he threatened to shoot the banker when we lost the farm. And the police thought he killed his father but I was never sure about that."

"But you think it's a possibility?"

Mom shrugged, seemed to be sobbing.

The reporter reached over to touch her on the shoulder. "We are sorry to distress you, Mrs. Isaacson, but we must ask you to respond to the suggestion that you were used as a courier or messenger between your son and other conspirators."

"If I was, I didn't know," Mom said. "They had me completely fooled."

"It sounds to us like any part you may have played in the conspiracy was as an unwitting dupe, not as a knowing participant," the reporter said kindly.

Mom nodded.

"Now, Mrs. Isaacson, as we conclude this painful interview, is there anything you would like to say?"

Mom straightened herself. "I just want to say that our family is very sorry for what happened. If we had known this would happen we would have gotten help for Harry a long time ago. He had a friend of his call his brother and threaten him if he didn't help with his bail money, but we aren't going to be afraid any more."

"Thank you, Mrs. Isaacson," the reporter said and looked into the camera. "As you can see, many complex issues combine to create the kinds of problems that threaten to tear our country apart. Again, I urge all of you to be alert to the signs of such mental disturbance in those around you. Get help for those who need it. It will take the best efforts of all of us to win this war against terrorism and drugs. Thank you for watching The Covenant Conspiracy: Terrorism Comes Home."

Another commercial break followed then the reporter returned, seated snugly in the studio. "We here at Live-Wire News hope this special program The Covenant Conspiracy: Terrorism Comes Home has helped you to understand the tragic events that have transpired in our area in the last few days. We want to remind you that no one has yet been convicted of any charges and the defendants have a right to a fair trial. The legal process has just begun its slow march to justice. Our intent has been to examine the processes that may lie behind the current wave of terrorism threatening America. Thank you once again for watching our Live-Wire News special The Covenant Conspiracy: Terrorism Comes Home. A fast-cut collage of scenes from the program were accompanied by "The Eve of Destruction" then faded into the intro for Wheel of Fortune reruns.

Harry could not sleep. He lay on the bunk, stared at the wall and reviewed his entire life. Like the reporter, he sought the answer for how he had come here, but the story was very different from the one he had seen on television. A part of him wished he had been violent and struck out instead of meekly living his life, hoping for the best and rolling with the punches. He thought of how much damage he could do in a few minutes on the streets of Seattle if he chose to. Then he thought of Judith and Rebecca and Little Joe, the farm, the horses, the river and he knew that all he wanted was his life back.

In his mind he went to the children's grove, listened to the soft murmur of those now-familiar voices. The words were unintelligible but the message was clear. "Endure. Life is fleeting, spirit endures."

He heard Long Joe say, "The covenants are all broken. Nations require enemies. If there are no enemies they will create one." He could see those eyes float before him in the darkness. "Death is just a change of status." He wondered if that was the answer, to end it and start the cycle again. But he thought of Judith and the children and knew he could not do it.

He thought of the family cemetery in Kansas and could feel the old man's hand hold his, hear his whisper, "People love to put their troubles on someone else, Harry, then hate them for it. That's what the Romans and the Sanhedrin did to the Lord. It's a way to buy a little more time."

He remembered all the stories of his ancestors who had survived in the West, had faced all the trouble that came their way and endured. He knew he, too, could endure, could see it through and in the end be not broken but stronger.

As dawn began to shine through the windows high above him and throw shadows of the bars onto the wall he felt his energy rise. There would be an answer, there must be. A part of him, in a strange way, welcomed the challenge, felt equal to the test. It was not fear but excitement that caused his heart to pound. He wished he knew a song to greet the day. He would ask Long Joe to teach him.

CHAPTER 26

Not long after breakfast the woman guard opened the door and called for Harry. He went to her and she snapped on the handcuffs, led him out. When the door closed, she whispered, "Something big is up. Good luck."

Jerry and Joseph waited in the visiting room. Jerry smiled at him. "Well, my grandma used to tell me every day is a new day. I guess she was right."

"What do you mean?"

"We have some new evidence," Jerry said. He glanced towards the ceiling. "I don't feel comfortable talking about it in here. But it could turn this whole thing around. We won't be ready until this afternoon. Judith's cousin, Nathan, is bringing a witness. And Little Eagle?" he asked Joseph. Joseph nodded. "Little Eagle," Jerry continued, "Is bringing some key evidence. And we hope they'll let us cross examine this Carlson kid."

"The problem," Joseph said, "Is getting a new hearing right away. Technically they don't have to do it. If the government doesn't agree, they could move you to Spokane and hear this later."

"So how do we get a new hearing?" Harry asked.

"Fred Lewis is talking to the Assistant US Attorney now," Jerry said. "He thinks he can convince them to agree to a hearing. Frankly, from the way Lewis talked, I think he knows something they don't want out. Your friend, Lasker, apparently offered him a bundle of money to help."

"So what do I do?" Harry asked.

"Wait," Jerry said, "And hope. If Lewis is successful we can go at about two o'clock. If the witnesses and evidence are here in time."

"You can't tell me who these witnesses are?" Harry asked.

"I'd rather not," Jerry said. "Sometimes jail walls have ears. Let's not take the chance."

"Does Judith know?" Harry asked.

"We'll talk to her as soon as they take you back," Jerry said.

It seemed forever until two o'clock. The woman guard came again, smiled at him when she put on the handcuffs. "You must have a guardian angel."

"Why is that?" Harry asked her.

"The bailiff says he's never heard of a second hearing this soon in a Federal case. He told me the US Attorney is really mad."

"So why are they doing it?"

"Nobody knows. But some of us are pulling for you. I know your wife's family."

The courtroom was less than half-full and there were only a couple of reporters. One of them Harry recognized as the star of The Covenant Conspiracy: Terrorism Comes Home. He studied Harry as though he were a zoo animal or museum exhibit.

Harry noticed someone wave for his attention and saw Ron Radford, then noticed that Jeff was beside him. Ron gave Harry a thumbs-up and Jeff shook his fist in the air.

The guard took Harry directly to the defense table and Jerry held a chair for him. Judith was brought to the table and she sat next to Harry, reached over with her cuffed hands to take his.

Harry looked around and saw that Johnny Carlson sat at the prosecutor's table flanked by two deputies. His father sat nearby. There was a commotion at the door behind them and Harry turned to see Long Joe come in. He carried a manila envelope then Harry saw Rebecca was with him.

"Hi Mom, Hi Dad," Rebecca called to them.

"Hi honey," Judith said to her.

"Quiet," the bailiff ordered.

Joseph went to talk to Long Joe and Rebecca, had them sit just behind the defense table.

A few minutes later Nathan came in. With him was Johanna Grant. They sat near Long Joe and Rebecca.

The bailiff came over and leaned near Jerry. "Is that it?" he asked.

Jerry nodded.

The bailiff knocked on the chambers door and soon the magistrate appeared. He asked them all to sit and began. "This hearing is a very unusual procedure but the court has been informed of extraordinary circumstances. Both the United States Attorney and the defense counsel have requested this hearing and the court feels that new information just brought to the court's attention makes it appropriate to proceed at this time. Defense counsel will begin."

Jerry stood and the courtroom was hushed. "Your honor, we have two witnesses to present as well as an exhibit consisting of a video-tape. We also have requested that we be allowed to examine the Government's witness, John Carlson Junior. We also would like to take another look at the video tape which the government showed to the court at yesterday's arraignment."

He took the envelope from Long Joe and asked permission to approach the bench. He handed the envelope to the magistrate who opened it and took out a videocassette.

"With the court's permission," Jerry continued, "I would like to call as a witness Rebecca Isaacson who recorded the video-tape you hold and ask her to explain the circumstances surrounding it."

The magistrate looked at the US Attorney who nodded.

"Proceed," the magistrate said to Jerry.

Jerry motioned Rebecca forward and she raised her hand while the bailiff swore her in. The magistrate smiled at her and asked her to sit in the witness chair. The bailiff adjusted the microphone for her.

"Rebecca," Jerry said, "Would you tell us how you came to take this video tape?"

"I was out riding when the cops, er... the police came to our place. I hid in the woods to see what was going on. I saw them take my Mom and Dad away and my little brother. They also took a lot of stuff out of our house. I was very scared."

"Then what happened?" Jerry asked her.

"I saw some of them go to Mr. Davis's house."

"And what did you do?"

"I waited for them all to go away but one car stayed there," Rebecca said. "It was getting dark so I rode up to the spring. I tied Shadow, that's my Mom's horse I was riding, and took the saddle off her and waited for morning."

"Did you sleep?" Jerry asked her.

"I slept a little on the saddle blanket," Rebecca said, "But it was cold so mostly I walked around and waited. When it was starting to get light I heard Reject, that's my dad's dog, barking down by the house. I wanted to see what it was so I jumped on Shadow and rode down there."

"Did you have your video camera with you?" Jerry asked.

"I always have my video camera with me," Rebecca said.

"What did you see when you got to the house?"

"I saw four sheriff's cars. One of them was one of those Blazers. They parked at the house and one man got out with a video camera and started taking pictures. The same man who did it the day before. They went in the house."

"What did you do?"

"I started taking pictures of them. I thought it was funny what they were doing."

"Where were you then?"

"I was in the brush right across the river. I let Shadow graze."

"What happened next?"

"I saw Mr. Carlson's truck coming and it went to our barn."

"And you took pictures of that?"

"Yes," Rebecca said. "And then they started unloading all these sacks, I thought it was fertilizer?"

"Objection," the Assistant US Attorney shouted, jumped to his feet.

"Overruled," the magistrate said.

"Who started unloading sacks?" Jerry asked.

"Mr. Carlson and one of the men from my Grandma's church. And the policemen."

"And you were still taking pictures?"

"Yes. I thought my Dad would want to know about it."

"Then what happened?"

"After they unloaded all these sacks into our barn, Mr. Carlson left in his truck and the man with the video camera went in the barn."

"Then what happened?"

"They were all laughing and talking loud. But I couldn't hear what they said. They all left except the one car. I could see the policeman sitting in his car."

"What did you do after that?" Jerry asked.

"I rode to Mr. Davis's house and told him what I saw. He said we should wait until the policeman was gone and then we would go call someone from our house."

"Did you call anyone?" Jerry asked her.

"No, because the policeman never left," Rebecca said. "Then Nathan came. He's my Mom's cousin. I told him what happened. He said we needed to talk to my Dad's lawyer so I hid on the floor of his pickup until we got past the policeman then we drove over here."

"Thank you, Rebecca," Jerry said. "That's all the questions I have, your honor."

The magistrate looked at the Assistant US Attorney.

"No questions," he growled.

The magistrate handed the video tape to the bailiff who put it in the videoplayer. There were some shots of the river and of various birds. Then suddenly a long shot of deputies going into the cabin, one carrying a video recorder. It zoomed in and Harry could identify Deputies Miller, Wilson and Brady. After about ten minutes the scene changed to John Carlson's truck backing up to the barn. John untied a tarp and pulled it back to reveal a stack of the brown paper bags of ammonium nitrate. The tape was almost continuous for nearly twenty minutes of unloading then the truck pulled away. Another break and the deputy with the camera entered the barn. Next came the scene of the deputies celebrating. Then the tape went blank.

There was a long silence then the magistrate said, "Thank you, Miss Isaacson. You can go back to your seat, now."

"You have another witness?" the magistrate asked Jerry.

"Yes, your honor, but I would first like to show the tape used as an exhibit by the government at yesterday's arraignment to point out some discrepancies that went unnoticed."

The magistrate looked at the Assistant US Attorney who frowned and nodded. He handed the video-tape to an assistant who carried it to the bailiff.

The tape came on with scenes of the raid and the interior of the cabin. There were close-ups of the computer system as the deputies yanked out wires and carried it away. Little Joe sat crying in Marlene's car. Two deputies used a pry-bar to rip the safe from its compartment.

"Your honor, I believe we could fast-forward through some of this," Jerry said. "The crucial part is a little further on."

The magistrate handed him the remote.

After about five minutes of rapidly flashing scenes Jerry slowed the machine to normal and said, "If the court will watch closely now, it is clear that the remainder of this video was taken at a different time." He backed the tape a little, paused the picture and said, "Look at the angle of the shadows here. Joseph Little Eagle pointed this out to us yesterday when we were reviewing a copy of the tape provided by the Government. The shadows here are very short and angled slightly to the east which would indicate that the tape was shot not long after noon which coincides with the time of the raid on my client's farm. You can see the barn in the distance and I ask you to look closely at the shadows at the back of the barn."

He started the tape again. The scene was again of the house. "One thing I just noticed," Jerry said and paused again, "Is that there was a sheriff's car right beside the cabin before. Now it's mysteriously missing. And notice the shadows. They are very long and angled towards the direction of the camera, that is, towards the west. These scenes were taken early in the morning which matches the time Rebecca Isaacson says she witnessed and photographed the planting of evidence."

"Objection!" the Assistant US Attorney said.

The magistrate looked at him. "You could rephrase that as alleged planting of evidence, Mr. Steinman."

"Alleged planting of evidence," Jerry said.

He rolled the tape again. Deputy Wilson smiled into the camera and pulled a bag full of white powder out of the back of a kitchen cabinet, held it up and turned it this way and that. There was a break, then a shot of Deputy Miller pulling bags of marijuana from a dresser drawer in the bedroom. Jerry stopped it again.

"This bedroom is on the east side of the Isaacson house. Notice the morning sun shining brightly though the window."

He started the tape. The scene moved to the barn and he set it on slow motion to point out the early-morning shadows and even a quick flash of sun into the camera lens. Inside the barn it was obvious that sun shone through cracks and a window on the east side of the building. As the camera panned to the stack of fertilizer bags, Jerry stopped it once again.

"Mr. Little Eagle also pointed out to us that these bags are stacked on fresh manure without any plastic or pallets or other protection underneath. Besides this being an unlikely way to store such material, if it had been stored this way, within even a few hours the liquid in the manure would have soaked into the bags and stained them. As you see these bags are fresh and clean just as they came from the warehouse. This tape had to be taken a very short time after the bags were put there."

"I believe that is enough of that to demonstrate your point," the magistrate said. "I believe you have another witness?"

"Yes, your honor, I would like to call as a witness Mrs. Johanna Grant."

The Assistant US Attorney stood. "Your honor, I want to go on record now that the United States Government had no part in any possible falsifying of evidence. The video-tape clearly shows that no officials of the government and no agents of government law enforcement agencies were present."

The magistrate frowned at him. "Mrs. Grant?"

Johanna came forward, was sworn and took the stand. She gave her full name and address.

"Now, Mrs. Grant, I understand you are a neighbor of the Isaacsons."

"Yes I am. I live just across the road and up a ways."

"Could you tell us the circumstances concerning something you overheard concerning this case just yesterday?"

"I heard Randy Jelstrup telling my husband about how they had blamed Harry—Mr. Isaacson for their plan."

"Where were you when you overheard this?"

"I was in my cabin and Mark, my husband, and Randy, were outside talking."

"What did you hear them say?"

"Randy said, 'We finally fixed that asshole Isaacson. He won't ever get out of jail.'"

"Did he say how they had 'fixed' Mr. Isaacson?"

"I knew what he meant," Johanna said.

"Objection!"

"Overruled."

"How did you know what he meant?"

"I heard them talking about it before."

"What did you hear them talking about?"

"The plan to blow up the dam. They all talked about it."

"Who is all?"

"The guys from the militia. They were always bragging, trying to get my husband to join."

"Did he join?"

"No, he thought they were just some overgrown boy scouts."

"Why didn't you or your husband report the plan to blow up the dam."

"We didn't believe they were serious. They had lots of crazy plans."

"What kind of plans?"

"To shoot missiles at the Federal Building in Spokane. And to shoot down a plane. They were always talking about some way they could start a war."

"Did they say why they wanted to start a war?"

"They said that if they could start Armageddon then Christ would have to come back and straighten everything out. They said that preacher, Bobby Baker, told them that."

"Did you ever see John Carlson Junior with the militia members?"

"Oh, he was always with them. He had this gun, my husband said it was an AK-47. They were always shooting in the woods and drinking beer. I was afraid they would shoot my dog."

"Did you ever hear John Carlson Junior talk about a plan to blow up Grand Coulee Dam?"

"Yes. Him and Randy were the main ones who talked about it. I always just thought they were silly."

"Did you ever hear any of them talk about Mr. Isaacson?"

"They hated him. They said he was a throwback. They were always trying to figure out how to make him move. And Johnny, John Carlson Junior, was always talking about how his dad wanted the Isaacson's farm so he could subdivide it."

"That's a lie!" John Carlson said.

The Assistant US Attorney turned to him, put his finger to his lips.

"Thank you, Mrs. Grant," Jerry said.

"Any questions?" the magistrate asked the Assistant US Attorney.

"Not at this time, your honor, but the government objects to the leading questions asked by the defense counsel and the conclusary nature of many of Mrs. Grant's answers. We also wonder why Mr. Grant did not come forward if he has no connection to the conspiracy."

"He's afraid of them," Johanna said. "They're always saying they will kill anyone who doesn't agree with them."

"Thank you, Mrs. Grant," the magistrate said. "You may step down."

"The defense would like to call John Carlson Junior," Jerry said. "Obviously he is not a witness friendly to the defense."

"Mr. Carlson will be considered a hostile witness," the magistrate said.

Johnny came to the front. His face was pale and he stumbled on the carpet. He raised his hand and said "Yes," to the bailiff's oath.

"Mr. Carlson," Jerry began, "Isn't it true that most of what you told FBI agents and other police officers was lies?"

"Objection," the Assistant US Attorney shouted. "He's badgering my witness."

"Overruled," the magistrate responded.

"Again, Mr. Carlson, most of what you told the police was not true. Am I right?"

"No," Johnny said. "Not all of it."

"Not all of what?"

"Not all of it was lies."

"So some of it was lies?"

"Maybe I was confused about some of it," Johnny said.

"Confused? How?"

"I might not remember the exact words someone said, or where I was when they said it."

"Okay, let's use an example. You said in your affidavit that Judith Isaacson first had the idea of blowing up the dam."

"Yes. She did. I heard her say it."

"Where was she when she said it?"

"At their stand, their little store. They were having a party."

"Who was there?"

"Harry. Mr. Isaacson. And Nathan, that's her cousin. And the hippies. And Eric Brown and his wife."

What did she say?"

"She said they always wanted to blow up the dam. She said they used to talk about it when they were kids."

"Who is they?"

"Her and Nathan and her other relatives."

"Did she say she had a plan?"

"No, but it gave me the idea."

"So you had the idea?"

"Well, I got it from her."

"Who did you tell about it?"

"Randy Jelstrup and the other militia guys. They thought it was a great idea."

"Did you ever hear any of them talk to Judith Isaacson about it? Or Harry Isaacson?"

"Well, no, but I think they did."

"What makes you think that?"

"I don't know, I just do. It seems obvious."

"But you never heard either of the Isaacson's talk about a plan?"

"No."

"Now, in your affidavit you also claimed that you knew that Harry Isaacson set off explosions. Can you give us an example?"

"One time when they were building a pond, Eric was helping them, they made a huge explosion that scared my Mom half to death."

"Did you see the explosion?"

"No, but I heard it and went over there to see what was going on."

"Was Walter Davis there?"

"Yes."

"Did you know that Mr. Davis had a license to set off such explosions?"

"Well I know he used to."

"And you also claim that you bought drugs from Mr. Isaacson. That was a lie wasn't it?"

"No, not exactly."

"What do you mean, 'not exactly?'" "I was told they came from Harry." "Who told you that?"

"Randy Jelstrup."

"So who actually gave you the drugs?"

"Randy did. But he said he got them from Harry, that he was secretly working for him."

"Did you ever see either of the Isaacsons use drugs?"

"Not really. But I heard about it."

"Where did you hear about it?"

"From Randy."

"So you never personally saw either of the Isaacsons use drugs?"

"No. But I know he was friends with this Jeff guy who used to come to Eliot's and everybody knows they sell drugs."

"Did anyone tell you that if you told these lies about Harry Isaacson that you could get out of the trouble you're in for setting all the fires?"

"Objection!"

"Overruled."

"Did someone give you the idea to tell these lies?"

"The police didn't tell me to do it."

"If the police didn't, who did?"

"I talked to my dad about it."

"Did your dad say you should tell lies about Harry Isaacson?"

"He said it might go easier on me if I did."

"Did he tell you what lies to tell?"

"He just said if I could come up with something on someone else, like Harry Isaacson, he could get the prosecutor to drop my charges. He said they do it all the time."

"Who does it all the time?"

"The police. He knows the judge. He said I would just be helping out the community."

John Carlson jumped to his feet. "You're a fucking liar," he shouted at Johnny. "I never told you to lie in court."

"You did, too," Johnny shouted back. "You said you could get me off if I did it."

The magistrate pounded with his gavel and the bailiff shouted "Order. Quiet."

"That kid is lying," John Carlson said. "He never was worth a damn."

"Mr. Carlson," the magistrate said, "If you don't restrain yourself, the bailiff will do it for you."

John Carlson sat, glared around the room.

Jerry started to ask Johnny another question, but the Assistant US Attorney stood.

"Your honor, I think we can dispense with any more of this. The United States will drop all charges against Mr. and Mrs. Isaacson. I am very disturbed by what I have seen and heard here today. I will repeat that it is clear that the United States Government had no part in any falsifying of evidence or directing witnesses to perjure themselves. From what I have seen I believe that we will be filing perjury charges, conspiracy to commit perjury, obstruction of justice and other charges against John Carlson Junior, John Carlson Senior and perhaps others.

John Carlson stood and headed for the door.

"I wouldn't go anywhere, Mr. Carlson," the Assistant US Attorney said.

John Carlson hesitated, sat back down and glared at Harry and Judith.

"I would like to apologize to the Isaacson's," the Assistant US Attorney said, "and point out that the government was as much a victim in this situation as were they. I would encourage them to seek civil remedies against those whom it appears conspired against them. The government considers such activity to be very serious and it will be prosecuted to the full extent of the law."

Harry didn't hear much of what was said after that. There was a commotion as the few reporters present headed out to find telephones. The star of The Covenant Conspiracy: Terrorism Comes Home sat in stunned silence. Harry was sure he could see his career trickling down the drain.

Jerry motioned for Harry and Judith to stand and the magistrate told them they were free to go. The woman guard came to them with a big smile, took off their handcuffs and led them to the elevator and up to the jail to sign release papers and recover their clothes and personal property.

When they walked out the front of the courthouse Jerry and Joseph waited for them. With them were Rebecca and Nathan and Long Joe. Rebecca ran to them, hugged Judith then turned to Harry.

She grabbed him and said, "Did I do good, Dad?"

"Oh, honey, you did wonderful."

"We're very proud of you," Judith said. Nathan hugged Judith, then Harry.

"Thank you, friend," Harry said. "You are always welcome in my home."

Long Joe shook Harry's hand. "Once again, an old Indian can be of a little help."

"Little Eagle," Harry said, "No one has ever helped me as much as you."

"That's what family is for," Long Joe said.

Joseph had a rental car, offered to drive them home. Jerry had to hurry back to Seattle. They drove to Electric City to get Little Joe. He was overcome when he saw them and could not speak. He and Harry held each other in the back seat as Joseph drove.

Judith turned on the radio, looked for news. A Spokane station interrupted a rock-and-roll song to announce that the government mysteriously had dropped charges against the key figures in The Covenant Conspiracy and released them. There would be a further report as soon as details were available.

When they reached the Manila Creek summit Harry asked Joseph to stop. Harry and Judith stood looking out over the river, arms around each other. Little Joe and Rebecca stood on each side holding their parents' hands.

"Home," Judith said.

"Home," Harry said.

Printed in the United States
1275400004B/88-102